BEYOND THE GYRE

Suzanne Francis is a captivating author. Her writing pulls you from the realm of reality and places you into the world of imagination so smoothly that you may not know you have arrived there.
Dianna Doles Petry, Sage Fire Reviews

Ms. Francis paints her setting with specific, colorful details that completely drew me into the land of Yrth and its ongoing civil war. I recommend it highly.
Dandelion, Long and Short Romance Reviews

Suzanne Francis, author of the "Song of the Arkafina" Series, is one of the best small press authors. Suzanne delivers an exceptional, unforgettable story every time. Her worlds are filled with colorful details and captivating characters that kept me turning the pages.
Pat Bertram, author of *A Spark of Heavenly Fire* and *More Deaths Than One*, from Second Wind Publishing

Also by Suzanne Francis

Heart of Hythea
Ketha's Daughter
Dawnmaid

BEYOND THE GYRE

Suzanne Francis

Published by
Bladud Books

This book is for Jill,
With love.

First published in 2008 by Mushroom eBooks

This Edition published July 2009 by Bladud Books,
an imprint of Mushroom Publishing, Bath, BA1 4EB
United Kingdom
www.bladudbooks.com

ISBN 978-1-84319-816-1

Printed and bound by Lightning Source

Contents

Prologue

Tristan rolled over in bed, opened his eyes and gave a moan of lonely frustration. Roseberry had gone to visit her mother in Kaisset again. Most of the time, he didn't miss her. His wife's enormous girth made her a frustrating and somewhat tiresome bedmate. She snored, for one thing, and when she turned over the bed creaked in a complaining way that Tristan could sympathize with. But right now, after the dream, even she would have provided some solace.

It always began the same way. Tristan would walk through a long hall, with many portraits lining the walls on either side. The faces were strange to him, and somewhat frightening, as their eyes followed his progress towards the far end of the room. In the distance he could see a bed—high, ornate, canopied. A sun and moon hung over the tented crown, shining on the brocaded curtains. His legs carried him onwards, and he felt a growing sense of anticipation—anticipation that centered itself in his groin, almost painfully so.

She had arrayed herself, as always, on the silken coverlet. Her long dark hair covered her nakedness like a dusky robe. Holding out her hand, she called to him: *Come to me, my love. I wait for you and you alone, to fulfill all my dark desires...*

He reached for her, and she threw her hair back, revealing her loveliness. Above them, the sun and moon began to glow—shining orbs of diamond and gold. They rose higher and higher until the chamber was brightly illuminated. Tristan felt the radiance enter his body, and soon he burned with the light of a million stars. Burned with lust for the Moon Queen that lay before him, ready to quench his desire in her cool dark mystery. *Come, my Sun. You are my Lord and Master. Take me...*

But always, just as she seemed within his grasp, the dream would end, leaving him trapped in physical need, miserably unfulfilled. Where was she? He had seen her face in a hundred chymike texts, and dreamed of her quivering loveliness many an insatiate midnight.

Tristan knew he had to find her—find her or go mad.

One

Holly

Katkin du Chesne Benet, common-law wife of Huw Adaryi, mother of Gwenn, Tristan, Poppy and Gwillam, felt every minute of her fifty-two years of age. She stared at her image, reflected back in wavy imperfection by a tarnished silver hand mirror. The mirror was magical—a gift from her Kymatre,[*] Neirin Mare. It had once been able to reveal the worlds between. But now it showed only Katkin's lined face and thereby the inevitable passage of time. There was nothing magical in that.

She tugged at her unruly curls, and noted that silver now mingled with the chestnut of her hair. A year had passed since she had last peered at herself in the mirror—a year since she had cared for the way she looked.

Huw stood in the doorway. "Hurry, my Queen. I know you don't want to miss this trip to the fishing shoals off Everruthe. Gunnar and Poppy are at the dock, ready to board. I have stowed our gear in the hold. We must go now, before the tide turns."

Katkin sighed and rolled her eyes, since she knew Huw could not see her. Then she turned her face towards him, and assumed a pained expression. "I am sorry, Huw. My head is feeling loathsome today. I guess I have the megrim. But I will be ready in a moment." Then, because she knew what his reaction would be, she added, "I am sure I can manage if I take some laudanum."

He sat beside her, his face a picture of concern. "Are you unwell? Why did you not say? I will tell Gunnar that he must go without us. There is no need to use the lilies of the field.[†]"

Katkin patted his hand. "Don't be silly. Why should both of us stay? I can lie here in bed with the curtains drawn. By the time you return I will be feeling fine again."

"I don't think I ought to..."

* Grandmother

† Firaithi name for any forbidden medicinal.

She broke in, perhaps a little too firmly. "I said go, and I meant it. With you to help Lut and Gunnar with the nets they will be able to fill the hold of the *Able Drake* in no time. We need the fish to dry for winter stores, and now is the best time to get them."

"All right," he agreed, with genuine reluctance. "I hope you will soon be better, Queen of my heart." His dark eyes gazed lovingly into hers, and Katkin felt an all too familiar jab of guilt. She had tried and tried, for the last sixteen years, to love him, as he loved her. Every day she struggled—except this one. The day of the summer solstice.

Huw left the room, with a last fond backwards glance. Smiling now, she slipped the ring from her finger, and buried it beneath the bedclothes.

Katkin watched with the spyglass from the top of Bird's Hill, as the boat bobbed up and down on the waves. Gunnar and his two sons, Lut and Jakob, were aboard, as well as Poppy, Katkin's adopted daughter. Her other daughter, Gwenn, and her granddaughter Myrie were at their house, Asavale, on the other end of the island. Gwillam, Poppy's little brother, would be there too; he never went anywhere without Myrie. But they would be busy getting the drying racks ready for the expected haul of fish. No one would miss Katkin, or think to look for her, for many hours. Only Kadya, Gwenn's husband, might be sitting by idly, but he was blind, and therefore no threat to her secrecy.

The sun rode high in the sky when she left the hill and walked across the wide plateau that occupied much of the island of Asaruthe. Over one arm she carried a woven willow basket. Her free hand smoothed the cream-colored linen of the new dress she had smocked and sewn. The material had come from Minbeorg. It had taken her all winter to embroider the yoke with an intricate motif of red roses and holly leaves.

Huw had admired it after she finished, saying, "Each year, you make yourself a new dress more ornate than the last, my Queen. But you have no one but us to show them off to. What is your purpose in this?"

Katkin had shrugged, saying she enjoyed the task and the pleasure of wearing the finished garment. Which was true enough, in its way.

A line of verdant holly trees camouflaged the cave opening. They loomed ahead of her, deep green in the sun, the berries glinting like many sharp red eyes. She stopped for a moment, looking about in all directions. The tumbled circle of rocks was deserted, save for a pair of black-backed gulls, and a dark-feathered juvenile. All watched her nervously, and then flew away, with mournful echoing cries.

Katkin squatted down and pushed her way through the thick foliage of the hollies. A thorn caught the skin of her upper arm, leaving a bloody scratch she did not feel. The shadowy land behind the trees hid a slender opening between two house-sized boulders. She sucked in her breath and squeezed through.

Though the mouth of the cave looked dark, a natural skylight, created by a fissure in the curving ceiling of the tunnel, provided enough pallid illumination to steer her steps towards the central chamber. There the fissure widened into a hole, which filled the hollow with shafts of bright golden radiance—enslaved sunlight, made to worship and warm this most sacred of spaces. Katkin stood for a moment, at ease, but filled with anticipation. Soon the sun would shine through the crack, and then...

She knelt, smiling, and unpacked the contents of the bag. A farl of oat bread, fresh-baked, and a stoppered jug of elderberry wine she placed on a flat rock that served as a table. Katkin hummed an old folk tune as she added a small crock of butter, and a pot of cowberry jam. Two plates and two earthenware goblets completed the setting. She frowned as she remembered the words to the song:

My love has gone for a soldier,
My soldier has gone for a love,
She is a beauty in satin,
With skin as smooth as a glove.

She stared for a moment at the wrinkled brown skin on the backs of her hands, seeing age spots where none had been last year. Sighing, she stood and checked the position of the sun, and then moved to the back of the cave, where a palliasse lay on the ground. The straw was damp and a little disheveled, so Katkin drew it together in a tidy stack. She reached into her pocket and retrieved a handful of dried rose petals and lavender buds. Carefully, she scattered them on the straw and then threw a quilt on top. Her hands came together, and nervous fingers sought to twist the ring on the third finger of her left hand. But she did not find it. Not on the day of the solstice.

She moved to a shadowed corner of the cave, and her makeshift shrine. Katkin spent her first winter on Asaruthe carving a tiny rough-hewn statue of the winged goddess. She had ruined many pieces of the soft cliff stone before she made a pleasing likeness. Huw offered his help, of course, but she had refused him.

Now Lalluna stood proudly on her pedestal, surrounded by bunches of dried flowers and foliage. Katkin returned to the basket and retrieved a fresh bouquet, composed of harebell and buttercup flowers that she had picked on her way across the meadow. She knelt and placed the flowers at the foot of the pedestal.

"Please let him come, my Lady. Please..."

Katkin had repeated this prayer sixteen times in the past sixteen years and in all that time Lalluna had failed her only once. She listened to the silence—it sounded like the soft breaths of a sleeping child. Satisfied, she stood and then moved to the center of the cavern, her heart beating in anticipation and fear.

The sun swung across the sky, until its celestial voyage took it over the hole in the cavern roof. She could feel its heat burning the top of her head, and she closed her eyes while raising her face upwards. The sun filled her vision with red—the color of heat, the color of passion. And then he came and laid her fears to rest.

Fyn stepped out of the sunlight, but his spun gold hair, so like Gwenn's, continued to shine, even in the shadows. Katkin crossed the cave, savoring the moment—that blessed moment of reunion. When she reached him, he took her into his arms and held her tightly. As always, they did not converse, though it had been a year since they last met.

But his kisses spoke of need, and hers of bitter loneliness.

His fingers found the fastenings on her dress and undid them, one by one. Katkin caught one of Fyn's hands in her own as he covered her freckled shoulders with kisses. Hurriedly, hungrily, she tugged at his shirt, and he removed it. Katkin noticed a new scar, thin and still angry-red, crossing his lean abdomen. She did not ask him about it.

He spoke for the first time as he unfastened his sword belt and dropped it to the ground. "Shall we, Katrione?"

"Yes, Tomas, we shall," she replied, with a smile. He smiled back, bemused at her stubborn use of his old name. Tomas de Vigny he had been, once in another life—before he became Amaranthine. But Katkin would have no part of that.

She led him to the palliasse, then stretched herself upon it and looked up at Tomas. He had left the land of the living at age twenty-four, and now remained frozen in time, immortal, but not immune to hurts. His body looked youthful still, strong and supple, but inside he was old, far older than she, ravaged by battle, loss and fatigue. It made the apparent difference in their ages a little easier to bear, knowing that.

She raised her hand and he dropped gracefully beside her on the quilt. Katkin shivered in expectation of what she knew would follow. He was, and always had been, the most skilled and satisfying of all her lovers. She cast herself adrift in the warm sea of his attentions, feeling the caress of his hands and mouth everywhere with intense pleasure.

"Tomas," she whispered. "Come to me. I am more than ready..."

The first time was always over too soon, but she consoled herself with the knowledge that they had four or five hours to spend together in the pleasurable search for satisfaction. Tomas rolled away from her, and rested on his back, and she passed the time by tracing every scar on his skin with her tongue, feeling his shivers of delight. Soon, he found her mouth with his own and kissed her roughly, then drew her on top of his body.

"Your turn," he sighed, and closed his eyes as she sank down and wrapped him in loving warmth.

Katkin wanted to hold on to the moment—to him—for as long as she could, so she took her time, letting the passion build, until they both ached for deliverance. The sun beat upon them, filling the cavern with golden light, and it felt as though the Gods had thrown wide the door to heaven. Katkin had only to close her eyes to imagine she rose on tongues of flame.

Fyn clutched at her, wordlessly begging for more. His hips thrust in time with hers, faster and faster, until the maelstrom of climax and release took them both.

After a time, when she had kissed the sweat and the tears from his eyelids, Katkin stood and stretched. Fyn lay on the quilt, watching her. "You are beautiful. Never more so than when your hair is wild, and your cheeks are still colored with passion, my lady."

She laughed at this, but it had a bitter ring. "And when I am old enough to be your grandmother, will you still think so, Tomas?" He stood and took her in his arms.

"You are unwise to disparage the turn of the seasons. Those of us who are so unfortunate to live outside of time cherish it. You are not the impetuous girl who once wetted an arrogant fool of a Captain with a jug of cold water. But to me, you remain just as lovely."

Unhurriedly, they threw on some clothes against the chill breeze that entered the cave through the fissure. The sun had passed behind a cloud. Fyn crossed the sandy floor and admired the table. "Cowberry? My favorite." Katkin joined him, and they sat together, sipping the wine and sharing a meal.

Katkin asked first, as she always did, about Lalluna, the goddess she had once served so devotedly. "When I saw you last, you said she had gone away. Do you know where she is now, Tomas?"

Fyn sighed. "I found her late last year. She has returned to the Temple and locked herself away from the outside world. When I visited her there, I begged her to go back across the heavenly plane and seek the companionship of our kind. But she would not. She says her people have need of her, and that she is at fault."

"Perhaps they do," Katkin murmured, as she spread some butter on a piece of the oat bread. "What is my son up to these days?"

"I know not. I may spend only a few hours in the living world, my dear. What little time I have I choose to spend here, with you."

"And I am very glad that you do," Katkin said, smiling, as she offered her wine in a toast. "To wicked liaisons," she added.

Fyn tapped his goblet against hers, but gave her a sharp glance all the same. "Indeed. But have you no shame, Katrione?" He smiled as he asked this, so she would understand it was a jest, but still she answered him very seriously.

"No, I suppose not..." she said, and then did not speak again for a minute or more. Fyn sat by her side, and sipped his wine, waiting for her to continue. "I love you, and I love Jacq. You both have been part of all my lives, and will be for all my lives to come, I hope. But Huw... Well, I just don't seem to have any room left in my heart for him. I mean, I care about him, of course. How could I not? We have been together for sixteen years on this cursed island."

"Why don't you leave here, if you hate it so?"

"What can I do? Would you let me go with you?" Katkin snapped back. He shook his head, as she had known he would, and she scowled at him. "I have my task, just as you have yours. The Dawn-maid has to come first."

Katkin sighed and rested her head on Fyn's shoulder. His hair was pungent with the scent of lavender and rose. It brought a blush of remembrance to her cheeks, knowing that the pressure and warmth of their bodies had crushed the petals and released their perfume. "I am sorry, love. I know you are not to blame. But I despise this place. It is windswept and barren, and very lonely. For me the sun shines but once a year, on this day—the day of the solstice."

He wrapped his arms about her as she shed soft tears on his bare shoulder. Silently, they finished the last of the wine, both aware of the sun's passage across the sky. They had another hour or two together, no more. After a moment, Fyn stood and approached the statue of Lalluna, then knelt before it reverently. He spilled the dregs of his wine into the sand, as a libation. Katkin joined him, and did the same. They stood and turned away as one, before walking back to the palliasse. Katkin undressed again, and Fyn pulled her on to the quilt. For a long time they lay together, and said nothing.

This time, this very last time, their lovemaking was measured— and sad. When it finished, they did not talk. Fyn dressed and re-buckled his sword belt. Katkin tidied her hair as best she could. Now they stood together under the rift in the cavern ceiling.

Fyn said softly, "I must go now, but my heart remains here— with you."

Katkin smiled through her tears. "Farewell, my love. I hope, someday..."

"Nay," he broke in, and for the first time his voice echoed the bitterness he harbored inside. "Do not hope for what will never be, Katrione. I am a walking corpse, and you have much life yet to live. Live it, in happiness, with those of your own kind."

She threw up her hands and cried, "My country lies in ruins, Dai has betrayed me, and you will not stay. What happiness have I? What reason to live?"

Fyn shook her shoulders. "Joy can be lost, and yet found again. But if it seems far away, then a noble duty may provide some solace."

8

"What do you mean?"

"Only this. My heart tells me that the final conflict is hard upon us, and this turn of the Gyre will soon be at an end. One we both love lies in darkness, bereft of hope. She needs you. Go to the Temple, as soon as you may."

Katkin nodded, and as he embraced her, she said, "Then we will meet again on the last battlefield, you and I. Even if it is in death, we will be together, and then there will be peace for all."

"In death?" Fyn closed his eyes and said forlornly, "I only wish it could be so. Farewell, my dear." He stepped away, and left her. Her surroundings now seemed monochromatic, and Katkin shivered. Slowly she drifted around the cave, collecting her belongings, and packing them away in the basket. There were no tears, only a brittle resolve that would soon be shattered in the secret spaces of the night, in silent lamentation for what she had lost, again and again.

Katkin exited the cave, and then made her way across the meadow, swinging the basket in the long grass. She swore and ducked behind a tor when she saw Huw in the distance, heading towards her on the same path. After a moment, he walked by with his head down, oblivious to her presence. She waited until he had passed from sight on the next rise and then hurried back home.

"Wait for me!" Poppy called, as she slipped and slid down a high dune. Gwillam and Myrie, who were well ahead of her, did not slacken their pace.

Her brother looked back. "Wait for yourself, sluggard. We will have finished all the gooseberries by the time you catch us."

He and Myrie dived behind a hummock of sand and shrubs, shrieking with laughter. Poppy slowed her pace, for she had seen another figure approaching. *Jakob. Or was it Lut?*

She could not tell the twins apart unless she talked to them.

"Hallo, Poppy!" he shouted, as he spied her from the bottom of a nearby dune. "Stop a minute. I want to ask you something."

Jakob then. Lut would never be so forward.

She stopped and waited as he strode up the loose sand towards her. He gave an easy grin when he reached her side. Poppy wondered to herself how two people as alike as Jakob and Lut could have such very different personalities. "Hello, yourself," she said. "Jakob, isn't it?"

He nodded. "Have you seen Myrie? Ma wants to cut her hair today. She has been looking all over for her."

Poppy lowered her eyes and studied a flowering vine that snaked along the ground at her feet. "No. I haven't seen her. Did you ask Ikor* Kadya if he knows where she is?"

Her lie fooled Jakob. "No, I will stop by his cottage on my way back to the byre. Are you coming over to help with the milking?" He gave her a sideways glance, his blue eyes half closed. "We can walk there together. If you want to, I mean..." His voice trailed off, and he thrust his hands into the pockets of his breeches.

She looked towards the gooseberry patch with longing, but decided there would be trouble if Jakob caught Myrie and Gwillam together. After tucking her arm through his, she led him back up the dune.

"I thought you said your Ma had a headache this morning," Jakob said. "But I saw her, a couple of minutes ago, when I was looking for Myrie on the tops. I saw your Pop, too. He sure looked angry."

Poppy frowned and changed the subject. Whatever difficulties her parents had, it was none of his business. She said, "I wish I had your long legs, Jakob. Look at you, you aren't even winded. It takes me twice as many steps to climb this hill. I am such a weakling!"

He laughed at this and peered at her legs, which were alluringly bare, for she had tucked her long skirt into her belt. Despite her complaint, her limbs were well muscled, the skin smooth and brown.

"What are you complaining about now? Let's have a look at those legs, Miss Brunner," he said. He dropped to his knees before her and squeezed her calf. "Feels pretty good to me."

Poppy let out a hoot of laughter. "Is that your best diagnosis?" she said teasingly. "Perhaps I had better get a second opinion."

Jakob's hand slipped upwards, past her knee, to the silky skin on the inside of her thigh. "Hmmm..." he said, more softly. "Do you have any discomfort if I press here?"

"No, Doctor," she answered promptly. "But I do have a pain."
"Where?"

"Right here!" With a quick twist, she flipped a foot-full of sand into his face and ran away, laughing. But the look that she gave him over her shoulder was frankly inviting.

_____

* Uncle

10

Jakob struggled to his feet and chased after her, while brushing the sand from his cheeks and eyebrows. She headed towards a copse of birches they both knew well. He caught her underneath their shapely white trunks. A second later, she was in his arms.

After kissing him for a moment, Poppy pulled away. She rubbed her chin and asked, "When are you going to start shaving? Every time we kiss, I get a rash on my face. Katkin is getting very suspicious."

Jakob pulled her close again. "Dad won't let me. He says a proper Northman must have a beard. I am sorry, Poppy." He stroked her chin tenderly, and she ruffled his long blond hair.

"Don't worry, I can always think of some story to tell her." She stared up at Jakob. "Don't you think we ought to be getting back? Bessie doesn't like to be kept waiting."

He gazed back at her. "Poppy..." He brought up his hand to touch her cheek. "Have you thought any more about what I asked you? You promised you would tell me your answer today." His face colored, leaving brilliant crimson streaks on his cheekbones that made his freckles disappear.

"Was it today I said?" she asked. "I guess I forgot. I... I need a little more time, Jakob."

His face fell. "But Poppy, you know I love you. I want to show you. Why won't you let me? We are both old enough..."

She shook her head. "I am, maybe. But are you so sure you are ready?"

This made him angry. "I am not a child!"

Poppy smiled and shrugged. "Don't get so huffy. I was only teasing."

Jakob was not mollified. "That's right. You were teasing. That is all you ever do, Poppy." His grip on her arm tightened and he lowered his voice to a whisper. "I want you so much. It is all I think about. It is driving me insane. Please say yes. Don't make me wait any longer." His left hand slipped down the front of her peasant blouse and groped for her breast. Poppy gave a cry and tried to back away from him, but he did not let her go.

Incensed, she raised her head and gave him a ringing slap across the cheek. He laughed and shook her by the shoulder. "Come on, stop being so coy. It isn't as if you have a lot of choice. Who else are you going to do it with? That idiot Lut?"

Poppy pushed him away and rubbed her arm. "I don't have to give myself to either of you," she said primly.

Jakob sniffed. "As long as we are all stuck on this stinking island it will have to be one of us. And obviously it is going to be me."

"Is it? And why is that?" Her big brown eyes flashed with annoyance.

"Because you want me. Just like I want you." He pulled her close again and kissed her. She did not try to escape. "See," he said, triumphantly. "It feels good, does it not? And I can make it even better. Let me please you, Poppy."

Poppy flushed. "Don't pretend you know what you are talking about."

"Oh, really? I've been with women before. I haven't had any complaints."

"I don't believe it. How could you..."

He said smugly, "Don't forget that I get to leave this backwater twice a year with Dad, to go to Minbeorg for supplies. Plenty of willing girls there, down by the docks. I took my first at age thirteen."

"Thirteen?" Poppy repeated in disbelief.

"Yes. So what? I was tall, even then. I told the woman at the bawdy house I was eighteen. The gold piece I gave her made sure she didn't ask any more questions."

She looked skeptical. "And I suppose Ikor Gunnar just waited outside the door for you?"

Jakob shrugged. "Dad was busy seeing to the loading and Lut was helping him, of course. I slipped away for a couple of hours. I caught hell when I got back, but I didn't care. It was worth it." He stepped closer, making her aware of the difference in their heights. Her head reached to just below his collarbone. He wrapped his fingers around her arm again, quite loosely, the promise of his strength and authority undeclared between them. But Poppy did not feel afraid.

"I don't care if you have been with a hundred girls," she said firmly. "I haven't made up my mind yet, so you will just have to go on waiting until I do." She glared at him for a moment, and then turned away, saying casually, "See you back at the byre."

She headed towards the cow shed, over by Ikora* Gwenn's big

---

* Aunt

house, Asavale, in a sheltered valley on the west side of Asaruthe. The afternoon sun beat down on her bare head, and she paused to pull her fichu over her long brown hair, and then wrap it around her shoulder. She considered Jakob's request as she did so.

Poppy was not naive. Her physician mother had made quite sure that she understood the ways of intimacy between men and women. Though Poppy had demurred at Katkin's offer of herbs to prevent pregnancy, saying she had no need of them, her mother, giving her a sharp look, had said, "Come to me when you do. With those boys of Gwenn's sniffing around, it is only a matter of time."

That had been three years ago, and since then she and Jakob had become more than friends, but she still could not convince herself that she wanted a sexual relationship with him. The herbs weren't always effective, for one thing, and then there was—

Lut appeared above her. His thick blond braids flashed in the sunlight as he made his way on the path, with his head down. She called, and he looked up without speaking in return. He waited while she scrambled up the slope towards him. Poppy smiled and a bright red tinge spread over the skin on his face and neck. "Hello, Lut."

He nodded in return, with his eyes locked on the patch of sand between them. She stepped a little closer, so she could make eye contact. "Are you looking for Myrie?" Another nod, accompanied by a quick backwards step.

"I saw her a while ago. With Gwillam. They went over to that patch of wild gooseberries by the long rill."

Lut cleared his throat. Poppy waited as he twisted the beaded wristlet he always wore. His Adam's apple bobbed a couple of times. Finally, he blurted, "Thanks." His blue eyes narrowed with worry. The feeling overcame his shyness. "You didn't tell Jakob, did you? Ma sent him to look for her, too."

Poppy smiled reassuringly. "Of course not. I wouldn't do that, Lut. We had enough trouble the last time he caught them together. Anyway, I saw him not long after. He was heading to the byre to see to the cows."

They stood for a moment in silence. The sun went behind a cloud, and a shadow passed over them. Poppy shivered. She let her shawl slip to her shoulders, and hugged it for warmth. "Lut?" she asked softly. "Do you want me to show you where they are?"

He shook his head.

Poppy gazed at him helplessly. "Well, I guess I will see you later then."

"Bye," he said, and turned away.

"Bye," she answered, as she studied his retreating back. His shoulders were wider than Jakob's, probably because he did most of the net-hauling on the *Able Drake*. Jakob was the quicker thinker of the two, always ready with an excuse to avoid hard work. He was a talker, was Jakob, and Poppy enjoyed his company, at least until he had started pressuring her to give herself to him. But Lut...

Poppy hurried after him. "Wait!" He glanced back over his shoulder, and slowed his pace. "I forgot something. I wanted to ask you how Jepper was doing."

His expression looked wary. "His leg is getting better. Your Ma splinted it."

"Is he out with the other goats yet?"

Lut shook his head. "Too little. I made him a pen in the yard."

He turned to go again, and Poppy laid a hand on his arm. "I think it is wonderful how you climbed down the cliff to rescue him, Lut. He would have starved to death otherwise."

Lut froze and looked at her hand. She dropped it to her side. Slowly, he turned to face her. "Poppy," he said softly, hesitatingly. "What do you want?"

Now it was her turn to stammer. "I... Nothing. I just want to talk to you. I mean, I want us to be friends, that is all." Lut continued to look at her seriously.

"I thought you just wanted to spend time with Jakob."

"Lut, why would you say that?"

"He told me so. He said that you were..." Lut stopped.

Poppy stared at him and a prickly feeling edged up the back of her neck. "What did he say? Tell me!"

Lut turned from her. "I got to go find Myrie. See you later." He strode away, and Poppy tore after him. She dove in front and thrust her finger at his chest.

"I asked you a question, Lut!" He didn't speak, so she demanded, "Answer me!"

"Jakob told me that he... that you..." He stopped again, in an absolute paroxysm of shyness.

Now Poppy felt certain she knew what he had been about to say. "He told you that he and I were lovers."

He nodded miserably. Poppy fumed, "That lying braggart. I never.... You do believe me, don't you?"

"Yes," he murmured. "Of course I believe you. Jakob lies about all sorts of things. A couple of months ago he said he had been studying all morning with Pop, when actually he took the *Able Drake* and sailed her to Everruthe. Dad thrashed him when he found out." Lut grinned at Poppy. She smiled back, thinking that she had never heard him say so many words in a row before.

"How did he find out?"

His smile grew wider. "Myrie saw him, and she told your brother. Gwill told Ma and she told Dad. He was plenty mad. We aren't supposed to take the boat out on our own." He paused and then raised his eyes to meet hers. "Do you want to show me where the gooseberries are? I really do have to find my sister."

Poppy nodded happily. They walked together in companionable silence for a few moments and then Lut asked, "What is Pop teaching you in the afternoons?"

"I am learning Secunian. Ikor Kadya has a manuscript that he wants me to translate. A journal written by a ship's Captain, named Josiah Tavish. Katkin took it from the Registrumhallen* in Scarfinda."

"Why is it so important?"

She shrugged. "I don't know, exactly. So far, it seems to be about cargo, and seamen. There is quite a bit I don't understand—entries on navigation and currents and things like that."

For a moment, it appeared Lut's shyness would get the better of him, but finally he offered, "I could maybe help you with that, if you want me to. I know a little about sailing."

Poppy gave him a brilliant smile. "Would you, Lut? That would be wonderful."

They reached the birch grove. Lut gave her an odd glance as they passed through, but did not say anything.

Myrie and Gwillam had finished the last of the gooseberries when Lut and Poppy rounded the side of the dune. Gwillam grinned and waved. Poppy's little brother was four years younger than she, but already the same height.

Myrie gave two clicks of her tongue as Lut patted her long dark hair affectionately. He knew she didn't like to be touched anywhere

---

* Hall of Registers

else. Myrie didn't talk like a normal person, although she was sixteen years old. Nor did she go to lessons with the others.

"Did you like the gooseberries, Myrie?" Poppy asked her, with a smile. Myrie smiled back, but her eyes were cloudy and unfocussed. She could look, no doubt about that, but she didn't always *see*.

"Click clack clicketty," said Myrie in reply.

Gwillam said, "That means she thought they were sour."

Poppy replied, "Well the both of you will be lucky not to get a stomachache after all the fruit you ate. Now come on. Ikora Gwenn wants to give Myrie a haircut."

Myrie lifted her head and shrieked, then dove down the hill towards the beach. Poppy shrugged when Lut frowned at her. "Sorry. I forget sometimes that she can understand what I say even though she can't speak."

Gwillam spoke. "Don't worry, Poppy. I can catch her. Tell Ikora Gwenn I will bring her to Asavale in a moment."

Poppy turned to Lut. "Do you want to walk to the byre with me?"

He nodded, shy again. Poppy, intent on cementing their friendship, thrust her arm through his as they walked to the top of the hill. At first he stiffened and tried to pull away, but after a time he seemed to relax, and started talking again. "Myrie is lucky to have Gwillam. No one else can understand what she says. He is a good friend to her."

Poppy nodded. "I wish Jakob felt the same way."

"Me too," said Lut, and sighed. "Ma has talked to him about it lots of times. She says Myrie needs someone to watch over her, but he always argues that it ought to be one of us." He snorted. "As if he would be bothered. He barely says two words to her in a day."

Poppy couldn't answer him for a moment. They were climbing the steepest part of the path that led up the cliff face and she needed all her breath as she clung to the rope rail that Gunnar had made for Arkady. Finally, they emerged on the top of the plateau that stretched east and west along the axis of the island of Asaruthe.

Panting, she turned back to admire the view. The sweep and curve of a sheltered bay spread below them, and beyond that, the ceaseless boom of the surf. Poppy gestured out to sea, "Look! I can see the *Able Drake*."

Lut shaded his eyes with his hand. "Dad and Pop are on board.

They must be going fishing again." That he had two fathers did not strike him as odd in the least, although he knew enough not to mention it when they went to Minbeorg.

Poppy tutted. "I hope Ikor Kadya will be careful. If he fell in..."

"Dad would fish him out again," said Lut, with the confident admiration of one who respected his father above all others.

"But he has only one leg. What if he couldn't get to him in time?"

"Then he'd throw a rope."

"Ikor would not be able to see a rope!" Poppy said crossly, but Lut shrugged.

"He is a good swimmer, Poppy, you know that. He could stay afloat for ages."

They left the cliff's edge and walked across the tops, staying well clear of the knots of sheep scattered about. Many of the ewes had lambs, which fled towards their mothers with bleats of alarm as Lut and Poppy passed. But a solitary lamb stood still, trembling, as they approached it.

"Where's this one's Ma, do you suppose?"

Poppy shrugged. "I don't know, but it seems very unhappy. What should we do, Lut?"

Lut stared past the lamb, to where a ewe lay sprawled in the green grass. "Od's Swallow! Not another one!" He strode past the lamb, which skittered away. Lut knelt and examined the dead sheep in disgust. A predator had torn out her throat. "Ma is going to have fits when she hears about this."

Poppy joined him at the dead sheep's side, holding her nose against the smell of decay.

"It is the second sheep she's lost in the last month. One of the dogs is getting at them. We keep Bridie and Wink penned, so it must be yours."

Poppy bristled. "It isn't our dog, Lut Strong Arm! How dare you suggest such a thing?"

"Well, what else could it be? There aren't any other predators on this island."

"I don't know. But Jolly would never attack a sheep. He is a good dog."

"Jakob said he saw your dog running loose on the tops just last week. If Gwillam can't keep..."

Poppy rounded on him. "Don't be such an idiot, Lut! You just said yourself that Jakob can't be trusted. He probably just wanted to get Gwill in trouble."

He backed away from her wrath, waving his hands. "All right! All right! You win. Don't take my head off." The orphaned lamb behind them bleated pitifully.

"What should we do? If we leave the poor thing out here it will die." Poppy's eyes filled with tears.

Lut grinned. "Quit worrying. I will carry it back to the house with us now. It can go in the pen with Jepper."

Poppy flashed him a grateful smile. "Thanks, Lut. I am sorry I called you an idiot." They converged upon the lamb, which took off towards the cliff edge. Poppy looked on in alarm. "Oh no! Lut, stop her, or she will fall, just like Jepper!"

Lut put on a burst of speed. The lamb had almost reached the edge, running flat out, bleating in terror. He dove clumsily, and just missed the lamb's back foot as it stumbled and headed in a new direction, skirting along the precipice. Poppy watched with her hand over her mouth as Lut gained his feet and chased the lamb again, calling to her to cut off its retreat. She hurried across the field, but not quickly enough to catch the fleeing animal. Just ahead, the ground fell away where a slip had claimed part of the cliff face.

The lamb disappeared over the side. A second later, so did Lut.

Poppy screamed in terror and ran for the edge of the cliff.

Two

Birch

Lut's blond head popped from below the rim. "What?" Then, seeing her stricken expression, he added, "Are you all right, Poppy?"

She hurried forward until she reached the break. Her relief at the sight of him standing unhurt on a wide ledge just a few feet from the edge made her shriek crossly. "Am I all right? I thought you had fallen down the cliff, you ass!"

Lut seemed not to notice her irritation. "Good. Give me a hand, will you?" He had hold of the lamb's back leg, as it dangled over the two hundred foot drop to the rocks below. "I'll pass it to you. Mind you hang on to it, eh? I don't want to have to run another race with that one. Once is enough."

Poppy did as he instructed. She handed the wriggling lamb back to Lut once he had scrambled out of the cut and he draped it across his shoulders, holding its feet in the front. The lamb relaxed, and lay on its side. Lut trotted across the field towards home.

Poppy cried, "Wait for me! What's your hurry?"

"Got to get this little one back to the house. It is probably dehydrated—and hungry, too. Ma's got some special mix she makes for the foundlings. We'll bottle feed it for a few days and it should be fine."

She smiled at him, much impressed. "You are full of surprises, Lut."

He blushed. "What do you mean? I am just Lut, the quiet one. Jakob gets all the attention around here." He stared at her for a moment, and Poppy thought she saw a flicker of jealousy in his eyes. Then he looked away again.

"I just meant that you know so much—about sailing and sheep herding, and..."

He gave her a shy grin. "Just because I don't talk doesn't mean I don't know things."

The high green roof of Ikora Gwenn's house came into view. Several goats cropped the sod on the top, crossing back and forth on the steeply sloping sides.

Gwenn was blond and rawboned, like her sons. She stood when she saw Lut approaching with the lamb, and Myrie, who had been sitting on a stool at her feet, scampered away. "Myriadne!" she called, exasperatedly, but the girl had already left the yard, running towards Gwillam's house. She threw the comb and scissors down in disgust.

"Shall I catch her, Ikora?" Although Gwenn was, in one sense, her adoptive sister, Poppy felt uncomfortable with the idea that the huge, ex-warrior before her could be as closely related as that. Ikora, for the fact that Gwenn had married Patre's brother, seemed so much *safer*.

"No, thank you," said Gwenn in resignation. "I was almost done.

She doesn't care what her hair looks like, anyway." She took the lamb from Lut. "What happened here?"

Poppy explained about the dead ewe. Gwenn burst into a torrent of colorful cursing, a relic from her days as a Fynäran raider. "If I find out which dog is responsible, I will tie a stone to his neck and throw him off the cliff!"

"Ikora Gwenn!" Poppy stared at her unhappily.

She growled unrepentantly, "Those sheep are our main livelihood, Poppy. Without them, we would not be able to trade for all the things we need from the mainland. Do you understand?"

Poppy sighed and nodded.

"Gwenn came over here earlier," said Katkin to Huw, trying to break the uncomfortable silence between them.

"Oh? Why is that, my Queen?" Huw stopped eating and looked over at Katkin, frowning.

"She thinks Jolly has been after the sheep. Jakob said he saw him on the tops."

Poppy threw down her fork and cut in hotly, "Jolly didn't do anything! Jakob is a liar."

Huw smiled at his daughter affectionately. "Now, Poppy, calling people names will not remedy the situation." He asked Katkin, "Has Jolly been running free?"

She shook her head. "Not as far as I know, Huw, but I can't watch him every minute. But Gwenn insists we should get rid of him anyway, since he is not needed for the herding."

Gwillam choked on his food. "No! He's mine. You can't..."

Katkin said, automatically, "Don't talk with your mouth full, Gwill."

He quickly chewed and swallowed. "I won't let you do anything to Jolly, Patre." He lifted his tear-filled eyes to meet Huw's.

"I will have a talk to Gwenn after supper," said Huw. "Now," he said brightly, "How were your studies today?"

Gwillam cheered somewhat. "I am learning trigonometry. Ikor says I have a great mind for mathematics." Katkin smiled and patted his head.

Poppy sniffed. "He would never say that about me. I can barely add two and two."

"But you are learning Secunian, are you not? Your gift is for

20

languages, Poppy. How is the translation going, anyway?" Katkin's eyes were bright and sharp.

"Well, I am trying, but it is difficult. Lut said he would help me though."

Huw and Katkin both spoke in astonishment. "Lut said?"

Poppy nodded. "I had quite a long talk with him today. He really is very nice, just shy."

A look passed between her parents. "Well, isn't that something?" Katkin said, after a moment. The talk passed to other subjects, and then Huw left the table, saying he would walk across to Gwenn's house. Poppy and Gwillam did the dishes, while Katkin mended one of the fishing nets. Once the sun sank below the level of the cliffs, she got out several oil lamps, made from large whelk shells, and hung them from the ceiling.

Poppy thought Gwillam still looked troubled, and when he went outside, she followed him. She found him sitting in Jolly's pen. "You didn't do it, did you boy?" he asked, and Jolly whined in return.

She sat beside them. "Don't worry, Gwill. Patre will sort it out. I don't think Jolly would hurt a sheep, and neither does he."

But Gwillam shook his head. "He's doing it to get back at me."

"What on Yrth do you mean? Who is?"

"That sneak, Jakob. Because I told Ikor Gunnar that Myrie saw him on the *Able Drake*."

"Gwillam, you don't know that."

"Yes I do," he said stubbornly, as his hands rubbed Jolly's thick fur. The dog licked his face. "Yes, I do. And I won't let anything happen to Jolly. You'll see."

The next day, Katkin, Huw and Poppy sat around the supper table, all staring at Gwillam's empty place. That morning, he had not been in his room, nor was Jolly in his pen. Huw and Katkin had hunted all day for him without success. Poppy picked at her fish and potatoes as they discussed plans for a more extensive search in the morning. She looked up when a curious noise drifted through the open windows. It sounded like the keening wail of some discontented beast.

Huw jumped from his chair as the sound grew louder, crying, "What in the gods' names is that?"

The door flew open and Myrie entered, dragging her breathless father by the arm. Her deafening wails subsided as she gazed around the room, and then started again as soon as Myrie realized that Gwillam was not there. Arkady shrugged hopelessly.

"I am sorry. She has been like this ever since this morning. Gwenn brought her to me when she couldn't stand it any more. Then Myrie made me come over here."

The girl's screams continued as she crawled into a corner, rocking back and forth with her eyes tightly closed. Katkin had to shout to make herself heard.

"We have been looking for him all day, Kadya. I don't know what else we can do." She frowned. "If Gwenn had not made such a fuss about that sheep, this never would have..."

Huw broke in. "It does not matter, my Queen. We must do something to help poor Myrie." He squatted before the girl and patted her hand awkwardly, which made her howl even louder.

Poppy said, "Patre, let me try." She grabbed her brother's oldest toy, a stuffed floppy-eared rabbit. It had been living on the mantelpiece since Gwillam abandoned it, five years earlier. She knelt beside Myrie and gently tucked the rabbit into her arms. Myrie hiccuped a couple of times, clutched the rabbit to her chest, and fell asleep.

Arkady gave a sigh of relief as Katkin explained what Poppy had done. Then he asked, "May she stay here tonight? Now that she is quiet, I don't want to disturb her."

Katkin said, "Of course. And tomorrow we will find Gwillam and then she will be happy again."

Sleep eluded her, though Poppy closed her eyes and forced herself to lie still. Finally, with a frustrated groan, she rose from her bed and crept down the ladder, then tiptoed into the kitchen, thinking a cup of milk might help to settle her nerves. Myrie still lay by the fireplace, with the rabbit clutched in her hands. She sighed, and muttered in her sleep, "Click, click, click..."

Poppy crossed the stone floor to check on her. Myrie had curled into a ball, hugging the rabbit to her chest. The room felt very chilly, so Poppy found a blanket and draped it over the sleeping girl's shoulders.

Myrie turned over and thrust her arm up, as her clicks became both mournful and more insistent. Poppy did not want her to wake in a strange room, alone and frightened, so she grabbed another woolen blanket and some pillows from the settle and stretched out beside Myrie. Her presence seemed to be a comfort, for Myrie's clicks subsided and she began to snore. A few moments later, Poppy slept too.

Poppy had a dream, and Myrie was in it. They both stood before a vast mirror, ornately framed in silver, and their reflections stared back at them. Myrie's reflection spoke, and she used real words. "When are you coming? We need your help!"

The real Myrie clicked questioningly. The mirror spoke again. "The Infirmarie. You must hurry, or there will be no one left to save."

The sparkle that flashed from the glass blinded Poppy, as though the sun had just come out from behind a cloud. It left an after-image on her retina—bright green and shaped like a flower. Her reflection cried, "Watch for us, in the mirror," as a second reflection joined the first. Suddenly Poppy looked down a long tunnel, with ever-smaller images of her and Myrie disappearing into its depths. She grew dizzy and then she fell, plummeting past her reflected selves, twisting and turning. At the end of the tunnel, she stopped, caught fast by some unseen hand.

Now she saw a room, dark and dank. A box, something like a coffin, lay in the center. The chill air smelled like decay, and Poppy felt very afraid. But her legs insisted on carrying her closer to the box, though she somehow knew the noisome stench issued from it. She looked down.

What she saw made her scream and scream, and then she woke.

Myrie patted her hair.

"I had a dream, Myrie," Poppy whispered. "It frightened me very much." She stared at the girl who lay at her side. Myrie's deep blue eyes were dark and opaque, like a pool of turbid water.

Myrie said, "Clack, click," sympathetically, and closed her eyes. Poppy, strangely comforted, did the same. After a little while, she slept again.

In the morning, Myrie pressed herself close to Poppy's side as Katkin said, "All right, is everyone ready? Today we are going to look all along the water's edge, and on the tops by the tors. We must not stop searching until Gwillam is found." She could not keep the worry from her voice.

Huw added confidently, "We will bring him home today, my Queen."

Katkin sighed. "I will never forgive myself if something has..."

He shook his head and looked towards Myrie, who stared vacantly at the rabbit still clutched in her fist.

Poppy took her hand. "Myrie and I will look on the south side, over by the old fishing shack."

"Good. We should meet back here at midday for a meal. By then we will have him, I am sure." Huw headed out the door, leaving Katkin standing in the kitchen. Her hands twisted her apron strings.

"Be careful with Myrie. Don't let her wander. I am going to the beach to meet with Gwenn and Gunnar. Just shout if you need help."

Poppy nodded and left the cottage, with Myrie trailing behind her.

They crossed the yard, and the chickens crowded around them, expecting their morning ration of grain. Poppy shoved them out of the way with her boot. The path to the south side of the island wound across the tops. They did not get far along it before Myrie stopped. She clicked at Poppy urgently, and tugged at her hand.

"Myrie? What is it? We have to go to the fishing shack. Gwillam may have slept there last night. If we get to him first we can help him hide Jolly."

"Mmmm..."

Poppy stared at her in surprise. "What are you trying to say?"

"Mmmm..." the girl said again. "Mirrr..."

"Mirror? Is that what..."

But Myrie was already running back towards the house.

When they reached the door, she flew straight in and up the ladder to Katkin and Huw's room. Poppy wondered how Myrie had known about the mirror. Her mother took it out of her keepsake chest only once or twice a year.

Myrie found the chest, and tried the lid, then clicked a few times in a thoughtful way. She closed her eyes and placed her hand over the keyhole. The next click came from within the box. She smiled and flipped the lid open.

Poppy stared at her, very quizzically. She forgot to whisper.

"Myrie, how on Yrth did you do that?" But Myrie only clicked happily, as she retrieved the mirror.

Poppy peered down, and saw her reflection right next to Myrie's, just as she had in the dream. Myrie blew a stream of moist breath on the glass, and it fogged. "Myrie!" said Poppy impatiently, and made to wipe it away. But the moisture evaporated on its own, and when the mirror cleared, their faces had disappeared.

Now Poppy could see Gwillam, huddled in a dark hole, with Jolly at his side. He held his arm close to his chest as though it were injured. She could see the tracks of tears on his grimy face. Poppy gave a cry of alarm and snatched the mirror from Myrie.

The scene in the glass changed. Jakob, or perhaps Lut, strode across the tops, followed by a rough-coated brown dog that Poppy had never seen before. He took the dog to the highest paddock and let it run amongst the sheep. Poppy watched in alarm as the dog caught a young lamb and shook it, as the other sheep fled in terror. Lut, or Jakob, smiled triumphantly and picked up the body.

Poppy sputtered, "That... That stinking liar! He owns the dog that has been getting after the sheep and he blamed it all on Gwill. Look, Myrie!"

She turned to show Myrie and then gasped in horror. Myrie had dumped out the rest of the contents of Katkin's chest on the quilt. A silvery robe lay in her hands, and she clicked excitedly. Poppy forgot her wonder at the strange mirror pictures, and hurried over to Myrie.

"You can't have that! Katkin will be very angry if she finds out we went through her things." She tugged at the robe, but Myrie held on to it. Poppy dared not pull too hard, in case it tore, or Myrie started to scream. Desperately, she grabbed Gwillam's rabbit and held it before her. "Look Myrie, here is the rabbit. We must find Gwillam and give it to him. He will be sad without it."

Myrie clicked agreeably and reached for the rabbit, so Poppy took the robe from her. The silver fabric felt smooth, almost uncannily so. It was warm to the touch and the warmth made it feel almost like a living thing. A tingling calm filled her, along with the deep, earthy scent of patchouli. Poppy could not imagine where her Matre could have gotten such a strange garment.

Azothe...

Poppy looked at Myrie. "Did you say something just then?"

Myrie clicked vacantly. Poppy shook her head. "Of course you didn't. I must be out of my mind."

Quickly, she folded the robe and put it back in the chest, then gathered the other small objects that Myrie had scattered about on the quilt. Several amulets lay there, including one made of some bright red, soft stone. But the image of Gwillam, hurt and alone somewhere, drove all curiosity from Poppy's mind. She dumped them unceremoniously into the box and then shut the lid.

"Come on, Myrie! We must find Patre and tell him about Gwillam."

Later, as all the residents of Asaruthe crowded into the small sitting room at Ruthecombe, Poppy told the story of Gwillam's rescue. "Myrie made it work. She breathed on the mirror and then I saw Gwillam. I didn't know where he had fallen, but Myrie recognized the cave right away, I guess because she and Gwill used to play there. And then I saw..."

Huw spoke. "Is there more to this story, my little flower? You must tell us if there is." Poppy's eyes filled with tears as she stared at Lut. He looked away from her. "I saw one of the twins—I don't know which one—on the tops with a strange dog. He killed the sheep that Lut and I found." Jakob's head snapped up.

"What is this rubbish? Poppy is just trying to protect that brat, Gwillam. Where would either of us get another dog from, anyway?" He stood, waving his arms. "You can't prove it was one of us."

Lut twisted the bracelet on his wrist. "It... It wasn't me," he said, finally, and no one doubted that this was the truth.

"Well it wasn't me, either," Jakob blustered.

"So," said Gwenn, intractably. "That leaves Jolly. Now, if we have finished here we can get on with..."

A high-pitched wail made them all cover their ears. Myrie ran to the center of the room. "Wait," said Gwillam. "Myrie has something to say first." Myrie subsided into clicking again. She went on for some time and then Gwillam translated. "She says that there *is* another dog on the island, named Dagger. A wild dog that belongs to Jakob. He brought it back from Everruthe."

Jakob could hardly speak at first. A muscle in his jaw worked rapidly as a bright red stain crept from his throat to his face. Everyone else in the room kept silent. At last he growled, "He is making it up. Myrie's as crazy as a blind magpie, anyway. Look at her! Her stupid clicks don't mean anything. I don't..."

Everyone started speaking at once, asking questions, making accusations. Arkady's voice rose over the din as he thumped his cane hard on the floor. "Let me speak! I heard a strange dog barking a couple of weeks ago. I told you about it, remember, Gwenn?"

Katkin raised an eyebrow at this. "You already knew of another dog on the island, Gwenn?"

Gwenn looked chagrinned. "Well, I just thought, you know... Kadya can't see and he must have made a mistake."

"But his hearing is excellent," Huw commented dryly.

Jakob, forgotten in all the excitement, tried edging out the door. His frowning father rose and limped towards him. "Tell me the truth. Is there another dog?" Jakob stood, eye to eye with Gunnar, and he could not look away. After a tense moment, he nodded and Gwenn swore in disgust. Gunnar said to his son, "Go and fetch it and then wait for us in the woodshed. Your mother and I will be along presently." Jakob opened his mouth to argue and Gwenn stood, shaking her head.

"We had better go with him now, to make sure nothing else happens, Gunnar." She looked over to Gwillam. "I am sorry," she said stiffly. "Jakob will be punished for this."

Gwillam buried his face in Jolly's fur and did not say anything in return.

Three

Yew

"How is Myrie, Lut?" Poppy looked up from the Secunian journal of Josiah Tavish.

He shook his head and shrugged. "Ma says she is getting harder to handle all the time. Just lately, every time she sees Jakob, she runs, like she is afraid of him. And he is so angry, I can't blame her."

"Well, he did get punished pretty severely."

Lut frowned at this, but did not speak.

Poppy went back to her translation. "What does it mean here, where he says, 'at south by southeast distant five miles, with breakers forward and on the weather bow?' I don't understand any of it!" Poppy stood and stretched. "I am hungry. Do you want some bread and butter and a cup of milk? It is time we had a break. I can't think straight on an empty stomach."

She crossed to the kitchen and took two earthenware beakers from the shelf above the sink. A big stone crock filled with fresh milk stood nearby, and Poppy used the wooden dipper to fill the beakers to the brim. Lut came up behind her as she cut two slices of barley bread from a round cob.

"May I help?"

Poppy stood on her toes, trying to reach the tub of butter, which resided on another, higher shelf. The greasy crock slipped through her fingers. She dived forward in pursuit and almost lost her footing. Lut threw his arm around her waist, and just stopped her from tipping into the sink, while nimbly catching the butter with his other hand.

She swayed for a few seconds, trying to regain her balance. The arm around her waist tightened, and pulled her closer. Poppy turned and looked at Lut, whose expression was a curious mixture of discomfort and desire.

Poppy quickly wrapped both her arms around his neck. As their lips met, the butter tub fell from his fingers and shattered on the floor. Neither noticed. Though his kiss was clumsy, and nothing like Jakob's, Poppy felt a new and breathless eagerness drawing her onwards. But after a moment, the cheerful sound of whistling floated in from outside—Huw returning from a fishing trip on the *Able Drake* with Gunnar and Arkady.

Lut dropped his arms from around her waist, put his hands in his pockets, and did not say a word. Poppy knelt and began collecting the shards of the butter tub. She whispered, "That was lovely, what we just did. Did you think so, Lut?"

"Yes," he agreed softly, just as Huw entered, loaded down with his fishing tackle and a wicker creel. "Yes I did, very much."

Jakob spied shamelessly from behind a tree as Poppy and Lut strolled along the beach path, holding hands. He saw his brother stop and pick a bunch of bright yellow yarrow flowers and present it to her with a wide, happy smile. She reached high and pulled his head down to meet hers, and they kissed for a minute or more, lovingly; longingly.

He turned away in disgust and sat with his back against the trunk. Was it not enough that his father had thrashed him with the leather strop for lying, or that his mother had cut Dagger's throat right in front of him? His parents had also forbidden him to sail on the *Able Drake* for three months and had given him many unpleasant extra chores.

But to lose Poppy to his idiot brother Lut was by far the worst of these unfair punishments. He could not bring Dagger back, or revenge himself on Gwillam—not yet, anyway. His parents watched him far too closely these days. Gwillam's repayment could wait—but Poppy's most definitely could not.

As they passed beyond his sight, Jakob muttered a curse and headed back to the byre. He had a lot of cow dung to shovel before nightfall.

That night, Poppy lay in bed, unable to sleep for all the thoughts crowding her pillow. Though she and Lut had been inseparable for the last two months, he told her for the first time today that he loved her. And Poppy had spoken through the magical stillness that filled her heart—she loved him too, even though he was sometimes inarticulately shy. They talked of marriage and children, and their own sturdy stone cottage on the island. Lut said he would speak to her Patre, whenever she wanted him to. Poppy, ever cautious, had told him she thought they should wait just a little longer, and he had unquestioningly agreed.

She shook her head in the darkness, wondering what on Yrth she had ever seen in his asinine brother.

Ikora Gwenn had marched Jakob over to the house the day after the meeting. He stood before them, red-faced and glowering. After a long time he mumbled, "Um sree..."

His mother said sharply, "What is that? Louder, please."

Jakob, his humiliation complete, had said slowly and clearly, "I... am...sor...ree."

He had not spoken to her since. Poppy could not have cared less.

Her room was warm, and quiet, but still she could not sleep. She stretched luxuriantly, feeling the love Lut had declared for her right to her toes. Perhaps tomorrow she would tell him she was ready. He could talk to Patre, and Patre would be pleased and say yes, because Poppy knew he wanted her to be happy...

A shower of taps sounded at her window. She sat up and opened the shutters. The darkness made it hard to discern the figure standing below. "Poppy?" he whispered. "Will you come for a walk with me?"

Poppy's heart began to beat rapidly. Why would Lut be out at this hour of the night? She rose and slipped her flannel robe over her nightgown, then crept down the ladder and out the front door.

He waited for her on the far side of the yard. She hurried over, full of questions, but he put his finger to his lips and pointed to the house. Then he grasped her hand firmly and led her towards the birch grove.

Once the house had disappeared behind the rise, she said, "Lut? It is you, isn't it?" He nodded and held up his hand, and she saw the beaded wristlet. "Is everything all right?"

"I just wanted to see you, Poppy. Don't be mad."

Poppy smiled and shook her head. "I wasn't sleeping, anyway. I kept wanting to get out of bed and dance on the rooftops and shout 'Lut Strong Arm loves me!'" She laughed. "Listen to me! I sound like a crazy woman."

He made a face, knowing she could not see it. The late summer darkness curled about them like a warm, soft blanket. They walked until they reached the shelter of the birches. Then he flopped on to the soft sand and pulled her beside him. "Lut, what are you..."

He put his hand over her mouth. "We don't have to talk, Poppy. You must know what I want and why I brought you here. And you came with me willingly, and that means you want it too." He uncovered her mouth and then kissed her roughly.

Poppy pulled away, quite shocked at the boldness of this request. "Lut! What on Yrth has gotten into you? Just this afternoon you said you were happy to wait until we got married."

He grasped her shoulders and shoved her back onto the sand. "I changed my mind," he said, and it came out sounding like a snarl. "I want you now. I will have you... Now." He ripped open the front of her robe as Poppy screamed. Panic-stricken, she fought him, raking her nails across his cheek. But he was far stronger than she.

He crowed as Poppy's breasts spilled forth from her torn

nightgown. As he wrapped his fingers tightly around her wind-pipe, she went limp and sobbed in his arms. "Lut... How could you do this? I thought you loved me?"

Triumphantly, he threw himself on top of her, only to discover that her capitulation was a ruse. Poppy grabbed his ears and then snapped her head forward in a vicious head-butt. He felt the bones of his nose split wide and he cried out in pain. As the blood poured from his nostrils she plunged a finger into his eye socket, and he rolled away from her in agony, almost blinded. Seconds later, she was gone, running back towards her house.

Her frightened wails wafted back to him on the night breeze, "Patre! Patre! Lut..."

When Huw got to the other side of the island, to where Gwenn and Gunnar shared the big stone house with their sons, he saw the lights ablaze and heard the dogs barking madly. He charged forward, with his knife in his hand. The door stood wide open. Huw roared, "Where is he? Where is Lut?" The chaotic scene that met his eyes robbed him of any further speech. Furniture lay upended, as though a herd of wild cows had stampeded through the room. Broken crockery decorated the floor.

The twins were sitting, but not voluntarily. Many coils of stout rope restrained them. Gwenn stood between, with keth'fell in her hand, glaring. Both the boys had bloody, scratched faces, and insanely angry expressions. One said, "Let me go! I am going to kill him. Do you know what he did?"

"What you did, you mean," the other interrupted scathingly.

"Shut up," cried Gwenn. "Shut-up or I will kill you both myself, I swear it."

"Faircrow," Gunnar growled. "That is not helping." He saw Huw standing in the doorway and frowned darkly at the knife in his hand. "Leave your weapon outside," he ordered. "Then you can come in. Is Poppy all right?"

Huw placed the knife on the ground, just outside the door, and walked through. "She is not injured, physically. But she is very, very frightened and upset. Katkin has given her a sleeping draught." His anger boiled over. "Which one of you scummy turds is Lut? I have some business to finish with you."

Huw clenched his fists and strode forward, then stopped in

31

confusion. When Poppy had come to him, weeping with terror and shame, she had identified her assailant as Lut. She said there would be no doubt, because she had broken the nose of her attacker, and gouged his eye. But the two boys who sat before him had almost identical bloody and swollen noses, copious bleeding and many, many cuts and bruises.

Gunnar said, "We don't know if it was Lut. They keep accusing each other. Gwenn can't get any sense out of them, and neither can I." The boys began shouting at one another again, hurling accusations back and forth.

Huw shook his head. "Poppy said Lut attacked her. He had the wristlet on. She saw it."

"I took it off and left it by my bed," Lut cried. "Jakob must have taken it." His voice grew plaintive, "I didn't do anything to her, I swear it. I would never hurt Poppy."

"Liar," retorted Jakob.

Lut gave an inarticulate scream of rage and struggled wildly against his bonds. Gunnar called over to Huw, "You had better go home. In the morning we will bring the boys to your house, and perhaps by then we will have sorted out who did what."

Huw's eyes narrowed. "I will do as you ask, for now, but know this—when I find out which one of those ruffians hurt my little flower, I will kill him."

Gwenn raised keth'fell. "The hell you will, Firaithi. Stay away from my sons."

Huw spat in disgust, turned on his heel and walked out.

The morning came, clear and cool. The sun shone brightly on the island, and the weather promised to be warm and calm. But inside the Adaryi household the atmosphere was tense, as though a tempest lay just over the horizon. The meeting took place in the sitting room. All the residents of Asaruthe attended, with the exception of Myrie and Gwillam, who had been sent to the beach with a picnic lunch. Poppy sat silently, though an occasional tear trickled down her cheek. Her Patre and Matre sat beside her. She looked over at Jakob and Lut, separated by the length of the sitting room, with Gunnar and Gwenn between them.

Arkady, appointed judge and arbiter by common consent, sat in the middle of the room. No one spoke for a long while.

Jakob, though he had a black eye and a grossly swollen nose, did not seem troubled. Lut stared at his hands, clenching and unclenching in his lap.

Arkady's scarred face looked grave. "In the sixteen years that our two families have shared this island haven, we have lived in harmony. Now that peace has been shattered by an attack on Poppy Brunner, which occurred sometime late last evening. We are met here today to determine the facts, so that we can take appropriate steps to punish the guilty."

Huw muttered under his breath, "He will be punished, all right."

Arkady continued. "I want each of the young people to speak to me, one at a time. There are to be no interruptions. Do I make myself clear on that point, Huw? We will begin with Poppy."

Poppy took a deep breath, as her Patre gripped her hand tightly. In a trembling voice, she told of Lut's appearance at her window, the attack in the birch grove and her spirited defense. Arkady asked few questions of her. When she had finished he asked, "Are you sure that it was Lut Strong Arm who came to your window?"

"Yes," said Poppy uncertainly. Lut's head sank even lower, and he put his hands over his face. Poppy gave an unhappy cry when she saw that his wrists were bound with cord. "I mean, no. I don't know!" she wailed finally, and burst into a fresh round of tears. She buried her head on her mother's shoulder as Katkin embraced her.

Huw jumped to his feet. "Kadya! What good is all this talk?"

Arkady, unperturbed, said, "Now you, Jakob Strong Arm. Tell me what happened last night."

Jakob's broken nose gave his voice an unfamiliar twang. "I was sleeping when Lut came into our room. He woke me, and I saw right away that something had hurt him bad. I asked him what happened. At first he tried to pretend he had fallen down the cliff, but when I saw the scratches on his face I knew there was more to it. Eventually he admitted he had attacked Poppy."

Lut made an agonized sound. "It isn't true. It isn't true. He was the one." He looked over at Poppy, his eyes red-rimmed and brimming with tears. She looked away.

Arkady said sharply, "You will have a turn to speak, Lut. For now, please keep silent. Continue, Jakob."

"Well," rasped Jakob. "Of course, I was angry with him. I told him what he had done was very wrong, and he went crazy. He punched me in the face several times. I had to defend myself, so I tackled him and we went down. Then Ma heard us fighting and she and Dad broke it up."

Arkady nodded. "Gwenn, would you please tell me what you heard? Do you know which of the boys started the fight?"

Gwenn stared at her sons pensively. "I did not hear anyone come in from outside. If they had an argument, they did so quietly. But when they crashed out the door of their room and down the stairs, I came running. Gunnar came too, as soon as he found his crutches. We tried to question them, but they only wanted to kill each other."

"How about you, Gunnar?" Arkady asked next. "Can you add anything to Gwenn's story?"

Gunnar shook his shaggy blond head morosely. "I cannot believe that either of my sons is capable of this terrible crime. They bring shame upon my household."

"And you, Huw?"

Huw spoke firmly. "When Poppy came home, she told me that it was Lut who had attacked her. I have heard nothing this morning that contradicts that. It seems obvious to me that he is the guilty one."

"Katkin? Did you examine Poppy after the attack?"

"I did. She had some bruising in the throat area, but nothing serious. But I think she was very lucky. Last year, when Huw taught her self-defense, I thought he was wasting his time. Now I am glad he did."

Arkady sighed and spoke to Lut. "You stand accused of attempted rape. Poppy has identified you as her assailant. What do you wish to say in your defense? Think before you speak, for I must take anything you say into account when I make my judgment. Take as much time as you need." He sat back in his chair.

But Lut began to talk right away, though his voice was very quiet. "Poppy and I spoke of marriage yesterday."

Katkin and Huw exchanged alarmed glances at this. Poppy kept her face hidden.

Lut shifted in his chair and spoke with his head down, as though addressing his hands. "I told her I would ask her Patre whenever she was ready, and she told me she wanted to wait a little longer. I walked her home in the late afternoon and then went back by the byre. Jakob was busy mucking out the stalls, and I greeted him as I went past. Then I went home, had some supper and got into bed. I read a book for a while, and then blew out the candle. Jakob still wasn't home, and I wondered where he had gone. I thought about getting up to tell Ma, but I didn't. Much later, maybe after midnight, Jakob came in our room and told me what he had done to Poppy. He gloated about it. I hit him—yes, lots of times, but who wouldn't? But now I understand that he provoked the fight so that I would have injuries similar to his. He set this whole thing up to get back at Poppy and me."

Jakob shook his head sadly at this.

Arkady asked, "Have you finished your testimony, Lut?"

"I want to speak to Poppy." She raised her head and stared at him with burning cheeks, remembering the feeling of his hands tightening about her throat. "I would never, ever hurt you. But if you do not believe me, then there is nothing else I can say."

Arkady tapped his cane three times. "It seems to me that the single piece of real evidence we have is the beaded wristlet that Lut wears. Poppy identified her assailant by the presence of this wristlet. Jakob does not own a similar bracelet, does he?"

Gwenn shook her head, and then said "No" so that Arkady could hear her answer.

"It is possible that Jakob could have taken the wristlet from his brother. Did Lut mention losing it the day of the attack?"

Gunnar offered, "He said he left it on the table by his bed yesterday evening."

"This morning I found it tucked under his pillow," added his mother.

"And does it show any evidence of the attack?" Arkady prompted.

"I can see the blood on it from here," Huw said loudly.

"Poppy?" said Arkady. "Was Lut wearing the wristlet when you had the conversation about marriage?"

Everyone turned to look at Poppy. She closed her eyes, thinking back. They had strolled together, holding hands, through the upper meadow. Lut had stopped by a yarrow plant and picked a tender stalk of light yellow buds. He handed it to her with a shy grin. In her mind's eye, she could see the bracelet on his wrist as he did so.

Poppy gave a choked sob and nodded.

"Please speak, Poppy," Arkady said gently. "You must have no doubts."

Poppy said, slowly and clearly, "Yes, he had the wristlet on."

Lut broke into anguished tears.

Huw stood and brandished his curved knife. "I have heard enough!"

Gwenn and Gunnar stood as well, stepping in front of their son.

Arkady cried, "Sit down, all of you! And put that knife away, my brother."

Huw looked at him in surprise. "How did you..."

Arkady gave a cheerless smile. "You said yourself I have excellent hearing." His voice grew brisk. "Based on the testimony I have heard today, I am not convinced that Lut Strong Arm is guilty. Nor am I sure he is innocent. For Poppy's sake, I do not think he can remain on the island for the near future. And I do not believe that he would be safe staying here, given Huw's need to revenge himself on his daughter's attacker."

Katkin looked at him quizzically. "Then what do you suggest, Kadya? It would not be fair to cast him adrift on the mainland, especially since you are not sure he is the culprit."

"My ruling is this—Lut shall be exiled to Everruthe for the next six months. His father can take him there on the *Able Drake*, and leave him with enough supplies to last for a few weeks. Then once a week, we will visit him again, with more food, and check on his health." He addressed Katkin and Huw. "Do you still have that canvas tent lying around? The one you took from the Black Guard?"

"Yes, my brother. But I do not think this plan of yours is the proper one. It only delays the final day of judgment," Huw said.

"This *is* my final judgment," Arkady said sharply. "You agreed to be bound by my recommendation. If he is innocent, Lut will come to no harm on Everruthe, but if he is guilty, neither will he be able to escape his punishment."

Katkin stood, frowning, and stared at Jakob. "Huw may be sure of Lut's guilt, but I am not. Stay away from Poppy, Jakob. You are not welcome here at Ruthecombe." Gwenn opened her mouth to argue, but Katkin turned her back and led Poppy out of the room.

Poppy took her Patre's spyglass and ran all the way to the tops, even though she heard Katkin calling for her. Now she lay on her stomach at the edge of the cliff, looking towards the rocky inlet that served as the island's harbor. The sun beat on the back of her head, making her feel tired and a little dizzy.

She could see the *Able Drake* tied to the little dock. Gwenn bustled back and forth, carrying boxes and bags. Enough food and supplies to keep Lut for a month or more. Poppy shifted, trying to catch sight of him. As she slid forward, the pungent smell of wild thyme surrounded her like a cloud. The smell reminded her of home, of happy evenings at the kitchen table, eating supper with her parents and Gwillam. In Poppy's remembrance of her former life on the island, Myrie came and went with sociable frequency, as did the tall sons of Gunnar Strong Arm. But the attack had locked that life away from her, as firmly as a forgotten dream. Everyone treated her differently, with solicitousness she neither wanted nor needed.

Lut shuffled forward, with his father at his side. Ikor Kadya stood on the dock, next to Ikora Gwenn. Poppy trained the spyglass on her, and saw that she was crying. Lut embraced her, and shook hands with his Pop. Then he stepped over the gunwale of the *Able Drake*, and turned to offer a hand to his crippled father. This unselfconscious act of courtesy brought tears to Poppy's eyes.

"Lut..." she whispered. "Why should you be going? I could forgive you, no matter what you did, if..."

They had not let her see him of course. Huw had been most adamant about that, though she had begged and begged for a chance to talk to Lut before they sent him to Everruthe. Poppy believed that if she had been able to look him in the eye, to speak with him in a soft voice, as she had done on the day they were betrothed, then she could have found the truth. But no one would listen to her.

Now they were taking him away, and there was nothing she could do about it.

The spyglass trembled in her hand as she began to weep. Perhaps the sun caught the lens, because Lut Strong Arm looked towards the tops, to where Poppy lay hidden amongst the thyme bushes. He stared, shading his eyes with his hand, for many moments, as his father saw to the sail.

As the wind carried the little boat out to sea, Lut raised his hand in a silent farewell.

Four

Chestnut

"But I don't want to leave," wailed Poppy. Her Patre frowned.

"Gunnar and Jakob cannot sail the *Able Drake* all the way to Citternia by themselves. And now that Lut..." Huw decided not to finish that thought. "Come now, my flower. It will do you good to get away from Asaruthe for a while. The journey to Minbeorg is not difficult in good weather."

"Why can't Gwillam go?"

"Because of Myrie. Don't you remember what happened last time they separated for a day? Our eardrums would not be able to stand it."

"Why can't she go as well?" Poppy continued obstinately.

Katkin and Huw exchanged glances. "Myrie is a special girl—in more ways than one. We have a responsibility to protect her, and that means she must stay on Asaruthe. Anyway, Gunnar would not want Jakob and Gwillam together on the *Able Drake*. That boat is too small for arguments and they are barely civil to each other."

"And Jakob and I are? I hate him! You know, Ikor Kadya never said for sure that Lut was the guilty one, and Katkin said she didn't..."

Huw broke in. "Poppy, we have been over this a hundred times. Your Matre agrees that you are needed on this trip. Is that not correct, my Queen?"

Katkin frowned, but held her tongue. It seemed best to leave hidden the heated argument that she and Huw had had on the subject.

"How is he? Ikor Gunnar took more food over to Everruthe last week. Did he say anything about Lut?"

Katkin gave her an exasperated look. "I don't know. We seldom talk to Gwenn and Gunnar anymore. But look at it this way—if you sail to Minbeorg you can ask him yourself."

Poppy brightened. "All right, I will. But if Jakob says one word to me about..." She subsided into muttered threats as Katkin and Huw sighed.

She packed a bag with two week's worth of clothes, her leather bound journal and Josiah Tavish's sea log. It had been sixteen years since Poppy had left Asaruthe, but the prospect of doing so now did not fill her with anticipation. Minbeorg, on the coast of Citternia, was a bustling seaport, home to forty thousand souls. In the days when she and Jakob had still been friends, he described the docks to her, and the rough accommodation that lined the wharfside streets.

"There are sailors everywhere. Huge hairy men with tattoos and scarred faces. They like to get drunk when they are in a port, so there are taverns on every corner. Lut and I went into one last time we were there."

"What happened?"

Jakob gave her a lazy grin. "They threw us right back out again! But I am going to keep trying. Gods, I wish I could just leave here and never come back!"

This declaration surprised Poppy. "Why would you want to leave Asaruthe? It is so beautiful here, and so quiet. I love being able to stand on the tops and look out to sea, to where the horizon meets the sky. It makes me feel like a bird, wild and free."

"Quiet? It is practically dead! In Minbeorg there are shops, and parks, and..."

"And women for hire?" Poppy had teased.

Jakob blushed but met her eyes boldly. "Yes, that too. You don't understand what it is like to be a man, Poppy. A man needs excitement; adventure. But here I am stuck in this cemetery with nothing to look forward to. Someday soon..." He had subsided into a glazed look of anticipation.

Poppy snapped her case closed and carried it downstairs to the main room. Her Matre handed her a long list, written in her untidy scrawl. "I am running out of some supplies. While Jakob and Gunnar are negotiating for the foodstuffs, I want you to find an apothecary shop. Try to get as many of these things as you can, but mind they don't cheat you!"

She nodded obediently and accepted a small leather purse full of silver. Katkin looked at her daughter apprehensively. "Be very careful with that. Minbeorg is a rough place."

"I know, you told me so already. So did Patre. About ten or eleven times," said Poppy with a frown.

Katkin gave her a sheepish smile. "I am sorry. I forget sometimes that you are twenty-two years old." She laid a hand on her daughter's arm. "Get yourself something in Minbeorg as well. Something to cheer you. A new dress, or a book or two. It has been ages since you had a treat."

Poppy shrugged and did not return her smile. "I don't want anything, except..."

"Except for what, my flower?"

"Nothing." She sighed and then tucked the purse into a pocket on the inside of her leather jerkin. Huw took her case and they walked to the dock. Gunnar was on board the *Able Drake*, checking the water casks and food supplies. Jakob lounged on the deck, swatting flies. Poppy ignored him.

Gunnar greeted Poppy's parents stiffly and announced that they would be casting off in a few moments. Poppy put her small case on board and thought about Lut.

"Is there anything I can do to help, Ikor?" she asked as Gunnar limped about the deck on his crutches.

He gave her a grateful smile. "Yes. Could you lash down the bales of wool in the hold? And check the empty barrels too. I don't expect we will have any rough weather, but we must be prepared."

Poppy turned back to her parents. "Well," she said tonelessly. "Good-bye. I will see you in ten days or so."

Katkin smiled, though it did not affect her worried expression. "Don't forget about the list."

"I won't," said Poppy, sighing, and crossed the deck to the cargo hold.

"And Poppy?"

"Yes?" she asked, impatient now to be on her way, and done with good-byes.

"Have a lovely time..." Katkin added wistfully.

"Yes," said Huw. "And be careful. May the Un-Named One protect you, my little flower."

Poppy did not answer them, and after a moment her parents turned away and trudged back up the hill. Gunnar sent Jakob forward to cast off. Just then, Gwillam and Myrie came tearing along the sandy beach and scrambled over the rocks of the breakwater. Myrie grabbed Gwillam's hand and pulled him on to the dock as Poppy came forward.

"Myrie has something to give you," said Gwillam, breathlessly.

Jakob frowned, but kept silent.

Myrie held out her fist. Poppy recognized the crow's foot periapt from Katkin's keepsake chest. "Myrie!" she said in alarm. "This isn't mine. Why did you take it?"

But Myrie pushed it into Poppy's hand and closed her fingers around it. She clicked excitedly and Gwillam listened with growing alarm. "She says you must take care in Citternia." He looked over at Myrie. "Death? Is that what you said?"

Myrie nodded gravely.

"She says..." Gwillam did not know what to make of this message. "She says Death walks the streets there, like a silent ghost."

"Death?" repeated Poppy, apprehensively.

Jakob went to stand beside her. "Why don't you take crazy Myrie somewhere else to play? Go on, get lost. Can't you see you are scaring Poppy?"

Poppy stepped away from him. "You get lost, Jakob Strong Arm. I can take care of myself."

Gunnar called from the steering oar. "It is time to get underway. We need to catch the tide."

Gwillam knelt and unwound the twisted rope from the bollards. Jakob strolled forward and snatched the rope from Gwillam's outstretched hand. Myrie clicked again, thoughtfully.

Poppy called over to Gwillam as the boat drifted sideways from the dock. "What did Myrie say?"

The wind filled the sails. Gwillam scratched his head. "She said the tide is... *turning*."

Poppy stood at the gunwale, a little disquieted by the wide vista of water that surrounded the boat and stretched, like an undulating grey-green blanket, right out to the wide horizon. The *Able*

Drake cut cleanly through the waves, making good time in the fine weather that had blessed the voyage. She looked back at Gunnar, standing rock steady at the steering oar, though the deck rolled beneath his remaining foot and the crutches he used to walk with.

He had been mostly silent in the two days since they had left Asaruthe, and Poppy had not yet summoned the courage to ask him about Lut. In truth, she felt almost as afraid of Ikor Gunnar as she did Ikora Gwenn. Though he had a nice smile that crinkled his blue eyes engagingly, and a fine singing voice, Poppy knew of the terrifying strength that lurked behind his calm demeanor. Ikor Kadya had told her tales of that strength, and of other powers. She shook her head at the vague remembrance of the leviathan that had come at his command.

Lutyond, the Mariner...

She felt a jagged ache in her chest. What were the sons of a God made of, the stuff of Yrth—or heaven?

Jakob joined her at the prow. Unlike his father, Jakob had been *very* talkative, despite Poppy's best efforts to ignore and discourage him. "Don't worry," he said. "Dad knows this journey backwards and forwards. He won't get us lost."

"I know that," said Poppy, crossly.

"What is eating you then? You have hardly said a word to me since we started out." He looked at her gravely. "It has been almost two months since Lut attacked you, Poppy. Everyone else on the island has gotten over it, except for you. Why don't you stop making life difficult for the rest of us?"

Poppy glared at him. "What do you mean?"

"Well, you know... I heard Ma and Pop talking the other day, saying how gloomy the island has become. It is like our two families are feuding, and it is all because you won't accept the fact that Lut is guilty."

"Ikor Kadya said that? Said I should accept that Lut is guilty?"

Jakob stared at the foam-flecked waves. "Not exactly that, no. But he did say that he wished he could come and visit Uncle Huw, as he used to. You should stop being so selfish, Poppy."

At this, Poppy fell into silent reflection. She hadn't thought how her behavior affected the others who shared the island with her. Was she being selfish?

"Do you want some help with that old journal you brought with you?" he asked after a moment. "We will be in port tonight, but I have some time now." He looked hopefully at her, and again Poppy was reminded of Lut. The pain in her chest returned, but she smiled in a determined way.

"Of course, Jakob. That would be fine. We can read it together."

They sat with their backs to the mast, and Poppy held the book open on her lap. The wind kept trying to turn the page, so she spread her fingers out over the paper. Jakob deliberately brushed his hand against hers as he pointed and said, "Now this picture shows a ketch. That must be what kind of vessel the *Briny Leviathan* was."

Poppy pursed her lips and slid her hand away. She noted that he had bitten his nails to the quick. "Hmm? What kind of a ship is that, Jakob?" she murmured, but did not listen to his answer. She was still gazing at his fingers, and remembering.

"It is a trading vessel, Poppy. The kind you use to cross the ocean with. It has two masts, one square-rigged and one lateen-rigged." He pointed to the sails, and she looked at his fingertips again. "I would love to sail on a ship like that. Just think of all the places you could go."

This brought Poppy out of her reverie. "Why would you want to go anywhere? Asaruthe has all we need."

He shook his head in amazement. "Asaruthe? I can't believe you, Poppy. That beastly island is cold, damp and dead dull. I can't wait to leave there. Don't you want to come with me?"

The hands that had attacked her had chewed nails, she felt almost sure.

"Why not?"

"Because I have Asparitus. I don't need anything else."

"What is that?" Jakob asked eagerly. "May I have some?"

She looked at him with disdain. "It is the Firaithi way. We walk lightly on the Yrth. We take little and return much."

"I'd rather go someplace where I can have everything I want. Aspari... whatever, doesn't sound like much fun."

"It isn't meant to be," Poppy said sharply. "When did you start chewing your nails, Jakob?"

"Huh? What has that got to do with it?" Jakob looked at his fingers. "I don't know. A while ago. After Ma gave me all those extra chores, I guess."

"Oh," said Poppy, and got up. She walked to the gunwale and looked out to sea, thinking of Lut.

"Don't you want to work on the book any more?" he called, confused by her frostiness.

"No," she said. "No I don't. Not with you, anyway."

Minbeorg had a fine natural harbor, which stretched inland for a mile or more, between the arms of a narrow peninsula and the mainland. A wide river, called the Caladrene, emptied into the head of the basin. As the *Able Drake* approached the outlying islands, Poppy looked through the spyglass at the many houses clustered along the hills and valleys of the mainland. She shook her head, wondering what it might be like to live amongst so many strangers, and thinking she would find it unpleasant after the wide-open spaces of Asaruthe.

Ikor Gunnar called her back to the stern. He said gravely, "When we berth in the town, try not to talk to the locals any more than you have to. We must not draw attention to ourselves."

"But... But Ikor, I have a list that Katkin gave me, for the Apothecary shop."

He smiled. "You can still go shopping. But if anyone asks questions, just say you live on an island to the south of Citternia, called Vangesu."

Gunnar called to Jakob to lower the sail and light the lanterns that hung from the bow. The winds had slackened during the afternoon, slowing their progress, and now as they made their way through the narrow mouth of the harbor, twilight's gloom lapped against the oaken strakes of the *Able Drake*. Two larger ships, festooned with many lights, blocked their passage. Gunnar cursed and hove to, just missing the leading vessel's stern.

"Ahoy!" A commanding voice rang from the ship, speaking Cittese, a close variant of Dalvolk. "How many souls on board? Where are you bound?"

Gunnar looked baffled. "Two others and myself. Why have you stopped us? We want a berth for a few days so that we may trade locally."

Several lanterns appeared, as men hung over the gunwales of the larger ship. "Any sickness amongst you?"

Jakob looked askance at them. "What? Are you mad? Of course not."

Gunnar murmured, "Let me do the talking, lad." He limped to the rail and looked towards the larger ship, called *Grosvenor*. "We have no illness."

"Stand by for inspection." The voice boomed out of the darkness, making it clear that this was no polite request. Three men, crowded into a small rowboat, crossed the intervening stretch of water.

"What is happening?" Poppy asked fearfully, and Gunnar shook his head in a warning for her to keep silent.

"This is strange," Jakob whispered. "We have never been stopped like this before."

"Shhh..." said Gunnar again, as the three men came aboard.

They wore kerchiefs over their mouths, making their voices indistinct. "Line up over there, all of you." As Poppy, Jakob and Gunnar obeyed, one of the men held up a lantern, searching for any others who might be aboard. The second man inspected the cargo hold. The third man looked at each of them in turn, holding the lantern close to their faces.

Gunnar grew exasperated. "Look, just what is all this about?"

"The Bludseth. Everyone who enters the harbor has to stop for inspection. Orders of our Master, Perriam. Now turn around and raise your tunics so I can see your backs."

"What in Od's name is a Bludseth?" Gunnar asked, with increasing concern.

The man's eyes narrowed. "Where be your home? I did not think I could meet a man from Yr who knew nothing of the Bludseth."

Gunnar kept his voice casual. "Well, now it seems you have, friend. Will you tell me or shall I call over to your Master on the *Grosvenor*?"

"First let me see your backs," the man insisted.

Gunnar, Jakob and Poppy followed his order.

"All clear," called the other two men, who had finished their inspection of the ship.

"Clear," echoed the third man, after he had studied their backs by lantern light. Gunnar turned and looked at the man expectantly. He shrugged. "There is a wasting sickness that plagues Yr. Some say it started in the South, but it spread quick-like, from Shadion to Danica. Some calls it the Bludseth, others—the walking Death."

Poppy paled and swallowed. "Walking death?"

"Aye, for a man can be dying unawares. It starts with a powerful thirst, so I've heard, and then a pain in the head. Red marks appear on the back, and sometimes on the face. Next thing he knows he's deader than a stone."

"Is this fell sickness abroad in Citternia?" Gunnar asked.

"Nay. Nor will it be, if we can help it. The Master has ordered checks on every vessel coming into the harbor. What is your cargo?"

"Carded wool, mostly."

"You'll do all right for yourselves then. Prices are high for such wares, just now. Not many ships coming in over the Reach. But if you want merchandise in return, expect to pay out royal for it."

Gunnar sighed, thinking of his own list of supplies.

They spent the night at an inn called the Guanock, with a bright yellow beacon painted on the hanging sign over the door. Poppy's room, little more than a cupboard with a grimy window, over-looked Wharf Street. It was furnished simply, with a narrow, lumpy bed and a small table. A cracked and somewhat dusty ewer sat on top, leading Poppy to the conclusion that the residents of the Guanock might not be overly fond of washing. She undressed and slipped beneath the covers, though it felt a little odd to be sleeping in a stationary bed after four days at sea.

The street noises outside seemed likely to keep her awake, but Poppy soon began to dream.

She wandered through a cold and forbidding landscape, where many white buildings stood forlornly empty, with boarded-over windows. On moving closer, she saw, to her dismay, that they were not empty after all. Many hands, grimy and scratched, with pale, bluish nails, reached out from between the cracks in the boards—reached out and caught at her clothing and hair. Poppy tried to run, but the bony hands held her fast.

"Hurry," a voice said. "Hurry, we are waiting for you."

Poppy thrust the hands away, and ran.

Many men, dressed in black, were marching across a paved square. They carried swords and guns, waving them at a band of raggedy skeletons who cowered before them. *Black Guard.* Poppy looked up as a vast shadow blocked out the light. A huge appa-rition hovered overhead, glowing faintly, and looking for all the world like some puffed up creature pasted against the sky.

A small, rotund man addressed a group of guardsmen. He fiddled with the wide golden circlet perched on his head. He said, "I need more. Bring them all to me. All of them." Then he pointed to Poppy. "Get her, she is one of them!" The Black Guard whirled in formation, like a flock of birds, and glided towards her.

A single man, brown-skinned and dark-haired like her own people, stood between her and the approaching soldiers. He drew his sword with a flourish, and then turned to give her a fetching smile. The hordes of Guardsmen trampled him into the dust.

She woke with a terrified moan and then lay very still, hoping she had not woken Ikor or Jakob, who shared the room next door. The sounds drifting in from outside, as the taverns emptied and carousing sailors made their way back to the ships, somehow comforted her. After a time, Poppy turned over and slept, untroubled by further dreams.

The morning dawned fine. The three travelers met in the dining room of the Guanock. As Jakob wolfed down greasy strings of sausage and about six fried eggs, Poppy sipped a cup of strong coffee and nibbled a sweet roll.

Gunnar asked, "Where are you bound today, Poppy?"

"To the Apothecary shop. Though I don't know where it is."

"There is a whole street full of them," Jakob said, with his mouth full. "Three blocks from Wharf Lane. I will show you after breakfast." He chewed and swallowed rapidly at a black look from his father.

"You will stay here and guard the boat, while I see to the trades," said Gunnar firmly. "Poppy can find her own way." Jakob looked disappointed.

"Of course I can. I will meet you back at the *Able Drake* when I am finished. How long will we stay here, Ikor?"

Gunnar shrugged. "I planned for us to stay three or four days, but the reports of this Bludseth disease trouble me. If we can finish our business soon enough, I think we will depart this evening."

Jakob's face fell still further, and Poppy guessed he had been planning another visit to the bawdy house. She gave him a wicked grin. "Don't worry; you will be back again—in another six months." He scowled at her as she marched out the door.

Poppy found the street of the Apothecary's Guild without much difficulty. She studied the elaborately painted signs, and then chose an imposing building with a pair of twined serpents executed in stained glass over the lintel of the door. High windows lit the wide counter dividing the main room. A young lad, of perhaps sixteen summers, stood attentively as Poppy wandered through the shelves. The familiar smells of woody herbs and powdered fungus made her think poignantly of home, and Katkin's sickroom.

"May I help you, Miss?" the assistant asked her in Cittese.

Poppy, who spoke Dalvolk well enough to understand him, said slowly, "I have a list of medicines and supplies that I need. Please tell me what it will cost to fill."

She handed it over to the boy. He raised an eyebrow and then called out, "Frater Berga, come forward a moment, if you please."

An older man, wearing dark robes and a pince-nez, bustled out of the back room. "What is it, Wulf? I am very busy." The boy handed over the piece of paper without any explanation.

Berga looked across the counter at Poppy. His hatchet-shaped face reminded her uncomfortably of a hawk. "Is this your list?" he asked. She did not like the way his dark, beady eyes were staring at her from over the top of his pince-nez, which dangled insecurely from the end of his bony nose.

Poppy flushed. "My mother made it for me, Sir."

"And why is your mother in need of such a quantity of arnica, if you don't mind my asking?"

Poppy, remembering Gunnar's warning, said primly, "Actually, I do mind. Now, if you cannot assist me, then pray return the list and I will trouble you no further." She could not help adding, "There are plenty of other shops on this street where I may spend my silver."

The older man signaled to Wulf, who vaulted the counter and got behind Poppy before she could even think of running. He slammed the door to the shop and snibbed the lock, then stood glaring at her.

Her eyes flitted from Wulf back to the old man. "Why do you detain me, Sir?"

"I have been given an order, by the Master of Minbeorg," said Berga, quietly. "I must report to him anyone who asks for all but very small quantities of certain preparations, including arnica and feverfew."

"W... Why?"

"These things are believed by some to be useful in the treatment of the Bludseth." He opened the hatch in the counter and stepped through, his black robes rustling menacingly. The hawk's face stopped right in front of hers. "Is that why you have asked me for them?"

Poppy shook her head wildly. "No! My mother is a physician. She may only trade for supplies a few times a year. That is why she requires a large measure of each of these items. There is no Bludseth on our island, I swear it."

"And where is this island, young lady?"

"Van... Vangesu, south of Citternia. Do you know it, Sir?"

"Indeed, I do," he replied gravely. "One of the worst outbreaks of the Bludseth occurred there, just a few months ago. Over half the population succumbed, I am told."

Poppy licked her suddenly dry lips.

By early afternoon, when Poppy still had not returned, Gunnar sent Jakob to the Apothecary Street to find her.

He gave his son a worried smile, "She has probably just gone shopping and forgotten the time. You know how women are." Then he turned back to his negotiations, frowning as a merchant said that he could not possibly fill an order for a hundredweight of rye flour, as the Bludseth had compromised their suppliers on the Main.

Jakob, given this unexpected opportunity to indulge himself, went straight to the first bawdy house he found. Two hours passed before he thought to look for Poppy and another hour slipped by whilst he made enquiries and found her whereabouts. When he returned to the *Able Drake*, out of breath and in a panic, Gunnar had already given up on his attempts to secure foodstuffs for the day. He sat on an empty barrel, smoking his pipe.

"Dad! Dad! Poppy is in the town lock-ups." Jakob skidded to a halt before Gunnar, who stood quickly, groping for his crutches.

"What in Od's Name?! Do you know why?"

Jakob shook his head. "Not exactly. Apparently, some of the things Grandmother put on her shopping list are banned or something. The Apothecary called the Constables and they took her away."

"How long ago did this happen?"

"I don't know. I have been looking for her all afternoon, but I just found out." Jakob cut his eyes away from his father, but Gunnar was far too worried about Poppy to notice.

"I had better get over to the prison. You stay here with the boat."

"But Dad..."

Gunnar dropped his voice to a whisper. "Listen, Jakob. We are in danger here, all of us. I have been hearing rumors from the traders all afternoon. They say the mainland of Yr is anarchy now, because so many of the ruling families have fallen prey to the disease. Only King Tristan of Beaumarais wields any real power."

Jakob swallowed. "*Uncle* Tristan, mother's brother?"

"Aye, the same. I never should have let Poppy go into town alone, not without looking at that list. She might have asked for remedies needed for the treatment of the Bludseth."

"And what? That doesn't sound so bad."

"Tristan has given an order than anyone found hoarding medicine is to be executed. Now do you see how serious this is?"

Jakob sat on the barrel, wondering if his ill-timed trawl of the district whorehouses might cost Poppy her life. "Look... We need to get Poppy out of the lock-ups, and you can't do it alone, can you? Not on crutches." His father stared at him, seemingly undecided, and Jakob pressed on. "If she is in danger now, it is my fault, Dad. I could have found her a lot sooner, but I..."

Gunnar frowned. "You can explain yourself later. Come on."

He limped away and hailed a horse-drawn hansom.

The Constables who brought Poppy to the lock-ups had questioned her once, gently, but she had not told them where she came from or the names of her companions. They were plainly annoyed at this, and had left her alone, saying they would return with a Magisterial Inquisitor.

Now she sat disconsolately in a square, stone-walled cell, wondering what would happen to her. The late afternoon sun shone through the half-moon window high above her head, creating a pattern of light and shade on the stone floor. She raised her hand and idly waved it about, making the outline of a bird that flitted through the shadowy bars.

A blue-uniformed Constable provided a welcome distraction. He approached the door, holding a diminutive young man by the scruff of the neck.

"Have you come to release me, Sir?" asked Poppy, without much hope.

He did not answer. After retrieving a bunch of brass keys from his pocket, he unlocked the cell door and shoved the boy in with Poppy. He slumped on the bench opposite her and sat silently, with his hands stuffed into the pockets of his threadbare breeches. "Cells are right full today, Miss. You'll have to share with this thieving wharf rat."

Poppy called to his retreating back, "I have done nothing wrong! Why will you not let me go?" The Constable ignored her pleas. Sighing, Poppy turned her attention to her cellmate. He had long, wavy hair, quite dark, and coffee-colored skin. The delicate features of his face were almost girlishly pretty. But something about him made her think of her Patre, so she asked, "Do you belong to the Kindreds?"

He scowled. "A stinking darky? Is that what you just called me?"

She blinked, taken aback by his reaction. "I asked if you were Firaithi, as I am. I didn't mean it as an insult. My name is Poppy." She held out her hand, but he glared at her and shifted further away on his bench.

"You?" he hooted. "A Firaithi? Don't make me laugh. You blue pots will have to come up with a better dodge than that to fool me."

Poppy looked very offended. "I *am* Firaithi," she insisted hotly. "On my mother's side. She belonged to the Kindred of Gitasha. What is a blue pot, anyway?"

The boy frowned at her for a moment. "Where did you get that from?" he asked and pointed to the crow's foot periapt that Myrie had given her.

"It belongs to my adoptive mother. She is Firaithi too. So is my Patre Huw..."

The boy suddenly looked much more interested. After putting a finger to his lips, he crossed the cell and sat beside her. "Shhh," he said, urgently. "Not so loud. You shouldn't go blabbing to just anyone about being Firaithi."

"Why not?"

He dropped his voice to a whisper. "What rock have you been under? King Tristan is hunting the Kindreds on the Main. Something to do with the Bludseth."

"Is that why you are in..."

He shook his head. "The blue pots got me for stealing at the Market." The young man watched her for a long moment, no doubt wondering if she could be trusted. Poppy held his stare unblinkingly. "My name is Rab," he said, finally. "Short for Rabbit. I belonged to the Kindred of Kiran. Until they were captured by the Ouzels."

"Ouzels? What on Yrth?"

He gave her a frankly mystified look. "Where have you been hiding out for the last ten years? You know, the Ouzels... The Black Guard."

Poppy nodded and said sympathetically, "They took your family? They got mine too, a long time ago. But how did you escape?"

"The Kirani knew the Ouzels would soon swoop from the sky in one of those infernal aermaran, so they sent us lathies* away— to Citternia. Our people don't travel here, because it isn't on either of the Ambits†, so they hoped the Ouzels would not look here either."

"So you are all hiding in Minbeorg?"

He sighed. "Not anymore. An older lad named Bear got the idea we should try and get back to the Main, and go to Bryn Mirain. Everyone was tired of living on the streets, so they agreed."

Poppy looked stricken. "But Bryn Mirain is gone."

"Don't I know it! Nowt but a burned out hole in the ground now. But there were Ouzels keeping an eye out. They got Bear and Mouse and Dog right away. I saw them being marched into an aermaran. The rest of us split up. I stowed away on a tradeship and came back here."

"What made you decide to trust me, all of a sudden? I mean, at first you accused me of being a blue pot, whatever that is."

He flashed a rakish grin. "A blue pot is a Constable, because their helmets look like upside-down chamber pots. I thought maybe they were trying to trick me, by putting me in a cell with a plant, but then I saw the necklace you were wearing. Only one of our people would have something like that."

---

* Firaithi children.

† The greater and lesser Ambits are the routes the Firaithi follow through Yr. Since Citternia is a large island off the coast, it has never been part of their journeys.

She looked about, but she could see no greenery. Rab guffawed loudly. "Have you been alone on an island all your life or something? Don't you know what a plant is? A stoolie? A snitch?"

Poppy, thoroughly baffled, shook her head.

"Ah well, never mind. You're with me now. What are you in for, anyway?"

She shrugged. "I don't know, exactly. I went into an Apothecary shop and asked for some medicine. Next thing I knew..."

"What sort of medicine?"

"Arnica, feverfew, bloodwort and a lot of other things. My mother made me a list."

He gave a low whistle. "They got you in here on a hoarding charge."

"Hoarding? What do you mean?"

Rab explained about the law and its punitive consequence. Poppy paled. "But they can't execute me! I haven't done anything wrong." She burst into tears.

"Don't worry. I said I would look out for you and I meant it. Now listen, this is what we have to do..."

Jakob loitered close by an imposing front door, keeping an eye on the constables standing guard. His father searched the darkened street behind the prison, looking for the back entrance. Earlier, a few judicious inquiries amongst the locals at a nearby tavern had given him a rough layout of the building. The cells were in the basement, with barred windows facing the inner courtyard.

Gunnar spied a narrow access tunnel that plunged straight through the building to the yard. A heavy iron gate blocked his way. After making sure he was unobserved, Gunnar stepped sideways and a little to the left, hoping to cross into the Vastness. It had taken him ages to get the hang of this movement again after he lost his leg, and he could not always manage it, even now. This time, after he opened his eyes, he could still hear the clang and rush of a passing horse-drawn trolley.

He tried again without success. Gunnar swore in frustration and wrapped his fingers around the bars. He pulled, straining hard, until the massive gate tore away from the hinges. The tunnel lay dark and silent before him as he limped through the opening and replaced the gate. He crept towards the yard, all the while regretting that he had not thought to bring his sword with him to Minbeorg.

"Help! Help!"

A Constable came running and held a lantern to the bars. "What is it?"

"I have been taken ill. My head, Sir. It feels about to burst asunder." With this carefully calculated appeal, Poppy slumped to the floor of her cell.

Rab cried, "Don't leave me in here with her. She's got the Bludseth, she has."

The constable cursed and fumbled for his key ring, then unlocked the cell door. As he knelt over the stricken girl, Rab darted by. The constable lunged after him, but he twisted away and escaped into the corridor before disappearing into the darkness.

Poppy sat up in surprise, crying, "Wait! You said you would help me escape!"

The constable gave her a hard, backhanded slap that rattled her teeth. "That'll teach you to play tricks on me, Missy. Not that it did you much good. You should have known not to trust a filthy little street rat like that 'un. Now get on that bench and don't let me hear another peep out of you tonight. The magistrate sent word to say he'll be here first thing in the morning."

Poppy curled up on the hard, wooden platform and wept, wondering whether Ikor Gunnar and Jakob would be looking for her, and what they would do when they found she was in the lock-up. Ikor had said that he wanted leave Citternia tonight, because of the Bludseth. Perhaps they would just sail back to Asaruthe without her...

An hour passed, and Poppy must have slept a little, for she jerked violently when a whisper drifted from the barred window above her head. "Poppy? Give three taps if you are in there."

She knocked on the bench three times and then watched in fearful amazement as Ikor Gunnar casually ripped her window bars away. He looked through the space, measuring the distance to the floor. Then Gunnar's head disappeared and Rab scrambled into the cell.

"Rab!" Poppy whispered joyfully. "You came back."

"Quickly, I hear the constables." Rab laced his fingers and Poppy placed her foot on the makeshift step. He flung her upwards, into Gunnar's arms. She gave a gasp of pain as the rough bricks scraped against her arms and chest, but she managed to scramble through as he pulled her backwards. They both collapsed in a heap onto the rough cobbles of the yard.

Gunnar got up first. "Come on! We must help the lad before the guards raise the alarm."

Poppy resourcefully dangled one of his crutches from the window. Rab caught the end and held on as Poppy and Gunnar dragged him upwards. Seconds later, they crossed the yard and fled back into the tunnel, just as a bell began to clang insistently. Gunnar waited until they had cleared the archway back onto the street, and then wedged the gate into the opening, cutting off their pursuers.

Jakob waited around the corner, at the reins of a hansom cab. "Get a move on. They are coming!" he hissed at them.

A solid block of the constabulary moved in his direction from up the street. The night air exploded with the sound of flintlock fire as Gunnar, Poppy and Rab hurried across the pavement. Just as they stepped from the curb, Rab gave a strangled cry and clutched at his calf. Gunnar snatched him up and threw him in the cab, and he and Poppy piled in behind. Jakob snapped the reins, soon disappearing into the maze of back streets and alleys that ringed the harbor.

No one spoke until they reached the wharf, and the *Able Drake's* berth. Jakob looked over to the young man who had helped them rescue Poppy and said casually, "So long. Thanks again. We never would have found her without your help." Rab stared at him a moment, then turned and started to limp away.

Poppy ran to catch him. "Rab, wait! Come with us."

Jakob said sharply, "Let him go, Poppy."

Gunnar frowned at his son. "We cannot abandon the lad here. He is hurt."

"How can we take anyone else to the island, Dad? There won't be enough food for us as it is."

Poppy set her mouth. "I don't care. He is a kinsman of mine, of the Kirani. Either he comes with us or you can leave me behind too."

Sounds drifted along the street—shrill sounding whistles, and many horse's hooves clattering on the cobbles. "None of us will be going anywhere if we don't man the oars and get out of this harbor," Jakob said urgently.

"I can help with the rowing," said Rab, quietly. "I know all about boats."

"Good lad," said Gunnar. "Welcome aboard."

The whistling pop of gunfire sent them all scurrying for the boat.

Five

Aspen

The sea outside the harbor lay dark and still, without a breath of wind stirring. Gunnar kept them at the oars for a long while before he put the boat into a narrow inlet far to the north of Minbeorg. "We should be safe enough here for the rest of the night," he said. "Now, lad, we should have a peek at that leg of yours."

Rab shook his head and his voice sounded curiously reluctant. "'Tis nothing, Sir. Just a scratch."

Poppy sat beside him on the deck, taking deep breaths to slow her labored breathing. She looked over to Rab. "I will bandage it for you. It is the least I can do after you risked yourself for me. Pass the lantern, Jakob."

Jakob rose, frowning, and unhooked the lantern from the mast. "I still think we should put him ashore."

"Put yourself ashore, oaf, and don't bother coming back. You won't be missed," Poppy snapped at him, as she tore the thin breeches material away from the wound. The ball had grazed the smooth flesh of Rab's calf, leaving a three-inch gash. Poppy used a clean cloth to bathe it with some seawater. Rab gave a muffled cry of pain, and twisted his head away before wiping tears from his eyes.

She gave him a reassuring pat on the knee. "Sorry. Katkin says saltwater is the best thing, but it does hurt like blazes." After finishing the bandaging as gently as she could, she settled back onto the deck with a sigh, thinking of her rescue.

"How did you know where to find me, anyway?"

Gunnar answered her question. "I was just about to step into the prison yard, when I saw your friend Rab appear out of nowhere, running towards me. He stopped and asked if I was looking for you."

Poppy turned her head to where Rab lay on the deck, with his eyes closed. "How did you know Ikor Gunnar was trying to find me?"

"Just a stab in the dark," he answered, without opening his eyes.

"Indeed," agreed Gunnar. "Once Rab told me which cell they had you locked up in, and what time the guards did their rounds, I sent Jakob to borrow a horse and cab. Once he returned, Rab and I went to fetch you."

"And I thank you for that," said Poppy quietly. "But what will we do now?"

"Head further up the coast," Jakob suggested. "See if we can buy supplies at some of the smaller villages."

Gunnar nodded. "Yes, I think that will be best. We cannot go back to Asaruthe with an empty hold. At least I got a tidy sum for the wool. But for now, we should get some sleep. The morrow can look after itself." Gunnar stretched out at the stern and soon began snoring. Jakob did the same.

Poppy, still restless and excited after her arrest and miraculous rescue, whispered over to Rab, "You will like Asaruthe, I promise. And my parents are very kind. They will make you welcome, and so will my little brother Gwillam."

"I shall look forward to meeting them, especially your Patre Huw. But who else lives on this island?"

"My Ikora Gwenn and her two husbands, and their children. Jakob and Lut are the twins, and they have a sister called Myrie. But Lut isn't actually there right now..." Poppy's voice trailed away and she changed the subject. "Did you see what Ikor Gunnar did to the bars of my cell? Sometimes he can be quite terrifying, but he is truly very nice."

"I know," said Rab matter-of-factly. "I do not fear him. His powers are great, but the Mariner is a good and gentle man."

"How did you..." Poppy began, but Rab turned away from her, and slept.

Gwillam and Myrie ran down the hilltop towards Ruthecombe. Katkin came outside, drying her hands on a rough towel, when she heard Myrie's excited shrieks. "What is it? Gwillam, is everything all right?"

"They are coming!"

"Who?"

"The *Able Drake*. Myrie and I saw it with the spyglass from on top of Bird's Hill."

Katkin frowned. "They are back early then. I hope everything went as planned."

Then Gwillam imparted a far more startling piece of news. "There is a stranger on board with Poppy and Jakob and Ikor!"

She looked very surprised at this. "Are you sure?"

Gwillam nodded. "He has long hair and dark skin, like Patre."

"Who has dark skin like me?" Huw came up and ruffled Gwillam's hair affectionately.

Katkin spoke worriedly. "Gwillam says there is an extra person on the *Able Drake*. He saw them through the spyglass."

"Truly, my Queen? We must send word to Gwenn and Kadya right away." He turned to Myrie. "Run home and tell your mother that the boat is coming back." Myrie clicked twice and set off along the track towards Asavale.

Gwillam trailed after her, calling back, "See you at the dock."

Katkin and Huw strolled across the tops to the cliff path. They could see the *Able Drake*, still far out to sea, but moving with the incoming tide. Katkin watched the billowing white sail pensively. "I cannot believe Gunnar would compromise our hiding place by bringing a stranger to Asaruthe."

Huw shrugged. "We should wait and hear what he has to say, Queen of my heart. But I can perhaps think of an explanation. Gwillam said the stranger was Firaithi. Is it possible this person might be known to one of us?" They reached the cliff, then slid down the steep path before fetching up on the sandy shore. The *Able Drake* closed rapidly as they hurried to the dock.

Gwenn and Arkady were already there, standing close together, with his arm encircling her waist. Myrie pranced about, whirling with her arms outstretched and head thrown back.

Gwenn snapped, "Stop that Myrie, or you will be sick." Myrie shrieked and turned even faster, until she collapsed on to the sand, and lay there giggling breathlessly.

Arkady smiled at the sound of her laughter. "Let her be, Gwenn. As long as she is happy, what does it matter?"

"That is not enough, and you know it. When will she grow

up—be normal, for the gods' sakes?" She dropped her voice to a whisper. "How can she be the one the Firaithi are waiting for? Maybe we have made a terrible mistake."

Arkady stroked Gwenn's hair. "No child that is loved is ever a mistake, my crow girl. You and I made Myrie together, and for that reason alone I love her. But she *is* the Dawnmaid. I know it in my heart, and you do too."

Gwenn sighed and looked at Myrie, running her fingers through the sand and clicking away to herself. "Perhaps she will change. Her time may not come for a long while yet."

"Perhaps," said Arkady. "Perhaps..."

The ship drew up to the dock and Poppy called, "Ahoy, land-lubbers! Stand ready for the mooring line." She tossed the rope to Gwillam, who wound it around and around the bollards. Poppy and Jakob hopped over the gunwale, and Gunnar handed over her case. Katkin and Huw crowded forward and embraced their daughter.

"You are back so soon, my flower," said Huw. "We were not expecting you for another two days." He called over to Gunnar, "How did the trading go?"

Gunnar eased himself over the railing and on to the dock. The young man known as Rab held his crutches as he did so, and then passed them over. "Not well," Gunnar answered. "There is a lot of news, and none of it is good. We had better have a serious talk up at our place, sometime soon."

Huw made a small distracted sound of agreement as Katkin said, "Poppy, who is your new friend?"

Poppy dragged Rab over to where her parents stood. He smiled diffidently and looked at the worn wood planks of the jetty as she introduced him.

Poppy spoke now in Firai. "This is Rabbit, son of the Kirani. He saved me."

"What on Yrth?" asked Katkin. "Did you get into some sort of trouble in Minbeorg?"

Myrie pushed into the middle of the group, with Gwillam just behind her. Rab looked taken aback as she pointed at his chest and said, "Clack, clack, click."

"That's Myrie," Poppy explained. "She always talks like that. And this is my brother Gwillam. He can understand her."

Gwillam flushed bright red and said in a shocked voice, "Myrie! I am not saying that out loud. Where did you even *learn* that word?"

Poppy shook her head, a little embarrassed by Myrie's bad manners, but Rab seemed not to notice. "This is my Matre, Katkin, daughter of the Anandi."

Katkin held out her hand, and Rab shook it. "*Tsmare onat shalomir,** Katkin of the Anandi," he said quietly.

"Welcome to Asaruthe, Rab. *Tsmare dila onarion.*"†

"And this is my Patre, Huw, first son‡ of the Chandrathi," Poppy said proudly.

A cloud chose that moment to scud across in front of the sun, casting them all in shadow. Rab drew himself up tall, though he was still a little shorter than Poppy's Patre. His deep hazel eyes caught Huw's and held them. The boy thrust out his chin and said, "*Tsmare onat shalomir*, Huw of the Chandrathi."

Huw did not give the proper reply. He merely gave Rab's hand a perfunctory shake and then said listlessly, "Please excuse me. I must check on some fishing lines." He hurried along the beach.

Gwenn, Jakob and his two fathers were leaving the jetty. Gunnar called over, "May the lad stay with you tonight? There are tales to tell today, and we all need rest."

Katkin nodded. "Of course. He can share Gwillam's room."

Gwillam did not look overjoyed at this idea. Neither did Rab.

Rab and Katkin walked up the path towards Ruthecombe together, with Poppy and Gwillam behind them. Poppy slowed her pace, and then whispered to her brother, "What did Myrie say?"

"You mean when she pointed at Rab's chest?"

Poppy nodded.

Gwillam's face went bright red. "She said... 'He's got tits.'"

Poppy sat in the living room, sipping tea, and spoke of her adventures in Minborg. Katkin shook her head in dismay when she realized that it had been her shopping list that placed Poppy in such peril.

---

* May the moon give you greeting.

† The moon shines on us all

‡ The son of the Tane

"So were you able to make any trades at all?"

Poppy sighed. "After we escaped from Minbeorg with Rab, we continued up the coast. We stopped at several small villages, but nowhere could we find the things we needed in the quantities Ikor wanted to buy. There is very little food in the hold of the *Able Drake*, I am afraid, and even less medicine."

Katkin patted Poppy's hand. "Don't worry, we will manage somehow, I expect. Now I should have a look at Rab's wound. I am sure you did a good job with the bandage, but I want to make sure it is healing well. Do you know where he went?"

"Rab went for a walk a little while ago. He said he wanted to stretch his legs after so many days at sea. I hope he won't get lost."

Katkin smiled. "He seems like the sort of lad who can look after himself."

Rab walked across the tops, following the same path taken by Huw some moments earlier. They would meet eventually, when Huw turned back towards Ruthecombe, but Rab felt content, for now, to defer that meeting and the unhappy words that would surely follow.

The view from the cliff top was breathtaking. The sea stretched away into the infinite distance, and the swell and retreat of the white-capped waves hypnotized Rab. It looked nothing like home—and home was a very, very long way from the island of Asaruthe.

Seeing Huw approach, the newcomer stopped and waited by the narrow path. The late afternoon sunlight still shone strongly, enough to make a sparkling brightness as it reflected on the unshed tears in Rab's eyes.

Huw's bare feet made no sound on the springy turf as he approached. For a long time the two figures stood together by the path, and neither could find any words to say. The harsh cry of a puffin echoed in the silence as it dove below the level of the cliff edge, seeking its nest and its young. Finally, Huw sighed and said, "Maia?"

"Yes, Patre?"

"Why have you come here?"

"Do you have no kind words of greeting for your daughter, my Patre? No matter," she shrugged. "I came because I miss you. Matre misses you too."

"I am sorry," he said, dully. "Your arrival came as a bit of a shock. I could not let the others know that I recognized you."

She smiled, though it did not reach her eyes. "I was not sure that you would."

"You look just like your mother, Maia. A proud beauty. And I see myself in your face as well. I had no doubts from the first moment I saw you step from the boat. But you cannot stay here, my daughter. You do not belong in this world."

"It is you who does not belong. Why do you not come away with me?"

"I cannot," Huw said, in an agonized whisper. "I have another life now."

She frowned at him. "What do you mean?"

He tried to explain, and the words came out in a flood that added little to her understanding. "Eira and I were given the gift of sight, long ago. We knew evil days were coming, when Tristan's wicked minions would hunt the Kindreds. That is why your Matre went with Shiqaba. She wanted you to be safe. So did I."

"Then why did you not come with us?"

He shrugged. "I wanted to, but Grigor, my Patre, was ill. I could not leave him, not like that. I begged Shiqaba to wait, but he left secretly, with many of the Chandrathi."

"You could have found us later, after your Patre recovered. But you stayed away for thirty years. Thirty years! I got tired of waiting so I ran away from Cara and came to look for you."

Huw looked stricken. "How is your Matre?"

"Very unhappy," said Maia, heartlessly. "And bitter. Bitter that the Amaranthine have kept you from her. She loves you and she wants you to come home. Do you think she will go on waiting forever? Will you not come back with me?"

"I cannot," he repeated. "My life is here now."

"With your new wife and children?" Maia spat. "How could you do this to us, Patre?"

"I wanted you to be safe," he insisted again. "And I paid for that. I wandered for many years in loneliness. Not a day passed when I did not think of you—or Cara. But then, when I met Katkin..."

"Don't bother to explain yourself," she interrupted coldly. "You met another woman and forgot about us."

"No! I still love your mother. But I cannot go to her. Hana has given me a task and I must see it through to the end." After a moment, he asked, "How did you find me, anyway? My sisters swore they would tell no one."

"I had no help from my Ikoran*, believe me. They would not tell Matre or me where they had hidden you away. But after I learned to gap shift, I spied on them. They spoke often to Lutyond, whom they call the Mariner. And he spoke of you. Finally, I left Mornguard. I ended up on Yr, traveling with the Kirani. I told them I was an orphan from another kindred. There are plenty of them wandering around Yr so they did not question me too closely. Later, I came to Citternia. I already knew that the Mariner visited Minbeorg twice a year with his sons, so I hung around and waited for my chance."

Huw fixed her with a burning glance. "And now you must go back to Citternia or where you will. I will tell Gunnar to carry you back across the Reach. If you return to Mornguard, tell your Matre I am well, and I think of her often."

"No! Let me help you with this task you must complete for Hana. Then we may return together."

"I must remain here, on Asaruthe, and protect the Dawnmaid. Maggrai is seeking her."

"How long will you have to stay?"

He shrugged. "I don't know. Until the Un-Named One sends us a sign, I suppose."

"There are signs aplenty. Yr is suffering from a deadly plague. King Tristan's men hunt our people like dogs and take them back to Isle St. Valery. No one knows why, but I have heard terrible tales, Patre, terrible! If the Dawnmaid is to redeem us, then she must go back to Yr now, while there are a few souls left to save."

Huw stared over the edge of the cliff, watching as the waves rolled and broke on the rocks far below. Huge clouds of spume appeared as the water found a blowhole and erupted into the air like a column of smoke. He stroked his greying beard thoughtfully. "If what you say is true, then no doubt the Dawnmaid's call will be coming forthwith. We have to be ready. You should come to the meeting at Asavale, and tell everyone what you have just told me."

She stared at him rebelliously. "As Rabbit of the Kirani, or Maia Adaryi of the Chandrathi?"

He sighed and looked away from her. "Please remain Rab, at

* Aunts

least for now. You must give me time to talk to Katkin and tell her the truth." Huw rubbed the back of his neck in agitation. "She will not be happy, Maia."

"Then why did you lie to her, Patre? You ought to have known this day would come."

He shook his head. "I thought... someday, at the end of this war, when Katkin had passed through Tsmar'enth*, you know... I would find your Matre in Mornguard, and beg her forgiveness. I believed that she and I might then be able to spend the rest of our allotted time together in peace."

"Faugh! You will be an old man by then. Look at yourself, Patre. You have grey hair already. Cara is still young and beautiful."

Huw laughed dryly. "I am but fifty-one. I think I have a little life in me yet. Still, I know the time in Mornguard moves more slowly. You are thirty-two in Yrth years, still you look no more than eighteen to me. But such things are unimportant. I swore to undertake this duty to the Dawnmaid, and I shall not desert her."

"Then I am staying with you," said Maia, flatly. "As Rabbit, of the Kirani, of course," she added, with a sly smile.

Everyone seemed to be distracted, and the promised meeting did not take place for many days. Huw spent a great deal of time with Rab, and both Katkin and Poppy watched the two of them with anxious eyes. Jakob also seemed taken with the newest resident of the island and gave up on his attempts to entice Poppy into a relationship. Poppy did not miss Jakob's company, but she did wonder what he saw in the younger boy. They seemed very unlike and yet she saw them fishing or hunting together almost every day, ranging far and wide over the island.

Summer had slipped into fall when the families finally met at Asavale. Rab stood in the middle of the room, and gave soft answers to the questions directed to him by Arkady and the others.

"How long has this Bludseth plague been troubling the peoples of Yr?"

Rab looked pensive. "I don't know exactly. For a long time it seemed only a fearful rumor, of the kind that parents tell their children in order to frighten them. Then we heard tales of men dying in the south and their families going with them. Some did

* The moon-gate, death

not believe these stories, but soon there were too many to discount. The tales spread as the disease spread, and soon there were fewer and fewer traders crossing the Reach. Now the Bludseth rules Yr, along with that evil *Gruagán* Tristan."

"And it is Tristan's Guard that is capturing the Kindreds?" Katkin wanted to know.

"The Ouzels, yes. I have seen one of their aermaran with my own eyes. It is a great and terrible sight."

Huw nodded. "You are right... Rab. But I wonder what purpose he has in gathering our people?"

"Some say it is because we are immune to the sickness. Some say he..."

Everyone waited in silent dread. Myrie stood and walked forward, until she stood very close to Rab. She clicked questioningly. Rab whispered grimly, "Some say that he and his Black Guard drink the lifeblood of our kind. In this way he hopes to keep safe from the Bludseth."

Myrie screamed and ran from the room. Gwillam followed.

Gwenn rose. "What has gotten into that child? I had better go and see to her."

"Leave her be," said Gunnar. "It will be better if she does not have to hear the hard words that we must speak now. We must decide amongst ourselves whether we will stay on Asaruthe, or leave this island that has sheltered us all for the past sixteen years. It may be that we will split up, if we cannot reach an accord. Each of the adults should speak in turn. I will begin."

He stood and spread his arms wide.

"I think I may speak for everyone in my family when I say that this island has become a blessed home for us. Here we may live in safety and freedom, untroubled by the trials of the rest of the world. It is true that we may not be able to trade for some of the foodstuffs that we have relied on in the past, but my wife assures me that we could grow more of the things we need on this island. I believe we should stay here."

Gwenn stood by Gunnar and said, "We have all sworn to protect the Dawnmaid until it is time for her call. And yet we know that she is unable to properly communicate or care for herself. I, too, think we should remain here, until she shows some signs of being able to do so. In any case, she cannot leave until she is eighteen."

Arkady spoke from his wooden rocking chair. "I wish to remain as well. I know the ways of our island intimately, and my blindness is no handicap here. On the mainland, I would be a burden to the rest of my family."

Jakob opened his mouth and Gunnar growled, "I said the adults, lad."

Jakob ignored him. "I should have a say in what we do! And I do not want to stay in this hole any longer than I have to. I want to see the world." He stared at Rab thoughtfully. "When I finish my boat I am leaving, no matter what the rest of you decide." Jakob had begun work on a smaller version of the *Able Drake* in the little bit of spare time he had when he finished his chores.

"Enough!" snapped Gwenn. "You will do as you are told until your eighteenth birthday as well, Jakob Strong Arm. Then you may sail away from this island and take a wife, if that is your wish."

Jakob flushed crimson.

"Now," said Gunnar. "What of our neighbors at Ruthecombe? What would you have us do?"

Huw stood and cleared his throat. "I believe the Un-Named One has sent Rab to us as a sign. The grave situation on Yr means the Dawnmaid must go soon, whether she can talk or no."

Katkin looked askance at him. "Are you suggesting we send her on her own?"

"Not alone no, but with those who are willing to accompany her. I don't believe we will gain any advantage by sending everyone on the island. One or two people would be enough."

Poppy spoke up. "Well Gwillam would have to be one of them."

"Were you not listening?" Gwenn spat. "I just said Myrie isn't going anywhere until she is at least eighteen *and* can look after herself."

"Gwenn, be reasonable," said Katkin. "What will be left of Yr in two years time? You heard what Rab said. The Kindreds need her now. What will happen if they all fall to Tristan? Our race will be at an end."

"But..." said Rab.

A quick look passed between Rab and Huw, and he shook his head. Poppy saw it, and wondered. "But what, Rab?"

Rab did not speak again.

Gwenn continued to argue, and both her husbands took her

side. The meeting grew raucous, with everyone speaking at once. Poppy, unable to stand the thought of another island-wide dispute, stood on her chair and cried, "Let me speak! I am an adult as well." Everybody stopped shouting and looked at her in surprise. "That is better. Now listen. It seems to me that we need more information. From what we heard at Minbeorg, things on the Mainland are bad. But none of us knows for sure if this is true, or not."

"I do," said Rab.

Poppy gave him a vexed look. "None of us who are trying to make the decision knows," she corrected herself. "But we have tools at our disposal that we have not used. Katkin's mirror for one, and the journal of Josiah Tavish. Let us consult them, and see what we can see."

Katkin said, "But I don't know if the mirror will show us any-thing, Poppy."

"Myrie can make it work."

"Very well," said Gunnar. "If you think these things may help us, then go and fetch them. We will meet back here in two hours, after dinner."

Poppy raised her hand. "Before we end this meeting I would like to ask one thing. What will happen to Lut if we decide to leave this island?"

Gunnar stroked his beard. "You need not worry. I know you still fear him, but if we leave then we will take every precaution to keep the two of you separate."

Poppy sighed, thinking he had no idea how wrong he was.

The Adaryi family walked back towards Ruthecombe. As they passed the path to the long rill, Huw and Rab exchanged glances. "We will be home soon, my Queen," Huw said. "I just want to show our visitor the best place to fish in the river." They disappeared down the path, walking close together, leaving Katkin shaking her head.

"What is it, Katkin?" Poppy asked.

"I don't know, but Huw has been acting strangely ever since that boy arrived. So has Jakob, for that matter. It all seems very secre-tive to me."

Poppy frowned. "I have noticed it as well. Do you think that Patre is coming down with melancholia again?"

"I don't believe so. It is the wrong time of year, for one thing. But I will watch him over the next few days."

"So will I," said Poppy thoughtfully. "So will I."

The front door stood wide open when they arrived. Katkin walked in, calling, "Gwillam! Myrie! Come and get washed up for dinner." When they did not appear, she said to Poppy, "Go and see where they are hiding. I will get started on the soup, and you can make some bannock in a moment."

She hurried back down the ladder almost immediately. "Myrie and Gwillam are not upstairs. And your keepsake chest is open. The dress—the talisman—everything is missing except for the mirror." Poppy sat on the bottom rung of the ladder and burst into tears.

Six

Beech

It had been Poppy who first thought to look at the dock. Now, as she and Katkin tore up the path to Asavale, Poppy cried, "I can't believe they would leave us behind like that. What on Yrth was Gwillam thinking?"

Katkin shook her head. "It does not matter. They have taken the *Able Drake*, and we have no way of catching them."

Gwenn had just served Arkady a bowl of stew when Katkin and Poppy burst through the door. Jakob had almost finished his first bowl and had asked his mother for seconds.

Gunnar said patiently, "Wait for the rest of us to eat our firsts, Jakob." He turned and spied Katkin. "I thought we agreed to meet after dinner?"

"Gwillam and Myrie have taken the *Able Drake*," Poppy cried. "Katkin and I saw the sail just as it passed out of sight over the horizon. They were heading west."

"What?" Gwenn dropped the ladle into the tureen with a splash. "If that son of yours has led her astray..." she spat at Katkin.

"Whisht, Faircrow. We need to think calmly—decide what to do.

How far have you gotten with your boat, Jakob?" Gunnar looked over at his son, who hadn't stopped shoveling stew into his mouth.

Jakob swallowed and wiped his lips on his sleeve. "The hull is mostly finished, but I haven't even started on the mast or the decking. There is a least a couple more weeks work in it, even if we all pitch in."

"Two weeks!" cried Katkin. "They will be long gone by then. My goddess, what are we to do?" She collapsed into a chair and covered her face with her hands.

"Gwenn, get the apple brandy," Gunnar ordered. "Where is Huw, Poppy?"

"I don't know. He went somewhere with Rab. Shall I go and look for him?"

Gunnar nodded distractedly and Poppy flew out the door. He sat next to Katkin and took her trembling hand in his. "Listen to me. Your lad is smart enough to know he cannot cross the ocean with Myrie in the *Able Drake*. You say they headed west? Then they are going to Everruthe to try and get Lut to go along with them. But don't worry overmuch; I know Lut—he will talk some sense into them. They will all be back here in a few days. You will see."

Katkin gave him a hopeful look. "Do you really think so?"

"I do," he said gravely. "Don't you agree, Inky?"

"Yes, absolutely." Arkady added, "Gwillam would never risk Myrie's safety."

Jakob coughed pointedly and held out his bowl. Gunnar stood and said, "Leave your dinner now, lad. We had better get to the beach and strip the bark from the tree that you felled for the mast. I think the young ones will bring my ship back ere long, but we had better ready another, just in case." Grabbing his axe, he limped to the door. With a last, longing look at the stew pot, Jakob followed him.

As the wide valley of the Long Rill opened below her, Poppy could see Huw and Rab, sitting side by side by the stony bank of the river. She opened her mouth, about to hail them, when she saw Rab bury his head on her Patre's shoulder. Huw put a comforting arm across his back and stroked his hair. Poppy felt a rush of heat to her face. Her Patre barely knew this boy. Where had this intimacy come from?

She slowed her steps and watched in fascinated horror as Huw placed a kiss on Rab's head. There was something very wrong about the scene transpiring below her, but Poppy knew she could not tell Katkin anything. She had enough to worry about. With a swift and silent about face, Poppy headed up the path and back over the hill. Then she stopped and called, "Patre? Patre, where are you?"

After a few seconds, his voice floated from the valley. "Over here, my flower."

This time, when she crested the hill, Huw and Rab were standing far apart, with their hands tucked in their breeches pockets.

Three days passed, and the new boat began to take shape. Jakob had finished the clinker-built hull some time ago, and now Gunnar supervised the laying of the decking and the smoothing of the mast and yard. Even Arkady helped with the sanding, using his sensitive fingers to feel the direction of the grain.

Everyone worked on Jakob's ship, except for Rab. He hovered just outside the busy circle of people in the cove, watching and waiting. Poppy watched him too, and her Patre. Although they spoke but rarely to one another, she saw secret glances pass between them— and in these glances, there were many things unsaid. Poppy had lain sleepless for the last two nights, wondering what she should tell her Matre. And each day, it seemed, she had more and more to tell.

She watched out of the corner of her eye as Rab stalked off alone into the hills. Huw was helping Gunnar step the new mast. Poppy dropped her adz.

"I am going to the house," she called to Ikora Gwenn, who stirred a cauldron suspended over a small fire. The melting pitch added a bitter tang to the air. "I will fill the water jugs at the well and bring them back with me."

Gwenn nodded and wiped the sweat from her head with a rag.

Poppy hurried to catch Rab, determined to find out the truth of his relationship with Huw. She followed at a distance as he passed through the spruce grove, and along a well-worn path that led to a special place in the hollows. Poppy knew his destination well— a perfectly round pool, lined with abraded stones, and filled by a gentle waterfall that cascaded down several tiers of rock. By the time she caught up, he had shed most of his clothes. Poppy did not wish to cause either of them embarrassment, so she dropped behind a rock and watched as Rab pulled his shirt over his head. With a quick knifing dive, he entered the water, popped to the surface and swam a few short laps back and forth under the waterfall.

Jakob did not seem so concerned with modesty. He hurried to the bathing pool and stripped, as Poppy, rigid with mortification, watched from her hiding place. After Jakob joined Rab in the water, she could not help overhearing.

"What took you so long?" This from Rab, who breaststroked smoothly over to Jakob.

"I couldn't get away. Ma was watching me like a hawk." He splashed noisily, and Rab gave a high-pitched shriek. Jakob lowered his voice. "I am here now though."

The next sounds were unmistakable. Poppy crept backwards, intending to slink away, shocked to her core. But the lovers finished quickly, and she had to remain in her hiding place. Jakob dressed and went back towards the beach, simpering over his shoulder, "Same time tomorrow, Sweetheart? Don't worry, next time I won't be late." Poppy shuddered in revulsion and waited for him to leave.

But when Rab stepped out of the water, facing her, Poppy jumped up with a scream of shocked rage. "Who the hell are you?"

Maia bent to retrieve her shirt. She slipped it over her head before answering. "What are you doing here? You had no right to follow me."

Poppy crossed the grass and stood before her. "I asked you a question first. Who are you?" She clenched her fists, breathing hard, and waited. Maia dried her long dark hair with her breeches and then pulled them on.

"My name is Maia. I am a daughter of the Chandrathi. Huw is my Patre." She peered at Poppy, and said mildly, "I am sorry. I expect my presence here is a bit upsetting for you. We were going to tell you and your mother the truth a few days ago, but when Myrie and Gwillam ran away, it seemed better to wait."

Poppy sputtered, "You are lying. You must be. Patre has been on this island for the last sixteen years. How could he have fathered a child?"

Maia insisted, "He married my mother thirty-one years ago, Poppy. I was born the following year."

"That is impossible," Poppy retorted. "You don't look any older than eighteen."

Maia shrugged. "Time passes a little differently where I come from."

"And where is that exactly?"

"Patre can tell you that, if he wants you to know. I suppose I had better find him and tell him you were spying on me. He won't be happy with you, Poppy."

Poppy stormed off, still fuming, and flung back over her shoulder. "I don't care! All this time I thought you were my friend, but you lied to me about everything."

Maia stepped in front of her and gave a smug little smile. "Why don't you just admit it? You are jealous. Not that I blame you. I guess I did steal your boyfriend."

Poppy shook her head in disgust. "I don't give a damn about Jakob. You can have him, with my compliments. Now get out of my way before I do something I might regret later."

Maia stared at her insolently, but finally stepped aside with a shrug. Poppy brushed her shoulder roughly as she passed. A covey of quail scattered in her wake—a mated pair with three little ones trailing behind them. They scurried into the bushes and cowered under the trembling leaves.

Katkin sat at the kitchen table, weeping bitterly. Huw stood over her, wringing his hands in distress. "Please, my Queen, let me explain..." He touched her hair softly and she slapped his hand away.

"All our years together were a lie! How could you?"

"I wanted to tell you! But my sisters made me swear I would not reveal the truth about Mornguard."

Katkin snarled, "You said you did not know where Cara went. You made me feel sorry for you. That was what you wanted all the long. I don't believe it had anything to do with Mornguard."

"I told you as much of the truth as I could—that she left me and took Maia. Yes, there was more to the story. But how could I have told you the rest without revealing the existence of their hiding place? It is the secret sanctuary of the Firaithi—the Dawnmaid's kingdom. Shiqaba has been leading a very few of our people there for millennia, so that they may be kept safe from the Angellus. They are the Kindred of Anjali."

Katkin remembered her own brief look at Mornguard, in the company of Shiqaba. She has seen evidence of occupation, though the Amaranthine at her side had denied it. Again, she had caught them in a lie, and this time Huw had been a part of it. She thought back on her hurried trip to Scarfinda, when she had tried to save his life, and the terrible attack she had suffered for his sake. All for a lie.

Maia lounged on the settle, close to Jakob Strong Arm. Poppy stood in the farthest corner of the room and regarded them both with loathing. Maia spied her and smiled purringly, then took Jakob's hand in hers. Poppy ignored this obvious provocation and went to sit by her Matre.

Katkin hissed, "Well, what are you waiting for? You said Maia came back here for you, so why don't you leave? Go back to your wife."

"Yes, Patre," said Maia breathlessly. "Do as she says. We can travel the worlds between. I can soon teach you and Jakob to gap shift."

Huw turned on her. "Listen to me, my daughter! I am not going anywhere, and neither are you—not by the worlds between. We could not leave by that method, even if I desired to go with you, lest we open a door that had best remain closed."

Katkin dried her eyes on her apron, more concerned with Huw's words than her own heartache. "What are you talking about, Huw?"

"When my *Kypatre** created this island, as a haven for the Dawn-maid, he placed it outside the middle azimuth, in the highest pellicula. My sisters and I knew..."

Katkin gave him a disbelieving look. "Your grandfather created this island? What on Yrth do you mean?"

He patiently explained, "He molded this land out of the stuff of the worlds between. It lies on Yrth, but it is not part of it, my Queen. That is why it does not appear on any chart."

Katkin and Poppy both stood and stared at him. Poppy shook her head. "Who is your other sister, Patre? Besides Ikora Eira, I mean?"

"Hana," he said quietly. "And, before you ask me—Shiqaba is our *Kypatre.*"

Katkin digested this information for a moment, feeling as if she

---
* Grandfather

were in a dream. "And you—that makes you Amaranthine, is that right, Huw? No more lies now, tell me the truth."

He raised his head, proudly. "I am the Firstborn. Did you not always know it?"

"Yes, it all makes sense to me now. That is why Shiqaba said I had to save you. But he wouldn't lift a finger to help me."

Huw rolled his eyes. "Please let me finish. When you or I cross the heavenly plane by gap shifting, it creates small holes in the fabric of the worlds. Usually these breaches close very quickly, but the person crossing always leaves a few bits of matter behind. An adept searcher could follow this residue from pellicle to pellicle, and thus find our island. That is one of the dangers we face. But there is an even greater risk. Because the island lies on the world of Yrth, but beyond the outermost pellicula, it may be that any hole created would be blown wide open by the forces of azimity.'"

Katkin looked at Huw doubtfully. "Azimity? What is that?"

Maia cried, "Enough of this wasted talk. May we not leave these small-minded folk to their business, Patre? I wish to show Jakob the beauties of the worlds between. Will you come with us or no? Cara awaits..."

Huw walked over to Katkin and knelt before her with his head down. He took her left hand and studied it. "I asked you something sixteen years ago, do you remember, my Queen? I asked if you would be my partner—equal in all things, and cherished above all things, until we stand before Tsmar'enth."

Katkin nodded as she stared at her hand and the bright silver ring she wore on her finger.

"I know I have not kept that promise as well as I should have, because there were things that I could not tell you. But now you know the truth—all of it, I still wish to honor my commitment to you. Will you have me?" He placed his hand, palm up, before her, waiting to receive her right hand in his.

Katkin hesitated only a fraction of a second before she slipped the ring from her finger and dropped it into Huw's open palm. "Go to hell, Huw Adaryi. I won't live with a liar."

Huw stared at the ring, shining light on his dark palm, as Poppy burst into tears. "Will you not?"

---

* The invisible force that holds the cosmos captive in its whirling dance around the Gyre.

Maia flashed Poppy a look of pure triumph as she stood and grasped Jakob's hand. "You see, my Patre, your pretend wife does not even want you to stay. Come with me now, back to Matre. *She* loves you..."

Huw spoke to his daughter, and now his voice was hard. "You are spoiled, just like your mother. I should have seen it, before now. But did you not hear me? You cannot leave this place by the worlds between. If you wish to go to Mornguard, you had best go there by boat. I am sure Jakob would be willing to take you, once his vessel is finished and we who remain on Asaruthe no longer have need of it."

Jakob spoke for the first time. His voice rose until it reached a tantrum scream. "But that will take ages! I am sick to death of this stinking island. Sick of my parents and their unfair punishments, sick of my goody-two-shoes brother and his uppish little girlfriend. I want to go now, and so does Maia."

"Don't be a fool, Jakob Strong Arm! You would risk everything we have worked so hard to protect?"

"You Amaranthine can keep your plots and plans." He placed a protective arm about Maia's waist. "Let's go, sweetheart. Don't listen to your old man. My Dad has gap shifted lots of times, and nothing bad has ever happened to him."

Maia nodded. "Farewell, Patre."

"No Maia, I forbid you!" As Huw dived towards her, Jakob stepped forward and a little to the left, dragging Maia along with him. Then they both winked out of existence on Yrth, leaving a spray of light that ominously illumined the shadowed sitting room of Ruthecombe.

Huw, Katkin and Poppy all stared at the space that Jakob and Maia had recently occupied. A thin, jagged scar of bright-rimmed blackness hung suspended in the air. An occasional puff of golden light leaked through, and lingered like a sunset-washed cloud. Huw swore. "Do you see it, my Queen? A discontinuity. Ach, my foolish, foolish children. What damage have you wrought?"

Katkin stood, mesmerized, and approached the glowing portal with her hand outstretched. Poppy cried fearfully, "No, Katkin! Don't go any closer to it." Huw took Katkin's hand and pulled her away.

He shook her, saying, "That is the pull of the azimity you feel.

Look no further at the discontinuity. We are all in danger as long as it remains here."

Katkin rubbed her eyes and stepped away from him. "What... What can we do to mend it?"

He sighed. "I will have to step through the hole, and close it from the other side. It is the only way."

Poppy looked at her Patre with shining eyes. "You can do that?"

A small smile played on his lips. "I can do many things, my flower, of which you know very little. I have mended quite a few such holes already since we came to Asaruthe, though they were much smaller."

"Sm... smaller?" Katkin's eyes narrowed in surprise and fear.

"Yes, my Queen. Tiny fissures left by someone with a great deal more skill at gap shifting. He left very little trace behind in the cave."

Katkin stared at him, shocked to the core. "You knew about him? You knew all the long? Why did you not speak?" Poppy looked back and forth between her parents, mystified by their conversation.

He shrugged. "Would it have mattered?"

"No," said Katkin, thoughtfully. "I don't believe it would."

Poppy, feeling excluded, cut in with, "What are you two talking about?"

Huw answered her in a monotone. "Nothing. Do not trouble yourself, Poppy."

She answered back, paying no heed to the sadness in his voice. "Well then, what are you waiting for? Do it, Patre. Fix the hole, so that we will be safe again."

A sudden surety filled Katkin. "If he does, then he won't be able to come back." She turned to Huw and stared at him, and her eyes were as cold as the ocean on a dark winter's day. "Will you? That is the truth, isn't it?"

He nodded. "But I have to go, my Queen. Otherwise the discontinuity will lead our enemies here, as surely as the moon sheds her silver flame upon the sea."

Poppy began to cry. "Patre, no! You can't leave us. What will you do? How will you return?"

"I intend to follow those headstrong youngsters, and erase all traces of their passage from here. Then I will come back to Asaruthe, when I am able, by boat. But if danger finds you here, you must *not* wait for my return. Flee and leave word for me, however you may. All right?"

Another brilliant shaft of light flooded the floorboards of Ruthecombe with a deadly spangle of color. "The crack is growing! I must go now, before it becomes too wide for me to stitch together. Farewell, Queen of my heart. I love you. Farewell, my flower. Take care of your Matre for me." He brushed his lips over Katkin's and placed the ring on the ground at her feet. Then he threw himself into the flaring void.

Katkin knelt and picked up the ring, then hurled it into the fissure. "Take that, you... you... lying Amaranthine!" She stared at the radiance, her face a battlefield of competing emotions. Suddenly, she rushed towards it. "Huw! Wait... Don't..." She fell to her knees, sobbing, as the blackness and the escaping shaft of light died.

Poppy's rising wail filled the room with the sound of her grief.

Gwenn glared at her mother. "I don't believe you! Jakob would never leave the island without saying good-bye to us first."

"He did, Gwenn. I don't know how much that bratty daughter of Huw's had to do with it, but he was determined to leave with her. Huw tried to stop them, I swear it."

Gunnar's eyes narrowed. "So that young man Rab was really a girl? I suspected as much, after Poppy treated her wound on the *Able Drake*. The skin on her calf looked far too smooth to be a lad's. And I thought it was strange the way Jakob took up with Rab after we got back here, especially after what he said on the boat." He looked over at Gwenn and patted her hand. "Getting angry is not going to help anything, Faircrow. The horse has already left the barn."

"Well I don't care. That Firaithi witch has stolen our son away. Who knows when we will see him again? And with Lut gone too..."

Poppy cleared her throat. "That's another thing, Ikora. Before Jakob left, he said he was sick to death of his goody-two-shoes brother. Don't you think...?" She paused and looked shyly at her hands, her fear of Gwenn getting the better of her.

"Don't I think what?" she growled.

"That... That... Lut is innocent?" Poppy finally managed to blurt out. "When I saw that Jakob chewed his nails..."

Gwenn scowled. "Honestly, Poppy! First, you lead Lut on like a wanton tart, and then you pretend he tried to rape you. And now Jakob has been kidnapped you think you can blame everything on him."

"Faircrow, calm down," Gunnar begged in exasperation.

Poppy looked at her with wide, shocked eyes. "Ikora! I never led..."

Katkin grasped her hand. "Come on, Poppy. We are leaving now."

"But..."

"I said, come on." Katkin turned back to Gwenn, who stood with her arms akimbo, while Gunnar looked on helplessly. She did not raise her voice, but still it sounded as hard as stone. "I won't have Poppy bear the blame for an unprovoked attack. Come over to Ruthecombe when you want to apologize for what you just said, Gwenn. We will not be back, until then. Farewell, Gunnar. If you need our assistance with the boat, then you have only to ask."

Gunnar shrugged sheepishly. "I need Lut's help to finish rigging the boat, but I cannot fetch him until I have finished it myself. What can I do?" He sighed and raised his hands in a questioning motion. "Let us hope they all arrive in the *Able Drake* soon."

Seven

Rowan

Six more days passed and still the runaways had not come back to Asaruthe. Nor did Gwenn go to Ruthecombe and beg her mother's forgiveness. She, Arkady and Gunnar toiled away on the boat, while Katkin and Poppy dealt with the farm chores as best they could. The work of managing the sheep, as well as milking the cows, kept them busy, but Katkin felt grateful for the distraction.

Poppy worked silently alongside her mother. Katkin tried to be cheerful, and spoke with a certainty she did not feel. "Don't worry,

Poppy. Gwillam and Myrie are probably on their way back by now, and your Patre will be doing his best to get home as well. You know he loves you dearly."

"I know..." Poppy still sounded angry. "But you don't love him, do you? Who is the *he* Patre mentioned before he left, Katkin? Answer me that."

Katkin ignored this provocation and carried the lantern across the barn to where her daughter sat mending an old woolsack with linen thread. The high crossbeams of the barn made leaping shadows across the ceiling, like frolicking beasts.

She willed her voice to sound warm and untroubled. "You look done in. Why don't you go on back to the house and get into bed? I will finish this." Poppy nodded tiredly and handed the curved needle to Katkin.

She walked back to Ruthecombe, thinking on the next day and the hard work it would bring. Asaruthe, their island sanctuary, had become somehow much less hospitable since Myrie and Gwillam took the *Able Drake*. Gunnar still seemed convinced that they would return, with Lut, but Poppy knew the journey there and back took less than a day with fair winds.

The startled cry of some fluttering night bird made Poppy jump. She stopped short of the narrow path that led to the house, and wrapped her fichu over her hair. The darkness that lay between her and the yard seemed almost solid. A slender moon rode high in the sky, but a thin bank of pearly cloud filtered its light into nothingness. Poppy forced herself to move forward again, determined to get home and into bed. The low walls of the courtyard came into view, and then the front door. It looked like a black square against the whitewashed walls of Ruthecombe.

As she moved closer, Poppy saw to her surprise that the door stood open, and a will-o'-wisp of light bobbed across the interior blackness from time to time. She did not feel afraid, exactly, but she did slow her pace, thinking that she should approach cautiously, from the side. As she slunk over the hummocky grass, trying hard to make her steps as silent as possible, she considered who might be in her house. A hopeful smile crossed her face.

"Patre," she whispered. "Patre has come home."

Poppy stopped under the window, and listened. Someone spoke within the kitchen. The voice made her heart race, for she did not know it. Suddenly she *was* afraid—very. She turned to flee, back to the barn at Asavale, where her mother sat alone sewing woolpacks. Strong hands caught her, and she screamed in terror.

"Poppy, no!" a familiar voice cried. "Don't run away from me, please... I won't hurt you, I swear it."

It was Lut.

She grabbed his hand and held it close to her face for a second. Long enough to see the nails were perfect. Lut buried his face in Poppy's hair.

"Ach, my blossom. You don't know how long I have waited for this. I missed you so much."

Poppy kept her arms wrapped tight across his broad back. "I missed you too. I thought about you every single day." She gave an unhappy cry. "Oh, Lut, what they did to you was so wrong. I knew in my heart you weren't the guilty one, but no one would listen to me. You must be very angry with us all."

He chuckled softly in the darkness. "At you? Never. But Jakob, well... I have a tidy score to settle with him."

"Jakob is gone. So is Patre," Poppy said unhappily.

"Gone? Where?"

"He went with... Gods, so much has happened since you left! I don't know where to begin."

Lut laughed and hugged her tight. "Kiss me. That is a good place to start."

She did, but only for a moment. Poppy asked urgently, "Who is that in the house? I heard a strange voice."

Lut shook his head. "We had better go back inside. There is a lot that you don't know either."

They crept in the front door. Gwillam and Myrie were sitting at the kitchen table, a half-burned candle between them, stuffing themselves with the remains of a loaf of bread and some butter. Gwillam spoke with his mouth full. "Hello, Poppy. Is there any milk? Myrie and I are starving."

Poppy's mouth opened and closed in utter astonishment. "Is there any milk? Gwillam Brunner! I ought to... Do you know how much...? Honestly, I don't know whether to hug you or strangle you." She dipped two cups of milk from the crock, and looked back over her shoulder at Gwillam. "Why did it take you so long to get here?"

Myrie shrieked with laughter as Gwillam groaned, and Lut said, "Not so loud, you two." He smiled at Poppy. "I found these lunkheads after they ran aground on some rocks off the south coast of Everruthe. They had banged the keel of the *Able Drake* pretty badly. It took me almost a week to fix it with the few tools I had with me on the island."

"May we make some toast?" Myrie asked. "We really are hungry."

"Just a minute, Myrie," Poppy said, obliviously. "I need to tell my little brother..." She stopped speaking and stood with her mouth open. Lut grinned and so did Gwillam. "What is going on?" she appealed to her brother. "That is Myrie sitting there, isn't it?"

"I *think* so."

"How did she learn to speak?"

Lut answered. "That is a long story, and we don't have time to tell it right now."

"Why not?"

Myrie explained. Her voice sounded oddly like a man's. "We have to go to the City of Isle St. Valery, where your mother used to be Queen. Lut is going to take us there in the *Able Drake* and Gwillam is going too. We came back here to pick up some foodstuffs, and to see you—of course. But the grownups won't want us to go, so we have to be secretive."

"You are right about that. Ikora Gwenn said at the meeting she would not let you leave Asaruthe until you were eighteen. But why is it so important to go now? You know how bad the storms can be in the autumn. We should wait..."

"We cannot," Myrie said sharply. "We have seen."

Poppy sat down at the table and stared at the younger girl. "What have you seen? Did you look in my Matre's mirror?"

The younger girl shook her head. "We have seen many terrible and dark deeds with our own eyes."

Gwillam muttered an aside to Poppy. "She's been going on like that ever since she found her voice. We this, we that... Lut and I think it is a little strange."

"How much food do you think Grandmother can spare?" Lut whispered across the kitchen as he dug through boxes and drawers in the pantry. "I brought everything I had on Everruthe. Still, if we hit any bad weather then we might need more. But I don't want you and Grandmother to go hungry."

"Me?" asked Poppy, in surprise. "I am coming with you. And Katkin can starve for all I care."

"No you are not. From what Myrie has been saying, Yr is an awfully dangerous place right now. I want you here, where I know you will be safe. And if Uncle Huw has gone, it would be wrong to leave Grandmother by herself anyway."

Poppy frowned obstinately. "I *am* going, and what's more, I don't give a damn if she is on her own. It is what she deserves after what she did to Patre."

In the end, Poppy left Katkin a note propped next to the still-lit candle on the kitchen table. Then she grabbed the last of the bundles, and walked out the front door. Poppy turned and gave her home one last backwards glance. "Farewell, Ruthecombe," she whispered.

When Katkin returned a few moments later, she was surprised to see a candle still burning in the kitchen. She stepped through the door, calling for Poppy. When her daughter did not answer, Katkin wandered over to the table and found the note. With a cry of horror, she fled back into the night, running for the dock.

"Either you let me come with you, or I go to Gwenn right now and tell her what you have planned." Katkin glared at the circle of dismayed faces that ringed the lantern in Lut's hand. Only Myrie seemed untroubled.

"But Katkin, we don't..." Poppy started to object, in a fierce hiss.

"None of you have ever even been to Beaumarais! How did you think you would find your way?" They all looked at one another and shrugged. "I thought so. Now, there is to be no more argument. Is the *Able Drake* ready to cast off?"

Lut nodded glumly.

They put out to sea shortly afterwards. Gwillam and Myrie manned the oars. Lut stood at the tiller, whispering commands to Poppy and Katkin. As the offshore breeze picked up, he called quietly, "Raise the sail. We will take her straight east, out to sea, and then wait for dawn before we start sailing southwards. There are too many islets scattered around this archipelago to risk a night passage."

Once he estimated that they were well out of sight of land, Lut dropped anchor, and walked forward to join the others. They sat on the deck of the *Able Drake* as she rode on the darkened sea, a speck in the wide, wide ocean that surrounded Asaruthe. A single lantern hung from the mast. It swayed with the gentle rock and swell of the waves, casting fleeting shadows. Though they had not yet slept that night, the crew were watchful and awake, sipping tea that Katkin had brewed with the little spirit stove in the hold. She passed a cup to Myrie, who sat by herself at the stern. When Katkin walked back to the others she turned her head and squinted back into the darkness, then rubbed her eyes.

"It isn't your vision," said Lut. "We can all see it too."

"A sort of blurriness," agreed Gwillam. "Like she is out of focus somehow."

Katkin nodded, though she felt no less confused. "What happened to her? When did she start talking again?"

"I can tell you that," said Gwillam. "After we left the meeting at Asavale, Myrie ran straight back to our place and got your keepsake chest. She did that trick that opens the lock and then dumped everything on the bed. I tried to stop her, but she would not listen to me. She took your funny dress, and that red talisman that Patre cut from the dead bird. It had a twisted piece of wire, remember?"

Katkin nodded, remembering the huge, black-feathered avisceti that had attacked as the two families attempted to leave the island of Starruthe, sixteen years previously. Huw had brought one down with his crossbow, and taken the talisman from around its neck.

"Well, Myrie sort of stared at the talisman for a moment, while she took the wire off—and then she ate it!" Gwillam shook his head in alarm. "I thought she would choke or something, but she just smiled in that strange way of hers and then hurried to the boat. Then, once we put out to sea, she started talking in that low voice. Now she calls herself *we* all the time."

"I think that red crystal must have had the life-force of some other soul bound within it," said Lut pensively. "Myrie has told us many tales of another life in St. Valery. She says she used to be an old man who died in a hunting accident. A man who knew you well, Grandmother."

Katkin's eyebrows rose sharply at this. "Did she say his name?"

Myriadne raised her head in a soft blur of motion. The lantern swung in her direction as a gust of wind brought the boat about on her anchor line. As the light hit her face, Myrie's eyes glowed fiercely—a thin band of blue bordering huge dark pupils. "We are Nicholas—Nicholas and Myriadne. And you, Katkin? Are you well, my dear?"

"F... fine. How is it that you are able to speak to me now, after all these years?"

Myrie moved closer to the others. She sat with her back propped against the boat, and stared at her bare feet. "We remember being shot, and we felt terrible pain. Death came for us, and we lay in the arms of the Uri'el that bore our dear Elisabeth's face. Then we slept, it seemed to us, but for a moment." She sighed, and rubbed the top of her head, in the way Nicholas was wont to do, Katkin remembered. "We do not understand what happened next."

"Tell us anyway. Perhaps we can help you make sense of it," suggested Katkin.

"We were roused again, in great agony, and instead of our beloved's face, we saw the feathered breast of a bird. And then, when we moved, we felt our arms had become wings. It was like waking to some terrible nightmare. But our mind... That was the worst thing of all. For we felt in our thoughts the red-stained frenzy of a bird of prey, always hungering, always seeking more flesh to rend. It was horrible... horrible beyond endurance. And yet it grew much worse."

"How?" whispered Poppy.

"Another power controlled us. He sent his evil desires into our mind, and the bird we had become did his bidding with eager willingness. For he wished us to kill, and we did, swooping on the unsuspecting, like some depraved hawk from the depths of hell. We feasted on the flesh of mortals, as much as our master would allow us, though the thought of that sustenance sickens me, even now. We did not think we could bear another moment of that existence. But then it grew worse again." Myrie stood and paced back and forth on the deck, with her fists clenched.

"What happened, Nicholas?"

"We were made to fly a long way, in the company of others like ourselves. Flying hurt us—we were heavy birds, much heavier than one of our kind should be. Ahead we saw a big island, and clinging to that island, a house with overhanging eaves."

"Feringhall," muttered Katkin.

Myrie's face twisted with anguish. "We dove, as we saw figures running on the beach. One broke away from the rest, and we followed him, shrieking hateful things in our bird tongue. Then we attacked, again and again, rending his face with our claws, and tearing at his eyes with our wicked beak. He fell, screaming. That is when we recognized him, from the white hair stained red with his blood. We wanted to dash ourselves against the rocks when we realized who we had slain. Our son... Our youngest son, Arkady. When the bolt pierced our heart we were glad beyond measure, knowing we would not have to suffer such torment any longer." Myrie burst into tears and flung herself on to the deck, her thin shoulders shaking.

This account had transfixed everyone, but Myrie's sobs brought them to life again. Lut crawled over and patted her back. "He didn't die. Katkin made him well, and he lives now on the island of Asaruthe. He is your father, Myrie, don't you see? Arkady is your Pop."

"Truly?" she asked him gravely. "You do not say this to merely comfort an old man's grief?"

"Nay," said Katkin. "Lut speaks the truth."

Myrie gave a happy sigh. "Then we can rest now in peace, for the first time since we woke again." She curled in a ball and closed her eyes. In a moment her jaw slackened, and she began to breathe deeply and evenly. Gwillam found a deerskin and draped it across her.

Poppy yawned. "I want to go below and get some sleep too. How will we divide the watches?"

After Katkin said that she and Gwillam would keep the first watch, Poppy climbed down the short ladder into the redolent darkness of the hold. As she felt her way forward to the pile of hopsacking she knew lay at the other end, her hand brushed against a soft bundle. All at once, the scent of patchouli filled her. Poppy picked up the dress that Myrie had removed from the keepsake chest, marveling at its softness and warmth. The sweet scent that surrounded her seemed to whisper. Poppy listened, struggling to make out the sound over the gentle slap of the waves against the sides of the *Able Drake* and the creak of the rigging. *Azothe...*

"Who are you?" she whispered fearfully.

"You..." the voice echoed. Poppy breathed in, letting the fragrance permeate her blood. She could taste it—mint and bergamot, spices and pepper. Color swirled in her mind, an earthy palette of shades, like the mountains and desert splashed across a canvas.

Sight and savor and scent dissolved into a haunting melody, feral and free, wafting her into a dreamless slumber as she stretched out on the sacks. But still she could hear the echoing cry—*Azothe*.

Eight

Ash

Gwenn wandered the cliff tops in a sun-lit haze, looking for missing ewes and their half-grown lambs. She wanted to dock the lamb's tails so that the wool on the rump would be tidy at shearing time. Bridie and Wink circled ahead of her, hunting in the brushy gullies and hollows and Gwenn gave a sharp, irritated whistle to call them back.

Arkady heard the whistle and turned his head. Gunnar, who stood beside him on a grey and black outcrop of rock close to the ocean's edge, asked lackadaisically, "Did you hear something, Inky?"

He nodded. "The dogs are barking on the tops. They must have found the sheep that Gwenn has been hunting for."

"Aye," said Gunnar, sighing. "She has been after them for days, but it won't help."

"Help what?"

"Well, you know... with the real problem. She is just missing Myrie and the boys. It is hard to lose your children all at once like that."

"She does seem a bit downhearted. I asked her to come fishing with us yesterday on the *Fair Drake*, and she just about bit my head off. Says she has too much to do now that Katkin is gone."

Gunnar nodded. "Gwenn is angry with her mother for leaving with the youngsters." He shaded his eyes and looked out to sea, searching for a sail.

"What about you? Do you think she did the right thing?" Arkady kept both hands on his fishing rod, feeling the imperceptible tug of a bite on the line. Slowly, he began reeling in the string.

"I am not angry with her, if that is what you mean. She is as level-headed and wise a woman as I have ever known. If Myrie and the others were convinced they needed to go to Yr, then Katkin would have felt obliged to protect them. She had to leave without telling us, because Gwenn insisted Myrie could not leave Asaruthe until she turned eighteen." He sighed. "I wish she had not done that. I would have gone with them, if they had asked me. Lut is a good sailor, but he does not know the currents as well as I do. Especially now..."

Though Arkady had lost his sight many years ago, he was by far the better fisherman of the two. His rod bobbed, and the two men worked together silently and efficiently for a few moments to reel in a lingcod. It flopped and gasped as it joined its brethren in the wicker creel.

"You are worried about the autumn storms?"

"Eh?" Gunnar slammed the creel lid and straightened his bent back with the aid of his crutch. "I suppose I was mostly thinking of the storms, yes. But something else as well. Ever since Jakob left, and Huw followed to repair the damage to the pellicle, I have had this vague apprehension. Something feels very wrong about our island, but I cannot put my finger on what it is."

"I know, I have felt it too. I wish Jakob and Maia had left some other way. Asaruthe does not feel like the haven it once did." Arkady stood still for a moment, listening. He could sense the surge of the waves, and knew that they would soon have to abandon their perch on the rocks for a spot higher up, beyond the tide line. "I even begged Gwenn to take keth'fell* with her when she went out this morning. She probably thought I was crazy." He nimbly re-baited his hook and tossed the line back into the ocean.

This brought a dry chuckle to Gunnar's lips. "Gwenn has not taken her sword from under the bed since Jakob and Lut..." He sighed and did not finish his sentence. "Anyway, what are we worrying about? No one knows where this island is and no one cares, now that Myrie has left us."

"I hope you are right." Arkady stiffened as another fish struck at the bait on his hook. He reeled it in, as Gunnar stood ready with the net.

"How do you do that? You have caught three times as many as I have, Inky. I am beginning to think you have some sort of uncanny power. Do you speak the language of fish, my clever friend?"

* Gwenn's sword, made for her by her stepfather, Jacq Benet.

"It is all in the wrist, Strawhead," Arkady answered back, laughingly.

That night they all slept restlessly, troubled by dreams. Usually Arkady enjoyed the experience of a clear dream, for in it he could re-experience the joy of sight—the beauty of the Yrth and his lover's face. But as he slept in his little stone cottage, lulled by the ceaseless rushing call of the ocean, he dreamed a dream of darkness—a darkness so thick and fearsome it felt as though he had been immersed in tar. He struggled forward with his arms outstretched, feeling far more handicapped by his blindness than he ever did in real life. The shrieks and cries of evil birds surrounded him, and he ran, clumsily, trying to evade their wicked talons. Then he heard more cries— cries he recognized. Gwenn, screaming in fear and pain. He tried to go to her, but he did not know the way, could not find her in that syrupy darkness that seemed to impede his every step.

"Gwenn!" Her screams grew ever more faint. "Gwenn!"

Arkady lay in bed, his heart pounding with anxiety. Though he wanted to get up and check on her, he forced himself to lie still. He knew she was with Gunnar, it being his week to sleep with her, and the unwritten code of their relationship dictated that Arkady would not enter the house they shared until she rang the bell for breakfast in the morning. It had worked for sixteen years, that code, had made their unorthodox three-way marriage almost trouble free. But now, lying chilled and sweating in his tangled sheets, Arkady needed to feel the comfort of her strength and the softness of her skin against his.

Gwenn slept in the curve of Gunnar's body, warm and secure. She heard someone calling her name, and she opened her eyes to see if he had spoken. But her husband no longer lay beside her. Tristan leered at her nakedness, and reached for her. Gwenn cried out in horror as she saw his clawed hands, swathed with shredded flesh.

"No! Don't touch me. Keep your bloody hands to yourself." He slid towards her on the bed, sneering, and she saw that he, too, was naked, and erect, full of loathsome desire.

"I want you..." he moaned. "You will be mine—all mine."

She screamed and woke herself up.

Gunnar snored on peacefully. His sleep took him back to the *Fire*

Drake, his old ship, burned and gone these sixteen years. He stood on her deck, in the rolling sea, admiring the carved dragon figurehead, the row of shields on the gunwale, the heap of weapons on the deck. An axe lay at his feet, and he hefted it, feeling the pleasant thickness of the oaken shaft in his hand. He swung it back and forth, faster and faster. With each slashing blow, his strength increased, until the heavy axe felt like a matchstick. With the strength came anger, towering and terrible. There were no enemies to fight, so he began to hack at the timbers of his beloved boat.

"Look what I have done! But you made me. You made me..."

She screamed like a living thing—like a woman—until she broke apart and sank, taking him with her. The bone chilling cold of the ocean drowned his rage, and left him choking and breathless. Darkness seemed to claw at him with nails of ice, dragging him deeper and deeper. His lungs begged for air. Just when he believed he would die, his head broke the surface of the water, and he awoke. A dark figure, tall and menacing, overshadowed the end of the bed.

Sudden real fear tore a grunt from his throat as he groped for his sword. "Who is there?"

Gwenn, whose eyes had been open for longer, said, "Kadya? Are you all right?"

The tears on his face shone in the moonlight. "I am sorry. I am sorry. I know I am not supposed to be here, but I had a dream. A terrible dream and I could not sleep for worrying..."

Gunnar lay back with a sigh of sympathy. "I did too. It was horrible."

"So did I," Gwenn said, in surprise. "What demon has visited our island this night, to bring such darksome terrors?"

"I don't know," Arkady said despondently. "But I am afraid—more afraid than I have been since I lost my sight. What can we do?"

Gunnar squeezed Gwenn's hand, and she shifted over in the double bed. "We can stay together, all of us, until this uncanny darkness passes." She grasped Arkady's sleeve and drew him to her. He climbed into bed, silently trembling. Gunnar pulled the covers over the three of them and they huddled together.

"Good night," said Gwenn, drowsily, a few moments later. "I love you both—very much. Now let us hope for pleasanter dreams."

"Indeed," said Gunnar. "Goodnight, Inky."

"Good night, Strawhead. I love you," replied Arkady, archly.

Gwenn stifled a giggle. Gunnar, somehow understanding the intention behind his words, answered entirely without mockery. "I love you too."

They all slept until the sun had cleared the tops of the trees that surrounded Asavale. Gwenn opened her eyes first, but lay still, wondering why the bed felt so hot and crowded. When she recalled her interrupted sleep, she smiled ruefully. The dark-winged dreams of the night before seemed like the fears of foolish children in the warm light filtering through the windows.

Arkady woke next and stretched, trying to relieve a cramp in his side. He whispered, "If we plan to make a habit of this sleeping arrangement, we will need a bigger mattress."

Gwenn snorted. "I don't think that will be necessary. Something just spooked us all last night. It won't happen again."

"Of course not," agreed Arkady, and rolled out of bed. "See you at breakfast." He walked back to his cottage, dressed himself, and scraped the razor over his bristles, all the while hoping she was right. But if anything, the feeling of imminent disaster seemed even more pressing this morning, for all the sun shone on the box of petunias outside his window.

When Arkady came back to the main house, Gwenn had just served plates of kippered herrings and sliced barley bread, spread thick with butter. Gunnar passed over a mug of coffee, saying, "I trust you slept well?"

Arkady maintained the same deadpan composure. "Very. And you, my friend?"

"Fine," answered Gunnar. "Never better." He handed Arkady a plate. "How about a fish sandwich for breakfast?"

Arkady snickered crudely.

"Knock it off, you two," said Gwenn, frowning at her own plate of fish. "I need some help tracking the last of those renegades today. The docking and crutching was supposed to be finished two weeks ago."

Gunnar patted her hand apologetically. "All right, Faircrow. What do you want us to do?"

Arkady added truculently, "Yes, sorry. We had no idea you were right in the middle of something." Now it was Gunnar's turn to chuckle, but he smothered it when he saw Gwenn's scowl.

She threw up her hands in irritation and strode from the room, crying, "Never mind, you idiots, I will do it myself! I have had enough of your little boy japes for one day." They heard her muttering as she went through the front door, "For goodness sakes, you would think that we were the first three people in history to share a bed..." Gunnar sighed as she passed out of hearing.

"Do you think we ought to stay here any longer? I don't believe those dreams last night were entirely coincidence." He shook his shaggy blond head. "It seems so foolish, but I feel as though we are in real danger. I wish I knew why."

"I agree, but you will never convince Gwenn. She won't leave the sheep behind." Arkady stood and began collecting the breakfast dishes. "It is my turn to do the washing up. Why don't you find Gwenn on the tops and try to talk some sense into her?"

Gunnar headed in the opposite direction, back towards the bedroom. "I will try, but you know how stubborn she is. But I am certain of one thing." His voice grew quiet as he disappeared along the hall towards the bedroom.

Arkady called, "What is that?"

"I am going to make her take keth'fell with her. And I will carry Ancarnen.* We cannot be too careful." He returned a moment later, and Arkady could hear the dull clink of metal upon metal. "Do you want to go fishing afterwards?"

Arkady nodded, up to his elbows in sudsy water. "Meet you at the jetty in an hour." He shook his head and smiled. "Good luck, Strawhead. You are going to need it."

The afternoon had turned hot, so Gunnar and Arkady buried their rods amongst the sand and rocks of the shoreline, and retreated to the shade of the cliffs. Gunnar had tapped one of the firkins in the cellar, and brought a stoppered earthenware bottle of ale to the beach along with his fishing tackle. He drank it quickly, still smarting from his acrimonious discussion with Gwenn. Just as Arkady predicted, she had refused to leave. Usually he deferred to her, but this time he had argued. She mocked his fears, saying that the island felt no different than it had six months ago.

Gunnar sighed, knowing this time she was wrong.

He nodded enthusiastically when Arkady volunteered to go

* The sword of the Mariner. See 'The Lay of Lutyond' in Book II.

back to Asavale for a refill of the ale jug and a cup of water from the well for himself.

"See if you can get Gwenn to come and have a drink with us. It would do her good." He blinked blearily in the bright sunshine, and took another long pull from his beaker, trying to drown the knot in his stomach. "She needs to unbend a little. Maybe then she will listen to what we have to say."

Arkady, who had fought his own battle with alcohol long ago, said resignedly, "All right, but mind you keep an eye on business. Don't get too relaxed yourself. I don't want to come back and find you napping while my rod is being towed out to sea by a whale, my friend."

"S'fine," Gunnar agreed. "I am not that soused." He drank again and added, "For now, anyway."

Arkady strode towards the cliff path, shaking his head. He heard Bridie's distant barks, and a torrent of cursing from Gwenn, faint but distinguishable. Arkady decided to fetch the ale first, and then try to find her. Gunnar was right—they had all been too wrapped up in worries since the children left with Katkin. Perhaps that was the only explanation needed for the recent spate of nightmares and anxiety.

A cry, echoing from behind him, brought his heart to his throat. He whirled and stumbled, sending the ale jug crashing to the rocks. Arkady began to run, holding on to the guide rope that followed the trail across the wide green pasture that covered the tops of the cliff. Though the path was a familiar one, the urgency with which he traveled made him slip and falter many times. Another scream—long, agonizing, gut wrenching—cut the air around him into darkened shreds of fear. Then he heard something far worse— the shriek of an aviscet, and another, and another.

He called for Gunnar as he struggled along the path, cursing his blindness. The sure knowledge that he could do nothing to help her—might indeed make things worse if she fought against the avisceti—did not slow his dogged progress.

"Hold on, Gwenn! I am coming..."

His voice cracked and trailed off as her screams continued unabated, mingled with the terrified yowls of the dogs. He heard Gunnar's panic-stricken calls from far below.

Arkady fell headlong as a pair of close-set stones trapped his boot. He went down hard, feeling the bones of his ankle percussively snap. He cried out in agony, but still tried to gain his feet. When he could not, he crawled instead. Gwenn's screams were fainter now, somehow drifting downwards from on high. He could almost feel her pain brushing against his face like the feathers of a bird torn apart in mid-flight.

She screamed Gunnar's name, again and again. Of course—he could help her. Arkady could do nothing, locked in the dark prison that had become his life. The knowledge tasted like the bitterest of draughts in his throat, more bitter even than bile. He stopped crawling and slammed his fist into the ground, again and again, sobbing in anguish.

Gunnar lay back, watching the gentle bob of the rods through half-closed eyes, as the swell carried the lines in and out. The ale had gone to his head—he didn't drink much or often now. Not like the old days, when he and Gwenn and the crew of the *Fire Drake* had raided the villages of Secuny for plunder and slaves. He had needed the drink then.

Nothing could allay the guilt that seeped around the edges of his now-virtuous life like an oily stain. Even his torture at the hand of his first mate, Arvid, and the loss of his leg had been a partial recompense at best. Gunnar sometimes wondered when the dark skald* would arrive, bearing his harp, demanding the coin due him. The 'sinner's tithe' his grandmother had called it. No matter how well you hid your transgressions, the skald played his harp, and you paid him.

A singular shadow passed overhead. Gunnar's eyes opened wide, and he looked up expecting to see the sun playing hide and seek with a bank of clouds. But the shadow was black, and many-winged, like some foul creature from the abyss. One of the avisceti turned its head, saw him, and gave a lazy shriek.

He struggled upright and cast wildly round for his crutches. The avisceti ignored him as he called to them, trying to distract their attention from Gwenn and Arkady. They streamed overhead, an impossible number, far too many to count.

Fear tasted metallic and cold, and turned his tongue to glue. "Gwenn, Inky, get down; hide yourselves!" He did not even know

* Bard

if they could hear him. Gunnar knew he had to get to the tops quickly, before the birds could strike.

But there is no quickness in a man with one leg, especially if he has been drinking. Cries of terror and pain from Gwenn punctuated Gunnar's time-consuming progress up the cliff—such heartrending cries as made him wish he could stop his ears, or tear them from his head. Each tumbled rock, each switchback, each sandy hollow, each hummock of grass, had to be negotiated in its turn, and all the while Gwenn fought a losing battle for her life above him.

When he reached the top, he saw her, or rather the maelstrom of feathers, beaks and claws that surrounded his lover. Keth'fell flashed in the sun, a molten blur of silver, but there were too many of the avisceti. As one fell, two more took its place.

Gunnar cried out to Gwenn as she turned and fled towards the cliff edge. The avisceti followed like a black tornado. "Wait, Faircrow. I am coming. Your right hand... Wait for me."

With a last anguished scream, she dived from the cliff.

"Gwenn..." he whispered, desolately proud in the knowledge that she had chosen her own death rather than defeat—a true warrior to the last.

But she could not cheat the skald—not like that.

Strong arms lifted Arkady and held him upright. The pain in his ankle made his vision blur red.

Gunnar hissed urgently in his ear. "Can you make fire?"

Arkady could make no sense of this. "Go to Gwenn," he cried hoarsely. "She is calling for you. Help her. Help her."

Gunnar shook him. "Listen to me! We need Hana's fire. The red kind. Can you make it?"

He understood. "How many are there?"

"A hundred at least. She tried to fight them, but there were too many."

"I cannot possibly make enough to kill..."

Gwenn's cries floated on the cooling breeze from the ocean. They were weaker now, and spoke unhurried words of excruciating death.

His voice sounded curiously flat, and very far away. "Just enough for her. They are tearing her apart, one piece of flesh at a time." The avisceti had dived below the level of the cliff—caught her before she managed to dash herself against the rocks. The skald wanted his silver.

Gunnar hissed insistently, "Make the fire, Kadya. I will throw it."

Arkady squeezed his empty eye sockets shut and felt the dryness, as though he cried grit instead of tears. *Just enough for her...*

"Hurry! She will soon be out of range."

He placed his hands before his midsection, calling on his center, praying all the while to Hana, his sister. The fire flowered red between his out-stretched fingers. "Now. It is ready."

Gunnar received the glowing orb, and did not feel the pain. The huge birds circled, driving closer, whirling, fighting amongst themselves for a shred of the sweet human flesh as it struggled weakly, held above the beach by the wicked, wicked talons of two of their number. Gwenn raised her head as Gunnar launched the fire, and her wide sky eyes seemed to bridge the distance, to look directly into his. She nodded.

The fire struck her, and she plummeted.

Within three seconds, nothing remained but a mass of angry and confused avisceti. They milled about in the sky, searching fruitlessly for their prey, before wheeling away with many disappointed shrieks, flying back across the ocean—towards the east.

Gunnar did not cry, even when he looked down and saw that the red fire had stolen three of his fingers in the time it took him to make the throw.

Arkady spoke very quietly at his side. "Did you get her?"

"Yes, I did."

"Then you aimed well and true," Arkady said, with grave courtesy. "I am so glad that she is not suffering any longer."

"Yes," said Gunnar again. "So am I. Very glad."

They held on to each other for a moment, while the Yrth turned below them—a different place than it had been ten minutes before. The enormity of their loss had not yet begun to penetrate and still Asaruthe felt like a mountain of ice, cold and forbidding. They were but two tiny broken figures clinging to her side, like insects.

After a time, Arkady asked, "Do you think you could carry me to the beach, Gunnar? My ankle is broken, but I would like to visit the place she fell. Could you do that?"

Gunnar picked up Arkady quite easily and slung him over one

shoulder, using his injured hand to steady him. Then he took up his crutch in his left hand, and limped along the cliff path to the beach, not hurrying. Arkady rode silently in his arm, like a sleeping child. Each tumbled rock, each switchback, each sandy hollow, each hummock of grass, was negotiated in its turn, but he had all the time in the world now. All the time he needed.

Gwenn's pain and Gwenn's blood had paid the skald, and paid him well.

When they reached the shoreline, Gunnar headed towards a patch of blackened sand, close to the place where they had been fishing earlier. Their rods still stood bolt upright and, curiously, keth'fell stood between them, point down amongst the rocks. But the irony of this and their ribald jokes at the start of this cursed day meant nothing now. Less than nothing.

Gunnar put Arkady down and stood with his arm about his waist to steady him. "Are we here?"

"Yes. But there is nothing left of her. Just some ashes. And keth'fell." Gunnar didn't say anything about the rusty splashes decorating the sand; a field of bloody poppies, borne of their beloved's suffering.

"Oh," said Arkady. "I hate to ask it, but could you do something else for me?"

"Of course, old friend." Somehow, they both kept their tidy composures from slipping. "What is it?"

"Could you shift, into the Vastness, to make sure she has reached there safely? I do not wish to know whose face her Uri'el bears, only that she is in its arms and at peace." Gunnar stepped away from Arkady, and did as he requested.

The Uri'el sat in the sand, its clear-veined dragonfly wings beating rhythmically, its scaly tail curled, like a cat's. Gwenn lay in its strong arms, immaculately whole, immaculately peaceful. Though he had not intended to look, Gunnar found his eyes drawn to the Uri'el's face, framed by strands of pellucid hair.

The features were a perfect blend of Arkady's face and his. Almost smiling, satisfied, he shifted back to the living world.

"She is there. And she rests easy." Arkady's expression relaxed. "Now we must go and see to that ankle of yours. Then I will come back and bury her ashes properly." Nothing would prevent his lips from trembling then, just a little, but of course, Arkady could not see.

"One more thing, my friend, and then I will trouble you no more. Could you go over to the side of the cliff where we left the jug? I would dearly like a drink of that ale." Gunnar had limped halfway there before he remembered that the Inkhorn had taken the empty jug with him. He turned back, just in time to see Arkady, his face pale and sweaty, bring his hands in front of his belly a second time.

It seemed the skald was not yet satisfied.

"No!" He stumbled backwards, his useless body again betraying him. But his pride no longer mattered now. "Don't leave me alone like this. I beg you..."

Arkady paused with his hands in mid-air. He did not bother to disguise his pain. "Don't grieve for me, Gunnar. I have been dead ever since that night on the beach at Feringhall. Why should I pretend otherwise, now that she is gone?"

Gunnar crossed the sand and drew level with him, but kept his hands at his sides. What good would it do to try and stop him? The skald would have his last piece of silver, whether today, tomorrow or next week. "So be it. Many men have chosen less honorable deaths."

Arkady gave him a mournful smile, and grasped his hand. "I give you my word that we will wait for you on the last shore. From thence, we will journey on together. But for now, you must take care of Myrie for me. Tell her that her Pop will always love her. Farewell."

He said nothing else, just closed his empty eyelids and bent his head. Gunnar would have embraced him, but as he stepped forward, a bright orange flower spread from Arkady's midsection. The heat was intensely painful, but cleansing in its way, and within seconds he was gone. Gunnar stared at the ground, at the molten puddle of sand that remained, still glowing red-orange. It coalesced and hardened into glass, as did the pain inside Gunnar's chest. After a few seconds, he threw his head back in a roar of utter brokenhearted sorrow.

Each warrior finds his carven throne,
Round the groaning table, full and free,
But the one-legged Mariner sails on alone,
In the dreary dark of the cold, cleaving sea. *

---

* The last words of the Lay of Lutyond.

Nine

Hawthorn

"What do you know about the river ahead?" Lut asked Katkin. They both stood at the steering oar, while Poppy, Myrie and Gwillam crowded the prow, watching for obstacles in the churning water. The River Ariane ran high, spilling over her banks, drowning the bases of the willows and other trees that hugged her sides.

"Not much," Katkin admitted. "I sailed this stretch of water a few times with Jacq, but never when it was running this high. But I do know one thing—now we have passed under the Mardon Bridge, we have reached Beaumaraisian territory. We had better be careful."

"Should I bring the *Able Drake* all the way to the City, Grandmother?" At a shout from Gwillam, Lut steered the boat to the right, as they shot through a narrow channel between two sand bars.

The river divided to pass around a small island. Katkin stared ahead, thinking of her former home—the City of Isle St. Valery, with its shining white ramparts and high Citadel tower. What would she find when she reached it?

Lut cleared his throat. "Oh, sorry," said Katkin. "I don't think we should go to the City just yet—not until we find out how things lie there. I want you to make for a village called Brooke. There is a serviceable jetty close by, as I recall."

Myrie floated back to the stern. "We have been to Brooke many times. Lut will find it easy to berth the *Able Drake* there safely and secretly. Once we are on land we can make our way to Acorn." She smiled at Katkin's stunned expression. "Yes, my dear. Your house still stands, though it has been empty for many a year."

"What then?" Gwillam called back. "What will we do when we reach Acorn?"

Katkin shook her head. "One thing at a time, Gwill. Let us get there first, and then we will make further plans."

"Except for Lut," said Poppy. "He should go back to Asaruthe as soon as we disembark at Brooke."

"Poppy..." Lut began, his voice already sounding forlorn. They had argued frequently on the long trip across the Reach, and past the mouth of the Gulf of Angar'et, and all along the Ariane about whether Lut would remain with them on Yr.

Poppy had insisted. "You cannot stay. We have immunity to the Bludseth, Lut. We don't know whether you do. And anyway," she added heartlessly, "I have a task to complete here, and you cannot help me."

"But Blossom, I can't just sail away and leave you here. Yr is dangerous. I want to protect you." Nothing he had said would dissuade her, then—or as he understood all too well—now.

"Grandmother, can't you talk to her?" Lut whispered to Katkin, but she shook her head.

"She won't listen. Poppy still hasn't forgiven me for what I said to her Patre."

They passed the first houses they had seen for several days, ramshackle dwellings on high stilts, with fishing dories tied close by. A fisherman stared in surprise at the unfamiliar-looking vessel and the tall blond boy standing at the steering oar. Lut raised a hand, but the man did not return his greeting. Instead, he dropped the net he had been mending and hurried up the steps to his house.

"We need to get off this river," Katkin muttered to herself. "It is too open. Too many prying eyes."

The Ariane widened as they approached the St. Germain Bridge, and Lut made preparations to step the mast. The bridge was a high-arched span of stone, two lanes wide. Katkin could remember when it had been constantly in use, as her subjects made their way along the Queen's Road, the main highway of Beaumarais. Now the grass grew rank and unkempt on its approaches.

"Soon we will come to another island," Myrie intoned in her gravelly voice. "You must take care, for the overhanging willows grow close over the river, and the way around is narrow. Also, there is a watchtower. *He* is often there, on the high parapet, surveying the countryside."

"A watchtower?" asked Katkin in surprise. "Split Island used to be wild and overgrown. Maybe we should put the boat ashore before we reach it."

Lut disagreed. "All of you get below. If I am at the oar, looking like a fisherman or a trader, we will attract less attention." He eyed the riverbank slipping past and saw high hummocky grass interspersed with rocks on both sides of the river. "I don't even know if I could land the *Able Drake* on the shore here without damaging her keel. It looks pretty rough."

They could see Split Island now. Trees grew right down to the steep shoreline. It surprised Katkin to see that a turreted fortification now crowned the rocky apex. As she herded the others into the hold, Katkin asked Myrie, "Who is he? The one you said lived in that tower?"

Myrie turned her glowing eyes back to look at Katkin.

"Our former Master," she said quietly. "Maggrai."

They were all pleased to escape the cramped hold when Lut whispered to say he had brought them to the bank of the river, close to the village of Brooke. Night had fallen as they made their way up the Ariane, making it easy now to creep away from the boat unseen.

Katkin hurried across the deserted jetty, following the others. A feeling stole over her, as if someone or something watched from the shadows. But she did not feel afraid. She slowed her steps, trying to part the darkness like a curtain, so that she might see what lay beyond it. Just then, she heard the faint sound of a dog barking in the distance and Gwillam hissed, "Hurry up, Katkin!"

A ramshackle warehouse stood just to the side of the jetty. Lut kicked in the door and they assembled inside, clutching their traveling bags.

Myrie spoke. "We have reached the end of the first stage of our journey. Now we must say good-bye to our dear ones. Lut and Gwillam will return to Asaruthe, so that they may console those that remain."

Gwillam swallowed. "I am staying here! Myrie, you and I have always been together..."

"And I don't want to go either," insisted Lut.

"You must," she insisted softly. "Your father will have need of you. We have seen. Now go," she repeated. "And take Gwillam with you. To one who is grieving the journey seems endless, but two may find comfort in each other."

Still unwilling, Lut went to stand before Poppy. "Should I leave?"

She nodded.

"Why, Blossom? I want to be here with you."

"You heard Myrie," Poppy answered coldly. "You are needed on Asaruthe. And I am needed here."

He turned away, not wishing her to see his anguish. Poppy's expression suddenly matched his. She raised her hand to touch him, but then let it drop to her side.

Katkin stared over at her, wondering what task her daughter had set for herself.

Gwillam hugged his mother and Poppy, then looked over at Myrie. She gave him a serene smile. "Do not grieve, my dearest," she said. "We will all meet again at the ends of the Yrth." She added some happy clicks, and Gwillam grinned grudgingly.

"Come on, Lut. Let's go." Gwillam tugged at his tunic, and pulled him from the warehouse. Poppy's eyes filled with tears, but she did not weep. Neither did Lut, until the darkness had swallowed the *Able Drake*, and she had carried them far downriver. Gwillam stood beside him and reached high to place an arm around his shoulders.

"What did Myrie say to you?" Lut asked, after a moment. "Why did you smile?"

"She said she would miss me, but the old man in her head could be her voice for now. And that we should wait on Asaruthe until we hear from her again. Then she promised she would never 'click' with anyone but me."

Lut burst into reluctant laughter. "Gods! What a terrible pun." He tightened his grip on the steering oar. "Now that the moon is up we should be able to make some headway. Go to the prow and watch for obstacles. I'd rather not meet whatever is haunting that tower face to face."

"Yarr, Cap'n," said Gwillam, cheerfully.

Katkin walked over to Poppy, who was still sniffling and rubbing her eyes, trying not to cry. "What are you looking at?" she asked her mother rudely.

"Poppy..." Katkin sighed. "I understand how you feel, but the only way we will be able to get through this is to work together."

"You have no idea how I feel. Don't pretend you care about me or Patre." She tried to turn away. Katkin caught her shoulder and shook her hard enough to set her teeth rattling.

"You are no longer a child, so stop acting like one! Open you eyes, and start thinking about other people. Myrie and I need your help."

Poppy raised her fist, incensed, ready to strike Katkin. Myrie glided over and placed herself between them. "Your Patre would want you to forgive," she said softly.

Poppy frowned. "All right. We work together. But it doesn't change anything," she insisted. Katkin shrugged tiredly.

"As you wish, my daughter. Nevertheless, I would have you know this—I do care for you—and your Patre, both." She sighed and then her face took on a determined expression. "Now, what is our first move?"

"Shall we wait here until dawn, or try to find our way to Acorn now, in the dark?" Poppy asked Katkin.

"We could go by way of the Vastness," Katkin replied thoughtfully. "Then we would not have to worry about being seen."

"No!" Myrie insisted. "The Vastness is no safe haven. Not anymore. The minions of Maggrai are everywhere."

Poppy's eyes darted fearfully and Katkin took her hand. "Don't worry. We have friends as well as enemies on Yr—somewhere close to us, I feel it. We must trust them to help when the way is dark." Katkin did not elaborate. She could not explain the feeling she had had when they stepped off the *Able Drake*—that some benevolent spirit watched over them.

They left the warehouse and melted into the flat midnight shadows cast by the brilliant full moon. Another figure, gleaming with its own undimmed luminosity, stepped from behind a stack of barrels, and silently followed.

The house, as Nicholas had promised, still stood, though it looked dilapidated in the dim light. But the huge oaks had sheltered Acorn from the worst of the winter winds, and the roof was intact. Poppy wrinkled her nose as she stepped over a pile of dark scat on the floor. Katkin poked at the cast-iron stove and screamed when three or four panicked bats flew from the chimney and winged their way around the room several times before heading through the door.

Poppy and Myrie were both laughing at her, so Katkin said grumpily, "Out, both of you! Go and gather some wood from around the oak trees."

Lut had given them most of the remaining food supplies from the *Able Drake*, saying that he and Gwillam could catch fish as they sailed back to Asaruthe. Katkin made a batch of girdle scones and some tea, then she, Myrie and Poppy sat around the scrubbed clean table. They had no butter, and no jam, but the scones were fresh and hot, and tasted good after a week of ship's biscuit and *blodmor**.

As they ate, they made their plans.

"We need to gather information, first of all," said Katkin. "All we know for certain is that the Kindreds are being rounded up by the Black Guard and taken to the Infirmarie."

Poppy chewed a mouthful of scone, swallowed and spoke with determination. "I am going to the Citadel tomorrow to look for work. Once I am employed there, I will be able to find out everything we need to know."

"Poppy..." Katkin began.

Poppy cut her off. "You can't be seen there, because you might be recognized. Myrie can't go because she has her own tasks to complete. I can speak the language, and no one in the City knows my face, so it has to be me." She sat back in her chair, satisfied that her arguments were unassailable.

Katkin nodded grudgingly. "All right, but how do you plan to get close to Tristan? His dealings with the Firaithi will be secret, I am sure of it."

"I will find a way. And when I do he will..." She stopped, remembering just in time that King Tristan of Beaumarais was Katkin's son—and her own adoptive brother.

"He will what?" Myrie asked curiously.

"He will tell me everything I want to know," Poppy said confidently. "Everything."

"What will you do, my dear?" Myrie asked Katkin, who sat opposite her at the table. "Poppy is right, you cannot be seen in the City, for though your arm has been restored to you, your lovely face is still the same. Your subjects will recognize their Queen Arkafina."

Katkin nodded. "I plan to pay my sister Willow a visit. She lives in a village, called Kaisset, on the Mistmere coast. Gwenn told me that Tristan married her daughter, his cousin Roseberry. And Yannick, her husband, is the commander of the Black Guard."

---

* Sausage made with thickened sheep's blood and intestines

Poppy twisted her hands together. "But surely you will place us all in danger if your sister is so close to the throne?"

"I don't believe Willow would betray me, Poppy. We used to be very good friends, once upon a time." She glanced over to Myrie. "That just leaves you, Myrie. What will you do?"

Myrie's dark blue eyes were blank and far away. Katkin shook her arm gently. "Hmm? Nicholas just said that there are many other avisceti here, suffering terrible pain and anguish, just as he did. We will assimilate as many as we can, and then make ready to free the remaining Autochthones."

"A... Assimilate?" Poppy asked her.

"Yes," agreed Myrie, impassively. "That is what we said."

Lut and Gwillam lay together on the deck, in the midst of the fathomless ocean. The *Able Drake*'s mast lay shattered in three pieces beside them, the sail a soggy, tattered lump. Gwillam had tried two days ago to wring the last bit of brackish water from it, but there had been only a little, and now they had drunk it all. The sun beat on them relentlessly and Lut raised his head.

"Gwill," he croaked. "Gwill, listen, we need to spread the sail out—make some kind of shelter."

Gwill did not answer, so Lut shook him. With a protesting groan he woke, and licked his cracked lips. "What? Why did you wake me? I was dreaming about waterfalls, and swimming, and..."

Lut shook him again. "Stop that! It isn't helping. We need to rig the sail into a shelter; otherwise this sun is going to cook us alive." Gwill rolled away from him and closed his eyes.

"Who cares? We are going to die anyway. The mast is broken, and you don't know where we are. There isn't any food, there isn't any..."

"I said stop it!" Lut growled. "We can't give up, Gwill. Now on your feet, swabbie, there is work to do."

"Yarr, Cap'n" said Gwillam, faintly, and staggered upright. Together they managed to form the sail into a rough tent, supported by the broken mast. This small amount of activity exhausted them, for they had not drunk any fresh water for three days, nor taken any food since their parched throats could no longer swallow ship's biscuit. Gwillam dropped to his knees and crawled under the sail, and Lut followed.

"Are you angry with me, Gwill? I would not blame you if you were," he said, once they had arranged themselves in the relative coolness of the shelter.

"Angry? No. I am too tired to be angry. Why would I be, anyway?"

"Because this is all my fault. If I hadn't sailed straight into the teeth of that storm, we would..."

Gwillam laughed, and it came out a terrible wheezing gasp. The sound of it made Lut want to cry, but he had no tears left. The sun and salt air had robbed them all. "Your fault?" he whispered finally. "You told me to lower the sail before the wind snapped the mast. I didn't do it in time. It is my fault. Not that it matters."

"What are we going to do?" Lut's voice sounded desolate.

Gwillam answered him with ruthless practicality. "Lay here until we die and then lay here some more."

Somehow, this hopelessness gave Lut a push of raw energy. "No! I want to see Asaruthe again, and Poppy. We aren't going to be beaten. I am going to try and catch a fish for us to eat."

"You are barmy," said Gwillam, and rolled over onto his side.

Lut grasped the gunwale, and pulled himself upright, trying to keep most of his weight on his uninjured arm. Part of the mast had fallen on his shoulder, rendering his left arm unusable. He had not mentioned it to Gwill. Ever since the storm had overtaken them, as they crossed the wide Reach between Yr and the island of Citternia, his shipmate had been stoically uncomplaining, even humorous at times. Now it seemed he had given up, but Lut would not. He baited a line with some ship's biscuit after soaking the rock hard bread in some salt water. Then he dropped it over the side. As he did, he prayed.

Father, if you can hear me, send your aid to us now. I am Lutyond, your son. We need sweet water and something to eat. No more would I ask of you, my Father, only enough to keep us alive until we reach land. Please...

The breeze stirred his long, blond hair, now unbound and disheveled, as Lut stared into the viridian depths of the ocean. He watched his line until it bobbed, once, and then again, more sharply. Lut hauled it up, feeling the play of the creature on the other end, his stomach churning at the thought of fresh fish. Another harder tug made the line slacken in his hand. Lut put his head down and wept.

Coolness filled him, like a draught of water, as a cloud appeared and blotted out the sun. "Step away," the wind seemed to whisper. "Step away, son of the Mariner."

"Who are you?" Lut cried in a panic.

"Step away..." the voice trailed away in the rising wind, as the first drops of rain fell.

Lut scrambled below the sheet again and shook Gwillam. "Come on! It is starting to rain. We need to catch some water in the sail and fill up one of the barrels."

After they had drunk, judiciously, and eaten a little of the remaining ship's biscuit, Lut said, "I thought I heard voices while I was fishing. I guess I really am barmy."

Gwillam took another sip of water. "What did they say?"

"Step away, or something like that. I don't know what it means." Lut shook his head. "I prayed for water and fish. We got the water, and some useless words we don't need."

Gwillam's head snapped up. "Useless? Maybe not. What do you know about gap shifting, Lut?"

"Nothing much, except that Dad knows how. It is how he rescued Ma from that ghoul, Maggrai, back when we were babies. Did you ever hear that story, Gwill?"

He nodded. "Do you think we could do it?"

Lut shook his head. "I don't think so. Dad told me it is very difficult to find your way around in the worlds between. There are things called azimuths, and pellicula, and... and... We could end up getting lost."

"And what? We aren't lost now? I say we try it." Gwill sat up and grasped Lut's injured arm feverishly. Lut gave a moan of pain. "What is it? Are you hurt? Why didn't you say anything?"

"You had enough to worry about. I think my arm is broken, or maybe my shoulder."

"That settles it."

"Are you sure about this? We don't know what we are doing."

Gwillam offered Lut a hand. "You just step forward and a little to the side. Isn't that right?" Lut nodded doubtfully. "Let's go, Lut." Together they staggered forward and the feeling of reeling discontinuity sent them both to their knees.

Suddenly the air seemed cool, and bone dry. "Gwill," whispered Lut. "Look over the gunwale and tell me where we are." Gwillam crawled forward and peeped over the rail.

He sounded very disappointed. "We haven't moved. I can see the ocean."

"Are you sure? Very sure?" Lut lay on his back looking at the sky. It was flat and white and totally without depth. "I think we are in the Vastness."

"The Vastness? Are we..."

Lut laughed aloud, filled with exultant optimism. "Nay, not dead. And what's more, we can escape! All we have to do is start the *Able Drake* moving. Katkin told me." Lut tottered over to the oars. "Help me, Gwill. Give the oars a pull."

"Which direction?"

Lut stood still for a moment, letting the very gentle motion of the boat settle into his bones. He closed his eyes. Another sense, that had lain dormant inside him, opened wide. He could feel the pull of the magnetic fields curving round the Yrth, could feel the force that lay to his left. Slowly he raised his undamaged arm. "That way is north."

"How do you know?"

"I just do," he answered simply. "But we should head east, back to the coast of Yr."

"If you know the way, why don't you just steer us home?"

Lut looked at him in surprise. "Do you think I can?"

"Aren't you the son of the Mariner?"

So Lut and Gwillam each grasped an oar, and gave a mighty pull. The *Able Drake* shot forward in the motionless water, and left no wake behind to mark her passage.

Lut took his position at the steering oar, feeling the smooth wood under his fingers. The tiller joined him to the boat, intimately, and he divined every shudder of her timbers. The currents, Orlinir and Rindras, flowed through his veins like warm salty blood.

"What is it like?" Gwillam asked presently.

Lut could feel the water, the deep, cold ocean of the Vastness as it caressed the sides of the *Able Drake*. From there it radiated outwards, until the ocean lapped the shores of many lands, and a chart came unbidden into his mind, showing him every coastline, every river and bay.

"Eh?" Lut drifted from his reverie. "What did you ask me?"

"What is it like, to be the son of a God?"

Lut looked very uncomfortable. "I don't know. I have never

thought of Dad that way, until just now. He was plain old Dad. You know what I mean."

"But he has powers beyond mortal men. So do you."

This made Lut even more distressed. "I do not," he insisted hotly. "I am just Lut, the quiet one."

"Then how did you know which way was north? How are you steering the ship right now?"

"I don't know," Lut bellowed. "I can just feel the way to go in my mind. But that isn't a special power."

"Of course it is, you idiot. I can't do that."

Lut dropped his eyes and stared at the tiller, thinking on his father's earnest, craggy face. "But I don't want it to be so, any more than Dad does. He told me once that his strength is his greatest weakness. It makes him a danger to the people he loves, and he has sworn never, ever to use it, unless lives were at risk." *And if his own father chose to reject his transcendency, should not Lut do the same?* "I am not a god, Gwill, nor the son of one." He sighed and added, "Please don't mention it again."

"All right. But denying something doesn't make it less true."

The *Able Drake* continued to cut cleanly through the cold, still waters of the Vastness. They felt no wind, heard no cry of bird or slap of wave—just an eerie, echoing silence that filled their ears more completely than any sound. After a time they stopped talking to one another, and studied the horizon, looking for land. The rippling distortion that appeared on the deck behind them caught them both by surprise. They stared, slack-jawed, as the wavering lines formed themselves into the shape of a man.

"Who... Who are you?" Gwillam asked fearfully. But Lut recognized him right away.

"It is Dad's cousin Fyn," he whispered to Gwillam. "They look alike, see?"

Indeed the man who stood before them was tall and blond, with bright blue eyes and a prominent cleft chin. But whereas Gunnar's face almost always bore a cheerful and phlegmatic expression, Fyn's looked grim. So grim that Lut asked, right away, "What has happened?"

"Much," said Fyn, tersely. "Your home has been attacked. We must go there now. Come, I will take you."

He would answer none of their panicked questions, just seized them by the hands and stepped forward. They felt the deck of the *Able Drake* spin away from under them. The scene flickered and changed. Gwillam kept his eyes squeezed shut, terror-stricken by the sensation of traveling the continua. But Lut looked about him in interest, feeling the careful way in which Fyn chose their path, shuttling in and out of the azimity interlacing the worlds between. In some places, the pull was stronger than others, and Lut soon found he could predict which way Fyn would turn next. It seemed his ability to navigate extended beyond the confines of Yrth, but Lut said nothing of it. It was bad enough already, what Gwillam thought.

They dropped on to the beach at Asaruthe. Gwillam opened his eyes and said reproachfully, "My sister Poppy said we were not to gap shift here. It might leave a path for our enemies to find the island."

"It matters not. I am very sorry to say they have found it already. Look you there..." Fyn pointed down the beach, to where a crippled figure stood forlornly alone, before two freshly dug graves.

Lut shaded his eyes with his hand for a second and then tore along the sand, hugging his broken arm to his side, crying, "Dad! Dad!" Gwillam followed more slowly, in no hurry; somehow knowing that the graves held the remains of Lut's Pop—and his mother, Gwenn Faircrow.

Huw located his quarry easily, once he had traced the fine particles of dust left behind by the fleeing pair. Jakob sat by the bank of a clear pond, tossing jewel-like pebbles into the water. Maia was nowhere in sight.

Jakob looked up as Huw came to stand beside him. "Oh," he said, tonelessly. "Hello, Uncle Huw. How did you find me?" A bright red spinel, splashed with chrysoprase, joined the others in the shallows. A floating plant, something like a lily pad, had a few stones resting on its slimy, tenuous surface.

Huw explained. Then he asked, "Where is Maia?"

"She left. Maybe a day ago." Jakob smiled grimly as he succeeded in flicking a small yellow jewel on to the leaf and reached for another. "We argued a lot, before that." Huw raised a questioning eyebrow at this. "She wanted to go on to Mornguard and I didn't."

Huw, who had thought he might be angry when he caught up with Jakob, found he was not. "Why did you not?"

Jakob kept his eyes on the ground in front of him, and selected a jewel to toss in the water. "I... I heard a cry. A terrible cry of anguish. Maia didn't believe me, but it sounded like Dad. I *knew* it was him, and I wanted to go back. But she wouldn't listen." The smoky topaz stone skipped across the pond. "She wouldn't listen," he repeated, and wiped his nose with the back of his sleeve.

"So she left you here alone?"

Jakob nodded, clearly miserable. Huw tutted in exasperation. "So spoiled, that one. Like her mother. What have you been doing since then?"

"Sitting here. Thinking what an idiot I am." Jakob replied. He stood and looked at Huw hopefully. "Can you take me back, Uncle? I did not want to try traveling the worlds between by myself, in case I got lost."

He shook his head. "Nay. If there is trouble on Asaruthe now, then gap-shifting would have been the cause of it."

"Then I *am* responsible for whatever has happened. I knew it," he sighed. "Everything is my fault." Jakob hung his head and stared at his bare feet. His toe found an emerald in the grass and kicked at it fretfully.

"Not yours alone. Maia must share in the blame, if indeed there is blame to be apportioned." He smiled and patted Jakob's shoulder. "Sometimes a sound or vision comes to us from another time or place, while we wander here in the worlds between. Often it is just the echo of a dream. Let us pray what you heard was such."

Jakob sighed. "What I heard was real, I know it. And anyway, Maia cannot be blamed for what I did to Lut... and Poppy." He got to his feet and then gazed into Huw Adaryi's startled eyes.

Huw took a deep breath, trying to master his anger. "*You*?"

He nodded. "I know there is no way to excuse what I did, and I am sorry. But I want you to know that I never meant to hurt Poppy—not really. I just wanted to frighten her and get Lut into trouble." Then he stood still, waiting for Huw punch him.

Jakob slammed backwards into the water, and scattered the shining stones on the slime pad. Huw stood above him on the shore, rigid with rage. "You mangy Gruagá dog! How dare you! How dare you say you never meant to hurt my little flower? Now get up," he roared. "Get up so I can hit you again." He flexed his fingers and waited, breathing hard.

The blood from Jakob's split lip mixed garishly with the dripping slime on his face as he dragged himself from the water. He stood silently, waiting.

Sighing, Huw dropped his hand, and turned away. "Get your things," he said, dully. "We will travel to Citternia, and buy a boat. From there we can make our way back to Asaruthe."

Jakob wiped his face on his sodden shirt, and picked up his boots. "Do you have gold? How are we going to...?"

Huw subsided into angry curses and then spat, "Gather some of the stones lying under your worthless lily-white feet, fool! They are worth a king's ransom on Yrth."

Ten

Poplar

Poppy gazed at the grim-faced housekeeper in dismay. "There is no work 'ere at the Citadel for the likes of you," she snapped, and made to slam the door in the girl's face.

"But... But Ma'am, I have to find employment in the City right away. My drunken father abandoned me here, and I have no place to go." Poppy let her eyes fill with tears, hoping to convince the hard-hearted supervisor to bend the rules for her. She had already talked her way past three guards and a page, but now that she had gotten this close to the throne room, one last stubborn woman stood in her way.

"I told you already. No testimonial, no job. I don't need any fresh-mouthed country lasses in here anyway. Go to the Widow's and Orphan's Society for help. This ain't a charity hall. Now get out, before I call the guard on you." The housekeeper's sour expression left no doubt she meant what she said.

Poppy turned to go, thinking that the walk back to Acorn would be long and tiresome in the dark. She had left there early in the morning, telling her Matre she would undoubtedly be able to secure employment somewhere in the Citadel before the day ended. Katkin had been skeptical of this claim, and Poppy did not want to give her the satisfaction of knowing she was right.

A young page approached, the same one Poppy had charmed her way past earlier. He gave her a shy blushing smile as she displayed her most winsome expression.

The housekeeper cleared her throat impatiently. "What is it, Andre?"

"The king, Ma'am. He wishes to seek his pleasure amongst his subjects this night."

"Again?" the housekeeper muttered. "Gods maintain us. That's the third time this week. Which one is it this time?"

"Madame Zomphadeus, I believe."

Poppy's ears pricked up. "Who is Madame Zomphadeus?"

The old housekeeper had forgotten about Poppy. She whirled and shouted, "I told you to get yourself gone, Missy."

Andre offered to escort Poppy back to the gate. "I'll see she don't bother you again, Miss Delchamp."

The housekeeper waved her hand and headed for the laundry rooms to find the special clothes Tristan wore when he went out on the town. The king liked to pretend that these visits made him one of the people, and he thought he should dress the part in a shoddy linen shirt and breeches, artfully patched and stained to look old.

Poppy walked along beside the page, wondering how she might find more information about this Madame to whom Tristan intended to pay a visit. She gave him a winning smile.

"I like your costume, 'tis very handsome," she began.

The page wore something like a squashed pillow on his head, and mismatched colored hose. The King, himself, had designed the uniform based on pictures in a storybook he had seen when he first took the throne. It looked thoroughly ridiculous. The page smiled back, pleased by the compliment.

"Sorry about old Grizzleguts back there," he said, slipping his arm through Poppy's. "What's a pretty girl like you doing looking for menial work at the Citadel anyway? You should be strutting about on the stage, you should!"

Poppy smiled inwardly at this transparent flattery and repeated the story about her wastrel father. The page tutted sympathetically.

"Mayhap I will visit Madame Zomphadeus," she suggested

presently. "She might give me some form of employment. Where is her establishment located?"

The page blushed, bright red. "I wouldn't know, Miss. She charges too much for the likes of me."

"The rent is high for her lodgings, eh?" asked Poppy, and the page shrugged helplessly, not wishing to elaborate further.

They had reached the tunnel passing through the high rampart walls of the Citadel. The page nodded to the guard, who produced a huge ring of brass keys, selected one and unlocked the portcullis. Poppy soon found herself on the bridge that spanned the dry moat that separated the Citadel from the Commons. She smiled at the page through the arched opening. "Thank you for all your trouble." Then she curtseyed prettily and turned away.

"May I see you again, Miss?" he called to her retreating back. "Just tell old Remy here when you find a room. He will bring a message to me." Poppy peered back over her shoulder.

"I am leaving the City tonight unless I can speak with Madame Zomphadeus," she said, with mock regretfulness. "I will go to one of the villages instead, and look for work as a dairy maid."

The page gave the guard, Remy, a pleading look. The guard pointed a grubby finger across the square to a narrow alley. "Down Tinker's Lane. Then left on to Lampwright's Street. Number 42. Big half-timbered house—you can't miss it." He leered at Poppy. "Maybe Andre and I will come and pay you a visit, when you get established there. You will give us an abatement on yer services, won't you? Cause we helped you, and all," he added hopefully.

Poppy nodded uncertainly. "Of course. I would be pleased to repay your kindness any way I am able. Now fare thee well. I must make my way to Lampwright's Street before night falls." She hurried away across the Commons, wondering what sort of arrangement she had just agreed to.

Katkin had told her that a flourishing market and many public celebrations took place on the Citadel Commons, but now, in the dull light of early evening, the plaza looked deserted. Weeds grew rankly between the cracked and stained flagstones.

Since Poppy had arrived in the City of Isle St. Valery, she had seen few people. Those she met on the pavement had passed her silently, heads down and mouths covered with cloth masks. Some bore angry red streaks on their cheeks and foreheads. Their closed expressions spoke of fear or mistrust, and anger at anyone still possessed of hope and good health.

She knocked on the front door of number forty-two—a heavily constructed, iron-clad affair, with a peep hatch at eye-height. It seemed oddly secure for a boarding house entrance. The hatch opened to reveal part of a man's face.

"What do you want?" he asked gruffly.

Poppy smiled at him. "I am looking for lodgings, sir. I was wondering if..."

"Get lost, this ain't a boarding house," he replied, with a rude sneer.

Poppy had prepared a ready reply. "I am an acquaintance of Madame's, come from the country. Won't you let me speak with her?"

The man shut the hatch, and then the main door swung open. He ushered Poppy into an opulent entryway, with potted palms, luxurious velvet drapes, and dainty slipper chairs. "Wait here," he instructed, and disappeared along the hallway. She stared at her surroundings, wondering what sort of business Madame Zomphadeus might be conducting, that would pay for all this extravagance.

The man returned, followed by a tall, elegantly dressed woman. She held a long golden lorgnette in one graceful hand. Her immaculately coiffed hair hung in soft tresses around her face. She smiled at Poppy, and her lips were very red, as red as the revealing dress that draped her slender figure. "You wished to see me, my dear?" she purred.

"Yes," said Poppy. "I am seeking employment and lodgings in the City. I heard at the Citadel that you might be able to help me."

"Really?" Madame looked over the top of her glasses at Poppy, taking in her well-scrubbed country attire, and pink-cheeked innocence. "I doubt it. I generally hire women with more experience. Have you worked as a courtesan in the past?"

"A... A courtesan?" Poppy flushed and felt very naive.

Madame laughed merrily. "Did you not know? Madame Zomphadeus keeps only the finest women in her palace of pleasure. Women who know how to fulfill a man's every desire and keep him and his wallet coming back for more. I hardly think a young lady such as yourself..."

Poppy stood a little taller. She knew the King, Tristan, frequented this place. It might be the perfect opportunity to meet him, face to face. She took a deep breath and said, "As you surmised, Madame, I have no experience. In fact, I am still a virgin. But I am free of any sickness, and quite comely. I understand that some men find such things appealing?" She stared at Madame, who raised one shapely eyebrow in surprise.

"Indeed they do. Perhaps I was a little hasty. We may be able to do business, after all. Stephane, please show this young lady... I am sorry, my dear, I did not catch your name?" She peered at Poppy through the lorgnette.

"Camille," said Poppy slowly. "My name is Camille de Rien."

This brought a small smile to Madame's lips. "And where are you from, Camille?"

"I am the child of the mysterious isle, east of the sun," intoned Poppy and Madame looked absurdly pleased.

"Excellent! You lie well and creatively. That is a talent we can put to good use here. Now Stephane will show you to the parlor, while I draw up a contract. Employment to begin at once, assuming you pass inspection." she added briskly. "You receive twenty percent of takings. I provide the clientele, security and physicks in the case of employment-related illness or pregnancy. Do we have an agreement?"

Poppy nodded firmly. "Yes, Madame. We do indeed."

Poppy stood in the center of a tiny attic bedsit, thinking it far removed from the luxury of the drawing rooms of Madame's, for all that it was only three flights up a narrow staircase. The room held a bed, a washstand with a chipped bowl and pitcher, and a small chest. The worn floorboards were covered by a tatty but clean rag rug. Obviously, Madame did not believe in spoiling her staff, but Poppy felt pleased, nevertheless. She had already heard from her employer that a special client had sent word to say he would visit them that night.

"He comes very secretly, this man," Madame had said, lowering her voice as she finished the last part of the examination. "We have to oblige him with our finest services."

"Does he always avail himself of the same courtesan?" Poppy asked, with mock-innocent curiosity.

"Indeed not," said Madame, with a smile. "Each time he visits we provide him with a tempting array of beauties, and he selects the one whom he desires. For this, we are paid handsomely—very handsomely."

"In gold?" Poppy asked, wide-eyed.

Madame gave a small, secretive smile. "Nay. A substance even more valuable than gold. So we must always do our best to make him happy."

Poppy turned to Madame, full of unfeigned enthusiasm. "Am I to be in the assemblage for this evening? Please say yes..."

Madame shook her head, quite decisively. "You are not his type, my sweet Camille. He likes older women, almost the motherly sort. I have heard that sometimes he does nothing but tell them of a dream that visits him often at night."

"Oh," said Poppy, disappointed.

"Do not worry your pretty little head overmuch. I have a scheme by which we will auction your initial services to the highest bidder." She smiled cunningly. "Since you are so young and beautiful, we will no doubt be able to hold quite a few such sales before anyone catches on."

Poppy tried to smother her horrified expression.

Madame added, "There are several very rich, older men in the City who have a particular... predilection, so I shall dress you as a child, with a frilly frock. They will pay well for the privilege of being your first lover, Camille, and you, of course, will receive your share of the profits."

Now as she stood in her tiny garret, Poppy shuddered, thinking she would never allow anyone to use her in such a perverse fashion. She must find a way to meet the King—tonight.

A sharp rap interrupted Poppy's reverie. A pale blond woman entered the room, bearing a tray with a bowl of soup and a hunk of black bread. Poppy judged her to be about thirty, somewhat pretty, but the heavy layer of powder and rouge she wore gave a hard edge to her features. "Supper," she said briefly, and dropped the tray on the bed.

Poppy tried a smile on her. "My name is Camille. What is yours?"

The woman put a hand to her face and massaged her temple. "I am Bettina. Madame asked me to show you around. Hurry and finish your soup. I have to be downstairs and dressed by half ten."

"All right," said Poppy, eager to find out what she could. "Will you keep me company while I eat? Tell me about this place."

Bettina shrugged. "There isn't much to tell. It is a whorehouse, only a little fancier than most, mayhaps."

"But you must have met many important and famous men," Poppy pressed. "Like the one who is visiting tonight. Isn't that exciting?"

"Famous men?" Bettina laughed scornfully. "They all looks the same to me—like a couple of silver pieces." She frowned and flipped her blond hair back. "You must be new to this business. There isn't anything exciting about it. It is drudgery, same as any other stinking job, plus we all have to worry about catching nasty poxes and babies too."

"But surely the money..."

Bettina gave a short bark of laughter and then rubbed her forehead again. "The *money*? What rubbish did Madame feed you? Twenty percent of the profits?" She grinned as Poppy nodded disconsolately. "Didn't you read your contract? Madame takes room and board and other "fees" from your twenty percent. Leaving you with..." She made a circle with her thumb and finger. "You'll work here for five years before you even pay for your outlay."

"She didn't tell me that! What is an outlay anyway?"

"You know that examination you had before you signed your contract? That is worth fifty pieces of silver to Madame, and you can't leave until you pay it back. Then there is your room and board. Some weeks we don't make enough to cover it, so we go further into debt. These days, especially, it is hard to break even."

"Why do you say that?"

"The Bludseth, of course, you ninny. Not so many men around to pay for our services and the healthy ones are worried about catching it from the likes of us." Bettina made an impatient noise and Poppy gulped down the rest of her soup. "That's better. Now let's go."

A quick tour of the upstairs area showed it to be as drab and shabby as Poppy's bedroom. There was a washroom with a cracked porcelain tub, a dark closet of a room with tables and chairs where the employees took breakfast—'around midday, because we work so late' Bettina informed her—and a very small sitting room with a tiny grate and a few moldering books on deportment and hygiene.

After Bettina led Poppy back to her room, she asked, "But what about downstairs? How do we get to the main floors?"

Bettina smiled grimly. "We don't, unless we are working. Madame likes to keep everyone up here. She says it is for safety's sake, but I think it is to make sure we don't run out on our precious contracts." Poppy watched as Bettina closed her eyes for a moment, and placed a hand to her face.

"Are you all right?"

"Fine! I am fine. It is just this damned headache. I will get some laudanum from Madame before I go to work."

"Headache?" Poppy stared at Bettina's face. The heavy powder had smeared where she had been rubbing her temple earlier. Underneath lay an angry red streak, looking like a claw mark of some ravening beast. "You... You have the Bludseth!" Poppy accused, as Bettina put a hand to her mouth. "Don't you?"

She nodded as her eyes filled with tears. "Please don't tell anyone, Camille. If Madame knew, she would wall me away, like Rowena." At Poppy's questioning glance, she explained. "Rowena used to be a courtesan here. She caught the Bludseth from a Secunian noble that visited St. Valery on a merchanting trip. Madame found out and locked her in her room. No one could go to her, even with food or water. She screamed and cried for a week. And then..."

"Then?" Poppy repeated nervously.

Bettina pointed. "She's still in there."

Poppy felt a creeping horror as she stared at the door-shaped section of bricks in the opposite side of the hallway. "But Madame said physicking was included in the contract!"

Bettina sank onto the bed, shaking her head ruefully. "If by physics you mean pennyroyal and laudanum, then you are right. She has plenty of *them* downstairs in the medicine cupboard. But nothing for the Bludseth. Not for the likes of us, anyway. Herself, on the other hand—well, the King makes sure she is safe."

"How?" Poppy whispered, half-knowing the truth, but still afraid.

"Our work is paid for in Broth."

"Broth, as in soup? What on Yrth? She said it was more valuable than gold!"

"Not soup, you idiot, Broth. It is the one true cure for the Bludseth. The King has a store of it, gives it to his friends and family, and the guardsmen."

Poppy's eyes narrowed. "How does he secure this... Broth?"

Bettina shrugged. "I don't know. But sometimes, if one of us has been extra good to him when he visits, he gives her some of it. That is why he has to choose me tonight!" she added fervently. "You can't turn me in. You can't!"

"All right," Poppy said reassuringly. "I won't tell."

Bettina gave a small pained smile. "Thanks, you are a true friend, Camille. And in return, I promise I will look out for you as much as I can. Madame runs a tough game here, but we girls try to stick together. I will introduce you around after work." She turned to go and Poppy laid a hand on her arm.

"Bettina? Could you help me get downstairs, tonight?" Bettina's friendly expression hardened.

"What for? You want Broth for yourself, don't you?" Bettina strode forward until she stood inches from Poppy's face. "Well you can't have it! I need it more than you do."

Poppy shook her head wildly. "No, it isn't that... Not at all! I just want to get out of here."

Bettina ran from the room, calling back, "I already told you— there is no escape, except in death, like poor Rowena. And I am not going the same way as she did, so keep your trap shut, hear me?"

Pensively, Poppy unpacked her small bag, wondering how she would manage to escape before Madame held the first of the promised "auctions" for her virginity. Her fingers brushed against a folded garment in the bottom of the bag. Katkin's dress...

She thought back to the morning. As she had packed her bag in the main room of Acorn, Poppy asked her Matre if she might take the silvery gown with her to Isle St. Valery.

"It bears a fragrance that is so calming," she had added, almost as an afterthought.

Katkin had been very surprised by her request.

"Fragrance? What fragrance? I have not smelled anything! But it is an uncanny garment, Poppy. I think you would find it disconcerting. Somehow, it can change to fit its surroundings. The Angellus gave to me, when they mended my arm. I don't know if..."

"I need it," Poppy had insisted, although inside she wondered why.

Now she removed the gown from her bag and spread it out on

the bed. Katkin was right—it did look disconcertingly *magical,* for it had no seams or fastenings, only a soft cascade of plain silvery fabric, so finely knit that Poppy could not see the threads. Trembling, she removed her clothes, and slipped the dress over her head. It fit perfectly, clinging to her curves, making her feel comfortably warm.

As she ran her hand along the fabric of the sleeve, she felt the whisper of a voice in her mind, and the scent of patchouli suffused her.

Do not fear. I am with you; you have only to surrender to me...

Just then, Stephane shouted, "First call before lockdown. If you are working, get downstairs to the wardrobe room, now!"

Poppy paced the hall, trying to find some other way she could leave the confined attic space. There were no windows bigger than a dinner plate, and no other stairwells. She met other women, hurrying for the door. They ignored her panicked questions. As she continued her search by the washroom, the reflection in a cracked and blackened full-length mirror caught her eye. The dress had changed!

It looked now like shot silk, shining like the scales of some otherworldly ocean dweller. The enticingly low bodice and nipped in waist showed off her curves to perfection. Ostrich plumes trimmed the sleeves and the cowl that draped her shoulders. Poppy raised it to cover her hair and part of her face, thinking to herself that in the darkened hallway it just might work as a disguise.

I am here...

Stephane's voice, echoing along the hall, made her jump. "Final call!"

Poppy, keeping her head well down, joined the last of the stragglers. No one paid any attention to her. She strolled past Stephane, and through the door. He slammed it behind her, with an ominous click.

"Oi! What are you doing here? Costumes are never to be worn upstairs," he growled. "Remember—any damage to that rag comes out of your paycheck. When you have finished your shift you put it back in the wardrobe pronto, understand?" She turned to face him, and nodded her head, trying to keep away from the flaring gas lamp that lit the upper stairs.

"I... yes. I will do that. I just forgot my rouge."

120

He stared at her. "You are the new girl. Madame ordered you to remain here. Get back to your room!"

Poppy spoke, though the voice seemed to come from somewhere else. "Bettina has the Bludseth. You should tell Madame right away." Stephane paled.

"Bettina? My gods! Are you sure?" he asked, his voice harsh with fear.

She nodded, her eyes betraying nothing. "I saw the marks on her face. She covers them with powder."

Stephane brushed past her without another word and ran down the stairs.

He sat in the finest drawing room, in his scratchy town clothes, waiting for the first of the whores to parade before him. Tristan took no notice of Madame as she sat beside him, offering drinks and sweetmeats from a silver tray, and trying to make simpering conversation. He grunted at her to begin, and she clapped her hands. A steady stream of women, mostly older, ostentatiously swayed his way. Some he recognized from former assignations, although Madame did her best to make each one look fresh and different, with elaborate costuming and hairstyles.

Bored and disappointed, he sat back in the dainty velvet chair, which creaked ominously. Not one of the women appealed to him. But the dream had visited him again last night, and the subsequent frustration made him ache all over. Ten offerings sashayed by, and he sighed. Five more came and went, and he frowned.

Madame looked on with increasing dismay. As a willowy blond, much taller than Tristan, pirouetted before them, she urged, "My Lord, what about Cherie? She is beautiful, and *such* a good listener. She can make your every dream come true."

"Enough! Get that gaudy tart out of our sight. We will take our custom elsewhere this night." Tristan rose and called for his guard, who stood in a knot by the vestibule door, looking longingly at the unaffordable treats before them.

"My Lord, please! There are others I might show you. Please wait while I..."

But Tristan had stopped listening. His eyes fixed on the inner doorway, the one leading to the wardrobe room. A figure stood there, wearing a hooded garment as silver and deliquescent as an enslaved shaft of moonlight. She did not speak as she lowered the cowl to her shoulders. Her skin looked like dusky peach silk in the low gaslight.

"Who in the gods' name is that?" Tristan murmured. "Why did you not show her to me before?"

Madame squinted and raised the lorgnette. "That is, um... I am not sure."

"Then order her to approach us!"

Poppy glided into the room, trying to look as regal as possible. She lifted her eyes to meet the King's astonished gaze.

"You!" Madame stepped between Poppy and the King. "I am sorry, my Lord. There has been a terrible mistake. This presumptuous hussy has offered herself without my knowledge or permission. She will be punished." Tristan thrust her aside as she cried, "Camille, go back upstairs where you belong."

"My name is not Camille," Poppy said softly. She cast her mind back to the voice she had heard, the voice of the dress, and a new name sprang unbidden to her lips. "It is Azothe."

"Azothe?" echoed Tristan, and he sounded as though he was talking in his sleep. "Azothe... Of course. My alpha, my zeta."

Poppy smiled mysteriously and inclined her head. Spices imbued the space between them, making the air almost viscous, and creating a sensual bond that held Tristan in stunned immobility.

Madame called, "Stephane, get in here! Remove Camille from this room at once."

The spell was, for the moment, broken.

The guards, at a barked order from their monarch, prevented Stephane from entering. Madame wrung her hands in dismay. "Please, your Majesty. This girl is not among those I have chosen for your pleasure."

He spoke very quietly, in a voice full of menace. "Does Madame wish to tour the inside of our Citadel dungeons? It can be made to happen—at very short notice."

She subsided at once into a pout. "Of course, if my Lord wishes to employ this inexperienced little chit for the evening, then I have no objection, but I cannot be responsible for his satisfaction. Are you sure you don't want..."

"Silence!"

Poppy stood still and said, in a husky whisper, "My Lord Sun.

The Moon awaits your command." Her dark beauty enthralled him, making his anger dissipate.

He licked his dry lips and spoke, never taking his eyes from Azothe's face. "I do not wish to employ her for the evening."

"Oh good," said Madame. "Because, you see, I..."

"I wish to own her," Tristan continued implacably. "She is mine, as of this moment. Whatever you paid for her contract will be reimbursed you in gold."

"My Lord!" gasped Madame, thoroughly alarmed at the prospect of losing her only source of the Bludseth physick. She clutched at his sleeve in a panic. "One of my girls has been taken ill. I need Broth to help her recover."

The King eyed her coldly. "Do not waste your sweet breath with such lies. I am not such a fool to believe any Broth would ever find its way into your unfortunate whores." He stepped away from her and spoke with finality. "I shall not be returning. Nor will there be any further Broth—just a single payment of gold, for Azothe."

Madame looked as though she might protest further, but only scowled at Poppy. "As you wish, my Lord. Stephane, ask the driver to bring his Majesty's carriage round the back. He is departing, with Camille."

"I'll get you for this," she hissed in Poppy's ear as she passed.

Poppy smiled impassively at Tristan. "Shall we leave this tawdry dwelling, my King?"

"We shall, my Queen," said Tristan softly. "We shall."

The sound of Bettina's anguished cries, filtering through the heavy brick walls, troubled them not one whit.

The carriage ride across the Citadel Commons was silent, save for the gentle clop of the horses' hooves on the cobbled pavement. Poppy stared into the darkness wondering fretfully what had come over her.

How could she have so callously betrayed Bettina?

She buried her hands in the sleeves of the extraordinary garment Katkin had given her, seeking comfort, feeling the warmth there, like a quickening spark of fire. Suddenly, she divined her alter ego, Azothe. She leaned back in the upholstered velvet of the carriage, letting the patchouli-scented persona wash over her. The fragrance grew more intense, until Poppy felt she could not breathe.

"Surrender to me. Surrender..."

At the moment she felt she must cry out, must claw open the window of the carriage, the scent overpowered the simple girl from Asaruthe, Poppy Brunner. Now there was no more revulsion and no more fear—just an icy, crystal clear awareness of how King Tristan Dinrhydan would meet his death.

Tristan continued to stare at his companion, drinking in her loveliness, still unable to believe he had found her, at last. In his mind, he reworked the interior of his private apartment in the Citadel Tower, making a suite of rooms for the intoxicating beauty who shared the carriage with him. A fragrant pool for her to bathe in, a dressing room filled with the most sumptuous clothes his treasury could procure, an elegant table where they might dine together. And a bed—arrayed with silken sheets and downy pillows; a high-canopied bed crowned with images of the moon and the sun. Just like the one of his dreams. He would make love to her—again and again.

Azothe turned her head to look at him and her eyes glowed like pools of liquid amber. He took her hand, and she felt his trembling eagerness.

"I have waited so long for you," he whispered finally. "Many dreams I have had, dreams that left me drenched with sweat, breathless, in pain. I have desired no one but you, my Azothe. And now you are mine." He groaned aloud at the crushing physical need that filled him. He would have taken her, right there and then, had she not spoken.

"My King," she said softly. "You must understand that you and I were brought together by destiny—to embark on the greatest chymerical experiment ever undertaken."

Tristan's mind reluctantly withdrew from the torrid fantasy world in which it had been frolicking. "Ex... Experiment?"

"Of course. Why do you think you felt such a powerful need, such agony? The fulfillment of all your desires is nigh, but that is but the beginning. We will achieve much more. Together, we will beget the Primeval Essence—the secret of immortality!"

Tristan sat back. How had she known of his secret yearning to live forever? He had told no one but his master, Maggrai, of this. His devotion to Azothe became absolute.

"Let me join with you right now, my Moon. Immortality will be found in the conjugation of our physical forms, will it not? That is what my dreams spoke of, over and over."

"Your dreams spoke truly, and they *will* come to pass. Nevertheless, in order to manifest the required energy, you must not spill your seed rashly. The desire must build... build until it becomes a raging furnace in your soul, the seat of the Sun's power. Then, my King, only then, will the unsullied, silver portal of the Moon open wide to receive your flaming scepter."

He eyed her hungrily while he considered the implications of this.

She fixed him with a burning glance and spoke, her voice as hard and smooth as volcanic glass. "Are you able to act with restraint?" she cried. "Or will you have me now and squander the priceless gift I would place at your feet?"

He shook his head, painfully and regretfully, wondering how much more torment he could endure. But the final triumph, the long sweet ache of release, would make it all worthwhile. Tristan had one desire more powerful than his physical hunger for the woman who haunted his dreams—the utter defeat of Maggrai, so that he might rule Yrth forever.

Azothe smiled triumphantly in the darkness.

Eleven

Locust

Willow stared hard at Katkin, too shocked for the moment to speak. At last she whispered, "My gods, it is you! It has been so long, I did not recognize my own sister."

Katkin smiled, thinking that Willow looked much the same, though it had been sixteen years since they last met. A little plumper perhaps, more careworn, but her eyes and tired smile were as kind as ever. "Yes, it is Katkin. May I come in?"

"Of course. But we will have to talk in the kitchen. Roseberry is upstairs, sleeping. I don't think she would recognize you, but we cannot be too careful. You are still a marked woman here, my sister."

She followed Willow through the house and down the stairs to a tidy, whitewashed kitchen. The cook gave her a cursory glance and went back to her pastry. Katkin put down the basket of apples she carried and unwrapped the fichu from her curly chestnut hair.

"How did you get past the guards?"

Katkin pointed to the apples. "I told them I had fruit to sell. I did not think I would be identified." She held up her arms and smiled. "Two hands now, see? The traitorous Queen of Beaumarais had but one."

Willow's eyes went wide. "How on Yrth? Has your healing skill progressed as much as that?"

Katkin laughed regretfully. "Nay, Willow. Some friends mended it for me, long ago. But tell me, how are you and Roseberry faring? And where is Emile? Not in the Black Guard, I hope."

Willow sat at the table across from Katkin and took her hand. The cook put a pot of tea and some cups on the table between them. Katkin glanced in her direction and asked, "Is she..."

"Inge has been with us since Emile was born. She is quite trust-worthy—just like another member of the family." She sighed. "Things are bad, Katkin. The Bludseth has taken many in Kaisset and in the other villages too. Only the Kindreds have any immu-nity to it. You have heard what Tristan has been up to, I take it?"

Katkin nodded.

"For all he is your son, and Roseberry's husband, I have to say I cannot abide that boy. He is conquering Yr, with the help of the Black Guard in their aermaran, and those frightening aviscet crea-tures. Nothing stands before him for long. Secuny and our old rivals, the Mardon, have fallen already. He has a force in Spanja now, and he is working steadily southwards."

"Is there no one to oppose him?"

Willow's voice sank into a whisper. "There is one brave man whose true name is unknown. They call him the Outlaw Glint. He and his followers, the Swallows, are trying to gather enough support to form an uprising. They wreak what havoc they can to Tristan's men and airships, but of course they are fearfully outnumbered."

"What about Roseberry? Whose side does she take in all this?"

"Roseberry takes no one's side but her own," her mother said sadly. "She has become rather... stolid, and thinks of nothing but food, and sleep. Tristan lost interest in her long ago. She spends most of her time here now, with me. Yannick is often away, so she is company of sorts."

"How can you bear it? Being married to someone who leads the Black Guard?"

Willow shrugged. "I still love him, in the same way you love Tristan. He is your son, is he not?"

Katkin traced a faded flower on the tablecloth with her finger. "I suppose so," she said, after a moment.

"Why have you come here after all this time? We heard nothing for so long I thought you must be dead, Kat." Willow's eyes filled with tears. "I am very glad to see you again."

Katkin gave her hand an affectionate squeeze. "I had to hide myself away for a time. But now I have returned, and I want to help restore order and peace to Beaumarais however I can."

"Can you heal the Bludseth?" Willow asked eagerly.

She frowned in disappointment as Katkin shook her head. "I have not been able to heal anyone since the old days."

They both took a sip of tea and sighed identically.

"How may I meet this man named Glint? I have a friend that I believe may be able to help him with his uprising."

Willow looked hopeful again. "Really? Who is this friend?"

"She is... that is to say, he is..." Katkin smiled sheepishly. "Well, they are a little hard to describe. Myrie used to be a commander of the Rising, so she knows a little about tactics and such."

"You have not lost your habit of talking in riddles," Willow observed tartly. "But no matter. Where are you staying? It is possible that I might be able to get a message to the Swallows." Willow's eyes brightened, and Katkin wondered what her connection to the outlaw Glint could be.

"I am hiding at Acorn. Myrie and I tidied up as best we could and moved in. Poppy went to the City a few days ago to try and find work. I am a little worried because we have not heard from her since then."

"Who is Poppy?"

"My adopted daughter. I have another son too, named Gwillam. They came from the Gitasha. Their parents were killed by the Black Guard, so Huw and I took them in."

Willow looked very surprised. "Huw? Huw Adaryi, the horse trader of the Chandrathi? Are you married to him now?"

Katkin shook her head. "Not married, no. We were..." She grimaced. "It is a long and not particularly pleasant story. I would rather not go into it if you don't mind."

The cook shot over to the window. "Miss Willow, the Master's coming. You had better hide your sister quick."

Willow's head flew up in alarm. "Gods! It is Yannick. He is supposed to be gone all day. Hurry!" She grabbed Katkin by the arm, dragging her across the kitchen and up the stairs to the second level of the house. "In here," she hissed, and shoved her into an unused bedroom. "Don't make a sound until I get rid of him. The guards may not have recognized you, but Yannick would. He still calls you a witch, and blames you for ruining Roseberry."

Willow shut the door in Katkin's face as she heard Yannick's voice calling from the stairwell. "Willow? Where are you, my wife?"

She cleared her throat. "Here I am, my dear. Just checking on Roseberry."

Yannick joined her in the hallway and said jovially, "How is the old mammoth, anyway?"

"Yannick!" Willow let her disapproval echo in her voice. "Don't call her that. You know it hurts her feelings. Why are you home so soon? I thought you would be gone all day."

"We heard a rumor that some darky tramps were holed up in Jacq's old farmhouse, so we raided it this morning."

Willow made a distressed sound, which Yannick misinterpreted. "I know. It is terrible the way that place fell into rack and ruin. Then to have tramps move in. But don't worry, we will get them."

She swallowed. "So... So they weren't there?"

"Nay. But we must have just missed them. There was a meal on the table, still warm. One of the men saw a girl with long black hair running into the Acre. I sent the dogs after her."

Willow could almost feel her sister's gathering horror from the other side of the door. "What will happen when you catch her, Yannick?"

He shrugged. "She will go in with the rest, at the Citadel, I suppose, if my Lord orders it. I did not speak to the King myself. He is still cavorting with that hussy of his. When will Roseberry get off her lard bucket and go back home? That new woman is going to steal her husband away from her. He has already installed her in Roseberry's room. How much longer until she becomes Queen as well?"

Willow did not seem worried by this. "What of it? Tristan has not been a good husband for our little girl anyway. He promised her years ago that the Infirmarie would reopen so she could resume her training, but he has done nothing but fill it with darkies."

"Shhh..." said Yannick, worriedly. "That is treasonous talk. There are hidden eyes and ears everywhere, my wife."

Willow shook her head, thinking he had no idea how right he was. She seized his arm and steered him back along the hall. "Have you news of the outlaw Glint, my husband? Tell me of your new scheme to bring him to justice."

Katkin listened as Willow's voice faded, and then she sank onto the bed, still reeling from Yannick's unexpected news. They had driven Myrie from Acorn and into the trackless forest that surrounded the shores of the Mistmere. What on Yrth must she do now? How could she find the Dawnmaid, all alone?

She sat there for what seemed a very long time, lost in hopeless rumination. Another door, which she had taken to lead to a closet, opened wide. The fattest woman Katkin had ever seen squeezed her way through, and stood in the middle of the floor blinking vacantly. Suddenly, she noticed the figure on the bed.

"Who in the gods' names are you?"

Katkin, guessing that this creature was Roseberry, answered, "I am your aunt, and your mother-in-law, if you like. My name is Katkin."

Roseberry's moon-shaped face wreathed into a smile. "Aunt! How very nice to see you." She winked conspiratorially. "Am I right in assuming you are in here hiding from Daddy?"

Katkin nodded nervously, hoping Roseberry would not betray her. But the girl merely plopped herself on the bed next to Katkin, causing the springs to quiver violently. "Have you been to Isle St. Valery yet? You won't be very pleased at the state of the Infirmarie, I can promise you that."

"No, but I wish to go there soon. I have some business in the Temple. But first, I must find the Outlaw Glint."

"What for?"

"I want to help him. Your husband has had his way in Yr for far too long."

Roseberry clapped her chubby hands in delight. "Hooray! Now things will finally get interesting around here. I haven't had anyone to talk to since Emile went away."

"Your brother? Where did he go?"

She frowned. "You know of the Swallows?" When Katkin nodded, she continued, "Emile joined them a couple of years ago. Then last month, the Guard arrested Emi for spying and sent him to the Citadel. He and Daddy didn't exactly see eye to eye, but even so, he tried to get him released. I did too, but Trissy wouldn't have it. But don't tell Mummy anything. She thinks he is still in the Acre somewhere. It would kill her if she knew the truth."

Katkin shuddered, remembering her husband's torture at the hands of the Guard after they charged him with the same offence. "Perhaps Emile has escaped," she said brightly. "Let us hope so, anyway. Now, how may I meet this man, Glint?"

Roseberry smiled. "You have only to wander in the Acre, Aunt. He will find you; nothing more certain than that."

Gunnar sat in the kitchen of Asavale, leaning back against the wall on a wooden chair. His heavily bandaged hand lay across his chest. Lut sat beside him, frowning. Neither spoke. Fyn paced the floor like a caged beast, his fingers clenched on the pommel of his sword. Gwillam stood in the doorway, feeling excluded, from both their grief and their anger at each other.

He tried again to make peace. "Ikor, if Fyn says that you are needed across the heavenly plane, then shouldn't you go? Even if you don't want to fight there must be..."

Gunnar let the front legs of his chair hit the flagged floor sharply, but kept his voice to a very low growl. "No. I have already said that I will not leave this island."

"But Dad," Lut said, angrily. "We have to do *something*. Ma is dead, and so is Pop, because of those foul creatures created by Maggrai. Do their deaths mean nothing to you?"

Fyn nodded in agreement. "Listen to the lad, cousin. Vengeance is the only fitting response to such a crime. Come with me. Together you and I can hunt that cursed moon-calf down, and put an end to him."

"No," said Gunnar again.

"Then let me go. If you don't care enough to avenge Ma's death, then I do!" He stood and smacked his fist hard onto the table, making the saltcellar rattle.

Gwillam paled at Lut's thoughtlessly cruel comment. "Lut, don't..." he began, but Gunnar rose from his chair and shouted over his words.

"How dare you? How dare you tell me what I do or do not care about?" Gunnar's eyes were so red-rimmed and hazed with fatigue and bitter anguish that they looked more grey than blue. They bored into Lut's until he had to look away. "I loved your mother, more than all the sundering seas. And I loved Kadya too. I would have done anything for the pair of them, anything..." Lut looked stricken as his father stifled a sob with his hand.

"Dad, I am sorry. I shouldn't have..."

Gunnar stabbed a finger into his chest, making his son grimace with pain. "You are damned right you shouldn't have. Nothing I can do now will bring them back. Nothing, do you hear me? The truth is, Maggrai's minions are not to blame for her death. I am. Do you want revenge? Then kill me!"

Fyn stepped between them. "Stop this foolish talk, cousin. Your grief has unhinged you. There is nothing you could have done against so many."

"I should have been there, at her right hand. I should have given my life for hers. What good am I, now? What good am I?" He put his hands over his face and turned away, and his wide shoulders trembled with brokenhearted grief.

"I am glad you are still here," said Lut, in a very small voice.

"So am I," echoed Gwillam.

"And I," agreed Fyn. "But if you will not help, then at least let the boy come with me. I can teach him to navigate the paths between. It is time he learned to be a true son of the Mariner." Gunnar turned back, wiping the tears from his eyes with the grubby bandage on his burned hand.

"Lut can go or stay, as he wishes," he said woodenly, and slumped back down on the chair again. "But why pursue this pointless revenge? It will gain you nothing, cousin."

Fyn's eyes blazed bright azure blue. "Pointless? Are you so wrapped up in your own grief that you forget I also lost a daughter? I gave my life so that she might grow up strong and untroubled by heartache. I would honor her memory by destroying her enemies.

131

She was a true warrior, worthy of the name. You, cousin, are nothing but a sniveling coward."

Lut saw his father's good hand tighten into a fist as he rose from his chair. "Dad... Don't," he begged. "He didn't mean it."

Fyn stepped back a pace when he saw Gunnar's expression.

He stared for a moment at the three of them, breathing heavily, his left hand clenching and unclenching. Then he slammed his fist into the foot-thick basalt wall of the kitchen, leaving a crumbling hole the size of a man's head. "*She... is... dead...*" he said slowly, emphasizing each word. "Nothing you do will change that. Now leave my house."

Fyn turned, shaking his head in disgust. "Are you coming, lad?"

Lut stared at his father for a long moment, and then drew himself up tall. "Yes. I will help you find Maggrai and destroy him. And then, when you have taught me how to travel the worlds between... I have some hunting of my own to do."

Though Lut did not say anything more, Gunnar seemed to know what he meant. "Leave your brother be. That is what Gwenn would have wanted. She loved you both."

"Dad, you can't expect me to forgive him! Not after what he did. Jakob is just as responsible for Ma's death as those cursed avisceti. He made the crack that led them here! And after what he did to me over Poppy..."

"What about Poppy?" Gwillam asked. "You promised you would wait here until she sent word."

Lut's look of angry despair made him seem ten years older, and wholly out of reach. "She sent me away, Gwill. I don't owe her anything, not now."

Fyn smiled grimly at this. "And you?" he added, in Gwillam's direction.

Gwillam went to stand beside Gunnar. "I will stay, Sir, if it is all the same to you. I am needed here."

"So be it." Fyn held out his hand to his cousin, who stared at it coldly, and then turned away.

Lut stood behind his father, and rested his forehead on a broad shoulder. "Farewell, Dad. I will return as soon as I can. Take care of yourself." He started to cry and Gunnar patted his hand awkwardly from the front.

"Go on, lad. Don't keep cousin Fyn waiting. I will be here when you come back." Lut stepped backwards and Fyn took him by the hand. With a sigh of displaced air, they disappeared. The silence in the kitchen deepened until it buried everything in twilit gloom.

Finally, Gwillam spoke. "Shall I see to the hole in the wall, Ikor? It is getting cold these nights."

"If you like," said Gunnar mildly. "And tomorrow we will finish docking the tails on those naughty lambs." He gave a small hiccupping sigh, then placed his arm over Gwillam's shoulders, and spoke with determination. "That is how I will honor her memory. By caring for the things *she* loved. Not by more death. Never that."

Twelve

Apple

Tristan and Azothe sat opposite one another at the dining table, feasting on baked fish and other fruits of the sea. Azothe ate sparingly, as always, but Tristan wolfed down his Coquille St. Jacques with evident relish. He pushed a platter of oysters towards her. "Try some of these, my dear?" he asked, hopefully. Their aphrodisiac qualities were well known. Azothe remained cool to the idea of lovemaking, although she had been at the Citadel for two weeks already.

Azothe raised her eyebrow in disdain. "I have eaten all I require of your excellent provender."

"Maggrai came back from the Watchkeep with some news this evening."

"Oh?" said Azothe, languidly.

Tristan slathered a piece of bread with butter and stuffed it in his mouth. Azothe frowned as he continued to speak. "He tracked a gap shift back to a heretofore unknown island in the middle of the Northern Ocean. He believes the Dawnmaid made her home there."

Her level of interest remained unchanged. "Did he find her?"

"Nay. He sent a great many avisceti, but they returned empty-handed; or should I say—clawed?" He giggled at this childish pun, and Azothe smiled tolerantly.

"Was there no one on the island, then? Was it deserted?"

"The avisceti made a single kill. The mother of the Dawnmaid." Another gleeful giggle escaped his lips. The knowledge that the avisceti had killed his sister Gwenn bothered him not at all. Nor did it seem to trouble Azothe.

She yawned and turned the conversation to the only topic of concern to her. "When will we be able to put our arrangement into place, my Sun? He must be out of the way before we begin our journey to immortality, through the congress of the Moon and the Sun." She fixed him with a hungry stare and raked her long nails on the bare skin of his arm. Tristan swallowed and closed his eyes, his body rigid with desire.

"I don't... think Maggrai has returned to the Watchkeep," he said, when he could speak again. Tristan frowned. "I caught him loitering outside your door last evening." He gave her a look of concern. "You will be careful, won't you, Azothe?"

She laughed, low and sultry. "I have nothing to fear from *him*! Bring him to the Chymericum this night. I think it is time I showed myself."

"Why?"

She just smiled and shook her head. "Bring him. Is not all in readiness?"

Maggrai paced the floor of the Chymericum, back and forth, back and forth. He clicked his long nails together nervously, though his face, as always, remained impassive. Tristan watched him out of the corner of his eye. He seemed upset—or even, perhaps... afraid.

Tristan had to try very, very hard to keep the exultation from his voice. "Are you ready to begin the amalgamation?"

Maggrai did not answer. He dragged his feet over to the workbench and stared at the small pile of corsfyre that Tristan had recently smelted. To himself, he muttered, "Is it enough? It must be enough." He pawed through the soft red crystals, and selected the three largest. "These ones, to begin with. Yes, they will do nicely."

Tristan turned the screw a little tighter. "I asked Azothe to join us, Master. She will be here soon."

Maggrai's head snapped up. "Azothe? What for, you idiot?" He turned to Tristan, and licked his fangs. Such a display would have reduced Tristan to jelly once upon a time, but now...

Tristan no longer felt any fear of Maggrai. In fact, though he continued to use the honorific "Master," it was Tristan who took the lead in the chymerical inquiries. It was Tristan who had found the distillation method that turned Firaithi blood into Broth. It was Tristan who had designed and built the apparatus that filled most of the room they occupied at the moment. The apparatus that would open the door to the future.

Maggrai eagerly awaited the day he would return from whence he came with the formula for Broth to save his ailing slave-kingdom. But Tristan and Azothe had other plans.

"Azothe knows a great deal about chymike, Sir. I believe she can help us."

His master frowned. "I do not need her assistance. My powers are potent enough to open the portal to the distant age. Once the chamber is lined with fire-clay, we will proceed with the amalgamation." He pointed to the three pieces of corsfyre that lay on the workbench. "These will provide the appropriate amount of energy..."

A tap on the door interrupted him. "Tell her to go away," Maggrai hissed. His pale skin exhibited a blue tinge, and Tristan could almost smell the fear infecting him. He *was* afraid—afraid of Azothe. In the time it took for Tristan to consider whether or not to engage in open rebellion, Azothe flung open the door and glided into the room.

Maggrai frowned again and muttered, "I locked that door myself. How did she...?" He saw Tristan look over at him quizzically and pulled himself together, though the sight of her made his scrotum retract, as if he had thrown himself into a pool of icy water. Maggrai cleared his throat and growled, "I suppose she may remain, but tell her to stay the hell out of my way."

Azothe did not speak to either of them. She moved smoothly over to the new apparatus and studied it with great interest. Tristan eyed her with unashamed lust. Though she had come to him with nothing other than the clinging silver gown she wore at Madame's, since then she had produced a dazzling array of frankly sensual garments. This one proved to be no exception—low cut, to reveal her pert breasts, wasp-waisted, and very closely fitted through the hips in a fabric that looked for all the world like the mail of some opulently argent fish.

She turned her deep brown eyes to gaze coolly at Tristan and Maggrai. "What is this contrivance, my Sun?"

Tristan went to stand beside her. Her musky scent touched his face like a caress, and stirred him. He stoically ignored the stimulation, and said, "This is the Chronagine, Azothe. I created it so that my Mas..." He decided he would bow before no one else in Her presence. "I meant, so that Maggrai may pass through the distant portal to his own time."

She raised an exquisitely shaped brow. Azothe had been at the Citadel for most of two weeks, but this was her first look at the dark-winged beast. Nevertheless, he had seen *her* before, many times. "Maggrai? Is that the name of yon unsightly creature?" Maggrai, very put out by this insulting inquiry, raised his hand in a way Tristan was sure would make Azothe clutch her temple in agony. But she merely continued to stare at him, and after a moment, he turned away.

A glance, no more, passed between Azothe and Tristan, as Tristan's assistant, Mungo, placed the last of the kiln-baked tiles in the chamber. The man stood by inattentively, awaiting his next order, and Tristan shoved him towards the corner.

"Why does he not speak?" Azothe asked.

"He cannot," Tristan replied. "Mungo once spied for the Swallows, I am told. The torturers in the dungeon cut out his tongue and shoved red hot skewers in his ears as payment for his transgressions. I believe he lost his wits somewhat as a result. But now he is the perfect trustworthy colleague for our little endeavor, wouldn't you say, my dear?"

Azothe nodded and smiled.

Maggrai fiddled with a series of dials set into the panel on the front of the Chronagine. He was muttering to himself again. Tristan strolled up beside him. "Let me help you with the calibration, Sir." His stubby, fat fingers flew over the controls, while Maggrai stood by, his useless claws clicking and clicking.

The transfer of power had been gradual. Perhaps ten years had gone by in which Maggrai had ruled supreme over Tristan, Beaumarais, and Yr. He had supervised the construction of many edifices dedicated to Prime God, and reveled in the worship of the sheep-like souls who frequented them. Then the dreams began.

They are two, and often come in sequence. The first is short. Maggrai sees himself restrained in some chamber with a small window. A face appears in the glass—beautiful, unforgiving, and deadly. The dark-haired angel smiles a smile of chilly satisfaction, such as one might take from pulling the wings from a fly. Then she turns red, and erupts into ferocious flame—only it isn't the angel who burns. Once the pain begins, he understands that, all too well. *He* is burning. As his flesh shrivels and splits, and screams claw their way from his flaming lungs, the last thing he sees is her face—cold, impassive, and smiling still.

In the second dream, he is still restrained, but this time his prison is a coffin. The pain remains—bearable only if he stays very, very still; like a fearful child who is hiding from some beast. The face comes again, the face of the angel. This time her eyes are warm, her expression one of pity for what he has become.

Tenderly she says, "I am sorry."

In her hand, she holds a curious object—a long thin dagger made of silver. She raises her hand high, and he sees for the first time that she is naked, and comely. The motion of her arm lifts her breast. Though his body is useless, burned to a husk, he still feels aroused by the sight—a phantom erection, for he has no sexual organs left. He stares, entranced, at the dusky nipple, surrounded by an even darker aureole, wishing he could touch it, or at least touch himself. It is the last thing he wishes.

She is both his angel of death and his angel of mercy. *Azothe.*

These dreams, following each other, night after night, weakened him, left him exhausted and distracted. Gradually Maggrai began to withdraw from activities in the Citadel. He built the Watchkeep on Split Island, and dedicated himself to examining every trace of azimity in the worlds between, trying to find the Dawnmaid. His failure to prevent her birth had remained a stinging welt on his pride.

He left the managing of the Firaithi and the production of Broth to his protégé, Tristan.

Tristan had become very adept at chymike and the smelting of corsfyre. Now, seventeen years since the day that Maggrai had first come to this time and place, he was ready to put that skill to use.

As he continued to adjust the controls for the Chronagine, Azothe glided over to the side of the apparatus. From the pocket of her silvery gown, she produced a small sphere, about the size of an egg, but clear, like crystal, with colored bars of light suspended inside. One red, one blue, one yellow, one white, one black. As Azothe held the globe, the heat from her skin caused the bars inside to swirl chaotically, like a ruined rainbow. She stared at it for a moment or two, and then placed it in the orifice meant for the corsfyre. It rolled down the conduit, and lodged out of sight close to the bottom.

Casually, she turned away.

Tristan said smoothly, "Nay my Lord, there is no need to test the Chronagine again. I, myself, placed a cat and a dog within the chamber last week, and sent them far from here."

"I disagree," said Azothe, quite unexpectedly. "We will not know with surety if it is safe for your Master unless we place a human test subject within and trigger the mechanism."

Tristan gave her a startled glance. Her words varied from the script they had so carefully written together.

"How do you propose to test it, without placing one of us inside the chamber?" Maggrai asked, with a testy shake of his wings.

"I think we should use…" She turned and glanced coolly at Tristan's servant. "Mungo. Yes, he will make a fine test subject. There is no harm in losing him if anything goes awry."

Tristan nodded in baffled agreement, then walked over to the corner and dragged the man he called Mungo back to the center of the room. "Here is our subject, Sir. I will place him in the chamber, and then we can engage the apparatus after I place the corsfyre in the feeding tube."

"I will see to that, little Tristan," said Maggrai, suspicious to the last. He carried the three pieces of crystal he had selected to the opening at the back of the Chronagine, and dropped them one-by-one into the orifice.

After opening the iron-clad portal, Tristan shoved Mungo inside and fitted the hatch firmly in place. A heavy wooden bar slid across the doorframe, locking it from the outside. A tiny window, made of clear selenite, allowed an observer to view the interior of the chamber. Mungo stood motionless within it, his usually vacant look replaced by one of abject terror.

Azothe placed herself between Tristan and the glass.

"It is ready." Azothe came to stand beside Tristan, and her

fragrance calmed his edginess. He engaged the master controls, sending the necessary energy into the chamber. The Chronagine began to pulse as it emitted a high-pitched whine. The sound grew louder as the vibrations increased, until Tristan and Azothe covered their ears. Maggrai stood at the controls, untroubled, watching the power levels build and build. The noise increased to a scream, and then a blinding flash came from within the chamber.

Maggrai shut it down.

The heat from the iron door had set the bar smoldering, and the smoke made him cough as he approached the viewing lens. He peered into the inside of the Chronagine and then chortled with glee.

He turned to Tristan. "The test subject has gone. The chamber is empty! I have found the mechanism for transcending the highest azimuth."

Tristan hurried forward, full of smiles, congratulations and a single question: "When will you use the Chronagine for your own journey to the future?"

"Soon, little Tristan, soon," he replied with a vague wave of his hand. "I must manufacture enough Broth to last until I may make more."

Tristan hid his disappointment well. "As you wish. I will make sure Guards watch the device night and day, so that no man may tamper with it. Now, goodnight, my Lord." He turned to take Azothe's arm, so that they might walk back to her rooms together, but she had already left without him.

The villages Katkin passed through were quiet, and many houses stood desolate and empty. She had taken shelter in one, in the village of Aix Acre, the first night after she left Willow's house. Four graves decorated the back garden, and they looked fresh. Fresh enough that the rank and weedy grass had not overtaken them, as it had everything else in the yard.

Willow had given her a haversack full of food, but Katkin had eaten most of it the first few days of her walk from Kaisset. Now, on the second week of her journey, she felt hungry and tired too. She should, perhaps, have accepted her sister's generous offer of a mare to ride. But Katkin had not ridden for sixteen years, and in any case, she had wished to search for Myrie and see the condition of her former kingdom on foot.

There had been a note on the dusty table at the last place she stayed.

Dear Mother, it began, in a neatly printed script.

Ben has come down with the cursed disease. Joseph and I put him in the shed and made him as comfortable as we could. The children seem well, so I sent them to the schoolhouse. I am going to St. Valery, to beg for some Broth. Fr. Bernard said they reward those who give them information on darkies. Our neighbors are hiding a family in their barn. Though I promised I would tell no one, now that my Ben is suffering from the Bludseth, I must do what is best for him.

Please see to Joseph and Libby until I return. Love, yr. Bella.

That house had five graves in the side yard, all in a row. Obviously, Bella's trip to St. Valery had been a fruitless one. She had not saved anyone in her family, nor even herself. Katkin shivered, wondering what had happened to the Firaithi she had delivered to the Black Guard.

She asked about Myrie everywhere she went, but no one would speak to her, even in Belladore, where there were many faces she recognized. The sharp-eyed Postmistress at the village shop ignored her questions, and announced she was closing early. Several people, with unfriendly faces, had followed Katkin from town, but she lost them in the fastnesses of the Acre.

Now she headed towards the grave of Tomas de Vigny. She did not have any real reason to visit there, but since Roseberry had said that the Glint would find her, it seemed as good a destination as any.

The wall around the gravesite still stood, but it had crumbled in places. Someone had tried hard to batter down the gate with a log, but the hasp and hinges held. Katkin removed the key from her kirtle, and turned it in the rusty lock. The gate opened with a squeaky whine and as she ambled along the path into the dell, it felt as though she moved through time as well as space.

Sitting on the marble bench by the grave, lonely and cold, she studied the ivy that had turned the carven headstone and the statue of Lalluna into shapeless humps. They floated in a sea of heart-shaped green leaves. Painful memories returned, but dulled—like a knife-edge that has cut too close to the bone. Tomas' last words to her; the explosive report of his pistol; the awful wreck of his face after the ball and powder had done their work.

And Jacq standing beside her, coldly rejoicing in his enemy's untimely death. Though she loved them both, they had been rivals for many turns of the Gyre.

Dai and Fyn.

And if the last battle was indeed nigh, as Tomas seemed to think, would he and Jacq stand shoulder-to-shoulder—or face-to-face? Katkin pondered this riddle for many moments, but found no answers. Nor did she did hear the men creeping up on her, until one had caught her hair by the ponytail, and placed a knife at her throat.

"Well, well, little darlin', and what have we here?"

Katkin shrieked and tried to turn her head, but the hand held her fast by the hair. But she soon saw the rest of her assailants. Five men gathered in a knot in front of her, and stared with frank glee. They were roughly dressed, in torn, filthy sackcloth trousers.

Katkin gave a moan of fear when she saw the red streaks on their gaunt cheeks. "What do you want?"

Their leader chortled at this, and his breath smelled foul against her cheek. "Hear that boys? The lady has a question for us. Tell her the answer, Briggsy." A tall, dark haired man with a mouth full of rotten teeth stepped forward and placed his face an inch from hers.

"Right-o, Davy. We want you, pretty lady. You ain't got the walking death, and that means you must be a darky. If we drinks your blood..."

"No, no! Please..." Katkin begged. "It doesn't work like that."

But the leader wrenched her head back, hard enough to silence her. "Get your cups ready, boys, while I cut her throat." Katkin screamed and struggled, but he held on to her firmly. The others dug in their pockets and grubby bundles for tin cups. Davy raised the knife high, but a flash of light from beyond the oak tree made him hesitate.

"Did you see something?" he asked nervously. The others shrugged and urged him to get on with business.

Katkin spoke with desperate certitude. "If you cut my throat, you will be cutting into an artery. Most of the blood will spill on to the ground. You won't get near enough for all of you to drink that way." The knife lowered a fraction, and Katkin forged ahead. "You need to find a vein, like the saphenous vein in the leg. If you cut it carefully then I won't bleed to death right away."

The men looked at her stupidly, scratching the welts on their cheeks. Davy still held her head, but the fingers holding the knife relaxed slightly.

"Listen to me! I am a doctor. I know what I am talking about."

"Do you think she's telling the truth?" asked the tallest man, to one of the others.

Briggsy answered for him. "A woman sawbones? Who ever heard of that? Course she ain't!" He leered at Katkin. "Come on, Davy. Let's have some fun before we kill her." He reached forward and groped for her breast. Katkin began to struggle wildly, cursing. A brightness flickered on the edge of her vision, perhaps from the pressure on her throat. The leader pulled a cosh from his boot and slammed it onto the back of her head, making the light fragment into a shower of stars. Katkin collapsed with a moan, and slid off the bench. Davy fumbled with his trousers, and dropped to his knees before her.

"Hold her tight, boys. Reckon she'll wake when I run my stallion between her thighs. When I have had my fill, you lot can have a turn too. We can cut her saf... safenoos vein afterwards." He reached for Katkin, intending to spread her legs wide.

A very tall figure stepped from behind the tree and drew his sword. He hadn't thought to kill the men, not at first. They were to be pitied—they had nothing to look forward to, except an agonizing death from the disease. He would have stopped them before they took her blood, of course, but only by frightening them away. Such desperate men frightened easily, as he knew from long experience.

But now he frowned. Rape was a crime of a different order. The men ringing Katkin had almost no chance to shout a warning to their captain before he came amongst them, slitting scrawny bellies and necks with his shining sword.

"Glint!" the stricken men cried to one another, in between gurgling shrieks. "It's the bloody Outlaw Glint. Save us!"

Through all their strangled curses and screams of pain, Katkin slept on, unknowingly awash with the warm blood of her attackers. When he finished and the six men lay dead, he picked her up, and stepped away.

Azothe answered her door in a hooded gown of silver, perfectly smooth, perfectly lustrous. "Yes? For what reason do you disturb my rest, O Sun?"

Tristan licked his lips, left speechless, as always, by the potency of her fragrant beauty. "I have just had word from the Infirmarie that Maggrai is on his way here. I believe he intends to use the Chronagine this night. We must be ready, Azothe."

She allowed herself one small, triumphant smile. "Indeed we must, my Lord. Has anyone touched the Chronagine since the last amalgamation?"

He shook his head. "It has been guarded every hour."

"Good." Azothe stepped very close to him, and spread her scarlet-tipped fingers wide on his chest. His flabby heart worked hard to vie with his mounting excitement. She looked at his flushed cheeks and smiled seductively. "Soon," she breathed. "How patiently you have waited, my Sun. The moment of fulfillment is at hand." And for the first time since she arrived at the Citadel, she placed her parted lips on his.

Tristan took her in his trembling arms and kissed her, but she stepped away far sooner than he would have liked. "Let us go. We should be at the Chymericum when he arrives. I would not wish to miss the culmination of all our hard work, would you?"

He shook his head, more in disappointment than anything else, but followed her along the hallway. A Captain stopped Tristan in the stairwell, and delivered a salute.

"A word, if I may, your Majesty?"

Tristan adopted a surly expression and nodded. "Get on with it, man. I have a pressing engagement."

"My apologies Sire. The gate detail had a report of trouble in the Acre, two nights ago—the Glint, out alone, and carrying his sword."

"Why have we had no news of this before now?" Tristan's scowl darkened.

The Captain's face went pale. "There has been a certain... unwillingness amongst the general populace to divulge his whereabouts. We had to resort to torture in order to extract any substantive details. But our investigation has revealed that he murdered six men."

"Our men?"

"Nay, Sire. Vagrants. And every man with the Bludseth too. Seems very odd."

From below them, Azothe cleared her throat, and began to tap her silvery slipper on the stones. Tristan started down the stairs, speaking back over his shoulder. "Double the patrols, and arrest anyone who refuses to talk."

"My lord, please," the Captain called. "I have not yet finished. There is another matter."

He stopped again, frowning. "This had better be very important, or the next piece of news you deliver will be to the gaoler in the dungeon."

The Captain nodded nervously. "There have been strange accounts, from several villages on the Mistmere, and within the Acre, Lord. I am concerned."

"Accounts? What do you mean?"

"Your mother, Sire. The traitorous ex-Queen Arkafina. Several people have seen her, from Kaisset in the north, through to Aix Acre. We thought the information must be false, but new sightings have come from Belladore, close to her old home."

Disbelief replaced the scowl on Tristan's face. "My mother? It hardly seems possible after all these years. Get an extra unit of Guardsmen in the Acre right away, and put a price on her head. Two hundred pieces of gold should do nicely. They should have no trouble tracking her. Her missing hand makes her easy to identify."

"But..."

"Enough!" Tristan growled, and hurried to catch Azothe's swaying hips.

He dismissed the Guardsmen standing before the Chymericum door, and unlocked it. Azothe drifted inside and stood in the middle of the floor, listening.

"He is coming, and soon all our hopes will be fulfilled. But remember, no matter what may happen this night, do not fear for me, my Sun."

Tristan looked alarmed at the somber, almost valedictory, tone she had adopted.

"Azothe... What do you mean?"

She smiled and placed a finger sensuously across his lips as Maggrai strode through the door. "Oh," he said, staring balefully at them both. "You are here to see me leave, I suppose?"

Tristan nodded. Maggrai clutched the flagon holding the Broth to his chest. His wings fluttered fitfully. "Well, get on with it then." He moved over to the control panel, but stood aside as Tristan joined him. "Everything... Everything will go to plan, of course? You have checked the integrity of the fireclay?"

"Everything is in readiness, Master."

"I don't trust her," Maggrai muttered. "Keep her away from the window. She always looks at me..."

"My Lord?" Tristan asked quizzically, and then hurried to reassure him. "Azothe means you no harm. She is as happy as I to see you return to your kingdom. This is the moment we have all been waiting for." Tristan meant this sincerely. Only since Azothe had come to him, with her superior knowledge of chymike, had he been able to look forward to this moment, the moment of freedom from Maggrai forever.

Slowly she crossed the room, like a glittering shaft of moonlight, and stopped before Maggrai. "Do you fear me? You should not. I will prove the safety of the device by my willingness to come with you, if you wish it." Tristan's triumphant expression turned to one of unreserved panic.

"Azothe!" he said sharply. "You cannot. I forbid it."

Maggrai stared at her, and licked his lips. She moved closer, until her body pressed close to his. "You are the one I came here for. You are the one I want—the one with all the power. Take me with you." The scent of patchouli surrounded them, and seemed to draw him ever closer. Sensuously, she stroked the sensitive skin of his leathery wings, and placed her lips at the moist hollow of his throat.

Off to the side, Tristan's mouth worked in anger. "Azothe..." he began again.

Maggrai's old jauntiness returned. "I underestimated this young woman. She has the grace and acumen to recognize the better man, after all. Why should she remain with a churl like you? In my kingdom she will be a Queen, the ruler of all my slaves."

Azothe whispered something in Maggrai's ear, and he smiled wolfishly. "Indeed, my sweet. I am sure that can be arranged, as soon as we arrive back at my eternal watchtower."

Tristan wondered bleakly what carnal act she had suggested. "My Lord. Don't take her away from me, please..."

Maggrai whirled to face him, and raised a clawed hand. "What are you whining about? I have given you the greatest kingdom in all of Yr. Without me, you would still be a spotty-faced boy ruling an insignificant backwater."

"But Azothe..." Tristan began to massage his forehead.

"Is coming with me. Farewell, little Tristan." Azothe gave him a calmly accepting smile, and followed Maggrai towards the chamber. "Now, secure the door, you idiot," he growled over his shoulder.

Once they had entered, Tristan placed the bar across the door, locking her inside with Maggrai. He could not reconcile her betrayal, not with knowing what would happen next. "Fine," he muttered to himself. "I don't need her. Once I have found the portal to immortality a thousand women will throw themselves at my feet."

But her voice and her scent lingered deep within him.

Tristan wiped his eyes and backed away from the door. His fingers fumbled with the controls, while he thought and thought of Azothe. *Why had she done it?* The whine of the Chronagine pulsed in time with the pounding in his temples.

"Azothe..." he said once more, desolately, as he flipped the secret switch she had helped him install.

The whine grew into a scream. The scream grew too painful to bear, and Tristan placed his hands over his ears. Even then, it seemed to penetrate his trembling fingers, boring into his brain like red-hot maggots.

A blinding flash of light—a searing, liquefying wave of heat.

A roar, which almost took Tristan's head from his shoulders, and filled his mouth with blood.

The silence and darkness that followed, as every machine in the room shut down, was a welcome relief.

The pounding on the locked dungeon door drove Tristan upright. He staggered along, feeling his way in the darkness like a blind man. When he found the door and unbarred it, a host of Guardsmen piled through, knocking him back to the floor again. "Get some light, you idiots," he screamed, and someone went to fetch a corsfyre lantern.

"Sire? Are you injured? The blast shook the whole west wing!" This from the Captain of the Guard, who hovered over Tristan.

"Stand away, man," Tristan snarled, and stood, rubbing his posterior where it had connected with the stone flags. "Where in blazes is that light?"

Once they had the room well lit, and Tristan had determined that he had suffered no injury, he sent the guardsmen away with muttered threats and curses. After barring the door he walked towards the Chronagine, or what remained of it. Two of the brick walls had caved in, and part of the roof, but the door was miraculously intact.

Tristan seized the door handle, and then screamed as the red-hot iron seared his hands. He found a pair of padded gloves and put them on, then tackled the bar again. This time he levered it from the brackets, and swung the door towards him. Inside was black, and sweet smelling—like roasted meat, scented with patchouli.

"A... Azothe?" he said timidly, wondering what the hell he was thinking, calling her like that. "Nothing could have survived that blast," he muttered to himself. The enormity of both his triumph over Maggrai and his loss of Azothe had yet to sink in.

A sound, like the light metallic clink of falling cinders, reached his ears. Something moved inside! He grabbed the lantern and held it close to the doorway, and then stared disbelievingly.

A silver sarcophagus, roughly human-shaped, stood propped against one wall of the chamber. As he watched, wide-eyed, it stirred, causing more ash and cinders to shower down on the blackened pile.

"Azothe?" he said again, still not trusting his eyes. The sarcophagus cracked open, and she emerged, unharmed and gloriously naked. With a cry of utter joy, Tristan caught her in his arms. "My moon Queen, I thought I had lost you!"

She disengaged herself from his embrace and spoke coolly. "I said you were not to worry, my Sun." Stooping, she picked up her silver robe, and slipped it over her head.

"Did the dress save you? Is that how you survived?" He was still marveling at this, when the black pile of ash at his feet groaned in agony.

"No..." said Tristan, suddenly afraid. "He cannot be alive. He cannot!"

Azothe nudged the heap with a perfectly manicured toe. "What if he is, my Sun? He can harm you no longer. Look!"

She held the lantern close. Tristan could not believe that the creature who stained the floor amidst the ruin of the Chronagine could still be amongst the living. The fire had taken his magnificent leathery wings, as well as his hands, forearms and feet—destroyed in the inferno that had melted the fireclay into shiny porcelain streaks on the walls.

"C...Cold," Maggrai groaned. "So thirsty..." His skin had mostly evaporated, leaving a charred layer of blackened flesh. Red fluid had begun to seep through in places, and pooled on the floor.

Tristan looked upon him with horror and dawning pity. "Should we help him, Azothe? Perhaps the royal physicians can..."

"No."

Maggrai screamed again, begging for water.

"But what shall we do then? Shall I fetch a knife? I cannot bear the sound of his suffering."

"No," she answered again, and her dark eyes grew still and very, very cold, like an icy mountain tarn. "He *will* suffer, and we shall offer him no succor, my Sun. Slowly he will die, in agony, and we will find enjoyment in his ordeal. Think on it, my Sun. It will be a joyous sport for us, to watch his life ebb away in an ocean of torment." She kicked the heap of burned flesh again, and Maggrai whimpered.

"Help me..."

Tristan stared at her, shocked to the core by this careless cruelty. But he dared not disagree with her. And why should he care if his former master suffered at her hand?

"Send the guards away and then fetch a box. We will scrape him into it, and carry it back to my rooms, secretly and silently. Let him listen to us making love this night, my Lord. That way he will know the most perfect anguish of both body and soul."

He hurried to obey, salivating at his brief glimpse of Azothe's perfect form. *Tonight...*

But of course, with Azothe, it would not be that easy. Once they reached her rooms, with the suppurating Maggrai carelessly positioned in a rough wooden box, she insisted he arrange it on a pedestal in the middle of the room. Tristan, still thoroughly discomfited by the agonized groans issuing from the faceless lump of blackened flesh, had argued with her. Again, she prevailed, and then, just as he thought she might relent at last, she insisted he must bathe first.

"The union of our bodies must be perfect in every way. We cannot sully ourselves with the grime of this world if we wish to cross into the eternal heavens." Tristan, sighing resignedly, had gone to wash.

When he returned, Azothe was not in her chambers. He stood still, for a moment, studying the magnificent canopied bed, with its silk sheets, and many soft pillows, picturing himself there—with her.

"Tristan…"

He turned, expecting to see her, but the whisper came from the wooden coffin on the dais. Utterly repelled, but still unable to resist the call of his former Master, Tristan crossed the room. He stepped to the edge of the box and looked down.

"Little Tristan." Maggrai painfully rasped each word. "Beware. She is a demon, that Azothe."

"Nay, Lord," said Tristan, lightly. "We planned your death together."

"Did you?" he wheezed. "Ungrateful little whelp. I loved you like a son." A spasm of pain wracked his body, and he shivered and stirred in his comfortless prison. "Listen to what I tell you! She desires your death as well, so that she may rule this world alone."

Tristan stood pitilessly above him. "I don't believe you. Azothe has promised to show me the path to immortality. She is the Moon, and I am the Sun. So it is written in every chymike text."

Maggrai lifted his stump of an arm infinitely slowly, and waved it before Tristan's horrified eyes. Blackened bone poked from the end, and Tristan thought he might be sick at the sight. "She will do to you what she has done to me," he croaked. "Unless you run away, now. Her heart is as black as the depths of the sea."

Tristan turned his back, and walked away. "You are naught but a dying old fool. Enjoy your last few hours on Yrth, *Master*. The last sounds you hear will be my cries of ecstasy, as I fulfill all my carnal desires with the beautiful Azothe."

Maggrai muttered, "Farewell, idiot. You have failed me for the very last time."

Azothe did not appear again that night.

Tristan woke in Azothe's room, in the bed he had made for the two of them. He lay coldly and disappointedly alone. Maggrai's groans of agony and the foul smell of his putrefying flesh did little to improve his mood. Though he reveled in his Master's utter defeat, Tristan had traveled only halfway to his ultimate goal of immortality. He felt ready, more than ready, to take the next all-important step. But for that, he needed Azothe. The guards had been busy all night, searching the Citadel at their monarch's snarled command.

He sighed and turned over, thinking it must be almost morning from the rose-tinted grey filtering through the narrow windows that pierced the stone of the Citadel Tower. Tristan closed his eyes again, firmly, and tried to get back to sleep. He could not. The scent of patchouli, seemingly wafting in with the dawn, enveloped him like a silken shower of petals.

Slowly, hardly daring to believe, he opened his eyes. She stood before him.

"Azothe..." he whispered, praying the dream had not returned to torment him once more. The door had opened soundlessly and he had not heard her cross the floor.

"My Sun. It is time."

Her clothing, all of silver shot with dark threads of purple and rose, clung to her curves with loving diligence. Tristan sat up in bed, unable to remain still through the surge of excitement that filled him to overflowing. "Where have you been? I waited all..."

She placed a finger over his lips. "You do not need to know. Only that I am here now. Only that." Azothe stepped back from the bed and began to undress. Tristan watched her, his anticipation mounting as she gracefully turned towards him, and lifted her gown over her head. She wore nothing underneath except a twisted silver cuff on her upper arm, cunningly crafted to look like coiled snake, with ruby-red eyes. Next, she untied the knot that held her hair, so that it fell in a glorious cascade to her shoulders, and brushed against her breasts. She was utterly intoxicating, utterly naked, and soon to be utterly his.

Inside his chest, Tristan's heart stuttered a little, and a nagging ache made him rub his left shoulder. But her next words put the pain far from his mind. "Are you ready to take me, my Sun? The moon anxiously awaits your flaming scepter."

He moaned with absolute ravening desire as she arrayed herself on to the silk sheets next to him. Then he fell upon her, covering her exquisite form with his flaccid bulk, not caring for the nice-ties of courtship or foreplay. Something thwarted his clumsy first push.

"You are still a virgin, Azothe?" he managed to choke out.

Her serene face gave no indication that she might be lying. "Whom else would I allow to drink from the pool of immortal-ity with me? But do not fear, my Lord. You cannot hurt me." He tried again, struggling with his almost incapacitating need to have her, while her hands seemed to be everywhere at once, inflaming him further.

"Yes..." she whispered. "You are almost there. Life everlasting awaits you, my Sun. Hold nothing back now, nothing..." She arched her back and thrust her hips forward and then he buried himself gloriously and deeply within the magnificent body of Azothe. The scent of patchouli grew sharp, almost overpowering, making his temples throb.

He plunged downwards again and again, until his flabby muscles trembled from exertion. She encouraged him with cries of ecstasy, whispered words of need—always wanting more of him, urging him to hurry towards his final release. Inside, his heart fluttered desperately, trying to keep up with his muscles' hungry demands for blood and oxygen.

Tristan gasped for breath, as Azothe's long red nails dug into his sagging buttocks. "Do not flag now," she cried. "We are almost there. I can feel it..."

With a magnificent effort he continued to move, though a throbbing pain in his jaw made him wince now and again. Abruptly his left arm went numb, and he had to hold himself above her awkwardly with one hand. A wave of nausea hit him hard, and for the first time he felt something other than desire.

Fear, tasting cold and metallic in his mouth, like blood.

"Azothe..." he began, but didn't finish—couldn't, as she fastened her lips to his with wild passion, and drove her tongue between his parted teeth.

His laboring heart could stand no more. Tristan screamed in agony as it exploded within his chest, at the same time as his shuddering hips thrust forward, caught within the instinctive strain of sexual release.

Thirteen

Redwood

When Katkin regained consciousness, she lay still and listened. No one was doing anything unpleasant to her, as far as she could tell, and that seemed a good sign. Nor had they tied her hands or feet. Her surroundings were quiet, except for the persistent drip of water somewhere close by, and she risked opening an eye. She saw mostly darkness. Turning her head slightly, and wincing from the pain, she opened her other eye.

A lantern hung from a ceiling hook, illuminating a table and two chairs. A man sat with his back to her. Katkin inhaled sharply with fear. Davy and the others must have decided to take her back to their lair. But why had they not cut her throat as they had threatened to? And why had they placed her on this comfortable pallet, and covered her with sheepskins?

As Katkin mulled the answers to these questions, the man at the table rose and turned towards her. Immediately, she closed her eyes and lay still, hoping he might leave the room, giving her a chance to escape. Soon, she could hear his light tread as he crossed the dirt floor and the creak of his knees as he squatted. She tensed, ready to fend off another attack. Nothing happened for a second or two, enough time for her to breathe in. The man kneeling beside her smelled clean and woodsy, of pine, nothing like the foul unwashed odor of her assailants. Then he sponged her face with a cloth soaked in cool water.

Her eyes flew open. "Who... Who are you?"

He was small, and dark, and strangely familiar. "Emile. Don't try to talk. You had a nasty bump on the head."

"E... Emile? Where am I?" Relief filled her eyes with tears. "Those men... They were going to..."

"Hush, Aunt. Do not think of it. They are dead, every one of them. You are in the Swallow's Nest, and safe."

"Dead?" she repeated, unbelievingly.

"Glint killed them all." Katkin struggled onto her elbows, and he offered her a sip of water. She looked at Emile, recognizing him now as Willow's son, whom she had not seen since he was a teenager.

Whereas his sister Roseberry exhibited little of the Firaithi heritage that Katkin and Willow shared, in Emile the blood of the Kindreds seemed to run almost true. His long dark hair and coffee colored skin made her think guiltily of Huw and she sighed.

"Did you save me? Are you the one they call Glint?"

Emile laughed at this, his even, white teeth shining in the darkness. "Nay, not me. I am one of the Swallows, nothing more."

Katkin frowned as her memory returned. "But Roseberry said you had been captured. How did you manage to escape?"

His smile disappeared, and he rubbed his ear, as though it pained him. "I was... sent away," he offered after a moment. "And then I made my way back here, yesterday. It is a long story," he added, quite unnecessarily. "But you should rest, so I will not tell it now."

He stood and turned away. Katkin fell back onto the pallet, calling drowsily, "When will I meet Glint?"

"Soon," said Emile, thoughtfully. "Quite soon, I believe."

When Katkin woke again, bright daylight showed her that she had been lying in a cavern rather than a room. The glare filtering in from outside outlined the low entrance. She stood, and found that her head felt very much better. The cave was a small one, perhaps designated as a dining room or meeting area. Maps and charts covered the table she had seen last night.

"Emile?" she called, but he did not answer her.

Katkin straightened her disheveled clothes and clicked her tongue disapprovingly at the bloodstains covering her kirtle. Then she combed her hair as best she could, and stepped outside. The sunlight blinded her, and she stood for a moment with her hand above her eyes. Eventually she saw that she stood before a rocky outcrop, deep in the Acre. Caves riddled the soft sandy stone, many occupied by men and materials. No one paid any attention to her as she wandered about, looking for Emile. She followed the line of the outcrop for fifty yards, and then stepped around a sloping shelf of rock.

Katkin believed she had not sustained any injury from her encounter with the diseased men, but the sight that met her eyes as she turned the corner left her doubting. A wavering apparition, with a blurry thatch of long dark hair, stood in the midst of a group of men. They kept their distance as the figure spoke to them.

153

The answer dawned on Katkin, seemingly from somewhere outside her own mind. "Myrie?"

The apparition turned.

She no longer had a face, not of the conventional sort, anyway. A haze of many-colored eyes, noses and mouths clustered in the vicinity of her shoulders and neck. When Myrie recognized Katkin, all the mouths wreathed into smiles. A rustling sound, as of many feet in motion, accompanied her as she crossed the grass. The men, standing well back, parted to let her pass through.

"You are feeling better, my dear?"

Katkin nodded, more than a little afraid. "Myrie... What has happened to you?"

The chorus spoke again. "We have assimilated many. Our voices have become one voice—our aims, one aim."

"And what is that?" Katkin asked, blinking and blinking, trying to focus on the cloud of eyes that watched her coolly.

"To rescue the suffering ones, of course. We shall do so, very soon. Very soon, when the Glint returns..."

In the end, Katkin had left the Acre without ever having the chance to thank her rescuer personally. No one seemed to know where the Glint had gone, or when he would return to the Swallow's Nest. Katkin had her business at the Temple to attend to. Emile walked with her along the path towards St. Valery, and they chatted like old friends as they passed through the high meadow, lit like a candle from the early light of dawn.

"How long has Myrie been with you?"

Emile scratched his head. "I was not there when she arrived, but I think about ten days. One of the Swallows found her wandering in the Acre and brought her back to the Nest." He grinned. "He said she was very hungry!"

Katkin laughed at this. "Was she, indeed? I am surprised the Swallows welcomed her. She has many mouths to feed nowadays!"

"Nay. That came later, after she found the first pile of dead avisceti."

They had reached the edge of a high, sandy bluff. Katkin approached the edge, and looked at the brambles clinging to the sheer face. Emile gave her a curious glance. "Are you all right, Aunt?"

"Yes, Emile. I was just thinking of someone whose acquaintance I first made at this very place." Katkin pointed to a spot on the river's edge, far below. "I climbed down there and retrieved his crutches after he threw them over the cliff."

Emile smiled. "A man then? Someone special?"

She gave a sheepish shrug. "I didn't think so at the time, but later, yes. He became my very good friend."

"Do you mean Uncle Jacq? It is strange, but Glint..."

"What about the Glint?" Katkin asked sharply.

"He reminds me of Jacq, somehow. Not only his fighting, which is fierce, just like the Dinrhydan's, but his eyes too. It has been a long time since I last saw Uncle Jacq, but I think that he must have looked like Glint."

Katkin closed her eyes for a moment, thinking of Jacq's homely face—his soft grey eyes, broken nose, and gentle gap-toothed grin. Suddenly she wished she had remained at the Swallow's Nest a little longer. Katkin thought of turning around, but her love for Lalluna prevented her. After a single backwards glance, she began to walk again.

"What do you know of this man Glint?" she asked Emile as they left the meadow by the steep path that wound down the face of the bluff.

"Not much. He came to us from a faraway land, or so he always says, if we ask. He is strong, as strong as I imagine the Dinrhydan must have been in his prime, and brave. Brave enough to take on Cousin Tristan's legions, and clever enough to evade capture for all the last year. They say the outlaw Glint is the most wanted man in all of Yr."

"But if he is not from Yr, then why did he choose to fight against Tristan anyway?"

Emile shrugged. "I don't think anyone knows the answer to that question. Glint offered his help, and we were glad enough for it, believe me. Mayhap it has something to do with the scars on his back."

"Scars?"

"Yes, wicked long scars, between his shoulder blades. I would say they pain him still, though they seem well healed over. He could have suffered some terrible injury at the hands of the Black Guard. Gods know, enough of us have." He tugged at his earlobe and fell silent.

They were passing close to the King's Road, and Emile stopped while they were still well within the shelter of the trees. "Farewell, Aunt. I hope you find what you are looking for at the Temple. We shall be coming to the Infirmarie ourselves very soon, if Myriadne has her way. If you still want to meet him you have only to wait until Glint leads the Swallows there."

Katkin took his hand and held it tightly. "Thank you for all your kindness. And please pass on my gratitude to the Glint. Tell him..."

"Aunt?"

Katkin gave herself a shake and continued softly, "Tell him I shall look forward to our meeting, very much."

Fourteen

Plane

Lut and Fyn hunted amongst the remains of ten astaren*. Their guardians, the Uri'el, shrieked and shrieked their distress. Fyn stepped over the spongy remains of a skull, and signaled Lut to follow. He did, keeping his eyes on Fyn's back—not looking down. The sight of the ruptured visage would likely make him vomit again. Lut clutched his abdomen with his free hand, trying not to picture the head, not to smell the vile scent of decay. But his imagination did the work far better than his eyes, and he doubled over in a fit of nausea. Fyn did not look back.

They left the shrieks behind, and Fyn stopped, waiting for Lut to catch up. "All right, lad?"

Lut nodded bleakly, though in truth he felt anything but. He took a deep breath to calm his queasiness and wiped the sour taste from his lips with his sleeve.

"Well, now you have seen what we must measure ourselves against. Keep your sword at the ready. We may find the Angellus or their minions at any time."

"Fyn?" said Lut, with trepidation. "What will we do then?"

* Spirit forms of the dead.

"Fight," said Gunnar's cousin briefly. "They can be beaten, if you meet only two or three. Otherwise, run." He glanced at Lut, and saw his pallor. "Is your injury giving you trouble? There is no shame in saying so. We can go back to Asaruthe."

Lut looked at his splinted arm and set his jaw grimly. "No, Sir. I want to stay here with you."

Fyn signaled for quiet, and dropped behind a dusty grey boulder. "Look you there," he whispered, pointing the tip of his sword to another cluster of Uri'el in the distance.

Dark figures moved amongst them. Lut closed his eyes in horror as he saw a voulge swing with lethal precision. The sound of the blade hitting the astarene's head was ghastly beyond belief. The shadowed figure then bent and rooted in the remains of the face.

"That is how they steal the anafireon," Fyn whispered.

"But... But surely, those men are of the Firaithi? Are they the enemy?" Lut asked in surprise, seeing their dark skin. "I thought we were hunting for fire-spewing black creatures shaped like young trees. That is what the Angellus look like, do they not?"

"Yes, but these folk are also the minions of Maggrai. And Maggrai is Lord of all the evil in this world, including the Angellus. Now let us go and put a stop to their game." He strode forth from their hiding place, with his sword at his side. Lut followed more slowly, loath to begin a battle with Katkin and Huw's kindred.

Fyn moved amongst the Firaithi, who fought back sluggishly with their voulges. One slash found its mark, leaving a deep cut on his forearm. Fyn gave a cry that drove Lut's leaden feet forward into the fray. He swung his sword left and right, feeling both awkward and somehow ruthless. The Firaithi men he fought against were emaciated and cruelly fatigued.

"Why are you doing this?" he cried to one, who swung his voulge weakly in response. Lut sidestepped it easily. "Why do you not speak? I don't want to kill you." But the man, who looked old enough to be Lut's grandfather, continued to stab mechanically with his weapon, until Lut had to put a sword through his belly. His foe collapsed on to the ground, with an oddly choked gurgle of pain. Lut saw his mouth fall open—saw the rotten black stump at the back of his throat.

He turned and ran blindly for the rocks.

"Never mind, lad," said Fyn consolingly a few moments later, as he wrapped a torn piece of linen around the wound on his arm. "Many men have suffered worse during their first taste of battle. I think you did fine."

"But, Fyn. Did you not see? Their tongues have been cut away. Even if they wished to beg for our mercy, they could not. How can it be right that we should kill them?"

Fyn's face darkened. "Have you forgotten that your mother lies dead and buried because of the likes of them?" He shook Lut roughly. "Listen to me! They harvest the anafireon that Maggrai uses to make corsfyre. And corsfyre animates the avisceti. The avisceti that shredded the quivering flesh from her bones! Do you think they listened to her pleas for mercy?" He stepped back, breathing hard.

Lut looked stunned, but only for a moment. Suddenly, he clutched his sword and raised it high. "Come on!" he growled to Fyn. "The rest of them went this way."

Katkin crept along the darkened passage, towards the sacred Temple of the Unity. As she felt her way forward, using her hands to search for stalactites and side passages, she thought about her former home, the Infirmarie and its fall from blessedness. Once it had been a healing center, a place of peace and comfort, where the white-robed Daminem* glided down the halls, and Juvenie† followed, learning the science and art of medicine.

Her distress grew and grew as she recalled the desolation that lay outside the door to the tunnel. Katkin had crept amongst the rank hedgerows like a beaten dog, past the main hospital wing— now a prison, with boards and bars over every high arched window. She could only imagine what horrors lay inside, amongst the cages and implements of Maggrai's laboratory.

She stopped, thwarted by a cave-in in the tunnel in front of her. But the loose rubble shifted easily, and Katkin soon cleared a path. She moved forward again, now and then calling quietly, "Lalluna? Can you hear me, my Lady?"

Only her voice reached her ears, eerily echoing *hear me, hear me*.

---

* Sisters of the Unity.

† Novice apprentices.

Katkin tried to remember the path to the Temple—how many steps, how many twists and turns? It seemed endless without the gentle light of the Goddess to guide her.

Deep in the heart of Hythea, Katkin shivered and stroked her restored arm fretfully. Her last visit to the Temple, to aid Lalluna, had not ended well.

Faint coughs, followed by a sigh, made Katkin's skin grow chill. She hurried forward, hands out protectively, feeling the closeness of the tunnel walls on either side. Then, by the movement of air, she could tell she had come into the open, though the darkness there was no less thick. She stopped in the center, close to the plinth that had once held an exquisite white marble statue of Lalluna.

It was empty now.

Beyond it, a radiance shone—so dim, at first Katkin thought her eyes were creating the comfort of light within the overpowering darkness. But when the cough came again, the light wobbled with it.

"Lalluna?"

"My vessel," came the answer, as faint and insubstantial as the light. "Come closer..."

Katkin crossed the sandy floor, feeling the imprint of small, jagged stones under her feet. They were the remains of the statue—the remains of Lalluna's beautiful wings, crushed to dust and pebbles.

When she came to the far corner of the Temple where Lalluna rested, Katkin knelt. "My Lady," she said softly. She could almost feel the effort as Lalluna gathered her fading strength. The light flared bright, and Katkin could see the Goddess lying on her side. One shapely wing covered her, like a downy blanket, with her face hidden well below the curve.

Another cough made the wing, and the light, shudder. "My vessel, why have you come to this place—this darkness?"

"I came to find you, Lalluna."

The voice grew plaintive. "I begged Fyn to tell no one where I could be found. No one! Why did he not listen to me?"

Katkin sought her hand. "Because he loves you. As do I. I could not bear the thought of you here—all alone. I had to come."

Faint laughter dissolved into another spasm of coughing. "Alone, you say?" she rasped after a time. "Nay, not so. I have my fears and my despair here with me. They keep me company." Her voice grew hard. "The only company I deserve."

Katkin chided her. "Do not say such things, my Lady. What have you done to deserve such companions? Your works on Yrth have been gentle, good and true."

A long time passed, as silence settled around them like the ash of a funeral pyre, before Lalluna spoke once more. "Have you seen what lays outside, beyond the door to the Temple, my vessel? A charnel house of death and despair, filled with hopeless souls who have nothing to live for—but for whom dying provides even less comfort. That is *my* final work on Yrth, and for that I deserve my suffering."

"What... What do you mean?"

"Remember what I told you in Scarfinda? That I felt my people calling for me once more?"

Katkin nodded in the darkness. "You said their voices were raised in worship."

Lalluna laughed softly. "How wrong I was! They were cursing us—me and my sisters, for we brought him here. *Maggrai.* His sins are manifest and I share in them all." Katkin made a sharp sound of disagreement but Lalluna continued on doggedly. "He has brought hunger and devastation to many on Yr. He trapped the Autochthones, bled them white, and left their bodies to stink in the high sun. But the theft of the anafireon—that is the worst crime of all. He steals their souls; their peaceful sojourn in the arms of the Uri'el. Ach! That I should live to see such wickedness."

"Lalluna! It is not your fault these things have happened."

"It is," she insisted. "But no matter. I have paid. And I shall pay again, when they come for *my* anafireon." The wing drifted downwards, revealing Lalluna's face, once the fairest of all faces, now covered in angry red weals.

Katkin, who had been straining forward to see in the dim light, fell back. "The Bludseth? But... How can this be? You are a Goddess—immortal! You must be..."

Her voice trailed away. There could be no argument with the evidence that scarred the ashen cheeks of Lalluna. It spoke its own truth—of pain and lingering death.

"Does Fyn know?" Katkin asked when she found she could speak again.

"Nay. And you must not tell him. I would have him think of me, across the heavenly plane, happy and free. Not like this." She coughed again, and then gripped Katkin's hand. "If you love me—then swear you will not speak of what you have seen."

Katkin squeezed her hand in return. "I swear on the heart of the Goddess. And I promise I will go to the aid of the Kindreds, once I get you away from here. There is a cure for the disease, a thing called Broth..."

"Stop! I would not drink such a vile potion, even if it would restore me to health. It is made from the blood of the Autochthones, a distillation of their suffering."

"Is that why Maggrai holds our Kindred in the Infirmarie?" Katkin swallowed hard, feeling her stomach lurch. *Broth...* "But then what can I do to help you? I won't let you die! I won't!"

"You were a healer once, remember?" Lalluna's voice sounded reproachful.

"But that all happened long ago," Katkin said guiltily. "I could only become so again through you, Lalluna."

Lalluna shivered violently, and Katkin took her own cloak and draped it over the Goddess. "Nay. Not so. There is something you must know, something my Grandmother and the others wished to keep from you. Your Gift..." Another fit of coughing took her, and this time a froth of red bubbled from her nose and mouth. Katkin could only sit by helplessly, stroking Lalluna's wing, until at last she gasped, "Your Gift—I had nothing to do with it. It belonged to you, all the while, and we Amaranthine do not know from whence it came. There is a tale, of Elleranne, and Ben'aryn..."

She didn't finish. Lalluna gave a horrible choked gurgle as her lungs hemorrhaged. She began to jerk spasmodically as her fingers clawed at her chest and throat. Katkin held her, screaming for help, pleading with Lalluna. The Goddess cried in agony and vomited red foam all over her cloud-white wings.

And then she drowned in her own blood.

"My Lady?" she asked in a trembling voice, but the Goddess lay cold and still in her arms, and Katkin knew she was dead. Heedless of the danger, she held onto her body, crying bitterly.

Lalluna's last words echoed in her mind. She could not understand them, could not allow herself—not if they meant she could have healed Jacq as he lay dying on the floor of Acorn. Such a thought could not be borne. Firmly, she put the past from her mind and tried to decide what would be best for her Lady, Lalluna.

161

With desolate sureness, Katkin knew what she must do, and that it would take all her strength. Gently, she laid Lalluna in the dust and shifted into the Vastness.

A diffuse light permeated everything, even the rocks of the cavern, and lit the Uri'el that held the Goddess in its arms. Lalluna's face and body looked perfect again, and so very, very beautiful. Katkin stood before the Uri'el for a moment; hoping it might get up and flee from her, so she might be free of her obligation. But it stayed still, studying its charge with absent concentration.

Katkin removed the dagger from her belt—the dagger with the pearl handle, that had once belonged to Tomas de Vigny.

Before she could think; before she could breathe; before she could stop herself—she plunged the knife into the middle of her beloved Goddess' face. She tore the head asunder, and the Uri'el began to scream. So did Katkin.

She could not help herself.

A tall gangly figure stepped from behind a pillar of rock, but remained partially in shadow. "Fyn! Over here. I have found more filthy scum hiding in the darkness."

Katkin stared and stared, unable to match the harsh words with the voice she recognized. "Lut?"

"Grandmother!" He gave her a look of uncomprehending disgust. "You? How could you?" Lut raised his sword.

Katkin stayed quite close to Lalluna. "I... I had to keep my Lady's anafireon safe." Quickly she bent, and dug the glowing red jewel from the wreck of Lalluna's face. Lut walked forward steadily, his sword at the ready, his eyes bright with anger and disappointment.

"I have killed many for such a foul deed as this. No wonder you wished to come to Yr with us, servant of Maggrai! You have harvested your last bit of corsfyre."

"I loved her!" she cried, but her words only echoed between them and did nothing to dispel his rage.

As Katkin backed away from him, Fyn appeared from the tunnel and hurried to join them. At the sight of Lalluna's face, he gave a cry of utter anguish. "Sweet Azimity! What happened here?"

"She did it," snarled Lut, and pointed his sword at Katkin.

"Katrione? No, it cannot be possible. How could you have done such a thing?" He turned away, weeping.

"Look there, Fyn. She holds the anafireon in her filthy, murdering hand."

Fyn stared at Katkin's closed fist in disbelief. "Is this true? Open your hand so I may see inside it."

She did, and his eyes went wide with shock. "How did Lalluna pass into the Vastness? Did you kill her with the dagger you hold?"

"I... cannot tell you."

He frowned darkly and raised his sword, though his hand trembled as he held it before her face. "Is there any explanation you might give, that will prevent me from slaying you?"

Katkin shook her head sadly. "I swore on the heart of the Goddess, Tomas."

His expression grew grave. "Then prepare to die. And do not think for a moment that our former friendship will stay my hand."

"Tomas, no! I loved her, as you did. Why will you not believe me?"

Fyn strode forward, implacable in his anger, as Katkin, terror-stricken, backed away from him. She could find nowhere to hide, nowhere that Fyn, the master of the worlds between, would not find her. He raised his sword high, ready to cut her down. Katkin fell to her knees and closed her eyes.

An arm encircled her middle roughly, and dragged her backwards, as the ringing clang of a second sword clashing with Fyn's filled her ears. Her eyes flew open, thinking that Lut had somehow intervened on her behalf. But it was not Lut who stood between her and Fyn, with bright sword drawn.

It was Jacq.

Katkin thought that terror had surely taken her wits from her.

"You!" snarled Fyn. "I might have known! One traitor always defends another."

They began to fight, swords clashing violently. Katkin stood and screamed at them, "Stop it! You don't understand!" Out of the corner of her eye, she saw Lut step forward, ready to wade into the fray on Fyn's side. Katkin grabbed a sizeable rock from the ground and lobbed it at his head.

It struck him in the temple and he crashed down, like a young tree. Fyn, momentarily distracted, turned his head, and his opponent lashed out with his boot.

"Tomas!" Katkin screamed, as he staggered backwards, stunned and bloody. Jacq whirled and grabbed her before she could run to Fyn's aid, and dragged her sideways and a little to the left. The Vastness winked out.

Katkin opened her eyes a moment later. They stood together on a beach, shingled with grey stones, perfectly round. The ocean glided in, washing against the stones, rolling them back and forth, in a symphony of pleasing chimes that sounded almost like music. When she lifted her eyes she saw that grey hues also shaded the water and the clouds. The imperceptible delineation between sea and sky at the horizon made Katkin feel like a figure on a vast flat canvas.

Jacq's arms were still around her. Katkin did not move or speak for a long moment; not wishing to break whatever magic spell had brought him back to her. He did not speak either, only brushed his lips against her hair—and waited.

After a time, she sighed and said, "Jacq?"

He wanted to respond to this greeting, but he did not. Instead Dai said gently, "Not Jacq, no. Your husband is dead, Katkin. But he and I share the same memories, as brothers will."

She looked at him and her eyes filled with disappointed tears. "You are Dai?"

He nodded and dropped his arms to his sides as she stepped away from him, scattering the musical stones. "Where are your wings then?"

He shrugged. "I cut them off."

Katkin looked at him in horror. "What on Yrth? Why?" But then, she understood. "You are the one they call Outlaw Glint, are you not? The one who leads the Swallows. Emile told me you had scars on your back."

"Yes, I am Glint. I came back to Yr, so that I could help the Swallows in their fight against Maggrai. What else could I do? His presence on Yrth was my fault." Dai turned and walked away from the water's edge, and Katkin followed him. Farther up the beach a flat table of grey rock made a bench of sorts. He sank upon it and patted the space at his side.

Katkin remained standing, with her hands on her hips. "So what is your game now? Will you betray the Swallows to Maggrai, the way you betrayed me?"

His grey eyes met hers. "I would *never* betray you. Never."

Katkin snorted derisively. He stood at once and caught her by the arm, then shook her, none too gently. "Listen to me! I could have let that hotheaded idiot Fyn cut you in half a moment ago, if I had wanted to. But I saved you! Just as I saved you from those foul brigands in the Acre. Why would I do that if I wished you ill?"

She stared at him, uncertainly. "I don't know! Each time I see you, I meet a different Dai Irrakai. How am I to trust what you say now?"

"You can trust this," he said, and pulled her back into his arms again. At first, when his lips met hers, Katkin stiffened, but after a few seconds she responded, wanting desperately to believe that Dai—this Dai anyway—loved her.

After a moment she pulled away again. "Where have you been for the last sixteen years?"

"Watching over your island."

"Why did you not come to me?"

His eyes flashed. "You thought of me as a traitor. And anyway," he muttered, "you had other company from time to time."

Katkin felt her cheeks grow warm, and said nothing in reply.

"But since you came back to Yr, I have been following you rather more closely. I had hoped to keep my presence on Yrth secret awhile longer, but when Fyn went after you, I had to intervene."

"You kicked him in the teeth," Katkin giggled.

Dai smiled back at her, saying dryly, "Yes, well, I owed him that, for the last time we met."

Katkin watched a school of small silver fish leaping playfully through the waves. "What is this place? It is beautiful."

"Xonea," Dai replied. "One of the worlds between. But we should not linger here. Fyn will soon discover our path, and I don't wish to meet him again just yet. His grief over what happened on Asaruthe has made him even more quick-tempered than usual."

She looked confused, but only for a moment. With sudden sharp fear she asked, "What happened on Asaruthe?"

Dai sat again and took her hand. He held on to it tightly as he described Gwenn and Arkady's deaths. Katkin seemed stunned, and did not say a word before breaking into anguished sobs. *More death...*

"And is Gunnar all right?" she asked finally.

Dai nodded gravely. "His son and yours are with him." Katkin sighed and straightened her back. Perhaps there would be time for mourning later, but for now, she must carry it like a burr, lodged deep within her. *Could she have healed them, if she had been...*

Katkin shoved that brutal thought away from her. She twined her fingers with Dai's again. "Where will we go? Back to Yr?"

He nodded and stared out to sea, shading his eyes with his hand. They were the same color as everything in the landscape around them. "The Swallows plan to attack the Infirmarie tonight and free the remaining Firaithi."

Katkin frowned. "But that is madness, Dai! You are hopelessly outnumbered. The Guard will cut you down like chaff. I will not stand by and watch you..."

"Stay then. You would be safer here anyway. But I must go. The Swallows depend on me."

Katkin shook her head. "I will return with you so that I can find Poppy, and look after Myrie, too." She realized her fingers still clenched the red jewel that held Lalluna's anafireon. "And I have to keep my last promise to my Lady." The remembrance of the Goddess' death brought fresh tears to her eyes.

"Moonlight has passed from the cares of this world," Dai said softly. "And you hold her soul in safekeeping. Rejoice, for she suffered much, and now she is at peace."

Katkin nodded, and wiped her tears away.

"I must meet the Swallows within the marches of the Acre within the hour. Will you come?"

"Of course. I don't plan to let you out of my sight, Dai Irrakai, lest the next one I meet be unfriendly."

Katkin followed Dai through the fringes of the Acre, heading towards the shores of the Mistmere. Behind them, sixty or seventy Swallows, led by Emile, crept along as quietly as they could. "How are we going to get across the water?" she whispered to her companion. "Do you have boats?"

Dai shook his head.

"Swim then?" she asked, only a little facetiously.

"We will fly," he answered gruffly.

She stared at him. "Fly? But I thought you..."

"You know that I did," he broke in, as he massaged his shoulder. "We plan to steal an aermaran from the landing field close to Frai Foret."

Before Katkin could object, Dai halted in the shadow of some trees, and held up his hand for silence. The Swallows clustered at his back, as he pointed to a broad expanse of green, just beyond the edge of the forest.

"This is the Valerslea. Our scouts have reported that an aermaran lands here at dusk each day to discharge a patrol of Guardsmen into the forest," Dai whispered to them. "We will capture the craft while it is on the ground and then fly it into the City. If we are careful to leave no survivors, then we should be able to attack the Infirmarie without any advance warning."

Katkin's eyed narrowed. "An aermaran can carry one hundred Guardsmen, at least. How will you fight against so many?"

He shrugged. "Most probably we will fail. But we have to try. Myriadne says the Firaithi in the Infirmarie will not be able to survive for much longer."

"Where is Myrie?" Katkin asked, scanning the cluster of Swallows at their back.

Emile answered. "She said she would join us here in a few moments."

Above them, the sky darkened as the aermaran hove into view, like a bloated bird of prey. A contingent of Guardsmen assembled on the landing field, ready to catch the ropes that dangled from fore and aft positions on the airship. This was Katkin's first look at an aermaran, and she studied it with interest. Wire netting now reinforced the gas bags, probably to deflect fire-tipped arrows. She remembered that Arkady had once destroyed an aermaran, and nearly himself, by setting fire to the gas inside.

The ship bristled with weapons, and Katkin wondered how many Swallows would lose their lives in this desperate attempt at its capture. As Dai gave the command to form up for the attack, she pulled the pearl-handled dagger from her boot and prepared to move with the rest.

Myrie stood in the middle of the Swallow's Nest, and closed her hundred eyes. Fifty mouths opened, and chanted in unison, as one hundred hands formed delicate mudras of supplication. "Come to us now, beloved one. The last battle is nigh, and we have need of you, and the Mariner."

A thousand miles away, the golden light that leaked into the kitchen of Asavale flickered, as though stroked by many unseen hands. Gwillam Brunner's head snapped up, and he dropped his knife and fork.

Jakob handed his father's plate back to him. "I cut up the meat for you, Dad. Do you want a drink of ale from the barrel in the cellar?" Gunnar shook his head and asked for water. Using his left hand, he began to eat the stew Jakob had prepared. His two-fingered right hand lay scarred and useless in his lap.

Gwillam sat still, as if listening to an unseen conversation. "Ikor. It is time."

Gunnar did not argue. He wiped his mouth with a napkin, stood and straightened his tunic. "Wait while I fetch my sextant."

Jakob stood too, and knocked his chair to the floor. "I am coming with you."

His father shook his head. "You have done enough, lad. Stay here and mind your mother's sheep until we get back." Gwillam passed him his crutches, and he limped away down the hall. When he returned, Jakob and Gwillam stood together in the middle of the room. They had stacked the breakfast plates and mugs in the basin.

Gunnar frowned. "I said..."

Gwillam came to Jakob's defense. "The sheep don't want minding, Ikor. They can go on eating the grass, just like always. We might need his help."

"What about Bridie, and Wink and Jolly? Will they eat grass too? And Bessie, can she milk herself now?"

Gwillam looked deflated. "Oh, I hadn't thought about that."

After he righted his chair, Jakob sighed and said, "Never mind, Gwill. Dad's right anyway. I *have* done enough."

Gunnar looked at him thoughtfully. Jakob had been a changed lad when he stumbled back on to the beach in the company of Huw Adaryi—quieter somehow, more measured, adult. He had confessed his crime against Poppy and Lut to his astonished father, and accepted his punishment stoically. He had visited the graves of his Ma and Pop, and wept many bitter tears.

Huw left shortly afterwards. Gunnar tried to stop him—he seemed lost and witless, devastated by the death of his brother. He abandoned the boat, *Spry Lass*, which he and Jakob had brought from Citternia and then carelessly gap shifted, leaving another small tear in the delicate fabric of the island. It lit the kitchen at night with ethereal golden shimmers.

"How shall we travel, Ikor?" Gwillam asked impatiently. "Myrie says we should hurry."

Roused from his reverie, Gunnar spoke. "The same way your Ikor Huw did. We will close the hole from the other side. That way we can leave *Spry Lass* for Jakob, in case he must leave the island."

Jakob clasped his father's hand. "Please take care, Dad. I don't want to lose you, too." Gunnar nodded and embraced him, then turned to go. "What about your sword? Will you not have need of it?"

Gunnar shook his head, as he stood next to Gwillam. "I gave Ancarnen to Lut. I will not fight any more in this world, lad. It solves nothing. Farewell."

Jakob bowed his head as Gwillam called, "Take good care of Jolly! Bye, Jakob..."

They stepped away, and the light in the kitchen died soon after. Jakob stood still, staring at the darkened corner. Then he went outside to see to the sheep.

So far, the Swallows had fared none too well in the battle for Valerslea. Though they waited until the aermaran landed before they attacked, a watchman on the bow side had seen their frantic approach from the trees, and sounded the alarm. A hundred or more Guardsmen poured from the hatchways, firing muskets once they were clear of the aermaran's nacelle. Though the guns were less than accurate, the blasts felled several of the Glint's cohorts. The weaponry aboard the airship proved far more devastating. Rays of searing heat cut swathes through the attacking Swallows.

"Fall back," screamed Dai, as another three Swallows collapsed from the heat and smoke. But the Guardsmen did not seem anxious to press their advantage. They withdrew, and huddled under the shadow of the aermaran.

Myriadne had come to Valerslea.

The Swallows regrouped behind her, and waited. Katkin watched as Myrie's hundred hands twisted in agitation at the plight of her companions.

Dai spoke softly. "They fear you, Dawnmaid. Would you have us attack again?"

The voices answered in unison. "They fear us for the way we

appear, but we are not invincible, Glint. Once they understand this, they will recover their courage."

Katkin stayed low, within the cover of the trees, watching the grass erupt into flame as the weapon on the aermaran discharged.

"What uncanny fire powers that gun?" one of the Swallows asked despairingly. "How can we fight against it?"

"Corsfyre," Dai replied. "And we have none of our own to answer it."

Katkin thrust her hand into her pocket. "We must do something. The aermaran will doubtless leave if we do not challenge the men on the ground soon."

"Do you have a plan, Aunt?" Emile asked.

Katkin drew a bright red jewel from the pocket of her kirtle. She stared at it and answered, "Yes. I think I do."

In her heart, she added a silent prayer: *Forgive me, my Lady.*

The forest of a hundred hands waved before her, and she placed the jewel within it. One of the fifty mouths opened, and then Lalluna disappeared. The heterogeneous creature known as Myriadne increased by one voice. More importantly, it grew a magnificent pair of cloud-white wings.

When Poppy woke, she felt hot and cramped. She tried to stretch, wondering why her bedclothes seemed so very heavy. Where was she, anyway?

A horrified shriek escaped her lips as she realized that a man lay on top of her—a man who was quite clearly dead. Poppy pushed and pushed, trying to shift Tristan's bulk. Finally, with a panic-stricken wriggle, she moved from under his corpse, off the bed and on to the floor. She stood there, panting wildly, thinking on his position in death and what it implied. The realization, when it hit, was not a happy one.

She vomited on the exquisite hand-loomed Cherumean carpet that the late king of Beaumarais, Tristan Dinrhydan, had bought especially for this room. Especially for Azothe. It had a design of trees, each with many branches intertwined.

Poppy pulled a silk sheet from under the still form of Tristan and wrapped herself within it. Then she sank on to a bench, upholstered in quilted velvet, and hugged her arms to her chest, trying to make sense of her situation.

She remembered Madame Zomphadeus. She remembered Bettina, with deep shame. She remembered sitting in a carriage, on a bench very much like the one she sat on now. She remembered the King of Beaumarais, close beside her, his living breath warm on her cheek. And the heady scent of patchouli.

What came after seemed darker than a moonless midnight.

Poppy sat rigid, trying to suck in air, as panic stole her breath away. When something brushed against her, she was too afraid even to scream. She scrambled to her feet, and tore off the sheet. A coiled serpent with ruby eyes wriggled against the bare skin of her upper arm. With a cry of disgust, she threw it on to the floor. Slowly, sinuously, it straightened itself, and slithered under the bed.

She backed away until she bumped into a table, still set from the previous night's meal. A jug of wine, half-consumed, beckoned to her, and she poured herself a goblet full. The wine warmed and calmed her. She wandered over to an opulent dressing table and sat before it. Although her reflection had extravagantly coiffed hair, the face that stared back at her looked much the same as she remembered. That was something, anyway.

Nevertheless, the King was dead, and she had probably killed him. Poppy felt no remorse over this—he was a bad man, and deserved to die. She took another sip of wine, considering what might happen to her when the Guard found out about Tristan. No accounting of dresses and patchouli and memory loss would help her—she knew that. She must hide the body, somehow, and then make her escape.

Quickly she stood, intending to throw on some clothes. Tristan's would do, if she could find none of her own. A muffled groan stopped her in her tracks. *Was he not dead, after all?*

But the man on the bed lay stiff and silent. The groan came from a rough wooden box that stood on a plinth in the center of the room.

Another whimper followed. She did not want to see what lay in the box, but Poppy felt her legs carry her closer, as though some unseen hand moved her like a marionette.

He was there, just as she had dreamed he would be.

She was there, just as he had dreamed she would be.

Poppy wanted to scream, but fear and revulsion made her heart hammer and her throat narrow to nothing. The sheet fell away from her trembling hands. "What... What are you? I saw you in a dream."

Maggrai grimaced, trying to smile. "Did you indeed? Are we playing a new game now, Azothe?"

"Why do you call me that? My name is Poppy. And I am certainly not playing a game. The king is dead, and they will blame me for it. But I didn't do it."

He struggled to raise his head, so he could stare at her breasts. "Then... you *are* my angel of mercy. You have come to save me."

She took a step back as he raised a withered black stump towards her face. "Help me! Please..." Though the sight and smell of his charred flesh sickened her, Poppy did not run away.

"Did I do this to you?" she whispered. "If I did, I am sorry. Something came over me. I don't know what."

Maggrai gave an impatient groan, so that Poppy would understand that her apologies were neither wanted nor of any use. "Will you help me?" he asked again. She nodded, and then disappeared for a moment. When she returned she held a shining silver knife—the hilt cunningly cast like a snake's head, with ruby jewel eyes.

Maggrai half-closed his eyes. "Is that the only way?" he asked with resignation.

"I think so. There is no physick in the land that could heal you now."

"So be it. Strike for the heart, and make it sure and swift."

She raised the knife high, but the sight of him lying there, so wretched and alone, brought tears to her eyes.

"Go to your rest now, and may it be peaceful," she breathed softly, and reached down to brush her mouth against his charred lips.

He felt a sudden, unreasoning need to help her survive. "You cannot gap shift from anywhere in the Citadel, there is corsfyre embedded in the walls. It will mean your death if you do not heed me. But still you may leave this room secretly, by the door behind the bed curtain. Take the stairs to the Chymericum in the third dungeon level. There is a door within—a *Mebbain*, gateway to my Watchkeep on Split Island. No one will trouble you there."

Then he closed his eyes and waited for her to end his pain.

The knife flashed. He did not make another sound.

Poppy looked at Maggrai's body. The silver snake-knife, its eyes shining red, still protruded from his bony, blackened chest. She left it there.

Myriadne took to the air in pursuit of the rising aermaran. Dai and the other Swallows watched as the creature dodged a blast from the heat ray mounted forward of the nacelle. Lalluna's strong white wings carried her higher, towards the hatchway. The Guardsmen on the ground, seeing her plan, began firing into the air.

"Come on!" cried Katkin. "We must attack, and give her some cover!" She charged across the choppy grass, through the pall of smoke, with a sword she had taken from one of the dead Sparrows. A musket ball whistled just past her ear as Dai threw himself on top of her and then dragged her over behind a low clump of brush.

"Stay down, you idiot! Let me do the fighting. You watch what Myrie is doing, and shout if she is able to get control of the aermaran."

Katkin nodded. He stood and charged towards the fray, with his sword held high. The Guardsmen turned and fled before his wrath. Up above, the aermaran tried to maneuver away from Myrie, but she flew with far more agility. Katkin shaded her eyes and watched in awe as she swung in great arcs, avoiding the fiery blasts of the corsfyre weapon, closing in on the main hatchway. Dai and the other Swallows attacked the Guardsmen on the ground, preventing them from firing upwards.

"Go on, Myrie!" Katkin shouted. "Head for the door on the side." The aermaran's hurried ascent had left the side hatch hanging wide open. Once she reached it, Myrie dove inside. Seconds later, an unlucky Guardsman came hurtling out, and plummeted one hundred feet to the ground, screaming all the way. He landed with a sickening thud, and screamed no more.

Another joined him, and another, and then a steady stream of Guardsmen jumped or fell from the hatch. The airship rolled like a sick pony. The corsfyre gun stopped firing, the sizzling hiss of its heat ray silenced.

"Look, Emile!" Katkin spoke to the young man at her side. "Myrie is bringing the aermaran to us. We have won!"

He stood and cheered. A Guardsman, fallen but still clinging to life, raised his pistol with sudden menace. Katkin screamed, "Get down!"

Emile flew backwards, and clutched at his abdomen in agony. Blood welled around his fingers and soaked his shirt. Katkin added her hands to the wound, to try and stop the flow.

"Aunt," he grunted softly. "Shouldn't have celebrated... quite so soon."

She knelt beside him, shrieking for help. The other Swallows, busy mopping up the last of the Guardsmen, did not hear her. Emile's face grew ashen as the blood left his torn arteries, and carpeted the grass like red jewels. Katkin knew she had to do something, or he would die.

Your Gift...

Slowly, she removed her bloodstained hand from his belly, and placed it on his chest.

It was yours, all the long.

It would not work, she knew that, had to believe that. She could not heal him on her own. But she would have to try, so that she could fail, and be at peace again.

Emile muttered, "Where are the Deres when you need them, eh Aunt?"

"Deres?" Katkin's eyes went wide. "What on Yrth are Deres?" And yet, as she asked it, the word seemed familiar to her.

"The trees," he groaned, and then gave a violent shudder, his face twisted in agony.

It would not work.

We Amaranthine do not know from whence it came...

Katkin felt her body tense, felt her mind spinning back—to a glade like this one, and Jacq, dying from a wicked iron ball in his chest. A towering oak, with its roots deep in the earth, its branches sheltering them all.

The trees. *Deres.*

She closed her eyes and focused the power in her hand. Sent it flowing into Emile. Felt the impact of the ball tear into her guts, and wanted to vomit. Held on to it. Held on to the pain, and then, let it go. Sleep overtook her, the sleep of pure exhaustion, but as her eyes closed she saw that Emile's face had relaxed and regained its color.

A dream. She walked with Tomas de Vigny in the silence of the Vastness.

Looking around her, she says in surprise—there are trees here, in the Vastness! How can they be here, if they are alive?

174

He nods and replies. The trees exist in all the spheres at the same time. No one knows how or why, for they are silent, and give their secrets to no one.

The trees. *Deres.*

Poppy found a wardrobe filled with luxurious silk dresses, all her size. She ran her fingers over the silky material, feeling the cool smoothness. After sniffing it carefully, she slipped a blue one over her head. Then she pushed her feet into a pair of dainty slippers, wishing she still had the sensible boots she had left at Madame's. She passed by the dressing table, and stopped to look at her reflection in the mirror. Though she wore Azothe's clothes and shoes, the brown eyes that gazed so seriously back at her were most definitely those of Poppy Brunner. Whatever madness had overtaken her had not been present in *this* dress.

Hissed whispers just outside left her thoroughly panicked. "He is in there, I tell you! I just heard a noise." Someone started knocking very persistently.

Poppy threw the bed curtains aside. The paneling concealed Maggrai's door, and it opened by a cunningly carved handle that looked like part of the molding. She stepped through the low opening. After rearranging the curtains, she shut the panel behind her.

Once she had sealed herself from the bedroom, Poppy looked around. She found herself in a narrow stairwell, fitted between two rough stone walls. A high slit provided a beam of light that barely lit the floor. The stairs plunged into total darkness, and Poppy was afraid to begin her descent. But the commotion from the bedroom, indicating that the servants were trying to break open the door, drove her onwards and down.

She kept a hand on the wall, and counted the steps as she went. *Three, four, five, six...*

Why had Maggrai helped her, anyway?

Twelve, thirteen, fourteen...

Where was the Chymericum?

Forty-one, forty-two...

What would she do when she reached the Watchkeep?

One hundred...

How would she ever find Katkin and Myrie again?

Poppy felt the ground level out and so she stopped counting.

The troubling questions remained. Her hands, held before her in the pitch darkness, felt solid panels—a door, with a stout bar across it. She lowered it to the floor, trying to be as silent as possible. Then she turned the handle, and opened the door a crack. She could hear voices, faintly, through the oak, and she waited, hardly daring to breathe, until they passed from her hearing.

The light from the corsfyre lanterns in the corridor blinded her a little. She paused in the shadow of the stairwell, letting her eyes adjust, straining her ears for any further sound.

Satisfied that she was unobserved, Poppy pulled the door open, and crept into the passage, somewhere deep in the bowels of the Citadel. Damp dripped from the walls and gathered in puddles on the stone flags. Poppy walked along the hall, picking a direction at random, since Maggrai had not told her the way to the Chymericum. She passed many closed and barred doors, some filled with moaning prisoners and recent torture victims, but she dared not stop to help them.

The staccato beat of marching boots made her heart race. She looked around for a place to hide, rattling a series of locked door handles with panicked frustration. A conversation drifted down the hallway. "...dead. You heard right, Breville."

"How?" the other voice inquired.

"In *her* bed. Looks like his poor old heart couldn't stand the strain." Crude chuckles followed his pronouncement, and Poppy felt her stomach churn. "But the Captain said to put the word out that the King was poisoned."

"What about his wife? Do she know yet?"

"That cow?" grumbled the first. They were very close now, about to turn the corner in front of Poppy. She raised her skirts, getting ready to run, when her foot brushed against the base of a nearby door. It opened and Poppy, with a relieved sigh, stepped inside and pulled it shut behind her.

The voices passed her by.

The room was dark, as dark as the stairwell had been, and very malodorous. Hoping she had stumbled upon the Chymericum, Poppy stepped back into the hallway, and removed one of the lanterns that hung from blackened iron hooks in the wall. After she entered, light in hand, she wished she had not. She had stumbled into a torture chamber, filled with a grisly collection of implements, and the decaying bodies of recent victims, some still cruelly locked within their devices.

Poppy placed her hand over her nose and mouth, then hurried back to the door. She could not exit. More voices carried down the hall, one high pitched and querulous. "I tell you I don't know anything! Please, I beg you, let me go."

Just as Poppy ducked behind an iron maiden, the door flew open and two Guardsmen entered, dragging an elderly woman between them. A black-robed man followed, carrying a rolled up cloth containing the tools of his trade. The woman continued to scream and plead until one of the Guards cuffed her. As her head lolled back in a faint, he strapped her into a stout wooden chair. He grumbled as he worked.

"We are wasting time! Why should this old girl know anything about the king's death? We locked her up in here last week. Azothe is the one we should be looking for."

The Captain answered, "No doubt that witch was involved, but I believe the ex-Queen had something to do with it too. Why else would she be skulking round Beaumarais after sixteen years? Someone saw her leaving the post office in Belladore and since this old bag is the Postmistress, I figure she might know something useful." He turned to the black-robed man at his side. "What do you reckon, Harry? The wheel?"

The torturer tutted with professional disdain. "Don't be daft. She wouldn't last five minutes on that. You need to persuade her to talk— not make her heart give out. Needles under the nails ought to loosen her lips. Then if that don't work, we'll give her the boot." He busied himself with the cloth, arranging it on the bench. Poppy looked on in horrified fascination as he withdrew several long, metal implements.

They threw a bucket of water over the woman, and she came to life, groaning weakly.

"What is your name and occupation?"

Her answer came out in a frightened whine. "I told you that when you arrested me last week. Tabitha Sinclair. I am the Postmistress of Belladore. Why are you doing this?" Poppy could not bear to hear what came next.

"Where is Katrione Benet? We know you spoke with her."

"I... I don't know! I haven't..." The torturer did his work, slowly and carefully.

The old woman's shrieks were horrible, like those of a terrified beast caught in a leg-hold trap. They continued unabated for several minutes.

"Now, Tabitha," said the first Guardsman, patiently. "Why don't you make it easy on yourself, and tell us what you know?"

She sobbed and gasped, unable to answer. The torturer produced more needles from the tray. Poppy covered her ears at the sound of the woman's agony. Abruptly, the screams stopped.

"Tough old bird," the torturer remarked casually. "Shall we bring her round again?"

They did. One of the guards, losing patience, seized her by the throat and shook her, hard. "Where is she? Tell us or we will start breaking your bones, one at a time."

Tabitha pleaded, "Mercy, please. I don't know anything to tell you."

She dissolved into sobs as the guard snapped, "Get the boot, Harry." As the torturer retrieved a menacing looking black object, he continued, "Listen here, Crone, we are through being nice to you. Since you won't cooperate, I will tell you what happens now. We are going to fit this lovely iron boot to your foot. Then I will twist this screw on the side here, see?" He thrust the boot under the old woman's nose, causing her to moan incoherently. "A few turns will crush your ankle bones. Now you have one last chance to..."

As the torturer bent to fit the boot to her withered foot, Tabitha screamed, "Help me, by the Gods! Somebody, please..."

Poppy could bear no more. "Stop!" she cried, leaping forth. "Leave her alone! I am the one you want. I am Azothe..."

Fifteen

Cedar

Jakob picked his way along the talus slope at the bottom of the cliff, hunting for crabs to cook for supper. The sun had sunk below the level of the horizon, but the sky still shone clear and bright, reducing the rocks and trees in the distance to black silhouettes. Jakob followed as Jolly, Wink and Bridie scampered ahead, barking at the gulls that gathered in the mouth of a small freshet. They rose into the air, shrieking irritably, and circled around their resting place.

Jolly stopped to sniff at the base of the oldest tree on the island, an ancient weathered cedar that had somehow survived in the harsh climate of Asaruthe for years uncounted. Jakob gave a careless whistle. Jolly shot in the other direction, heading towards his old home—Ruthecombe. Cursing, Jakob followed.

Once they reached Poppy's old house, the dog pushed the door open and stood at the bottom of the ladder, growling and barking. Bridie and Wink hung back, with their hackles raised.

"What is it boy? Is someone there?" Jakob, thoroughly discomfited by the thought that some stranger might be on the island with him, paused to grab the nearest weapon—a long-handled toasting fork with metal tines—before he climbed the ladder to the second floor.

The quiet and dark attic gave him no reassurance. Jakob checked Poppy's room first, but it was as she had left it, with a rag doll resting on the neatly made bed. Gwillam's untidy room was just as empty. But Jolly's insistent barks continued to float up from below, so Jakob went into his Grandmother's room. By now, the light had almost gone, but he could see that the room had not been disturbed for some time. It looked cheerless and lonely, the only occupant a pile of discarded clothing.

Jakob turned away, thinking he ought to get home, and see to his crabless supper.

His eye caught the flash of a mirror, half-covered by the clothes on the bed. It winked invitingly at him, though the light had gone from the room. He picked it up. A moment later, with a cry of dismay, he gap shifted, leaving a golden sheet of light leaking across the bed. Below, on the first floor, the dogs began a deeply distressed howl.

She dreamed she could fly. Lalluna floated at her side, peaceful once more. Katkin sighed and touched a downy wing. "You were right, my Lady. The Gift was mine all the long. I wish I had known in time to heal you."

Lalluna gave her a sad smile. "Such a Gift should not be squandered. Save it for those in need. As for me, I am happy to be one with the Dawnmaid. Now I can make amends for all my transgressions in this life."

Katkin was just about to argue, when she caught site of a lonely figure on the ground far below, trudging along a winding ribbon of road. She dove downwards, irresistibly drawn.

He looked at her, with tear-filled eyes. "I am trying to get back to Elleranne, but it is so far. I have lost my wings..."

With a jerk, she woke. Dai crossed the sloping floor, squatted by her side and took her hand. "Are you all right?"

Katkin looked around her, baffled by her strange surroundings. The low ceiling had a dull metallic sheen. A tracery of struts and columns divided the small space, leaving little room for the Swallows who sat on the floor, murmuring together.

"Where... Where am I? I felt as though I were flying."

He smiled at this. "You are. Inside the capsule of the aermaran. It is taking us to Isle St. Valery."

Katkin sat up, catching sight of a familiar blond figure at the helm. "Gunnar! How on Yrth did you get here?" He gave her a friendly wave and returned his concentration to the wheel.

"Have you no words of greeting for me?" Gwillam stood above his adoptive mother, hands on hips. With a cry of joy, she jumped to her feet and folded him into an embrace. After a moment, feeling embarrassed by the snickers of the Swallows, he pushed her arms away, saying firmly, "That is enough greeting for now, Katkin!"

Gwillam sat beside Katkin and answered her questions. "I heard Myrie's call, so Ikor and I traveled the worlds between. He hurried me along fearfully quick, and we arrived just as the aermaran touched back down on the Valerslea. You were still sleeping, so Dai picked you up and brought you on board."

Katkin shook her head in wonder. "And... And Emile? Is he all right?"

Dai said, "He is very well. But how did you—"

"I don't know. And until I do I don't want to say anything more." Then, remembering her vision of the oak tree in the glen, she asked, "Has Emile ever mentioned the Deres to you?"

"Deres?" Dai repeated. "There is a legend, from the earliest time of the Autochthones, of something called the Deres. The Elders describe them as the pillars supporting the Gyre, but I know little else. Emile has never said anything about them, at least not to me."

A barked command from Gunnar—"Hold fast! We are descending"—brought the conversation to an end. The floor assumed a much steeper slant, and Katkin had to grab for the nearest handhold to keep herself from sliding downwards.

Dai whispered in her ear, "We are going to drop on the roof of the main wing of the Infirmarie. From there we will fight our way in, and save as many of the Autochthones as we can. The Swallows who remain will escape St. Valery by boat, leaving the aermaran to transport the captives to freedom."

"Where will we take them?"

He shrugged. "I believe Myrie knows, but she will say only that we must set a course due west."

"And then?"

He touched her cheek. "One battle at a time, my love. One battle at a time."

Poppy sat in the chair that had once held Tabitha Sinclair, in the same dark nightmare of a room. A contingent of guardsmen, led by General Yannick Abelard, stood before her. She swallowed as the black robed torturer swept in.

But she had known it would come to this, from the moment she leapt out to save the old woman.

The second-in-command spoke. "We have been instructed by those acting for the interests of Queen Roseberry to torture this woman, Azothe, also known as Camille de Rien, until she confesses her heinous crime—the murder of King Tristan of Beaumarais—and implicates those who assisted her. Do you wish to observe the proceedings, General?"

Yannick frowned. "Of course. Begin at your convenience."

The torturer had been heating a pair of iron tongs in a portable brazier. He withdrew them, and the red-hot iron filled the room with the metallic smell of pain. Poppy struggled uselessly against her bonds as the Captain of the Guard addressed her.

"Do you wish to tell us who helped you murder the king?"

"No one helped me," she said in a parched whisper. "I acted alone."

Her interlocutor sounded almost apologetic. "I do not believe that to be the case, young woman. Are you sure you will not speak further?"

Poppy nodded.

"Then we must persuade you to be more forthcoming." He turned to the torturer and ordered, "Pull out her teeth, one at a time."

They clamped a band cruelly tight around her forehead, and forced her mouth open with a felted rod. Poppy prayed she would faint; or better yet, die before they could get very far. She closed her eyes in terror as the tongs drew near.

With a roar of fury, a blond-headed warrior appeared, seemingly from nowhere. He carried no weapon other than a toasting fork, but he made short work of the men who tried to prevent him from reaching Poppy Brunner. A single twist of his hand broke the torturer's neck, while a kick crumpled General Abelard to the ground. He howled in agony, clutching his shattered kneecap.

Poppy opened her eyes, uncomprehending, as gentle hands removed the gag from her mouth. "Lut? Have you come to save me?"

Jakob slipped a finger under the metal band, and tore it like a crust of bread. Then he ripped the leather restraints from the chair, and picked her up, without answering her question.

"Wait! Don't try to gap shift again. It won't work. There is corsfyre here, embedded in the walls."

Jakob frowned, remembering his father's harrowing tale. "How can we get out of here, Poppy?"

"Put me down! We will have to make a run for it. Try to find the Chymericum." She explained about Maggrai as she rifled through the pockets of the fallen gaoler and removed his keys.

The General remained on the floor, whimpering in pain. Jakob took Yannick's sword from him. He held it up to the light of the corsfyre lantern, admiring the engraving. The sound of hurrying boots brought his head up. "Let's go then. Stay behind me." Poppy unlocked the heavy door.

They hurried through the threshold, and came upon another group of guardsmen. Jakob threw himself amongst them while Poppy sheltered in a doorway, more than a little in awe of his strength and his wrath. As the last guardsman fell, clutching at his slashed throat, Poppy began unlocking the dungeon doors to the left and right of her.

"Poppy, what are you doing? We don't have time to..."

"I have to help them, Lut." The prisoners stepped forth and took stock of the situation. They all ran like frightened rabbits, heading for the upper levels. All but one.

Madame, looking considerably worse for wear, staggered forth from the last cell. "You!" she screamed, as she recognized Poppy. "At last, I can make you pay for what you did to me, you lying little whore."

"Wait," said Poppy. "I am sorry for what happened. Please believe me. I wasn't... myself. But now that I am helping you, can you not forgive me?"

Madame looked at her with loathing, and raised her prison issue blouse. The skin underneath had livid red streaks. "Can you help with this, my dear?" she spat, and then called along the corridor— "Help! Help! Prisoners escaping."

Jakob silenced her with a vicious thrust of his sword, but not before her cries had summoned reinforcements. Three more guardsmen appeared, running with swords already drawn.

"Halt!" their leader cried. "Halt in the name of the King!"

Jakob shoved Poppy behind him and fought his way forward. They passed the door through which she had originally entered the hallway. The second one along from it hung crookedly from its blackened hinges.

"In here." Jakob kicked the remaining timbers apart, pulled her within, and then blocked the door with the huge Chronagine control panel. She paid attention to his unusual abilities for the first time. "Lut? How on Yrth did you..."

"No time to explain. Where do we go from here?" The persistent sound of hammering echoed between them.

Poppy hunted around the room, looking for the portal. Finally, she pulled open the door of what appeared to be a supply cupboard. A mist of stars lay within it, swirling just out of reach. "I think this is it. Maggrai said I could escape to his Watchkeep through something called a *Mebbain*."

The Chronagine panel, pushed from behind by at least twenty guardsmen, toppled forward onto the slates and smashed, sending sparks arcing through the dim light. Jakob grabbed Poppy and jumped between the stars.

* * * *

Katkin watched from a porthole window. It felt as though she remained still, trapped within the aermaran, as the roof of the Infirmarie loomed closer and closer. Gunnar studied the same view with intense concentration, both his whole and injured hand gripping the wheel, trying to bring the unfamiliar craft in for a soft landing. He hoped, by this gentle approach, to dupe the guards standing below, who would have seen many aermaran stop to discharge captured Firaithi. The roof of the main building had a high peak, but the wings on either side were flat-topped and graveled. At Myrie's direction, he aimed for the left one, and drifted to a halt.

Forty Swallows disembarked, dressed in the uniforms of fallen guardsmen. Dai stood amongst them, in his own clothes, pretending to be their captive. They marched across the rooftop in double time, and hammered on the locked door to the stairwell.

"Open up!" Emile shouted. "We've got the bloody Glint here."

As Katkin looked on from the window, with Gwillam at her side, the door opened. The Swallows surged forwards, overwhelming the guards within. Abruptly the door shut, and blocked her view. She sighed and twisted her hands together.

Gunnar called over from the wheel. "See to clearing some space for our guests. They will be coming soon, and we must load them and depart." And this, to Gwillam—"You are a clever lad, are you not? See if you can divine how to operate this corsfyre weapon. Looks like quite a contrivance, but if we can use it against its makers we might just pull off this fool stunt."

Gwillam, smiling broadly, hurried to the cage on the bottom of the nacelle that held the gun. He lowered himself gingerly into the control seat, grabbed the handles and swung the gun round in a vicious arc. A blast of heat set the rooftop door blazing.

Cries echoed from within the Infirmarie.

"Careful, lad. You hit one of the gas bags with that weapon, and we will all be blown to Skyre and beyond."

Gwillam grinned and shrugged sheepishly. "Sorry, Ikor." He settled down to study the controls, while Katkin hurriedly removed anything she thought would not be necessary for the trip west.

Each time she passed a window, she paused, hoping to see the Swallows filing out with the Firaithi—and Dai. When fifteen minutes had passed, she wondered if they had met more resistance than they had bargained for.

"Gunnar," she began, worriedly. "Maybe we should..."

The door, still smoldering, exploded outwards, and Dai strode forth, a young Firaithi girl cradled in his arms. "Open the hatch!" he cried. A stream of gaunt, wraith-like people followed, supporting each other, herded and encouraged by Swallows.

Katkin hurried along the gangplank, and took the child from Dai. She lay still and cold in her arms. He walked back to the end of the line, sword drawn, ready to defend the flank of the retreating Swallows. Katkin could see at least a hundred guardsmen crossing the greensward in front of the main building.

"Dai! We must hurry. There are more men on the way."

She laid the child on a blanket just inside the door and pulled her knife from her boot, ready to help with the defense. Then the corsfyre gun sizzled and spat, and a wide swathe of flame appeared before the approaching reinforcements. They scattered in alarm.

As the last of the prisoners gained the gangplank, Dai called, "Swallows! Go to ground."

One spoke as he gathered up a coil of stout rope and threw it over his shoulder. "You will return to us soon, Glint? There is still much to be done." Dai nodded noncommittally as he waited by the hatch, embracing each of the departing Swallows.

Emile hugged Katkin, saying, "Goodbye, Aunt. My mother told me once that you had great powers, but I never expected to see so for myself! Thank you for saving me. I pray we will meet again in happier times."

Dai clasped his hand. "Farewell, true heart. The Swallows are yours to command now. I will not be returning to Beaumarais."

Emile seemed unsurprised by this. "May the gods bless you, Glint. But is there a boon I might ask of you before you go?"

"Of course, Emile."

To hide his embarrassment he studied his boot tops intently. "Could I have a lock of your hair?" he eventually blurted. Dai looked so surprised by his request that he added, "It isn't for me. A friend asked for it, in return for his help. He thinks very highly of you."

After unbinding his long silver-brown queue, Dai wrapped three strands of hair about his fingers and removed them with a tug and a wince.

He passed them to Emile with a smile. "Tell your friend I am happy to oblige."

Emile folded the gift into a handkerchief and tucked it into his jerkin, then moved away. A mysterious darkness seemed to swallow him long before he reached the edge of the roof. Katkin sighed as she watched him disappear, wishing her own son had been as honorable and upright as Willow's seemed to be.

As Gwillam kept the guardsmen at bay, the remaining Swallows climbed down the side of the Infirmarie that faced away from the greensward. When Katkin went to stand by Dai at the hatchway, they had already melted away into the deepening dusk.

"Farewell!" Katkin called. "Thank you." As the last of the light died, she walked up the gangplank with Dai at her side.

Once inside, she gazed at the raggedly dressed Firaithi huddled against the walls of the passenger compartment. Most looked too stunned and too ill to appreciate the change in their circumstances. Katkin moved amongst them, offering reassurance as Gunnar sent the aermaran whistling skywards.

One elderly woman, clutching the hand of a young child, screeched, "Where are you taking us?"

Myrie, who had remained hidden behind a bulkhead, glided into the open. Many of the Firaithi shrank back at the sight of her, and several cried out in terror. "Well, Dawnmaid?" Dai asked. "Where would you have us go?"

She shook her head. "I do not know."

Katkin approached her, stunned by her words. "But... But you are the Dawnmaid, the beacon of light for the Kindreds! If you don't know, then how will we find your kingdom?"

Fifty mouths smiled back at her. "We have only to head westwards. One is coming who will help us."

"Who?" Dai asked her, impatiently.

"You will see," she answered, in a lilting chorus of voices. "You will see."

The *Mebbain*, after a disorienting few seconds of star-streaked blackness, had deposited them at the Watchkeep, as Maggrai had promised. The stone tower stood over a hundred feet high, rising like an obelisk from the top of a rocky prominence on Split Island. The Ariane, hemmed in by the narrow passage, coursed by on either side of the cliff-like banks. Maggrai had chosen Split precisely because no one had ever been able to land a boat on the island.

Poppy wandered around the top floor, which seemed to serve as both living space and observatory for Maggrai. It held little in the way of furnishings—a low bed covered in skins, a worktable littered with plans and drawings, and the cupboard that held the entrance to the Mebbain.

She could not help thinking, somehow, that she had been there before. The bed, especially, provoked a warm blush on her cheeks, but she could not imagine why it would be so. She trailed her fingers over the silky coverlet and a very familiar scent filled the air. Profoundly disturbed, Poppy hurried to the center of the room.

Everything looked very tidy, as though the owner expected to be away for some time, except for a blue globe that lay on the trestle table that served as a workbench.

She picked it up. "What do you think this is?"

"I don't know. But I would guess it is probably a weapon. Maggrai was an evil creature. I am very glad you made an end to him."

Poppy placed the blue orb back on the table and turned to face him. Her deep brown eyes gazed thoughtfully into his. "Do you think so? He seemed quite harmless to me."

"W... What? That monster? He killed my..." The realization struck that she did not yet know of his mother's death, or of her Ikor Kadya's. His heart told him that he must not disclose it—not yet, while they were so far from the comfort of home and familiar objects. He cleared his throat and continued, "I mean... a lot of Firaithi." Then, to distract her, he asked, "What happened in the Citadel, Poppy? What were those men after?"

Her expression changed, and he could tell the question had upset her. She sat beside him, and sighed. "Would you mind if I didn't tell you? I would just rather forget about it."

Jakob squeezed her hand. "Of course not."

She brightened immediately. "I suppose we should see about getting out of here. Katkin and Myrie will be wondering where I am." They explored the room and found a single wooden door that led onto a high balcony. A low stone parapet protected it from a sheer drop. Looking into the gathering dusk, they saw that the wild fastnesses of Split Island grew right up to the base of the tower.

Jakob scratched his head in confusion. "How in Od's name did he come and go?"

Poppy smiled. "He could fly, remember?"

"But we cannot. And though it is hard to judge in this darkness, I think it must be at least eighty feet to the ground."

"Maybe we could climb down?"

"No chance of that, I am afraid. Do you see how closely these stones are set together? Not a hand or foothold anywhere." They went back inside, and wandered around the main room disconsolately. After a time, Poppy sat before a large convex mirror and studied her distorted reflection. "What are we going to do?"

"I don't know," he said, and slumped beside her on the bench. "We can't use the *Mebbain*. That would only take us straight back into danger again. Maybe we should try gap shifting?"

"There is probably corsfyre here, too. Otherwise, why would he bother with the *Mebbain*?"

"I guess we will have to stay here until someone thinks to rescue us." Jakob fiddled with a rounded projection on the table before them, trying to think of something more helpful to say. The mirror gradually grew hazy before his eyes, and their reflections disappeared. A dark landscape appeared, with many high evergreens, and a glassy lake. Four Uri'el sat tranquilly by the shore, ignoring the group of men that moved steadily towards them.

Poppy leaned forward. "This must be another mirror like Katkin's, showing us things from other places. I wonder where Maggrai..." Her eyes went wide as she pointed at the mirror, where two figures armed with swords massacred the voulge-wielding Firaithi. "There is Jakob! Look, Lut! He is killing that old man. How could he do that? Oh, this is terrible... Terrible!" She burst into tears and buried her head on Jakob's shoulder.

"Poppy." Jakob felt the softness of her hair against his cheek. Somehow, he willed himself to continue. "There is something I must tell you." He stared through narrowed eyes as the blond warriors in the mirror mopped up the last of the Firaithi harvesters. "That is not Jakob."

"What? Of course it is. One is Uncle Fyn and the other one is Jakob. It looks just like him! Who else could it be?"

"It is Lut." Jakob placed his fingers before Poppy's face before she could think to argue. She stared at the bitten nails in shock.

"You... You are Jakob?" Poppy stood hurriedly, and backed away from him.

"Yes. I am sorry. Sorry for everything..."

She threw the first thing that she laid her hand on, which happened to be an empty glass retort. Jakob ducked and it shattered against the wall, only just missing the mirror. A beaker full of yellow powder followed. While she hunted for something else, he frantically tried to calm her. "I know you are angry, and I don't blame you."

"What are you doing here? Why didn't you tell me who you were before now?" She reached for a second retort, and found the blue globe instead.

"I gap shifted from Asaruthe after I saw you in the mirror. Should I have stopped to introduce myself first, while those butchers pulled your teeth out?" He glared at her until the hand that held the sphere slowly dropped to her side.

She grimaced, thinking of those red-hot pincers again. "No... I suppose not. You saved my life, Jakob," she added grudgingly. "I suppose I ought to be more grateful. But how did you get back to Asaruthe? What happened to Maia?" Jakob frowned, remembering Maia, and their unhappy parting. He was about to explain, when the scene in the mirror shifted.

He tugged at Poppy's sleeve urgently. "Look!"

Black smoke and flame showed first, and then, rising like a buoyant bubble, an airship appeared. "That is an aermaran. Rab told me about them."

Jakob's eyes went wide. He had spied the tiny figure steering the vessel. "There is Dad, at the wheel! How on Yrth did he manage to capture an aermaran?"

Poppy stood. "It looks as though it is passing over the river. Maybe we can hail it! Come on, we should go back to the balcony."

They could see the approaching aermaran in the distance, brightly lit, fore and aft, by massive corsfyre lamps. It moved slowly towards them, following the course of the river. Poppy screamed and shouted, waving her arms, but the airship did not deviate.

"Oh no! They can't see us in the dark. It is no good. We are going to be trapped in this stupid tower forever." Poppy burst into tears.

Jakob watched the progress of the airship, guessing that its course would take it right over the tower. He spied a heavy mooring line, carelessly left dangling by the Swallows in their hurried ascent, swaying back and forth in the wind.

In that narrow thread lay salvation—or death. Jakob figured he had less than five seconds to determine whether or not he could catch it. In three seconds, he had decided he could. Swiftly, he wrapped his arm around Poppy's waist, threw her over his shoulder, and then stepped on to the balcony.

She beat her fists into his back, crying, "What are you doing? Put me down!"

With careful timing, Jakob caught the trailing rope. Poppy screamed as the line jerked tight and she and Jakob soared into the darkness. She clung to him with her eyes closed, as, hand over hand, he climbed until they were well above the level of the trees. "It is all right, Poppy. You won't fall, I promise."

She sputtered incoherently," You... Just wait until... I will never forgive you for this, Jakob Strong Arm. Never!"

Jakob smiled to himself and tightened his grip on the rope. "Ahoy!" he called to the aermaran's capsule. "Ahoy! Stand by to receive boarders." The fierce wind created by the airship's passage whipped away his words.

"Poppy, I am going to have to climb higher. Hold on to me, all right?" She did not answer, and he began to worry that she might have fainted. He shook her. "Poppy?"

"All right," she shrieked through gritted teeth. "But if you drop me, I'll..."

Another twenty hand-over-hand pulls brought them much closer. Jakob called again and prayed his newfound strength would not fail.

A square of light appeared above them. Jakob shouted joyfully as a second rope snaked down. This one was a ladder. He hung on to the mooring line with one blistered hand as he shifted sideways, trying to get his feet onto the rungs of the ladder. A gust of wind sent it flailing away from him, leaving him dangling off-balance. Shoving with all his strength, he got Poppy on to the rungs as it swung back.

She clung to him as he scrabbled for purchase. The wind swung the ladder away again. Poppy cried out in terror, frantically trying to hold on to him and the rungs.

He knew his weight would quickly prove too much for her. "Let me go!"

"No!" she shrieked, against the wind. "I won't let you fall."

"I won't," he lied desperately. "I have my hand on the ladder, right now."

She didn't loosen her hold, and he could feel her muscles trembling with the strain. He prised her stiffening fingers away, one by one, praying she should not fall with him.

"Jakob! No..."

His voice, only a breath in her ear, sounded gentle and sad. "Don't forget me, Poppy." He might have been saying farewell at the coaching house.

Jakob pulled the last of her fingers away from his tunic. Poppy screamed as he spun away from her. Well within her sight, he winked out, like a falling star.

Sixteen

Nutmeg

Poppy, still shrieking Jakob's name, clung to the ladder as it rose. She could see Katkin's anxious face framed in the light streaming from the capsule door, and beyond that, Gunnar, hauling the rope up hand over hand.

Once she reached the door, they helped her inside. Gunnar asked sharply, "Where is the lad? Did I not hear Jakob's voice calling?"

"He fell. I am so sorry, Ikor. He fell trying to save me."

Gunnar put a hand to his face and turned away. Katkin put her arms around Poppy. "Thank goodness you are all right," she murmured.

"But Jakob... We have to go back. See if we can find him. Maybe he didn't..."

His father growled, "He could not have survived that fall. And we would never find his body in the wild lands below us. Anyway, the skald never gives anything back. Not to me. Now we had best get on with this journey. I have the sheep to tend at home." He limped back to the wheel, and stood there, grim-faced, as silent and rigid as stone. Poppy did not dare offer him any words of comfort, or question his confusing words about the skald.

She dried her tears, determined to believe that Jakob *had* survived—and that they would someday meet again. Then she peered around the capsule, taking in the sick and frightened survivors. There looked to be fifty or sixty in all. "Is that all who were left?" she whispered to Katkin.

Her mother nodded. "They are mostly Gitashaen, and Rajnathi. I know none of them. They say many others died in the Infirmarie, of sickness brought on by the making of Broth. I cannot believe my own son..."

Poppy stared at Katkin, then slowly laid a hand on her arm. "Tristan is dead. So is Maggrai."

Katkin closed her eyes, feeling the bitter heartache of loss once again. "You... killed my son?"

"It was the dress. Your silver dress. I know it sounds impossible, but something lived in it, something that made me do things I wouldn't have done on my own." She peered at Katkin, willing her to believe.

"Did he... Did he suffer?"

Poppy's cheeks colored violently and she swallowed before answering. "I don't think so."

That felt like enough. Katkin sighed and let her shoulders relax, telling herself that even if she had been there, she wouldn't have healed him—not Tristan. Poppy continued to apologize, and Katkin cut her off. "I am not angry with you. It is for the best that he is gone. Now perhaps Yrth will have peace."

Gwillam, who had been sleeping curled up on a pile of skins, asked, "Who is gone?"

Poppy, once she had accepted his joyous greeting, explained.

"So Jakob fell?" he asked sadly, as her story came to an end. "I guess you can't be mad at him any more."

"No. I am not angry with Jakob. But I wish we had spent more time together. I never got a chance to thank him properly for saving my life. He seems to have changed a great deal since he left with Maia."

"So has Lut," said Gwillam, unexpectedly.

"You are right about that, Gwill. Jakob and I saw him in the mirror. He fought our people, and killed some too! He looked really angry, as though they had done him some great wrong. But the Firaithi are not the enemy!" Gwillam gave her an anxious look.

"Are they?" Poppy frowned as an uneasy feeling crept over her. "Why will you not speak?"

Katkin took her hand and stroked it. "Poppy, a very bad thing happened on Asaruthe after we left there. Your Ikora Gwenn and Ikor Kadya..."

She had taken it better than either Katkin or Gwillam expected. The news of her Ikor Kadya's death made her sit back, but she did not cry, not in the crowded stuffy hold of the aermaran. There were too many others there, already upset and weary. Poppy could almost smell the scent of despair that infected them.

"Will you be all right?" Katkin asked, her green eyes warm with worry.

Poppy nodded and squeezed her hand. "Katkin, I... just wanted to say I am sorry for blaming you for everything. I should have opened my eyes and seen the truth long ago. I guess I was just too wrapped up in my own troubles."

Katkin gave her a tired smile. "All of us on Asaruthe were, Poppy." Just then, Myrie glided into view from behind an iron strut.

"Holy Star! What has happened to her?" Poppy gasped.

Myrie stopped right in front of her, and fifty-one mouths smiled. "Welcome back," the voices chorused, and Poppy could only smile and nod in return. "We have need of your skill, my dear. You must show us the way to our destination."

"My... My skill? I don't know anything useful."

From within the cloud of arms, a single hand extended. It held the small leather-bound journal belonging to Josiah Tavish, Captain of the tradeship *Briny Leviathan*.

"None of us speaks the language in which it is written, but you can read this, can you not?" Poppy took the book and opened it. Josiah's crabbed handwriting looked as difficult to decipher as ever.

"I will try," she said, uncertainly. "I have translated some of this already, but it would take a long time to do it all. Can you tell me what am I looking for?"

The faces nodded in unison. "The way to a certain isle, in the far West, over Golden Ocean. The place that Josiah first met a traveler known as Shiqaba."

Poppy sat in the corner, and Gwillam sat beside her with paper and crayon ready to transcribe her words. Myrie hovered over them, her eyes bright with impatient interest. Half an hour passed in silence, while Katkin tended to the survivors, offering them water and ship's biscuit from the hold of the aermaran.

"What about my Harry?" asked one young woman tearfully, as she cradled the sickly child whom Dai had carried from the Infirmarie. "They made him harvest corsfyre, along with five other men. He wasn't at the Infirmarie when you took us. Are we going back for him? We have to!" She dribbled a little water into the child's mouth, and she sputtered weakly. Her body went into spasm, jerking violently, as her mother tried to hold her down. "Help her," she cried to Katkin.

Katkin backed away, shaking her head, unable to face the torture of healing the child.

"Elleranne! Help her!" the woman said again.

Stunned, Katkin stared at her. "What did you call me?"

The child's seizure had ended, but she breathed with difficulty. Katkin, unable to resist the mother's pleas for her dying child, fell to her knees. She placed a hand on the girl's bony chest and closed her eyes. Then she saw a room, shadowed and filthy, with barred and boarded windows. They had tied her hands but not her feet, and she lashed out with her boot as Maggrai approached her. He carried a scalpel and a basin in one hand, and a tiny stuffed doll in the other.

"This is yours, I believe?"

Katkin nodded, trying to reach for the doll. He smiled wickedly. "You would like to have her back?" He waggled the doll before Katkin's face. "Then do not fight me, sniveling brat."

She looked on in terror as the rusty scalpel lowered to just above the throbbing vein in her wrist. Behind her, she heard her mother's voice, hoarse with panic. "No! Please... Not my wee one. Take my blood instead. Take it all, you monster."

Katkin felt the sharp sting of the scalpel as it sliced through her skin and veins. The blood welled up, dark and thick. She screamed at the sight of it—dripping and pooling into the bowl held below her wrist. Katkin sobbed and retched, reaching for the comfort of her doll, as Maggrai tossed it casually on the floor and stepped down hard. The delicate porcelain face crumbled to dust.

"No," she cried. "Let me go!"

At once, she stood amongst the trees, and they whispered to her. She placed her forehead against the bark, feeling the power that pulsed just inside, within the phloem.

"Elleranne..."

"Deres?" she whispered to them. "Deres?" Dizziness overcame her, and she fell in a crumpled heap amongst the gnarled roots.

When she woke, Katkin's heart leapt as she saw Dai's face.

"You are here?"

He nodded and helped her stand, then gestured all around them. "I don't understand it. One moment I was standing on the deck of the aermaran, watching you heal the little girl, and then I saw you fall. When I stepped forward to help you I found myself here."

Katkin touched the tree. The contact of her fingers against the cinnamon colored bark gave her a curious thrill. "They brought you. The Deres. They brought you to Rythis."

"Why?" he whispered.

The answer came from somewhere outside her. "Because of Elleranne and Ben'aryn." Sighing, she took Dai's hand, and strolled with him under the trees. The murmured refrain caressed the breeze. He did not understand her words, but the bittersweet joy of being with her in this place—Rythis, his favorite of all places in the Cosmos—drove all questions from his mind.

She breathed deeply of the air—cool, dry and curiously redolent of nutmeg. "You don't recall bringing me here that first time do you?"

Dai shook his head. "I do not know which of my future selves saved your life that day you fell from the Infirmarie, but I am very glad he did." He brought her hand to his lips and kissed it softly.

She pointed up high to where the trees disappeared into the mist, remembering it all, as if it were a dream. "We flew, like angels. Down through the trees. I thought they looked like the pillars of some giant hall."

Dai closed his eyes and shuddered.

Katkin stopped walking and wrapped her arm across his back. "Oh, love, I am sorry. I never meant..."

His eyes opened, and she saw the anguish there, but still he spoke with pride. "I know you did not. And I gave my wings gladly. I would give much more to make amends for all the grief my folly has brought to Yrth."

She stared at him and said with bitterness, "I was your folly, was I not?"

He smiled at this, and gently wiped her tears away with the edge of his thumb. "Nay, not you. How could I regret the life we spent

195

together? In all my journeys between the stars, I never found anything that moved my heart as you did, love. Never." He drew her into an embrace and they kissed. Then Katkin pulled her mouth from his, and gazed at him, her eyes shining with excitement.

"I can give you back your wings!"

An expression of hope crossed his face before he frowned. "I won't have you suffer more pain on my account. And anyway, I don't need them anymore." He stared into the distance, considering his fate.

She shook his shoulder gently. "How can you say you have no need? You loved to fly, you told me so once, long ago. Please let me help you. The pain would be a pittance to pay for such joy. Together we could explore the silence of the stars..."

"No! You do not understand. We have to return to the aermaran and pass with it to the last Isle."

"Why? Maggrai is no more."

Dai smiled at this, but his eyes did not change. "He is dead in this life, in this turn of the Gyre, but who is to say he will not return? There is only one way to be sure of the future." But what this way would be, Dai did not say.

"Come now!" she chided gently. "Let the future take care of itself. You and I have done our part already. Surely we deserve some reward? Stay here with me."

Katkin wound her arms about his neck and buried her face in his shoulder, tracing her lips across his collarbones and the hollow of his throat. The whispering in the trees subtly increased, captivating Dai, urging him to accept. He stroked his hands across her back, and felt her fingers gently seeking his scars in return.

"Katkin, my love." He could hardly bear to speak, between the whispers and his own desire. "You know I would, if I could. But there is a last task for me, something that I alone may accomplish."

She raised her deep green eyes to meet his, and in them, for the first time, he recognized the forest from which she had sprung. He saw it all—ages and ages of roots, bark and leaves entwining and supporting the Gyre within and without.

Deres... In her eyes.

"Who are you?" he whispered, and the green flickered with sparks of gold and red.

"I am only Katkin. Must I be something more?"

196

"You *are* something more. And you know it. Am I wrong to question you so?"

She laughed at this, and her eyes glowed light green, with insouciant joy. "It doesn't matter, Dai. Our fate remains our fate. But here, amongst the trees, there are other possibilities." She placed her hand on his heart and closed her eyes before he could think to stop her. For a moment, it seemed darkness had shuttered the forest, and then he felt the exuberant growth of new flesh between his shoulder blades, tearing his tattered shirt apart.

Katkin did not flinch or faint. Not this time. But she instinctively understood that there would be no other healing like this—the Deres had given her a gift, free of any pain. *Was it a reward? Another unfathomable part of their all-encompassing design? Or something else again?* Katkin did not know, but the expression on Dai's face as she stroked his newly unfurled wings brought her more bliss than anything she could have imagined.

With an exultant cry, he caught her up and soared into the azure sky.

The aermaran silently parted the clouds, like a frolicking Leviathan of the deep. Gunnar kept his eyes fixed on the forward window. They were well over Golden Ocean now, further west than his people had ever sailed. He did not know what lands, if any, lay before them, but he did not want to risk coming upon some heights unaware. Brightly lit shreds of cloud showed briefly before streaming past the airship and back into the dark of the midnight stars. He studied them in silence, feeling the subtle play of azimity on the meridians of Yrth.

Behind him, Poppy's voice droned on and on, as she translated the journal. "Our fresh water is almost gone. Spivey, Drogue and Pell died yesterday. I've never seen three more pitiful specimens. They had lost their teeth from the scurvy, and could no longer chew ship's biscuit. Didn't take long for them to starve after that."

The remaining Firaithi murmured amongst themselves. "Where are they taking us?" "I'd rather go back to that prison than starve to death in this flying pickle jar!" "I heard one of them say we was headed for Tsmar'enth—the moon gate. They mean to kill us all..."

Gunnar, who stared into the starry void outside with intense concentration, growled, "Keep the passengers quiet!"

Myrie smiled as she glided to the center of the capsule. "Do not concern yourself, my father. We will sing to the anxious ones, and bring peace to their troubled hearts."

"What about Katkin and Dai?" Gwillam asked. "How will they find us in all this darkness?"

Myrie did not seem concerned. "The Irrakai knows the way to the Isle. He will bring Katkin when the time comes."

Then Myrie began to sing. The sweet sound of all her voices, joined in harmony, silenced all further questions and unrest:

> *So willingly did he take flight, beyond*
> *The sacred spires and the naked stone.*
> *Wings of golden gossamer he donned,*
> *And vowed to journey ever on alone.*

Poppy, eager to help her Ikor if she could, continued with her translation, murmuring now in Gunnar's tongue, Dalvolk. "Master Penro equipped the Leviathan well for this journey, and crewed her with the finest darkies. But neither he nor I told them the real reason for this voyage—to find the legendary Western Isles, where the trees are said to be fruitful beyond the measure of any on Yrth."

> *He sought the stars; he set himself apart,*

"The ship drifts due southwest, and the darkies grow ever more fearful. A high wall of cloud before us drove them close to mutiny, and when the streaks of white fire appeared, I gave the order for Fenwick and Drury to break out the small arms. Thus, we compelled them to man the oars, and carry us forward towards the island that First Officer Brett said he saw through the spyglass when we passed this way six years ago."

> *Braved both the zenith and the cold abyss.*

"If this island hath no fresh water or foodstuffs then I believe we will all perish. We are eighty-five days from Scarfinda, and have been becalmed for twenty-three."

> *As seasons passed, no sorrow touched his heart.*
> *He thought to find no greater joy than this.*

"A storm approacheth, of such magnitude that I fear the darkies, as weak as they are, will not be able prevent damage to the sails and rigging. I have ordered them to lie us ahull until it passes."

Until, by chance, he glimpsed a smallish star,
Inconsequential, backward planets, too.
He lingered long, and studied from afar,
A pleasing orb, clad all in cloudy blue,

"The gale hath driven us south, beyond the wall of cloud. Now the sea is still, as still and smooth as green glass. The sky is dark, the stars faint and though the moon was hale when we met the storm, now she is wan—as wan as a sliver. No man hath traveled so far, and though the strongest among us is weak from thirst, we go on hoping the island lies just over the horizon. But the darkies no longer need to pull the oars, nor do winds fill the sails. The *Leviathan* moves of her own volition, carrying us to the furthest shore."

Her solitary moon held close aligned.
As tight as lover's hearts may be entwined.

"We have searched for this Isle on three other voyages, but only now, with this crew, have we come close. Master Penro believes that they have some uncanny ability to cross the spheres into a land where silence reigns. But I don't know how he learned this."

He longed to touch that misty mantled sphere
Whose beauty pierced the crystal span of night

"The white winged creatures that appeared on the deck three days ago must be figments of my fevered mind. No sound of wave or bird. No water. No food. Death stalks us, like a spectre."

And she in turn desired to draw him near,
To join his lissome dance of fearless flight.
Yet beating, beating, beating 'gainst the race,
He fell, and falling stripped his pinions bare.

"The Gods hath given heed to our prayers. For a day and a night, the most gentle of creatures have visited us. Doves, resting upon the yardarms, cooing and calling. Gawain saw much weed floating in the water. Can there be any doubt that the Isle lies just ahead? Bryst is taking soundings every ten leagues. The bottom lies at twenty-five fathoms."

The Yrth was hard; pitiless her embrace,
And wounded now, he lay in deep despair.

"The Isle is paradise. It is lush and bountiful, with trees such as no man or myself hath ever seen with his own eyes. But many of the darkies have disappeared since we came ashore, before I thought to lock them below decks. I do not know if we have enough able seamen remaining to make the long journey back to Scarfinda."

But soon his love had gathered up each pin,
And as she wept, she wove the rainbow shrouds
To soft enfold the broken god within,
And ferry him once more beyond the clouds.

"The new man can speak the language of the darkies, though he is tall and as clean-limbed as a God. They respect and even fear him, and there have been no more desertions since he joined the ship, four days ago. With his help, Gawain took a sighting, and at last found our position with the Ship-Star. He assures me that he can navigate our path homewards."

Now only in her secret dreams he flies,
Circling, always circling, and never more to rise.

The last ringing trebles in her voices faded away as the Firaithi sat spellbound, some with tears flowing. The song of the Dawn-maid had soothed their fears, and many now sought to touch her hands.

Gunnar, whose fierce concentration had made him immune to the power of Myrie's song, asked sharply, "Does he give coordinates?"

Poppy frowned and scanned the remaining entries. "Yes, Ikor. Thirty-nine degrees west by eighteen degrees south. But from the description I would say they must have been somewhere within the Vastness. Will those strange numbers work in the living world?"

He smiled grimly. "That is all I need to know. Even if the Last Isle lies beyond the Vastness, the Ship-Star will guide us. Now let us hope this uncanny craft can get us there without running out of magicks. I would not like to be cast adrift in this ocean of air on which we sail."

Gwillam passed the transcribed journal to Gunnar and then went to stand by Myrie. "What was that song called? It was so beautiful."

Myrie slipped into the language of clicks that he alone could translate. He listened intently and then shook his head, silently, in sorrow.

After a time they returned to the bracken strewn forest floor, and walked again amongst the impossibly tall and slender boles. Katkin asked, "Do you remember your last words to me—before you died? You said that flying was your greatest joy, but that you loved me more."

Dai nodded gravely. "Yes, I do remember, though the memory is a painful one."

Katkin gazed at him unblinkingly. "Huw once told me a story, of an eagle that fell in love with a human girl. The story of Elleranne and Ben'aryn. Your words—they were in the story, just as you said them. How could that be?"

He smiled and shrugged. "Remember the time of the Autochthones is not like ours. The echo of their tales passes backwards and forwards through the Gyre. The story might well have once been true."

She looked askance at this. "But you did not visit a sorcerer named Nys, nor give away half your life force to be made human!"

He came to a halt, beside the hammered grey-green bark of a high rimu. His moonlit eyes peered downwards into hers. "Did I not?"

"N... No. Did you?"

"Yes. Of course, the passage through the Gyre has distorted the tale somewhat but the basic facts remain. I made a sorcerer out of science, and I did lose a great deal of my power when I became human."

"But the story said you were ugly and wracked with pain on

the inside! That Nys made you handsome so that Elleranne would love you. That isn't true..." The deep sadness in his eyes made her pause. "Is it?"

He traced his fingers over the bark. It was long before he spoke again. "I did disguise myself and it did cause me pain. Not physical, of course, but I suffered a great deal of anguish for what I had done to Jacq's mother and to you. I tortured myself with the knowledge that you were meant to marry the son of Shiqaba, and if you had seen my real face, you never would have chosen me."

She placed her hand over his, and felt the green pulse of the tree through his skin. "Is this not your true form that I see now?"

He shook his head sadly.

"Show me, then. I want to know the man I love as he truly is."

His eyes widened. "You won't love me—not if you see the truth. I am not of your kind, Katkin, not a man at all. I never was."

"I don't care. It will not change the way I feel." He sighed and touched her forehead with the tips of his fingers. Katkin felt dizzy for a moment, and closed her eyes. When she opened them again, Dai had disappeared.

And yet not so. The creature that stood before her still retained his grave and noble essence, but not his humanity. The wings remained the same—grey fletched, possessed of magnificent grace and veiled power. But whereas the Dai she knew bore feathers only on those quick and powerful wings, soft bluish-grey down clothed this creature's entire form—solid on his back and barred with white and tan on his chest and groin.

She could not help a sharp intake of breath.

His head was sharply streamlined, with huge wide-set eyes—the sharp, unblinking eyes of a predator. Dai turned his head so that he could see her properly. He ruffled his feathers in agitation as he waited for her to scream, to flee, to give voice to her disgust.

She did none of these things.

Katkin raised her hand and touched his bill. It was decurved, wickedly hooked on the end, blue-grey like his feathers, with a distinctive golden stripe where it met his face. The feeling of her fingertips on the sensitive hide of his maxilla made his eyes half-close, and he shuddered.

"Can you speak?"

His voice echoed in her mind—the same voice, though now

filled with wonder. "Not in this form, no. Why do you not run from me?"

She blinked in surprise. "Why should I? I have seen eagles before."

His eyes crinkled at this, and it almost resembled a smile. He said proudly, "No eagle, me. I based my form on the falcon—a peregrine."

"Oh. I just thought, since the eagles came to our aid in Brunner's Valley..." She stopped and gazed into his dark eye. "You are so very beautiful. Why have you hidden yourself away all this time?"

He shrugged and his feathers fluffed luxuriantly. "I thought you would fear me." She took a step closer, so that the top of her head rested just under the curve of his bill.

"I am not afraid," she whispered, as her fingers stroked the incredibly downy feathers of his breast.

"Katkin..." he began as her hands continued to wander, finding pleasure in the movement of his feathers, the softness of his skin beneath them. "Katkin, don't. There is no future for us—for this."

Her fingers moved to caress the dark feathers on the crown of his head, making him want to cry out with desire. "Why not? May we not have a single moment of happiness? Something to remember, when we travel back into the darkness once more?" She stepped closer, and slowly raised her arms, so that they rested on his sloping shoulders. "Make love to me, Dai."

He couldn't fight her or his hunger any longer. Slowly he lowered his bill, and stroked her cheekbones softly, first one side and then the other. The simple need he made plain brought tears to her eyes.

"Like this?" the voice in her mind asked. "Or would you have me transform back?"

"Just like this."

He threw back his head and gave a piercing cry that echoed through the trees—a falcon calling for his mate. Katkin shed her gown and stepped forward, trembling a little in wonder—and fear. They found a soft place, covered in the greenest grass that she had ever seen and lay upon it. Katkin shivered and moaned as he caressed her throat with his feathers, and flicked his tongue over her breasts. Her hands sought to please him in return, as she explored his body.

When she dared to plunge her fingers into the downy shade

between his legs, his voice whispered, "Do not fear, love. I have not completely given up my human form."

Katkin lay back, and raised her arms to him, saying, "I am ready, Dai. Come to me." The scent of the trees filled her with spicy-sweet desire as Dai buried himself between her thighs. Instinctively, she threw her arms about his neck, and wrapped her legs across his back.

"Hold on to me tightly," his voice cried in her mind. "Don't let go, no matter what."

Then with three powerful beats of his wings, they left the ground, and soared into the sky. Dai's hips thrust in time with his wing beats, and Katkin screamed, half in passion and half in terror. He climbed higher and higher, beyond the towering treetops, his wings never faltering as she dug her nails deeply into his shoulders. With each cycle of his magnificent wings, Katkin felt them enfold her completely. She relaxed into the sweeping flow, while her arms continued to hold him tightly.

The air grew chill, and she never felt it, though it was hard to breathe this close to the firmament. Katkin let her head fall back, and looked over Dai's shoulder at the stars that hung like white jewels before her eyes.

His voice spoke again in her mind, strong and quiet, as he stayed perfectly still within her. "Do you remember the dream I once spoke of, my love? How you and I flew up and watched all the stars fall?"

"Yes, of course." He cast her mind back to the night she first heard Jacq speak of his dreams of flying—and how he feared them. "You said it was the end of the world."

"And so it will be—for us." He spoke now in his own tongue, slowly and sadly. "*Passeme nalaneralans sang rure truirn. Deres. Deres. Palos candicat sanien, iraos karimad tellubys ad anhanir. Geanfe iraos Dai.*"

"What do those beautiful words mean? You said them in your sleep the night you told me of the dream."

"I said this prayer: 'Would that I could stay here with you always, love. Here amongst the silent stars, with our bodies entwined. Soon, so soon, we must part, before your strength is gone. And the trees await our presence.'" He tightened his arms about her and said, "But before we depart this place forever, I wish you to feel the enchantment of the Irrakai when he flies."

She buried her head on his downy breast and nodded in reply. He reached the zenith of his long climb, and they hung, suspended in space, for one heart-stopping moment. As a climax swept through her, Katkin's legs tightened convulsively, burying him deeply in her body. With a scream of pure delight, Dai swept his wings back and dived down, down towards the trees.

The speed with which they plummeted, the shrill rushing of the wind, Dai's high-pitched cries of ecstasy, all gave Katkin the eerie sense of standing still as the world exploded up and around her. She closed her eyes tightly, letting the passion of this wild freedom take her to places she could never have imagined.

It seemed it would last forever, and yet the knowledge that they soon must part became a weight that dragged them relentlessly towards the surface of Rythis. They fell and fell together, tumbling across the azure. From some untouched place within her, Katkin thought that surely Dai meant to kill them both—to dash them mercilessly against the hard cold ground. But she felt no fear at this, none at all.

At the last possible second, he threw his wings wide and braked. The resulting change in momentum tried to tear Katkin from his grasp, nevertheless his strong arms kept her close to his breast. Within a few seconds they lay on the ground again, in the lush grass, with his wing folded about her.

Neither said anything for a long time. Dai brushed her face sadly with the sides of his beak, and blinked his wide eyes, trying to burn her features into his mind. Katkin stroked his trembling wings, and sighed.

All around her, the trees murmured, *Elleranne, you must leave us now. Elleranne...*

The scent of the forest turned unpleasantly metallic, like rust, and a cold wind stirred the branches over their heads. A shower of dead leaves spiraled down, brushing her naked skin with stiff, dry fingers.

"What do the trees whisper?" Dai asked Katkin. "I do not understand their words, but it seems to me they sing of loneliness and regret."

"They say I have to leave here," Katkin whispered sadly. "This world is no sanctuary for us."

"It is so," he agreed. "Come, the last battle is at hand."

Seventeen

Larch

Gunnar rubbed his eyes wearily with his hand, keeping the other attached to the wheel. Exhaustion made his good leg tremble, and put a new ache in his stump. Helming this unfamiliar vessel through the strange ocean of the sky had drawn on all his skill as a mariner.

The journey to the island had been smooth for the last two days. The passengers had dozed, too ill and malnourished to take much interest in their surroundings, with the exception of those whom Gunnar had called to watch for obstacles through the forward porthole. Poppy and Gwillam had taken their turns too. Myriadne stayed with the remaining Firaithi, soothing their fears and their children, and telling them of the beauties of their new home beyond the sea.

The airship pitched and rolled as the first crosswinds from an oncoming storm reached her. The solid wall of cloud that shone darkly in the morning sun filled the forward view of the airship.

"Come now, *Wind Beast*," Gunnar muttered, using the name he had given Maggrai's craft. "Do not fight me. We must work together to save these good folk."

Gwillam came to stand beside him. "May I help, Ikor? Why don't you let me steer for a while, while you get some rest? You have been standing here all night."

Gunnar patted his head. "Nay, lad. I had best be at the helm when we pass through yon storm. Anyway, *Wind Beast* and I have come to an understanding, have we not, old girl?" He patted the throttle as Gwillam smiled and shook his head. "Why not see if your sister needs help with the feeding of the passengers? I saw her brewing cold tea not long ago. You could bring me a cup too, if you don't mind."

Gwillam nodded and hurried aft, to where Poppy stood, doling out the last of the ship's biscuit to the hungry Firaithi. The passengers muttered amongst themselves as the ship continued to roll like a colicky horse. Several of the younger children vomited, and the sour smell filled the cramped and stuffy hold.

"When is Katkin coming back? I wish she could fix those babies who are sick."

"I don't know," said Poppy crossly. "Help me serve these cups of tea. She disappeared with that man they called the Glint after she healed the little girl. Myrie says we are not to worry about them."

"Does... Does Myrie know about Ikora Gwenn yet?"

Poppy shrugged. "Katkin told her before she went away. She didn't seem too upset."

Gwillam watched the cloud of arms and legs as it moved through the cabin trying to calm the unhappy Firaithi. "Myrie is many people now. The only one who would care is lost among them all."

Poppy gazed at her brother, surprised at his perceptiveness. "Do you really think so?"

He nodded. "She has imprisoned herself within the others. She gave her life for them." Gwillam sighed. "I miss her so much, but I don't think she will ever be as she was."

"But at least she can talk now. Don't you think she is happier because of it?"

He didn't answer, for at that moment the airship gave a metallic squeal of protest as the struts twisted in a vicious crosswind. As the airship entered the stormy skies east of the last Isle, Poppy listened fearfully to the scrape and squeak of the huge gas bladders. The capsule grew dim. Lightning flashed against the portholes, giving the pale faces of those inside an eerie glow.

Gunnar remained at the helm, unyielding, and fought to keep *Wind Beast* level and on course. He shouted, "Hold fast, everyone!" just as an earsplitting peal of thunder shook the ship from stem to stern.

The terrified passengers clutched at each other and anything else they could find, as a nightmare of darkness and howling wind enveloped the ship. Poppy clung to a pillar as the ship dove straight down like a hawk in pursuit of its prey. She watched helplessly as her brother rolled along the steeply sloping deck and fetched up in the lap of a Firaithi Kymatre.

The storm raged around *Wind Beast*, lighting the tracery of iron with Deathfire. A ball of glowing lightning blew in a window, showering the floor with shards of crystal. It shot about the inside of the cabin before dissipating with a distinct popping sound. Nevertheless, the band of clouds was a narrow one, and in fifteen minutes, no more, they had come through to the other side. Now the sky above them looked flat and white, the sea below as still and green as glass.

Gwillam, with many embarrassed apologies, extricated himself from the old lady's grasp. "We made it!" he crowed to Gunnar. "You steered us through the storm, Ikor."

But Gunnar looked through the window, frowning. "We are losing altitude. The storm must have holed one of the gas bags. And I still don't see the island." He spoke with determination. "Open the hatch and throw out everything we have no need for. We must lessen *Wind Beast's* burden as much as we are able."

Poppy dragged herself upright and struggled with the door. Gwillam helped her unlatch the bar. The door fell open, letting in a freezing blast of air. Between them Poppy and Gwillam dragged a heavy box of ammunition and dropped it into the green waters far below.

"Help us!" Poppy cried to the Firaithi, who still seemed pinned to the floor in terror. Several of the younger women struggled forward, as the airship continued to glide downwards. They threw empty biscuit and water barrels out the hatch.

The descent leveled slightly. Myrie pushed through the crowd. "Let us through. We will fly forward, on Lalluna's wings, and look for the island."

A moment of tense silence passed as she floated through the door and disappeared. Gunnar worked hard to stop *Wind Beast* from heeling over as the pressure in the breached bag dropped further. Poppy and Gwillam continued to remove and throw out anything not fixed in place.

Gwillam moved down the sloping deck, to where the corsfyre gun lay. "You don't want me to dump this too, do you? We might need it when we get to the island."

Gunnar frowned. "That weapon will be of no use to us under the waves, lad." He passed over an iron wrench, left behind by the aermaran's former owners. "Loosen the bolts and let it fall."

Gwillam sighed and went to work on the fastenings.

Just then, Myrie returned, smiling triumphantly. "The island is less than three leagues hence," several voices announced.

"How can that be?" Gunnar growled. "It would be well before the horizon. I should be able to see it from here."

Much laughter ensued from Myrie. "Do you doubt us? It is shrouded in mist, Mariner."

Gunnar squinted towards the window and scratched his head. "I pray you are right. I don't think *Wind Beast* would make much of a sailing ship, and she may become one if we do not strike land soon."

"We will not need to float. The island lies just ahead. There is a high cliff on the side that we approach, but the top will make a fine landing site."

Excited cries from the Firaithi who clustered by the forward hatch put proof to Myrie's words. The mists parted to reveal a rugged isle, the outlier of an archipelago stretching into the unexplored distance. Gunnar slid the throttles to full stop, and the propeller slowly reduced its revolutions. But *Wind Beast* continued to barrel forward, carried on the momentum generated by the storm.

"Ikor! We are not stopping. Where are the anchors?" Poppy cried.

He waved distractedly at her to be quiet as the airship, still rapidly losing altitude, approached the cliffs. It was impossible to tell if the vessel's cabin would clear the edge, but it looked to be close. "Everyone get back to the stern!" Gunnar ordered.

Poppy, Gwillam and the rest of the Firaithi scrambled up the sloping deck to the rear of the capsule, and hung on. The weight shift raised the front of the cabin slightly, leaving it just above the cliff side. A few seconds later the bottom caught on the rocky brow of the cliff, flinging everyone to the deck. The shrieks of the terrified passengers mingled with the scream of tortured metal as the airship broke apart.

Their forward progress came to a halt. Many of the passengers looked dazed—and some were injured, but none severely. Gunnar dragged himself from beneath the wreckage, and wiped a trickle of blood from his lip. His crutches were still inside the twisted hull of the cabin. He sighed as he surveyed the remains. "Farewell, *Wind Beast*," he muttered. "You were a fine craft."

Gwillam hurried over, bearing a single crutch. "Sorry, Ikor. The other is broken."

"Never mind, lad. I can manage with one." Gunnar stood, with Gwillam's help, and wedged the crutch under one arm. "Are Poppy and Myrie all right?"

Gwillam nodded. "What should we do?"

"I am only the navigator. My job is finished now. You should find the Dawnmaid and ask her."

He hobbled over to lend his strength to the rescue of those still trapped inside. After throwing several huge pieces of twisted metal aside, he left Poppy and the others to crawl into the remains of the cabin. On the far side of the airship, Gunnar gazed into the distance, wondering about this strange land they had come to.

Not far from their landing place, many magnificent trees stood in a rough semi-circle. Swirling hues shaded the lower trunks, while the upper branches were pure white and shapely in their nakedness. The massive green crowns looked to be a thousand feet or more above his head. An opaque whiteness filled the space between them, making it almost impossible to see the trees on the far side of the circle. Gunnar thought it uncanny, since the tree's habit seemed open enough to let in plenty of light.

They were taller and more beautiful than any trees he had ever seen, or even imagined seeing in his dreams, and yet he felt somehow oppressed by their presence.

"That is Deres Tama," said Myrie, who had appeared at his side, with the whisper of many moving limbs. "The fastness of the Trees."

"How do the Firaithi fare?" Gunnar asked wearily, wishing he were back on Asaruthe and away from the mysterious threat of those trees.

Myrie's voices called back over her shoulder, as she approached the grove. "Katkin is with them. She has healed the hurts of most already."

Cries of recognition and consternation came from the distance. Another group of Firaithi hurried towards Gunnar, well away from the shadow of the towering trees. He recognized Huw, and the girl he had known as Rab, but not the strikingly beautiful woman who walked between them.

Huw hurried up, out of breath, and embraced him. "Are you alright?"

Gunnar didn't answer, only stared pointedly at Maia, who dropped her eyes. "Is Jakob with you?" she mumbled to her boot tops.

"Nay, he fell from the aermaran, trying to save Poppy. You'll not see him again in this life." Maia's head drooped and she turned away from Gunnar without speaking further. She walked rapidly back along the path to Mornguard and did not look back.

Huw twisted his braids nervously, and exposed a bright red feather. "I am sorry for what happened," he said softly. "Though I suppose it makes no difference to you."

He shrugged and said enigmatically, "The blame lies between me and the Skald. Apologies will not change anything."

Huw looked ready to argue, until the woman at his side cleared her throat impatiently. "This is my wife, Cara," he said quickly.

Gunnar raised an eyebrow at this, but made no comment. As the silence became brittle, Huw said, with forced cheerfulness, "We have plenty of room at Mornguard for the newcomers. Cara and I will see that they are made comfortable."

"That is well," said Gunnar, with a fierce twinkle in his blue eyes. "Katkin is with them now. Why don't you see if she needs any help?"

Huw stared towards the wreckage as his wife's expression turned to a pout. "We should go back and make preparations. Shiqaba can lead the others there when they are ready."

Cara walked away without speaking further. Huw would have followed, but Gunnar caught his arm. "You will have to face her eventually. Better to be a man, and do it sooner. She deserves that much from you."

"I... I know. And I will, I swear it, but now is not the right time." He pulled his arm from Gunnar's grasp and ran to catch Cara and Maia.

Poppy saw Jakob first, standing alone under the shade of the gigantic eucalypts. She ran to him, leaving Gunnar in her wake, and threw her arms about his neck. "You are alright! I knew you would be. I just knew it!"

Jakob pulled her close, happy that she had put their enmity aside. Gunnar limped up next to them and patted his shoulder. "Well done, lad," he offered quietly. "I thought I had lost you, as well. But how did you escape? Poppy said she saw you fall."

"I did. But a tree caught me." He grinned sheepishly at their surprised expressions. "I know how it sounds, but it really did seem as though the branches just reached out and held on to me. Once I stopped falling, I gap shifted. Eventually I found my way here."

Katkin stood as far away from the trees as she could, watching the reunion and waiting, but for what she had no clue. The air felt humid and somehow edgy. "What is going to happen?" she asked Dai.

"There are many coming. I feel the disturbance in the spheres. But why the Deres have called us all here is a mystery to me." He sighed and looked to the west, towards Mornguard. "At least the Autochthones are well out of it. They have suffered enough." After Katkin healed the last of their wounds, Shiqaba and the Dawnmaid had taken the dazed Firaithi across the cliff tops to the ancient haven of the Kindred of Anjali, the offered ones.

"Those are the Deres?" Katkin asked, pointing to the tall eucalypts. "I thought they existed only on Rythis. That is where I last heard their voices." But even as she said this, she heard the whispering of leaves in her mind and shivered. "I don't like this place. There has been sorrow here—great sorrow and anger too. The trees speak of it. They want something from us, some payment in return. Do you know what it might be?"

Dai stared towards the center of the grove but did not answer her question.

Fyn and Lut were the first to arrive. Lut gave a cry of rage when he saw Jakob, still with his arm about Poppy's waist. "Get your murdering hands away from her!" He strode forward, with his sword drawn. Gunnar tried to block his progress, but Fyn pulled him aside.

"Let them be, cousin. They have business that needs tending."

Poppy stood between Lut and Jakob, with her hands on her hips. "Leave him alone! He saved my life, Lut. You must forgive him."

Jakob gently moved her out of the way, saying, "Thank you, Poppy, but I can speak for myself." As soon as he had a clear path, Lut slammed his fist straight into Jakob's abdomen. His twin doubled over and fell, then lay on the ground, groaning.

"Lut. Listen to me. I am truly, truly sorry about what happened to Ma. That is all I can say. Please can you not..."

Lut waded forward, gave him a bone-shattering kick in the ribs and then stomped hard on his unprotected neck. "Sorry isn't enough, Jakob."

"Fight back, Jakob," Poppy cried. "Use your strength to defend yourself. Please..."

Another brutal kick from Lut broke Jakob's nose, and it exploded in a shower of blood.

Gunnar decided that this one-sided fight had gone on more than long enough. He carefully disentangled himself from Fyn's grasp, though his increasing rage made it hard for him not to injure his cousin.

"That's enough, Lut," he roared. Lut continued to kick Jakob, who seemed unable or unwilling to put up any defense.

Gunnar was very surprised when Lut raised Ancarnen and pointed the tip at his throat. "Stay out of this, Dad," he growled in a voice very like Gunnar's own. "I am sorry, but Jakob must be punished for Ma's death. You wouldn't do it, so I will." His foot swung forward again.

With a scream of rage, Poppy launched herself at Lut, and knocked him off-balance. He struck her cheek as he shoved her aside, and Gunnar moved in, grasping Lut's wrist. With a quick twist that made Lut yelp with pain, he disarmed him. "Fyn!" Lut cried in dismay. "Help me..."

But Fyn's attention was elsewhere. "Well, well," he said, quietly. "What have we here?" He drew his sword with a flourish as Dai and Katkin hurried forward, intent on helping Gunnar with Lut. "Lord and Lady Turncoat have decided to join the party."

Katkin ignored this provocation and went straight over to Jakob, who lay moaning weakly with Poppy at his side. Gunnar had Lut backed against the tree, with Ancarnen at his throat. Dai and Fyn stood face to face.

Fyn's eyes lit with a cold blue fury. "Retribution will be mine at last. I give my oath before all present that I shall not rest until I see you fall, Irrakai."

"Don't be a fool! How long will it be before we are under attack? We can fight each other some other time." Dai stepped backwards, but Fyn followed, right in his face.

"That is a pity," he spat, and swung his weapon in a vicious arc. Dai flew upwards to avoid losing his head. "I want to fight *right now*. Once I am done with you then I can finish what I began with that murdering whore, Katrione."

"The hell you will," Dai muttered, and drew his own sword.

"Belay this madness, cousin," Gunnar cried, but he could not intervene without leaving Lut, who stood ready to attack Jakob again.

Katkin screamed as the two Amaranthine crossed swords with a crash of tempered metal. "Use your wings, Dai! You don't have to fight him. It doesn't matter."

"Yes, Dai," Fyn said mockingly. "Why don't you fly from me, you craven piece of shite?"

"I won't let you hurt her. She has done nothing to deserve your wrath. Save it for me, you hotheaded halfwit." A bloody slash appeared on Dai's upper arm, as Fyn answered this insult with his sword.

The contest continued. Katkin closed her eyes to block the terrible sight of her two lovers fighting one another, and tried to bend all her thoughts to healing Jakob.

Dai cried out in pain as a shallow thrust of Fyn's sword pierced his shoulder, but he did not return the blow. Instead, he let his wings take him just outside Fyn's range, then hissed, "Lalluna died of the Bludseth, you idiot! Katkin saved her anafireon from Maggrai's minions."

Fyn swung his blade again. "Liar!"

"Cousin! Listen to me!" Gunnar roared. "Look up, man. Look up!"

Fyn ignored him, thinking that Gunnar must be a fool if he believed that he would fall for such an infantile ruse.

A second later, he narrowly missed being burned alive. Dai, seeing his peril, snatched him up and away. A fiery downpour announced the arrival of the Angellus. The wingless stave-like creatures arced in tight formation and came back around for another attack.

Katkin screamed a warning but did not leave Jakob's side. Keeping her hand on his chest, she tried desperately to focus her healing power on him.

"Come on, Katkin. Please don't let him die..." begged Poppy, as she fought to keep Jakob still. He thrashed from side to side, his lungs fighting to get enough air through his crushed windpipe.

The Angellus emitted high-pitched whistling clicks as they blasted the ground outside Deres Tama with searing bolts of red lightning. Anything it touched burst instantly into flame.

Fyn struggled wildly as Dai held him above the fray. "Put me down, you misbegotten moth! I don't want your help. The Angellus and I are old friends. I know how to fight them."

"How?" Dai demanded.

"Nothing slows them for long, but they fear the trees. If we stand beneath their canopy and wait, the Angellus will come close, but they will not attack us."

Dai flew to the grove of eucalypts and set Fyn beneath them. Gunnar released Lut and handed him Ancarnen, saying, "Use this only on our enemies, lad. If you go after Jakob again, I will kill you myself." He glared at Lut, who paled. "Do I make myself clear? No more revenge. It won't bring your mother back."

Lut swallowed and nodded. "Yes, Dad, I understand."

Dai and Fyn stood side by side. Out of the corner of his mouth, Fyn said, "Wait until they come down. You will see the fire dim as they get close to the ground. That is the moment to attack. Strike hard with your sword and you can cut one or two of them in half before the rest scatter."

Dai smiled grimly. "You attack from below. I will be waiting above. If we cooperate, perhaps we can kill more than one or two. Agreed?"

Fyn glanced at him, opened his mouth to argue, and then merely shrugged. "As you wish. But remember, when they are flying they can use the fire. You will not be able to avoid it for long."

A wave of thirty black branches dropped from the sky, firing pulses of red light. Nevertheless, as Fyn predicted, they would not enter the space under the trees. When the Angellus came to rest close to the ground, Fyn leapt forth and cleaved two neatly in half with his sword. Lut tried to do the same, but cursed in frustration as his weapon cut thin air.

"You have to move quicker than that, lad," Fyn cried, as he strode right to the edge of the tree canopy, risking another fiery assault. He managed to destroy one more before the Angellus rose again, clicking frantically. Dai dove amongst them, chopping and slashing. A rain of black splinters fell as Fyn hurried back under the deep shade of the branches.

Dai joined him. "Will they attack again?"

Fyn nodded grimly. "They never stop attacking. Eventually we will have to retreat, and then they will destroy everything in their path. Our only hope is to gap shift and lead them away from Mornguard, so that we can save the Firaithi."

Forty more Angellus had replaced the ten that Dai and Fyn slew between them. They hovered out of range, with implacable menace, waiting for the Amaranthine to move away from the shelter of Deres Tama.

They unsheathed their swords, and stood side by side. Despite the overwhelming odds, Fyn's expression turned to one of wry amusement. "Eydis told me this would happen, long ago. She said you and I would draw swords together before this turn of the Gyre had ended. I did not believe her."

Dai smiled and shook his head. "I would not have believed her either. You and I have been enemies through every gyretime."

"Mayhap it is time to change that," said Fyn thoughtfully. "If it is true what you said of Lalluna."

"Mayhap," agreed Dai. "Doubtless many things will come to an end before the battle is won."

Katkin could feel Jakob's strength ebbing away under her hand. With a cry of frustration, she sat back on her heels. "I am sorry, Poppy. There is nothing I can do for him."

Poppy burst into tears. "Please try again, Katkin. Please... We can't let him die. He risked his life for me."

The Angellus dove towards the shelter of the trees, and Fyn strode to meet them. Dai took wing, and between them they managed to slay a few more and drive the attackers back. But the Angellus continued to appear in the sky in vast numbers. A hundred or more new ones dropped with a whistling rush of displaced air, and began to click tauntingly, just out of reach. The singed grass and shrubs filled the air with thick, choking smoke.

Lut, in overzealous pursuit of one of the stragglers, strayed from underneath the shelter of the trees. A bolt of red lightning went wide as Dai caught the firing Angellus in mid-air. A second searing wave of fire engulfed his wing and he tumbled downwards, just as Fyn dragged Lut back under the safety of the leaves.

Katkin did not see Dai fall. She had her eyes tightly closed, in one last desperate attempt to save Jakob's life, and sought to connect to the strength of the Deres. She found it, unexpectedly, beneath her knees. The power welled from within the dark soil, coming from the roots of the eucalypts. As the pain from Jakob's wounds tore through her, Katkin screamed and collapsed forward over his prone form. But within seconds, the bluish tinge left his face, and he stirred.

Dai hit the ground hard as five Angellus hovered above him, their fire at the ready. With a fearsome war cry, Fyn exploded from beneath the tree, and attacked, trying to disperse them before they could strike.

"Move, Irrakai! I have your back."

As Fyn fought to cover his retreat, Dai crawled painfully towards the circle of trees, his left arm and wing blackened and smoking. Gunnar limped forward to help him, but Jakob beat him to it. He picked up Dai easily and threw him across his shoulder, then ran back towards his father.

"Lut!" he called. "Use Ancarnen. Help Fyn get away from them."

Lut looked on in horror as a fresh influx of Angellus drove his uncle further into the open. Fyn whirled this way and that, trying to avoid their fiery exhaust. His boot caught on a rock half-buried in sand. With a cry of pain, he sprawled forward, just as a deadly blast of flame turned the ground beneath him into an inferno.

Eighteen

Fir

Fyn disappeared. The Angellus continued to drop from the sky, in ever-increasing numbers. There might have been a thousand circling overhead, but as long as Dai and the others remained beneath the trees, they were safe enough.

Dai said to Poppy, "Do not step out of the circle of trees. There is nothing to do but wait until the rest join us. Perhaps they can help fight these cursed creatures, if they are not ambushed first."

Poppy paused her restless pacing. "Where is Gwillam?"

"He went with the Dawnmaid," Gunnar answered her, without taking his eyes away from Lut. He had resumed his watchful stance between his two sons. "To Mornguard. He is no doubt better off there than here with us. I think the Firaithi village will be a safe haven, until all else fails."

But even as he said this, Poppy cried, "Look, Ikor! Myrie is coming now." She pointed to the southwest, beyond a line of low sand dunes. Myrie, using Lalluna's wings, fluttered towards the cloud of angry Angellus. They left their circling and wheeled in perfect formation.

"She will be killed," Lut shouted to his father. "Let me go. I have to help her." Gunnar nodded and stepped out of his way. Lut, followed closely by Jakob, tore out from under the trees, whooping and shouting, trying to attract attention away from Myrie. They were partially successful. Some of the Angellus sheared off and came after them, dropping pulse after pulse of the deadly red light. Jakob and Lut were forced to abandon their rescue and retreat back to the refuge of the trees.

Dai and the others watched as Myrie fearlessly approached the attacking Angellus. Surprisingly, when she reached their airborne column, it parted so that she could fly through, and then reformed behind her. When she same to rest on the sandy greensward to the east of the trees the Angellus continued to circle above, but made no move to fire upon her.

An out of breath Gwillam joined the others under the tree. "Did you see that, Poppy? They fear her! The Angellus will not attack."

Poppy shook her head. "But they certainly don't fear you, Gwillam Brunner! What were you thinking running into the open like that?"

He shrugged. "I heard Myrie tell Shiqaba that she wanted to talk to the Angellus. I had to come with her."

"To talk to them?" repeated Poppy in surprise. "How does she think she can do that? They don't even have mouths!"

Myrie raised her many hands and clapped them together, in a pattern that sounded something like the clicking language she used to speak with Gwillam. Above her head, the Angellus slowed their frantic circling, and then came to a stop. They hung in the sky like dormant saplings, waiting for the warm breath of spring.

Katkin stirred and stretched, then sat upright with her back against the tree. Dai walked over, cradling his burned arm, and squatted by her side. Her eyes filled with tears as she saw the ravaged remains of his wing. The choking stench of burned feathers filled the air between them. She struggled to her knees before him and raised her hand.

He took it and placed it to his lips. "Not this time. You would sleep again, and very soon there may be those who need your touch more than I." He pointed to the smoking field, where Myrie still stood alone, below the Angellus. "They respect the Dawnmaid, but for how long?'

Dai's face was a study in pain, and more than anything Katkin wanted to free him of it. "But Dai, your wing..."

"No! I don't need my wings anymore. If we prevail this time, I know in my heart it will not be through battle."

Katkin gazed across the field as, one by one, the others appeared. Shiqaba came first, with Eydis by his side. Then Hana and Eira, with Geya between them. They held her hands tightly. Behind them glided a whole host of unfamiliar creatures. Some were almost transparent, wavering like naked flame. Some were like strange beasts with horned brows, others like fantastical plumed birds. They stood, waiting, watching as the Angellus began to circle like vultures overhead.

A vibration thrummed through the air as the black stick figures turned in formation and dove downwards. Already their fires were bright with the spark of their rage. The Amaranthine drew their weapons, and stood grim-faced and silent.

Myrie threw up her many hands and cried, "Stop!" with a host of voices.

She began a series of rapid clicks that caused the Angellus to wheel about and come to rest on the ground. One black figure, taller than the rest, moved to the fore. Though it looked as featureless as the rest, it bore a talisman—a single green leaf, carved from some emerald-hued adamant. It clicked questioningly to Myriadne, and she tried several other sounds in response, in a chorus of lilting voices. An edgy silence followed, as each side struggled to understand the other, but the fires of the Angellus remained dimmed.

"What is she saying?" Katkin whispered to Gwillam.

"Myrie is asking them what they have to gain by attacking us. But I don't understand their leader's response, and neither, I think, does she."

The Angellus with the talisman continued to click in a persistent drumming rhythm.

"Click, click," she hazarded in return, but her reply did not seem to move the tall Angellus.

With a clack of something very like disgust, he turned from her, and his fire grew bright once more. The Angellus rose smoothly into the air, and made ready to attack.

Gwillam watched in dismay. Suddenly he called, "Myrie! Speak to them again. Just you alone, this time. Not the multitude. Find yourself."

The blurred features struggled with this, mightily, as the first bolts of fire rained on the Amaranthine. They huddled beside Myrie and beneath the Deres, but the Angellus seemed to have lost all hesitancy. Several delicate deer-like creatures were consumed in flame, while Myrie tried to disentangle her singular persona from all those that inhabited her form.

Shiqaba charged forward to protect the remaining Amaranthine, his two-handed sword held before him. The leader of the Angellus swooped low and sent three red pulses his way. Eydis screamed in horror as Shiqaba burst into a sheet of brilliant yellow flame. He staggered forward and then fell face down into the molten pool of metal left by his weapon. A fourth pulse made sure nothing remained of either.

Finally, Myrie's face resolved into a single visage, and her blue eyes shone fierce and bright. She clicked now in a solo voice. With a deeply authoritative tone she commanded the Angellus to cease firing and come to rest.

They obeyed at once. The leader moved to the front and waited.

Myrie spoke again, and this time it answered quietly. They held a rapid conversation. Gwillam listened, but the clicks were too fast for him to comprehend. He turned to Katkin in dismay.

"I hope she can reason with them. They seem not to like what she is saying." Indeed the Angellus were stirring with something like anger, and their fires grew bright.

Katkin, who had remained within Deres Tama during the last skirmish, now ran forward until she stood at Myrie's side.

"Why are you doing this?" she cried. "You saved my life. You even gave me back my arm! Why are you destroying these good souls? They have done you no harm."

She held her breath as the tallest Angellus approached her, clicking questioningly. The glowing green spot that danced from side to side on its black bark-like hide seemed to focus on her face. A thin branch swung from the main stem and extended towards Katkin.

She stiffened, but did not flee. It touched her forehead and she felt a tingling burst of energy, like a bolt of static electricity.

Nothing moved for a long moment of silence. Then the branches of the eucalypts stirred, though no one felt a breeze.

"Emma na Deres," said the leader of the Angellus slowly and reverently. "Elleranne. We salute you." With these words, it bowed, into a U shape. The other Angellus followed.

"What are they doing?" she hissed to Myrie. "How do they now know our tongue?"

"They took the words from your mind. Now, at last, we understand."

"I don't," answered Katkin flatly, and Myrie smiled.

"Speak, friends," she told the Angellus as they straightened themselves. "Tell us what you sought to protect, here in the Vastness." The Amaranthine murmured aloud at this, and several drew weapons.

"Foolish child! Do you not see that they are evil?" Geya cried. "They are no one's friend but Maggrai. We should destroy them utterly."

Eydis cuffed her.

Slowly Myrie seemed to shrink. Sighing tiredly, she sat on the sandy ground, and Katkin sank beside her. Dai crawled over and took her hand. Gwillam joined them and placed his arm across Myrie's back. Gunnar maintained his watchful position close by, with Ancarnen at the ready, lest Lut should try to undo Katkin's healing of his brother.

"My name is Bastet," it said. "The first leaf-holder of *Na*-Inais. Who speaks for the Fenacrist?"*

"You do not call yourselves Angellus?" Dai asked.

"Kek!" said Bastet, forgetting itself for a moment. "It called us so—the one of your kind who closed the portal and trapped the Sutun-*Na*. *Na*-Inais, the guardians, sought to free them. That is why we fought."

"What... What are Sutun-*Na*?" asked Katkin.

"The Uri'el," said Myrie, with certainty. "That is their name for them."

"So you thought that we were allied with Maggrai? Is that why you fought us through every turn of the Gyre?" asked Katkin.

Bastet agreed. "It is so. But what were *Na* to believe, when your

_____
* The living ones.

221

kind destroyed so many of the *Na*-Inais, Elleranne? *Na* consulted the leaves, and they said *Na* must protect the Sutun until the Vortice could be opened once more."

Dai shook his head. "If only we had known the truth. So much death could have been avoided."

Now Bastet posed a question of its own. "Why did you steal the anafireon from your own kind? Many Sutun were deeply distressed, for they could not protect their charges."

Katkin grimaced at this irony. "They who harvested the corsfyre were the slaves of the tyrant, Maggrai. They had no choice but to carry out his evil wishes." Her voice grew strong with new hope. "But now he is dead and can harm no one. There will be no more war—no more destruction."

There were many excited clicks from the ranks of the *Na*-Inais who clustered behind Bastet. Their leader asked slowly, "Who took its life?"

Poppy stepped forward. "I did." Her voice trembled a little in fear. Bastet glided towards her until it stood very close.

It said, "Did you make use of Tanithi-*ka*, Azothe? The silver serpent?"

Poppy nodded, but she felt discomfited by the name it called her. The glowing green eye brightened. "You have done all we hoped," Bastet continued, in a low voice. "Elleranne chose her daughters well."

"It was not me at all. A spirit named Azothe haunted the dress. From whence did it come?"

Bastet gave something like a shrug. "Tanith, the silver serpent, is the servant of the trees. It dwelt in the garment the Deres gave to *Na*. And *Na* dressed your mother in it, rather than the bloodied rags she wore."

Just then, Eydis, looking old and frail, shuffled forward into the circle with Eira at her side. Dai rose and supported her arm as she spoke in a quavering voice.

"Hear me! I speak for all Amaranthine when I say we are humbled and ashamed to find we have waged war against those who were not our true enemies. Such folly has a high price, and many on both sides have given their lives." Eydis closed her eyes briefly, remembering her brother's fiery death. "We beg for their forgiveness and understanding, and seek to make amends."

Bastet said, "*Na* also regret."

Eira asked, "How may *Na*-Inais and Sutun-*Na* return to their own proper time and place?"

"*Na* were able to make our way down the Vortice from above, but the way back is impassable. Thus have *Na* been trapped here in the Gyre for many turns."

Poppy tried to understand. "Maggrai closed the Vortice so that he could keep the anafireon here—within the Gyre?"

Katkin answered. "That is what he told Gwenn, long ago. He wanted the corsfyre to power his kingdom. But after he blocked the passage, his slaves began dying of a terrible disease—the Bludseth. He came to the past himself to seek a cure, and then became trapped, for he did not have enough power to return."

"And *Na*-Inais came through the Vortice, to protect Sutun-*Na*—the Uriël?"

Myrie smiled encouragingly. "That is right, Poppy."

"But what will Sutun-*Na* do with the astaren if the Vortice is opened again? Where will they go?" Everyone looked expectantly at Bastet.

"Beyond the Gyre," it answered softly. "Into the Nowhen."

Poppy seemed dissatisfied with this explanation. "Don't they ever return to life again?"

"Anafireon is always conserved. Moving between states of Radiance and Shadow. Radiance exists in the Gyre, formed of the Fenacrist. The Nowhen holds the Shadow anafireon. And Sutun-*Na* are the bridge between."

"Then why can we not remember our former lives? We must have many of them," Poppy asked.

Bastet looked towards Katkin. "There are some here who are able. They possess anafireon with great integrity. But most often when anafireon disperses into the Shadow it combines with that of many equally weak astaren. Perhaps a memory or two may remain, like bubbles in a clear mixture."

Now the green light focused piercingly on Dai. "Are you the Fenacrist known as Irrakai?"

Dai nodded.

"*Na* have seen another. We met it far from here, in a different place. It gave us some words to bring to you."

Though the others spoke in shocked whispers, Dai did not look at all surprised at this. "What is the message you bear?"

223

"It said to tell you that the end is the beginning of all."

Katkin whispered, "What does that mean? Do you understand it, Dai?"

"Yes. I understand." But he did not explain Ben'aryn's words to her. He spoke instead to Bastet. "Maggrai had a dispersal device, called the Anafiremad. Is it powerful enough to clear the Vortice?"

"Dai, what are you...?" Katkin began, but Dai signaled her to be quiet as Bastet spoke again.

"*Na* believe it to be so," it said. "*Na*-Inais have known of it for many turns, but *Na* could never ask your kind to make use of it."

"Why ever not?" asked Katkin. "It seems we could have solved this quandary long ago."

"One must bear Maggrai's weapon to the center of the Vortice," Bastet answered sadly. "And for it there will be no Shadow."

The Amaranthine cried out in horror. "Do you mean that one of us would never be reborn?" Such an idea seemed profoundly distressing to Eydis, who sagged between Eira and Dai. They laid her gently on the ground. "It is impossible," she whispered weakly. "I will not allow it."

The Amaranthine who stood in a circle around Myrie and the others muttered fearfully. Several winked out of existence as they gap shifted away from Deres Tama. Geya, seeing a chance to escape her punishment, also disappeared. Even Hana, the Eastern Star, could not face the thought of such destruction. She embraced her sister and left with a sigh. Others followed, one by one, until only Eydis, Eira and Dai remained.

Katkin watched this retreat with rising antipathy. "Is there not one amongst you with the courage to do what is right?" she hissed to Eydis. "Why did you not stop them?"

Eydis gave her a wan smile. "How could I do so? We cannot give up our anafireon. Even to consider such an idea is an abomination."

Katkin caught Dai staring at her with eyes as dark and bleak as the sea on a winter's day.

"There is one with the courage." Now the field seemed empty save for the two of them. "My folly created this ruin, and it will be my last undertaking to make it right."

"Dai..." she sobbed, as he took her in his arms. "Is there no other way? If it only meant your death, then I console myself with the knowledge we would meet again. But this is for all eternity!"

"Yes. And it cannot be helped. I have known it since I learned of Maggrai's presence here."

"Then let me go with you."

Dai frowned at this and shook his head. "You have many lives left to you. Live them in happiness and peace."

Katkin gripped his shoulder hard and he winced with pain. "Why would I wish to go on living my lives if you will not be a part of them? What happiness and peace have I? This is the only way we can ever be together! Please, let me do this."

Dai sighed and took her in his arms again. He had loved her for so many lives, so many turns of the gyre. "Are you sure?" he asked finally. "Anafireon as pure and bright as yours should not be squandered. There will be no going back."

She laughed briefly, with deep bitterness. "Bright, you say? Nay. The cares of this Yrth have tarnished it, like cheap silver. What is it worth now?"

"Much—to me. More than the Gyre and everything in it." He spoke quickly, now that he had made up his mind. "Very well then—we will go together, into the silence of the stars. May the Gods forgive me for taking from them one so favored."

The field came back into view and all upon it stood silently, waiting for Dai's next words. He stood by Katkin and squeezed her hand. "We will use our anafireon to clear the passage," he offered quietly. Poppy gave a cry of distress.

There was distress, too, in Bastet's voice. "There can be but one. Too much anafireon will destroy this world and everything in it. Which of you will go?"

Katkin looked utterly despondent as Dai said, "I will. Alone." She tried to argue, but he walked away from her.

The *Na*-Inais bowed low before him. Bastet said, "*Na* must first find the device made by Maggrai. Its evil will be turned to good."

Eira, who had stayed on the ground by Eydis' side, spoke for the first time. "How will you find it? I thought Maggrai had died."

"*Na* will ask the Deres," it replied. A series of rapid clicks brought twenty-four of the *Na*-Inais to its side. One by one, they removed their leaf amulets and laid them on the ground before their leader. Each unique shape glowed with hues of green, gold and auburn.

Eira studied the radiant leaves with wonder and fascination. "What do you call these amulets?"

"*Folium*. They were a gift from the Deres. With them *Na* can find the truth."

Eira removed a pouch from her kirtle and shook three red spinels from within. They rested in the palm of her hand. "I, too, have a way to find answers. But I would very much like to know more of your folium."

"Watch and listen and you shall learn," it urged her. "And later, if there is time enough, *Na* would be honored to understand your stones too." The leader of the Inais clicked something like a song over the stone leaves gently and quietly. "I ask the Deres to bless the folium with their knowledge. Then *Na* must wait for the folium to speak."

Finally, it waved a hand-shaped twig, and three of the leaf stones began to shine, blazing in the flat white light of the Vastness. The resonating song that followed sounded like nothing they had ever heard before. Only Katkin gave a smile of recognition, for she had heard the same air on Rythis.

"*Matre on Di*," muttered Eira. "The trees sing a song of their beauty."

Bastet studied the three, and then spoke aloud. "Aspen, hawthorn and olive," it said, with wonder. "So the Anafiremad is already here, amongst those present. *Na* knew the Deres would provide."

"But that is impossible!" sputtered Lut. "None of us has been close to Maggrai."

"I have," said Poppy quietly. "But he didn't..."

Then she fell silent and placed her hand in her pocket. Slowly she withdrew a blue orb and held it before the company. "Is this what you are searching for?"

"Where on Yrth did you get that?" Gwillam asked her.

"From Maggrai's Watchkeep. I planned to throw it at Jakob," Poppy answered with a sheepish grin. "Then I put it in my pocket and forgot about it. I guess it is a good thing he stopped me."

Bastet's voice sounded almost dry. "Indeed. Maggrai has used such a weapon on *Na* many times. The rupture of an Anafiremad would have destroyed the Watchkeep and most of Beaumarais as well." It scanned the Irrakai's face intently. "You are determined?"

Dai nodded.

"Then *Na* give you gratitude. But heed this. *Na* fear you will feel great pain before the end. You must not let go of the Anafiremad until the moment of dispersal. Can you do this?"

He shrugged, remembering his ordeal at the hands of Tomas de Vigny long ago. "It would not be the first time. I won't fail you."

Bastet clicked approvingly. "When you are ready, move to the center of the trees and you will feel the pull of azimity. Let it carry you upwards, until you reach the crown. You know what to do then."

Katkin stood under the trees watching despondently as, one by one, he said solemn farewells to the others. Eydis embraced him, saying, "This last journey will be the greatest, Dai Irrakai, though it does not lead to the stars. We who remain will honor your memory with each breath."

Eira added, "You and I might have been brothers rather than enemies. I wish it had been so—for now I see what we have lost."

Dai faced Gunnar's two sons. "Farewell," he said. "Make your father proud, for you are the sons of the Mariner—and he is mightiest of the Amaranthine." Jakob shook his hand warmly. Lut turned away without speaking.

Gunnar limped forward and said humbly, "Your spirit is far mightier than mine, Dai. May Mother Ocean receive you into her peaceful embrace."

Dai gave him a wry grin. "When next you see your cousin, tell him I will miss our jousts. Farewell."

"That I will," answered Gunnar gravely.

Though Gwillam and Poppy barely knew the tall, grey-eyed Amaranthine before them, they both shed tears of regret at his farewell. Then Dai and Myrie spoke long together, and neither told anyone else what words they shared.

Finally, after making his last goodbyes, he stood once more before Katkin. She bit her lip hard to stop her tears, but Dai let his fall unashamedly. "Grieve gently at this parting, dear one. I go to my end with pride, knowing I have been able to undo some of the harm I caused. Goodbye, love."

With trembling hands, she unfastened the crystal feather talisman that had once belonged to Jacq and placed it around his neck. "Farewell, my husband. I love you always."

This time—the last time he would hear her voice—he did not argue with her words.

He embraced her and then strode towards the center of the eucalypt grove. "Wait," she whispered. "Please let me go—instead of you..." But Dai did not stop, nor did he look back.

Katkin buried her face in her hands and sobbed. A dream came to her, from long ago, as clear as a series of pictures in a gallery. *Jacq had saved her from her enemies and then left her on the ground. He held an orb, poisonous and green, loosely cupped in his palms. The light from it increased until it almost blinded her, and as it increased, she could see Jacq's form dissolving into nothingness.*

She opened her eyes, forcing herself to watch Dai's last moments. "Go gentle, love," she whispered as he reached the center of the grove. He stood tall, though his burned wing hung painfully crooked. The orb he held looked just like the one in her dream, save for its color—this one was of a soft blue. It did not seem possible that something so small could be a weapon designed to destroy a soul.

As he rose, he rubbed the Anafiremad between his hands, stripping off the protective coating. It began to glow green, like putrid swamp gas, lighting his face. His expression betrayed no fear, only intense concentration.

"Stand away from the trees and cover your faces," Bastet cried. "*Na* must not watch the Anafiremad do its work."

The rest fell back, but Katkin did not move, nor did she close her eyes. Instead, she waited for the explosion, with the perverse hope it might still reduce her to dust. She stayed rooted in place to the very end, even when the green light seemed to burn through her retinas and into her brain.

Dai screamed as first his skin, and then his subcutaneous fat burned away. But though his body glowed incandescently with agonizing radiation, he did not release his hold on the Anafiremad. A brilliant blast of violet and ultraviolet light accompanied the final destruction of his epiphysis. It shimmered wildly through the trembling leaves.

The others had covered their ears and eyes in terror, but other than Dai's last tortured cry there was no explosive report. Only the gentle movement of the air as it passed through the trees, up the column of pure white light that had appeared between them.

In the silence that followed, Katkin realized that someone had thrown their arms about her, providing shelter from the deadly power of the blast. She opened her eyes to find her face buried within the folds of a heavy linen robe of deepest black. It smelled sweet—of frankincense, sandalwood and myrrh. Then she stepped away, trembling in fear and wonder, with the sure knowledge that Death had embraced her.

Nineteen

Olive

It was over. The rising breeze flowing through the trees told them so and yet no one moved. They had all seen Death standing by Katkin, and they were afraid.

Katkin stayed at Death's side, oddly comforted, waiting to see what would happen next. He neither stirred nor spoke, and seemed to be waiting too, but for what she could not fathom.

Finally, Bastet spoke. "*Na* salute the memory of the Irrakai." The other thousand or so Irais behind it clicked three times, with melancholy precision. Then they took to the air, and circled the crown of the eucalypts. Their flight became a farandole, like black clouds woven amongst the shining leaves. Many birds, large and small, joined them, and their piping cries provided a mournful tune to the dance.

Katkin watched them fly with tear-filled eyes. It was beautiful and sad, a moving tribute to Dai. She left Death's side, letting the breath of wind draw her to the center of the trees until she stood in their midst. The rising draft carried the scent of summer rain, and the sea. An object lay at her feet half-buried in the sand, and Katkin knelt to retrieve it. Her once-clear crystal feather, transformed by the power of Dai's anafireon, had become a pure dove grey with flecks of green. The fire had consumed the leather thong, so Katkin placed the talisman between her breasts, hard by her heart.

Bastet approached her, but kept a respectful distance. "Elleranne. Sutun-*Na* approach."

Katkin had her hand over her heart, feeling it beat through the talisman, but at Bastet's words, she opened her eyes and looked down from Deres Tama. A vast white cloud approached—so vast it defied the efforts of her mind to comprehend it. At this distance, she could not divine its swiftly moving substance. But in the time it took to bring her hand up to shade her eyes she could see the multihued glints of a million sets of dragonfly wings.

"It is the Sutun-*Na*," Poppy cried. "And look, they are bringing their astaren." She hurried down the hill, back towards the cliff edge, as the first of the Sutun reached it, like the shreds of mist that presage the coming of a storm. They flew with their long tails trailing behind them, cradling their charges to their scaly bodies.

"Mother of Ods," said Gunnar as he stared wide-eyed at the stream of Sutun stretching out of sight over the horizon, along the way the aermaran had voyaged across Golden Ocean. A million or more souls in flight, all heading for Deres Tama and the newly reopened Vortice. He turned to his grandmother, Eydis, who stood by his side, leaning heavily on her staff. "How many astaren did Maggrai trap with the closing of the portal?"

Eydis shrugged. "I do not know."

He gave her a sharp, sideways glance. "You are eldest amongst the Amaranthine, are you not?"

"But the Vortice has been closed through all my turns of the Gyre. "Only Moera knows how many unhappy souls have lingered here—and how many have perished," she added bitterly. "For those sacrificed to the corsfyre furnaces there will be no Radiance, and no Shadow. They are forever lost to us." As the first of the Sutun reached Deres Tama, she could see that although most bore their astarene burdens with carefree joy, there were some whose arms were unhappily bare.

"The *Periri*,*" Bastet said from behind them. "For *Na* there is no rejoicing."

A steady flow of Sutun passed between the boles of the trees, approaching from all directions. Once they reached the towering column of light in the center their wings grew still, but even so, they rose toward the crown of leaves. One by one, they disappeared with a quiver of their translucent rainbow wings. But those that Bastet had called the Periri clustered in a forlorn knot at the bottom of the Vortice, not attempting to enter within.

"Poor things," murmured Poppy. "May nothing be done for them? Why aren't they given new souls to watch over?"

"Each Sutun has one astaren it may care for in each turn of the

---

* The lost ones.

Gyre," Myrie explained. "Bastet told us so, just now. But do not worry, Poppy. When the *Na*-Inais make ready to depart, they will take the Periri with them, back into the Nowhen."

"But surely there will be others—many others," Gunnar pointed out. "It may be a hundred years before all the Sutun who have been trapped can make their way up the Vortice." He scanned the rising ranks of astaren anxiously, looking for Gwenn and Arkady.

She seemed to understand his thoughts. "Do not fear, Mariner-Father," said Myrie. "We will stay here, at the Vortice, and become its Guardian. When lost ones arrive, we can help them find their way." She dropped her voice low. "And when the Sutun bring your dearest ones, we will send you a message, and keep them here until you may join them."

The relief brought tears, and Gunnar rubbed his eyes before speaking. "Thank you, Dawnmaid. I don't want any special favors. But if you could just tell me when they pass this way..."

Myrie laughed at this. "You have earned a boon for your careful handling of *Wind Beast*. We are happy to oblige."

"What about me?" asked Gwillam, who had been standing by, listening to their conversation. He looked stricken by Myrie's announcement that she planned to remain at Deres Tama. "Do you have a boon for me, too?" Myrie turned to him, her face unfocussed, her dark blue eyes muted.

"We hoped you would perform a task for us; something very important."

Gwillam sighed, wishing somehow he could bring back Myrie, singular. "What do you want me to do?"

"There are still many avisceti at large in Beaumarais and throughout Yr. We wish that you would bring us their corsfyre."

"And if I do? Will you assimilate them, as you have the others?" Her blurred head bobbed a time or two. Gwillam frowned and reached out his hand. He wanted to seize the girl called Myriadne and wrench her free of all the others. But there remained nothing to catch hold of, only a smudge of unfamiliar arms and legs. After a moment, his hand dropped uselessly to his side. Yet he could not abandon this girl whose life so closely intertwined with his. "When I bring them, will you talk to me, as you used to?"

"Of course we will," Myrie insisted, her face garlanded in a flood of smiles.

He turned away without smiling in return.

Poppy and Lut left the hillside and walked together on the stony beach. They might have spent five minutes in uncomfortable silence before Lut summoned the courage to speak. He stopped on the shore of an inlet and watched the waves washing the narrow banks, smoothing the roughness of the sand with its gentle touch. She stood beside him, waiting, as a sea bird broke the stillness.

"Blossom, we need to talk..." Lut kept his hands in his pockets, and his eyes on the ground. "I... wanted to apologize for hitting you when you got in the way of Jakob. Can you forgive me?"

Poppy nodded, warily. Lut didn't say anything else for a long while.

"Is there anything else, Lut? Katkin said we should not be gone for too long."

He cleared his throat to keep the next words from sticking. "A lot has happened since we spoke of marriage."

Poppy drew in a sharp breath. She had almost forgotten about that happy afternoon on Asaruthe. It seemed like a memory from another lifetime. "That is true. We are different people now." Poppy nudged a scallop shell with Azothe's tattered slipper.

"I am not." He took her hand and stood before her. "I am still Lut, the quiet one. And I still want to marry you and build a house on Asaruthe for us to live in together."

Poppy raised an eyebrow at this. "The Lut I knew on Asaruthe would never have kicked a fallen man in the throat! You *have* changed and you are a fool if you don't see it, Lut Strong Arm."

His eyes flashed with anger as he let go of her hand. "Jakob richly deserved a thrashing after what he did to us."

"He said he was sorry. I believed him."

"Because you love him?" Lut spat. Then he took a deep breath, determined to speak more reasonably. "Try to understand. I had to grow up pretty quick when I lost Ma and Pop. Some of the things I saw with Fyn made me sick, sick to death, but I could not take the coward's way out. There is so much evil in the world." His eyes softened with sadness. "If you want Jakob, just say so."

"No! Jakob is my friend, and I care for him, but you are..." Poppy paused, finding it difficult to express her feelings. She thought of evenings in a snug stone cottage, with quiet conversation as they mended the fishing nets. The sound of laughter as the children ran up the hill to visit their grandfather's house. The smell of fresh bread mixed with the salty tang of drying fish. The taste of the wind off the sea.

Was that what she wanted?

Something tugged at her—a blurred vision of another face, the feel of another mouth on hers. Poppy shuddered, thinking it must be a suppressed memory of her time in Tristan's bed. And yet it did not fill her with disgust, only longing. She could not fathom how she might feel so, so she firmly put the reminiscence behind her.

Lut, impatient to hear her answer, asked, "I am what, Blossom?"

"You are my future."

Poppy threw her arms around his neck and kissed him. He closed his eyes, and relief washed away his anger and doubt. Nevertheless, somewhere deep inside him, a voice keened softly of other battles, and a reckoning left unpaid. Resolutely, he damped it down, thinking her love would be enough.

Back at Deres Tama, Katkin wandered disconsolately around the Vortice, wishing she could join the steady stream of Sutun that rode the beam of light. She watched Myrie and Gwillam standing close together, deep in conversation. Poppy and Lut were on the beach, no doubt making plans for their future. Jakob followed Gunnar as he limped about, the two of them using their strength to clear the remains of the smashed aermaran from the cliff top. Eira and Eydis sat in the shade of the trees, and Huw spoke quietly with them.

Only the dark figure of Death stood solitary, as she did.

Katkin wondered if she would ever get used to the feeling of being alone. Not just lonely—she had been that many times in this life and others. But *alone*, without any hope of finding her true love again. How would she go on, life after life, without Jacq? The pain had only just begun, and already it seemed fathomless. In between her breasts, the feather felt cold, like a shard of ice. It burned against the skin of her sternum, and a dull ache followed, one she tried to ignore.

Jakob hurried towards her, calling, "Grandmother! Come quickly, we need you."

The fear in his voice made her swallow her grief. The tightness in her chest remained. "What is it? Is Gunnar hurt?"

Jakob shook his head as he pulled her towards the aermaran. "Fyn," he said breathlessly. "It is bad, Grandmother. Please hurry."

A thrill of fear shot through her, but Jakob's words did nothing to prepare her for the awful reality. When she saw Gunnar kneeling next to a shapeless mass, Katkin thought at first he had wrapped Fyn in his cloak. A closer examination left her reeling. He had not been covered—the blackened heap of ash and bone was all that remained of Fyn. The fires of his enemy, the Angellus, had caught him as he fell.

"Get something to shroud the body with," she muttered to Gunnar, forgetting, in her desperate grief, something important that Tomas had told her long ago.

"Blessed Brigga, open your eyes," Gunnar said, horrorstricken. "He is not..."

The darkness stirred, and Katkin felt acid burning in the back of her throat as her stomach contracted violently. No, he *couldn't* be...

It wasn't possible, and yet...

Fyn was alive.

He did not feel pain. There were no nerves left to carry the impulses to his brain. Nor could he move. He lay face down, in the place he had fallen on the field of battle.

"I was unconscious when Tomas disappeared. Dai told me he gap-shifted before the fire hit him," Katkin babbled to Jakob, but she might have been trying to convince herself. "I believed him. I should have checked for myself." Her voice rose to a shriek. "I should have..."

His lips were gone, his teeth charred stumps, but his voice still worked, a little. "Katrione," he whispered. "Don't..."

She fell silent at once and lay on the ground, so that she might put her ear next to the husk of his face. To do this she had to close her eyes—to see what remained of Fyn was simply unendurable. "Oh, love. I am so sorry."

He spoke with many pauses, as his strength allowed. "No need. I deserved it... Shouldn't have... jumped to conclusions about Lalluna." Then his voice sounded almost jaunty, like the Tomas de Vigny of old. "Always a bit of a hothead, in this life. But what happened after I fell? Did we lose?"

Gunnar spoke from above them. "Nay, Cousin. In all the turns of the Gyre, I have never seen such a victory. You may be proud of your part in it."

He grunted his approval and waited for Katkin to speak again.

She lay silent for many minutes, as she fought another bloody battle inside herself. Courage won, but only just. "Tomas, I can heal you, as I did once in the Mistmere. Do you remember?"

"No."

"Of course you do," she rambled, her resolve already melting away, like ice on a warm spring morning. *Goddess, his flesh is completely gone.* "I swam out and found you in the darkness." *The pain must have been terrible.* "Lalluna was there too." *So much pain...*

"No," he said again, his voice rising only slightly. "No healing."

"But Tomas, I have to help you. How could I leave you like this?"

"Leave me," he echoed dully. "Nothing you can do. Not this time."

"How in the name of Ods can he still be alive?" Jakob hissed, shocked out of all discreetness.

"Whisht, Jakob," his father snapped, but Katkin had already heard the question.

"That bitch Geya stole his death from him, long ago. He has no Sutun-*Na*." Her eyes filled with tears, and they spilled through the closed lids. She leaned close again. "Tomas, listen to me. There are beings here, called *Na*-Inais. They are the guardians of the Uri'el, whom they call Sutun. I am going to talk to them. Perhaps they can help you."

"Help me die?" he asked, with pathetic hopefulness. "Want to... so much."

She hurried away, shaking her head, trying to erase the image of his charred face. It did not work.

Bastet listened sympathetically, but could offer no aid. "*Na* have not the power to give the unfortunate one a new Sutun," it said regretfully. "There is only one who might, but do you dare to ask it?" A thin, black arm extended from its side, and pointed to Death.

But to relieve Tomas de Vigny's suffering, Katkin would dare anything at all.

He stood by the Deres, watching the endless flow of Sutun up the Vortice. Katkin stamped her foot in frustration. Death ignored her.

Anger trumped fear. She spoke. "How could you have abandoned Tomas to an endless Hell of existence like that?"

He did not look down.

"Why don't you answer me? Say something, anything! Tell me how I can help him or strike me dead, right now."

He seemed, at last, to hear her and lowered his head. Katkin felt her heart rise into her throat as she looked upon the face of Death for the first time. It was as sweet and wrinkled as a winter apple, wholly benign. Her anger and then her fear evaporated.

"You protected me from the power of the Anafiremad. I wanted to die, I suppose. Because of Jacq. Now I believe you saved me for a reason. Is that right?"

He nodded.

Katkin, encouraged, spoke hurriedly, lest she should lose her determination. "I want to give my Sutun to Tomas de Vigny. May I do that?"

He nodded again.

"Then make it happen."

Death raised his hand and touched her face, and though he spoke no words, she understood he wanted her to be very, very sure of her decision.

It was her turn to nod. His expression remained impassive as he turned away from the trees. Katkin followed. By the time they reached Tomas, the Sutun already floated at his side.

"May I speak to him once more?"

Gunnar stared at Katkin though narrowed eyes. "Who are you talking to?"

"Death," she answered in surprise. "Can you not see him?"

He shook his head. "Has he come for Cousin Fyn? I thought you said..."

Katkin replied tersely. "I did. But I was wrong. Say your goodbyes now. I don't think he has much time left."

Gunnar squatted and spoke to his cousin in an undertone. Fyn said only a few words in return, but they sounded almost lighthearted. Jakob mumbled an awkward goodbye and then the two of them retreated. Katkin knelt by Tomas' side and willed her voice to sound tranquil. There was never any doubt in her mind that she would send Tomas de Vigny to his final rest with a lie.

"I have good news. The Inais have a new Sutun, just for you.

Death is waiting here, at my side. He is ready to take you on your last journey."

He gave a heartrending cry of relief. Katkin knew she must hurry, but there was so much that she wanted to say. "You and I have shared many lives, love. Until this last turn of the Gyre, we sailed always on parallel courses, close but never touching. I am very glad that we intersected at last." She was crying bitterly now. "Farewell, my gallant Captain. I will never forget you."

He would have held her if he could, and given her comfort. But he could only murmur, "Nor I you. In my heart, I know we will meet again, on some other sphere, my dear. Until then, may the gods protect you, Katrione."

The shadow of Death loomed over the two of them, the Sutun by his side.

Katkin stood and backed away, covering her face with her hands. The pain of this final loss tore at her heart like the claws of a ravening beast. *Had she felt alone before now? Then what would she call this feeling—desolation? Utter hopelessness?*

No—there was nothing left of her to feel. Nothing left but a cold, cold emptiness, a hebetude that permeated her very soul.

The gentle touch of a hand on her shoulder brought her back, but offered no comfort. Katkin dropped her hands from her face and opened her eyes. Death stood by her, and together they saw that the Sutun had done its work. Its strong arms cradled Tomas like a sleeping child. Stepping forward, Katkin brushed the blond hair away from his eyes and gently kissed his forehead. She gazed at his face, wishing she could feel the same peaceful serenity.

Then the Sutun beat its diaphanous wings and rose. It flew towards Deres Tama. Katkin watched it until it disappeared at the top of the shining column, taking Elfair Ap Fyn on his long-awaited journey to the Shadow lands.

When she turned to speak to Death, to give him her thanks, he had gone.

The *Na*-Irais gathered on Deres Tama, lined in orderly ranks, making ready to depart. Some, joined in pairs, held Periri between them. Slowly, silently, they rose through the Vortice, until the space between the trees was bare, save for the Sutun that continued to stream from across the ocean.

"Farewell, my friends," Myrie called. "We will not forget your valiant fight to free the Sutun. May your voyage carry you beyond the stars."

Only Bastet remained. It flew across the field towards Katkin, who still lingered close to the place Tomas de Vigny fell. She and Jakob had dug a rough grave, while Gunnar found a blanket amongst the detritus of the aermaran. They wrapped what was left of the body and laid it gently in the shallow pit. As Jakob scraped the dirt back, Katkin and Gunnar collected rocks to make a cairn.

She was standing before it when Bastet came to find her.

"You have made an arrangement with Death." It was not a question.

She nodded, wondering how it knew, and then bent to replace a fallen stone from the top of the cairn.

Bastet continued, "The one named Ben'aryn gave *Na* a message."

"I know. I heard when you told Dai."

"The message is for you, Elleranne."

She stood, brushing the ashes from her hands. "For me?" she asked, without real interest. "What did he say?"

"It told *Na* to speak these words to you: *You have given away your death, but if you wish to leave this life, you have only to call upon me.*"

She stared at Bastet. "Is that all he said?"

"Yes, Elleranne. That is all."

"How did he know?" she whispered. "Is Ben'aryn a God?" She thought back to the day he had saved her life, catching her as she plunged from the third story of the Infirmarie. She had believed him to be so then, though he had tried hard to dissuade her.

Bastet clicked thoughtfully in answer to her question. "Certainly it has the favor of the Deres. And it lives within the Shadow, though it is not part of it."

Katkin understood this at once. "He is immortal? But he told me the Amaranthine could die—and I have seen it myself, many times."

"It gave away its Sutun long ago, just as you did, Elleranne."

They stood side by side, looking at the second grave of Tomas de Vigny, and Katkin wondered for whom Ben'aryn had given his death.

"You have saved your kind, Elleranne, but great suffering remains. *Na* must go now, back to the Darkness. You will return to your home too, and help those who are left behind."

"There is nothing I can do, Bastet," Katkin disagreed, with a desolate sigh. "My country is in ruins. It is too much for me to do alone and there is no one else, not now."

Gently, he clicked in opposition to this. "The leaves say it is so, and they do not lie."

"What do they say?"

"*Willow.*"

A bright burst of flame carried it away from her before she could think to reply. Bastet flew up the Vortice, and the branches soon hid its form. A long time passed before Katkin stirred again.

Not until a terrified scream tore through the stillness.

"Goddess above, what is it now?" cried Katkin as she ran back towards the trees. The screaming continued. The bright column of light from the center of the Vortice backlit the scene, and at first, she could see nothing.

"Don't come any closer." The voice was high-pitched rather than menacing, and Katkin recognized it right away. She stepped forward, shielding her eyes from the glare. What she saw made her shake her head in absolute disbelief. *How could Poppy have been so wrong?*

Tristan stood under Deres Tama, smiling triumphantly. He had Poppy's ponytail firmly wound about his fingers, and a knife at her throat. Poppy continued to scream and he shook her, until she went limp in his arms.

Katkin, thinking she had much less to lose than her daughter, said, "Let Poppy go, son. I am ready to accept whatever retribution you wish to give me."

He laughed at this. "The time I wanted you has long since passed, Mother. Now you are nothing to me."

As Gunnar and his sons hurried forward, Tristan waggled the ten-inch dagger he held at right angles to Poppy's neck.

"Stay back, all of you, or rest assured I will cut her throat." Poppy seemed to wake at this threat and struggled. Tristan tightened his grip. "Tut tut, my dear. Why are you so coy? Last time we met, you spread your lovely legs for me quite willingly, remember? You begged for the pleasure of my kingly rod of state."

"No…" whispered Poppy, sick with humiliation and horror. "You are dead, I saw you. You can't be alive. You can't."

Lut pushed his way to the front of the little knot of people that had gathered before Tristan. "Take your filthy hands off her, fiend. She never gave herself to you!"

Tristan gave him a cocksure grin. "Are you her betrothed? What a pity I already plucked her first sweet fruit from the vine. I hate réchauffé, don't you?" Jakob grabbed Lut's collar and struggled to hold him back. Gunnar limped over to lend a hand as Lut stared, mouth working, absolutely rigid with fury.

"I don't believe you. Poppy would never do that. Would you, Blossom?"

Poppy paled, but did not answer his question. Suddenly Lut's expression turned wintry. "I see," he said, grinding out the words with brittle precision. "But there is still the small matter of my mother's death between us."

Tristan looked aggrieved. "It was *so* regrettable that your mother got in the way of my avisceti as they sought the Dawnmaid. But why blame me? Your brother Jakob led them straight to the island. He even managed to get rid of you first." He glanced over at Jakob with a conspiratorial wink. "Well done, my dear boy."

"Lut," Jakob said desperately. "He is lying. It wasn't like that. I never…"

Lut turned, much faster than Gunnar could react, and dealt Jakob a vicious blow with the hilt of his sword. He reeled sideways and fell, clutching his eye. Lut strode on without a backwards glance.

Tristan watched him with interest. "Wait, Strong Arm! Now that your idiotic brother has crippled General Abelard, I need someone like you. Together we could raise a mighty army. Will you join me?" Tristan's face wore a cajoling smile, but death lingered in his eyes. Lut never faltered in his advance.

"Go to hell. I would never ally myself with the likes of you, troll spawn." He stepped resolutely under the circle of trees. He could hear Katkin's voice behind him, begging him to stop, for Poppy's sake. A red haze clouded his vision, as her words sank into the quickening drumbeat that filled his ears. With a bloodcurdling cry, he charged forward, with Ancarnen raised high.

Tristan's smile had frozen, but now it turned cruel. He raised his hand and thrust a stubby finger towards his attacker. Lut gave a choked gurgle of pain and fell to his knees.

"Foolish boy! There is no way you can win. This world *will* be mine. Ironic, isn't it? Your very own mother gave me the necessary skills to begin my ascendancy." Tristan gave a coquettish chuckle. "*Fess Tun Me Doha,** indeed. Now I have all the freedom I need to despoil this world and its occupants, again and again." He ogled Poppy's heaving breasts. "With the lovely Azothe as my Queen and helpmate, of course. Isn't that right, my dear?"

Poppy spat the words through gritted teeth. "Never! I would rather die."

"Would you, indeed? I could arrange that. But for now, I have a different entertainment in mind. Perhaps this will help you recall your former devotion."

Tristan pointed at Lut once more. He gave a cry of agony and clutched at his sword with both hands. The tip of Ancarnen nosed around until it lay against his breastbone.

Poppy could see every muscle straining in his forearms as Lut fought to keep the sword from plunging straight into his own heart. "Don't hurt him. Please, Tristan! I will do as you ask."

The tip had already pierced Lut's chest, and his blood flowed freely along the gutter of the blade. "Try harder, my dear," Tristan insisted. "Let me hear you beg. Tell me how much you want me."

The words she spoke next seemed to come from somewhere else—a distant echo of Azothe, like the scent of perfume lingering in an empty wardrobe. "Very well, my Sun. You shall have all you desire. I am your most willing slave."

Tristan laughed. "That is better, my lovely Azothe." He waved his hand limply.

As Lut fell forward onto his face, with Ancarnen underneath him, the others clustered around. "He is alive," said Katkin, after she sought the pulse in his neck.

Gunnar turned to Eydis with desperation in his eyes. "Grandmother, do something! You have the power to stop him, do you not?"

Eydis spoke, her voice soft and frail and utterly without hope. "I can do nothing. Maggrai has closed the circle."

"Maggrai?" Katkin wondered if old age had robbed the woman's wits from her. "But that is only my son, Tristan."

---

* Tristan's mantra, given him by Gwenn. It means *freedom lies within.*

She shook her head. "I see it now, all of it. We believed the child that Raven bore would become Maggrai, but we were wrong. *Your* son Tristan came back from the future to prepare himself for his upcoming conquest of Yrth. We can kill him, again and again, but it won't matter. Do you not see? The circle is closed."

Smiling malevolently, Tristan raised his hand again. Eydis clutched at her heart and slumped against Gunnar's side. He caught her as she fell.

Tristan was too busy gloating to see the murderous expression in Gunnar's eyes as he laid Eydis beside Lut. "It has certainly closed for you, old woman. I shall travel between the spheres, gathering my *new* minions. Soon we will join in battle once more. My victory will be glorious, of course..."

Gunnar's towering cry of rage shook the trees to their very roots. "You will have no victory, shite stain. By the Gods and all that is sacred, Gwenn did not die for that!" He threw his crutch aside and hopped forward. Gunnar bore no weapon save for his formidable strength, and his wrath, and yet he looked every inch a warrior from the tales of old. "Let her go. This will be your last chance."

The warning had no effect. Tristan only frowned in concentration as he raised his hand and willed Gunnar to stop. The Mariner came on relentlessly, though his face showed his agony. Three more hops, and he would be upon his enemy.

Tristan stiffened, and tried to step to the left. At that moment, Poppy plunged her hand into his groin and twisted viciously. He staggered, momentarily disabled, but kept his knife close to Poppy's neck. "You will die for that, bitch" he grunted, and slashed the blade across her throat.

As Poppy collapsed he shoved her towards Gunnar, then Tristan stepped forward and a little to the left. He felt the ground spin away from him, felt the welcome rush of nausea that always accompanies a gap shift. A relaxed sigh escaped his lips as he closed his eyes, prepared to let azimity take him wherever it would.

Poppy staggered forward as Gunnar swung wide, his fist connecting with nothing but air. Tristan had disappeared.

"Go after him, Mariner. Make an end to the monster once and for all," Eira urged. Gunnar stood over Poppy, swaying with exhaustion. Katkin knelt by her daughter's prostrate form and tried to stop the bleeding.

Jakob handed Gunnar his crutch. "Thank you, lad. Now stand aside. You are in no condition to be moving around." Lut's assault with the hilt of Ancarnen had left one of his brother's eyes a bloody wreck.

Jakob shook his head. "My turn, Dad. Stay here with her." Lut had ruined one of his eyes, but Jakob figured he could follow Tristan well enough with the other one. His uncle had shifted hastily, leaving a sparkling trail of dust behind.

Tristan stood before the bank of a stream, listening. He could hear no sound but the gurgle of the icy water as it poured over the lip of a fall and into a rock pool. He relaxed, and the hand that held the bloody knife dropped to his side. The fools would never find him now, and he would soon be able to gather together a new army of minions. Then the Amaranthine would fall to him, as they had done so many times before. There would be no one left to prevent him from blocking the Vortice again, now that heroic fool Irrakai had blown himself to crumbs.

He smiled, thinking on the old hag's last words: *Maggrai has closed the circle.*

This plan occupied him for a moment, as he watched an army of blackened leaves march along the flowing water, and sink out of sight.

When an arm snaked through a hole in the fabric of the world, he never saw it coming. Jakob snatched him by the collar, twisting it tight, so that Tristan could barely breathe. Though he swung with the knife, and connected with Jakob's thigh muscle, his pursuer did not release his hold. Tristan screamed as Jakob squeezed the bones of his wrist into pulp. The knife dropped from his nerveless fingers. Thus did Jakob drag him back across the worlds, crying and struggling all the way. Back to Deres Tama.

Gunnar gave a cry of relief when Jakob appeared again, still holding Tristan by his collar. He sagged, holding his crushed wrist close to his chest. "My dear Jakob. I had no idea you were so powerful. Obviously I made an error by offending you, but do you..."

"Kill him!"

This from Lut, as he struggled to stand. "Do it, Jakob. Don't let the maggot get away again." Jakob nodded and wrapped his arm around Tristan's neck, intending to snap it.

"No, Jakob," Katkin called from her place at Poppy's side. "He will escape with Death, and this time you won't be able to follow him."

"What should I do?" Jakob cried in confusion. "What should I do?"

"Kill him, you coward," Lut shrieked again.

"Don't!" bawled Gunnar and Katkin in unison.

He caught a flash of silver from the corner of his eye, and that somehow helped him decide. Jakob never hesitated. He raised Tristan high above his head and hurled him towards the column of light—straight into the Vortice. It scattered and sparkled like shards of broken glass as he hit, and then re-formed. As soon as Tristan realized where he had landed, he slammed his bulk against the wall of light again and again.

"No! Don't send me away. Not into the darkness. Please, mother, you must save me. I am your one true son..." Katkin covered her face and turned away, weeping. Tristan rose, twisting like a fly on a strand of spider silk as he struggled against the Vortice. One last wail echoed from amongst the shivering leaves, "You haven't seen the last of me. I'll find my way ba..."

Twenty

Elm

Lut had insisted they return to the beach again, and now, in the strange cold light of the Vastness, his face looked pale and stern as he marched along beside her. Poppy waited for him to speak. When he judged they had put enough distance between them and the hilltop, he stopped and turned to face her. Two blotches of color appeared on his cheeks.

"Did you do it?"

Poppy pretended not to know what he meant. "Did I do what?"

"Lay with that filthy mongrel, Tristan."

She believed if she told him the truth he would understand. "Yes, I think so. But I don't really remember."

But Lut was unforgiving. "Filthy slattern! How could you?"

Poppy stepped back a pace. "It wasn't really me..." she tried to explain, but Lut only shook his head in disgust. "The dress..." she began again, more desperately.

"Save your stinking excuses. You gave yourself to my mother's murderer." He glared at her. "Just now I heard you agree to serve him."

"To save your life! What would you have had me do?"

"Would that I had died rather than hear those foul words from your lips!" He shook his head angrily.

Poppy's eyes filled with tears. "Lut," she whispered. "Nothing has changed, truly. I still want to marry you."

"Do you think I can pretend it never happened? Don't be a fool. Every time I touched you, I would remember that *his* murdering hands had been there before me."

She drew herself up, angry now at his pig-headedness. "Fine! Blame me for everything. Do you wish to break our engagement?" Her brown eyes blazed at him, and he looked away. "Answer me!"

The frosty silence stretched long between them. Then he thrust his hands in his pockets and gave a brief, sharp nod.

Poppy tried to look untroubled. "Speak. I wish to be sure of your intentions. For if we are estranged, then I believe Asaruthe would be too small for the two of us."

He shrugged. "Why should I care? I am not going back there anyway."

"Not going back?" Her determination crumbled. Poppy's lip trembled as she struggled to understand. "But Lut, you love our island. You have said so many times. How could you have changed so?"

His expression did not soften. "That was *before*. I was a child then—a stupid child in love with someone I barely knew."

Poppy let this petty cruelty pass without comment. Instead, she asked, "Then where on Yrth will you go?"

He snarled, "Nowhere on this Yrth. That craven piece of shite Jakob gave Maggrai another chance to run, so now it is up to me to find him. I will make him pay for Ma's death, once and for all. Goodbye, Poppy."

"Lut, don't..." she began, but he had already walked away from her. Poppy wept as she trailed him along the beach, dragging her slippers in the sand. As the distance between them grew and grew, Lut never once looked back over his shoulder.

He brushed by his brother without a word, and went to talk to Gunnar. Jakob watched from a distance as Lut argued animatedly with their father. After a moment, he threw up his hands and then walked resolutely towards the Vortice, with Ancarnen sheathed at his side.

Jakob called, "Wait!"

Lut stared at him as he approached. "What do you want, Jakob?"

"Are you leaving? What of Poppy?" Jakob placed himself between Lut and the Vortice.

Lut fingered the pommel of Ancarnen and frowned. "What of her? I broke our engagement. Now get out of my way or I will kill you, I swear it."

"But why? I thought you loved her."

"Do I have to remind you what Uncle Tristan said?"

"Don't be a damned fool, Lut! Whatever Poppy did, she had a good reason for it."

"Why don't you have her then? I am sure she will be just as happy to spread her legs for a rapist as she was for a murderer."

Before he could think to stop it, Jakob's fist shot out. A quick cry of warning from Gunnar caused him to soften the blow before it landed, otherwise he might have killed his brother outright. Even so, Lut staggered backwards, with blood streaming from a cut above his eyelid.

Gunnar and Poppy both converged on the pair. "No more fighting," he roared, as Poppy threw herself between them.

Lut stood still, his breath coming in great, ragged gasps. "You will pay for that, Jakob. When I finish with Maggrai, I will be coming for you. You can't hide behind Dad forever!"

Jakob spoke with genuine regret. "I am sorry I lost my temper, but I couldn't let you say that about Poppy." He extended a conciliatory hand, but Lut glowered at it.

Gunnar frowned at Lut. "The lad has apologized. Now shake hands and make it right with him. If you insist on pursuing this fool quest of yours then you should be at peace with your family before you go."

Lut spat copiously on the ground before the three of them, then turned and threw himself into the Vortice. "I was always the quiet one. Well, no more! You can all go to hell for all I care." Holding

Ancarnen straight above his head, he rose through the trunks of the eucalypts, and vanished from sight.

Poppy stared at her slipper tops, trying not to cry. Jakob patted her shoulder awkwardly, saying, "Don't worry, Poppy. He will come back."

"I don't think so, Jakob." She took a deep breath and straightened her head. Her pride would prevent her from saying just how much Lut's defection had hurt. Instead, she turned to Gunnar and asked, "How is your grandmother?"

"Eydis is dead," said Gunnar dully. "The strain Tristan put on her heart was too much for her."

"Oh, Ikor, I am so sorry. But what will happen to the Amaranthine now? Will you lead them?"

"They already asked me, but I said no. All I want to do is go back to Asaruthe. I have responsibilities to tend to there. Things that cannot wait." But what those things were, he did not say. Worry etched new lines in his face as Gunnar shook his shaggy head.

Poppy looked back to Jakob. "How about you? What are you going to do?"

Jakob threw an arm over his father's shoulder. "I am going back to Asaruthe with Dad, of course. He will need someone to help him with the farm."

Poppy seemed surprised by this. "You told me you couldn't wait to leave there."

He shrugged. "I know. But that was *before*."

"Before what?" She stared at him, disturbed by the echo of Lut's words to her.

"Before I left with Maia and ruined everything."

Jakob sighed, and Poppy recognized the hurt in his eyes. She grabbed his arm and pulled him a little way from Gunnar. "You still love her, don't you?"

"Of course, but it doesn't matter, not now. Dad needs me, and anyway Maia—well, she and I have our differences."

"Why don't you talk to her? Maybe she would be willing to come to Asaruthe with you."

Jakob laughed cynically. "What do you think we fought about? She said she never wanted to set foot on that island again." He looked at Poppy thoughtfully. "And you? What will you do?"

Poppy gazed into the distance, back across Golden Ocean,

wondering. *Could she be happy on Asaruthe, without Lut?* "I wanted to return to Asaruthe, but..."

"You don't think you can live there with me?" Jakob finished for her, with an unhappy sigh.

"It isn't you, Jakob, honestly. I just thought I had my future all planned, and now I don't know what I should do any more." She frowned and changed the subject. "I see Patre coming."

He drew level with them, nodded briefly to Gunnar and Jakob, and threw his arms around Poppy. "Are you all right? Eira has just told me of the terrible danger you faced, my flower."

Poppy hugged him, smiling at his worry. "I am fine. Katkin said it was only a scratch. Jakob's wound was much worse."

Huw did not seem reassured. "I should have been there to protect you. But now, you must come with me. We will gather your things and go back to Mornguard, where I know you will be safe."

"Patre..." said Poppy, hesitantly. "I don't know if I..."

Huw released her, but spoke firmly. "Of course, you will stay here with us, my flower. Maia and Cara will be very pleased to welcome another member into our little family." Somehow, Poppy could not convince herself of this. He must have sensed her doubts, for he added, with a cursory glance at Jakob, "I am sure you would be happier in Mornguard, with your own kind."

Poppy stood silently, watching the three of them, trying to make up her mind. Her Patre wore a wide band of gold on his finger, and the Tane's scarlet feather in his hair. The silver at his temples and beard had somehow disappeared, making him seem ten years younger. He looked as happy and prosperous as she had ever seen him. But, though Jakob had placed his arm around his father again, it was difficult to tell who was supporting who. The two of them seemed hopelessly bereft.

Her mind cleared. "Thank you for your kind offer, Patre, but I think I am needed more on Asaruthe."

"Are you sure about this, Poppy?" Huw looked over at Jakob with obvious disdain. "There are many fine young Firaithi men in the village for you to choose from."

She smiled at this clumsy lure. "Yes, Patre. I am quite sure."

Eira stood before Deres Tama, and called in a deep, clear voice. "Return to me, brothers and sisters." One by one the Amaranthine winked into existence and stood before her in a rough semi-circle. There were cries of dismay when Eira announced, "The Numen* is no more. She has passed through Tsmar'enth and now lies sleeping beside her brother, awaiting the next turn of the Gyre. I would fill her place as Stavebearer, and lead you henceforth."

Almost all of them murmured their assent. Only Geya spoke out. "I should be the one! My clever designs brought the Dawnmaid to Deres Tama and saved us all."

Raven stepped from behind her and spoke for the first time. "Always I have stood in your shadow, my sister. But I will speak now, and tell the others the true nature of your foolish plan."

Geya glared at her. "Don't you dare!"

Raven continued, "Geya tried to fulfill the prophecy by bringing together north and south, and almost destroyed the true Seed Bearer as a result."

"That was just a silly mistake," Geya insisted petulantly. "Everything else I did..."

"Was even worse," Hana interrupted. "You forced your sister to bring death and destruction to Yrth in the form of the battle crow, Keth Dirane. Many humans died as a result, but there is one whose name deserves special mention—Jacq Benet, known to us as Dai, the Irrakai, seeker of the paths between the stars..." Katkin's head snapped up at this and she stared at Raven with burning eyes. "Had Eydis not intervened, and sent Shiqaba to prevent the loss of his anafireon, Dai Irrakai would have been no more."

"And who else among us would have sacrificed themselves to clear the Vortice?" Eira cried. She turned to Geya. "Would you?"

Geya pressed her lips together. No one else spoke.

"So be it. I accept the mantle of leadership. Now, I have but one thing left to say. For many turns of the Gyre, our kind have used the people of Yrth. We gave them many marvels, 'tis true, but they also suffered much at our hands, and the hands of our enemies. My first directive is that we remaining Amaranthine will retreat to the outer pellicula, and remain there until the Autochthones have developed enough to join us."

"But what about the Anjali?" Huw asked anxiously. "We at Mornguard still need your protection."

"No, you do not. The future is no longer in doubt, thanks to

* Eydis

the Irrakai's sacrifice. I am Eira and I have spoken." She clapped her hands three times and stepped away. The others followed, one by one, until Raven stood alone. Katkin walked to her side, half-expecting Raven to gap shift before she came within speaking distance. But Geya's sister remained rooted in place, with her eyes to the ground.

She tried hard to reconcile the evil Keth Dirane with the disheveled, childlike woman who stood before her. "I just wanted you to know I feel no hatred towards you. You were only a tool in the hands of others—perhaps even Dai, himself. I am not sure I will ever understand my husband's last moments on Yrth. But there is a question you could answer for me. What happened to the child that you made with him before he died?"

Katkin had to bend her head very close to hear Raven's anguished reply. She seemed to be talking to herself. "Geya convinced me it was right—that we would bring him back as one of us. That he would be a traitor no longer. But it was she who was the traitor. She paid, 'tis true, but so did I, who never wanted Dai's death."

"What do you mean?"

Raven's dark eyes brimmed with wretchedness. "After Eydis tore me from my vessel, I crossed the heavenly plane. She took me to one of the outer azimuths, and there we stayed, waiting for the child to be born. Eydis made no secret of the fact she planned to make an end to it. I did not wish her to, for even though she told me again and again that the child was an abomination, I... I loved him, as any mother would love her first-born child. Was that so wrong?"

Katkin shook her head unhappily, thinking how misplaced her lingering anger had been.

"When I felt the first birth pangs, I hid from my grandmother and the rest. I went to Rythis—and there I squatted under a tree like a common animal and pushed my baby into the world." She paused to dash angry tears from her eyes. "When I held him in my arms for the first time I felt such joy; for he was a tiny copy of the Irrakai, with perfectly formed wings. And then Death..." Raven turned away, her shoulders heaving, fists clenched.

Katkin spoke clumsy words of comfort. "He was stillborn? I know it is very hard, but sometimes it is for the..."

Raven turned to face her. "No! He lived, but Death took him anyway."

This seemed an unfathomable injustice. "Why? Did he say why?"

Her words were bitter. "Death does not speak. Not to the likes of me. He merely held out his hands. I knew I could not hide, not from Death, so I had to give my child over to him." She broke into anguished sobs.

Katkin put her arms around her, understanding all too well her grief. "Perhaps he only wanted to protect the child from Eydis."

"Perhaps," said Raven, not persuaded.

"And you never saw him after?"

From within her arms she felt Raven's head shake. "But I have heard his name spoken from time to time, so I know that he lives—somewhere."

"His name?" Katkin asked, with trepidation. "What did you call him?"

Raven stepped away from Katkin and disappeared, but her voice echoed through the intervening space and time. "Ben'aryn. I named him Ben'aryn—son of my sorrow."

Then Katkin understood, for the very first time, just how wrong they had been—about everything.

A grove of poplars stood in the distance, their golden leaves shining in sweet contrast to the dark green of the firs beyond. They seemed to call to her with gentle voices, and once Katkin walked beneath them, she felt somehow calmed and uplifted. The damp leaves beneath her boots gave off an earthy rich smell, almost like bread, reminding her that she had eaten nothing since they left St. Valery three days before.

A wide lane ran through the copse, and Katkin knew it led to Mornguard. She stood well back as many Firaithi passed back towards the village from Deres Tama. But though the last of them hurried by, with his head down, she could still see the red Tane's feather in his hair. Katkin stepped from the shadows.

"Hello, Huw. I wish to speak with you a moment, if you don't mind."

He looked surprised to see her there. "Katkin! I thought... you must have gone already."

Though she had meant to say many bitter and angry words to Huw Adaryi, she found they had fled. She only tilted her head at him reprovingly. "Without saying goodbye? I would not do that. Anyway, we have something important to discuss."

"We do?" He raised an eyebrow at this. "I assumed you said everything you wanted to say when I left Asaruthe." He held out his hand as a golden leaf fell, and it landed neatly on his outstretched palm. Katkin saw the ring on his finger and frowned.

A caustic comment sprang to her lips and she bit it back. Why should Huw not wear a token of his wife's esteem? Katkin herself had never given him a ring, nor kept her marriage vows. She could not mend that now. The leaves continued to shower down, adding a new plating of gold to the ground.

Huw asked softly, "What do you wish to speak of, Katkin? I must hurry back to Mornguard, for Cara will be waiting."

They had owned nothing between them. Only the children remained in the final, sad dissolution of their sixteen years together. Katkin cleared her throat and spoke. "Poppy is going back to Asaruthe."

"I know of this already. I wanted her to remain here with me, but she feels responsible for that worthless *Gruagá*, Jakob."

"Well, he did save her life, Huw. I am content for her to go there if she wishes. She says she still loves Asaruthe, but I wonder if it will seem so welcoming without Lut. But she is twenty-three—quite old enough to do as she pleases. It is Gwillam I am worried about."

"And why is that?"

"Did you know that Myrie has appointed herself a guardian of the Vortice? And she has asked Gwill to hunt down and kill the rest of the avisceti? She wants to assimilate their anafireon." As Katkin stared up into the poplars, she saw that many small birds flitted through the branches, lighting and alighting with silent grace. This gentle touch brought the golden leaves spiraling to Yrth.

Huw frowned. "That is too big a task for one young man to accomplish, even one as resourceful as Gwillam."

"I agree, but he is determined to carry it out, and rescue the rest of Maggrai's Firaithi slaves as well."

"I will find two or three *kylathie** from the village who are handy

---

* Older children in their teens

with a crossbow. If they are willing then I will send them with Gwillam."

Katkin gave him a grateful smile. "Thank you. That is what I hoped you would say. When he has finished his work, Gwillam wants to remain at Mornguard, close to Myrie and Deres Tama. I hope you will find room in the village for him."

"Of course. As my eldest son, one day the Tane's red feather will be his."

"What about Maia? I am surprised she does not want to inherit the position."

"In our world," he paused and cleared his throat. "In *my* world, I meant to say—a woman may never be Tane. But in any case, Maia has made it clear that she does not wish to stay in Mornguard."

Huw stared at the golden carpet. Katkin knew he had a question of his own, and that he did not want to ask it. Finally, he blurted out, "Where will you go, Katkin?"

She did not have a ready answer for him. Huw continued, "Of course, as one of the Kindreds, you are welcome to live in Mornguard with the rest of our people." He gazed at her directly for the first time. Katkin recognized something very like fear in his eyes.

Although nothing much mattered, there *was* something she could do after all—some small way she could make amends for all her careless cruelty to Huw Adaryi. She spoke with determination. "There is still much sickness in St. Valery. The people there need my help. I won't be coming to Mornguard."

He had the grace not to show his relief. His eyes were sad as he spoke to her for the last time. "My Queen... I know I was not what you wanted—not really. But still you gave me sixteen years of your life, and for that I thank you. I will carry your memory in my heart until I pass through Tsmar'enth. May the Wayfarers guide you wherever you wish to go." He looked up the path, towards Mornguard, and his foot took an expectant step forwards.

They had nothing left to say to each other. "You had better be going then. Goodbye, Huw." She gave him the briefest of hugs and then turned back to Deres Tama. Behind her, the little birds took wing and flew out of sight.

And yet, once she had decided to go back to St. Valery, Katkin found it was not so easy to get there. The crash had left the aermaran a hopeless ruin and the Firaithi had no ocean-worthy vessels at Mornguard. Though it took her completely out of her way, she had no choice but to return to Asaruthe by the worlds between, with Gunnar as her guide.

Many wonders filled the journey, but she did not see them. Katkin thought only of Dai, and how they had once traveled the worlds between together. She spoke little to her companions. Poppy and Gwillam watched their mother anxiously, hoping that when she reached Ruthecombe she might decide to stay.

The island was much as they had left it. Three starving dogs waited faithfully by the front door of Asavale, and greeted the travelers with pathetic barks and tail wagging. Gunnar slaughtered a sheep and gave them a huge pile of offal to make up for Jakob's desertion. Once he saw they were well fed, he disappeared, leaving Poppy, Jakob and Gwillam to throw open the doors and windows and air out Asavale.

Poppy wrinkled her nose in disgust at the smell of rotten potatoes issuing from the larder.

Gwillam scratched his head. "I know when Jakob left the island to rescue you. How can all this food be bad already?"

"Time passes differently in the Vastness, remember?" Poppy answered him. "I think there has been no one on Asaruthe for several weeks. Certainly the poor dogs were hungry enough!"

By the end of the afternoon, they had the dusty house tidy again and a joint of mutton roasting on a spit in the hearth. Gwillam brushed Jolly, while Jakob tried to comb the worst of the burrs from Wink and Bridie. Poppy sat contentedly by the fire, supervising the dinner and darning a huge pile of woolen socks. When Katkin came back from Ruthecombe, she saw Gunnar in the doorway, watching this domesticity with a sad half-smile on his face.

"Will you walk with me, Katkin? I have to tend to something on the south shore."

She nodded, a little mystified as to why he needed her company. On the climb down, he spoke little, and deflected questions about their destination. But by the careful way he gathered wild flowers along the route, Katkin felt sure she knew where they were going.

The sun slipped towards the horizon, bathing the sky in radiant shades of mother of pearl, shot through with cerise. Katkin and Gunnar reached the graves. A pair of wave-sculpted boulders marked the final resting place of Gwenn Faircrow and Arkady Svalbarad. It lay well above the spring high tide mark, in a sheltered hollow of the cliffs. Someone had placed a necklace of shells over each marker stone.

"It is such a peaceful place," Katkin offered quietly. "You chose well, Gunnar."

"Yes. Kadya loved the sound of the sea."

He bent his remaining knee clumsily and placed the flowers in a crumpled heap before the graves. He kept his head bowed for many minutes, gathering up sand and letting it spill through his fingers, in an intensely intimate expression of mourning. Katkin stood well back, wishing the bitter dregs of her own grief could be touched so readily.

After a time she inquired softly, "Why have you brought me here?"

He didn't answer her question. Instead, he spoke of Gwenn's death and his own part in it, as he brushed the grains of sand from his wounded hand. "Nothing remained afterwards. I buried keth'fell and..." he took a deep breath, trying to force the words to come. "Some ashes. And as for Inky..."

Gunnar awkwardly turned to face Katkin, still on his knee and stump. His eyes were as blue as the ocean and as deep—deep enough to hold all the suffering of the Yrth within them.

"When his body burned away, Hana's fire melted the sand underneath into glass. I dug it up when it was cool enough to handle. That is what I buried in his grave." Gunnar gently smoothed the sand again before groping for his crutch. His cheeks were wet with tears by the time he had struggled upright.

"Gunnar..." began Katkin, wanting to help him, but not knowing how.

He kept talking, as though he knew there was nothing she could say. "I found it hard, losing them like that. And yet in an odd way I felt happy too, knowing they were together, and at peace. Both of them had suffered so much..." He wiped his eyes and sighed. "But when I heard what you said about Fyn, I felt afraid. For Kadya. Because he died once before. Do you remember?"

She nodded her head, wondering why she had not thought of it herself. Arkady had succumbed to liver failure after he saved Gwenn's life on Starruthe.

"As soon as we reached the island this morning, I came here, to the gravesite. I could not bear the thought that he might have become a living ghost, like your Tomas de Vigny, alone in the Vastness. But he was *here*, with his Sutun, next to Gwenn." His eyes were imploring. "I want to be comforted by it, but I don't understand. Do you?"

Katkin nodded again, thoughtfully. "Maybe I do. When Kadya and I traveled together, after he left you and Gwenn on Starruthe, I asked him how he had come back to life. He had been hitting the bottle pretty hard so I did not pay much attention to his answer. Especially when he told me that he had not really been dead at all."

"But we all saw him. You are a doctor, and you believed him dead, did you not?"

"Yes, I did, but..."

He frowned. "Then I still don't understand."

"Kadya said that he had learned something from Dawa—a discipline of the Eastern Star called Firemma.* With it, he could hold on to his anafireon, and keep it with him for many days after it left his physical form. That is why he waited there, close to Dawa's house, when you went to the Vastness."

"And when Death opened the door, then he rejoined his body?"

"Yes." Katkin smiled, glad she could help after all. "Now do you see?"

He did, but he did not smile in return. Gunnar muttered, "The Skald did not like it—being cheated like that. No wonder he took Lut from me. Well, I have only a little silver left to spend. Mayhap he will play for someone else now."

That night as they sat around the kitchen table, Katkin asked Gwillam, "Can you find the way to St. Valery? By the worlds between?"

He shook his head. "I have only been there by boat. Lut took us, remember? And then on the way back, Fyn brought us back to the island."

"The time for travel between the worlds has passed," Gunnar growled. "You heard what Eira said."

"How will we get there then?" Katkin sighed. "Gwillam will want to meet the lads from Mornguard, and I have to get back to

* Lit. spirit devotion.

Willow's house. She will know who is running the country now. If anyone is."

Jakob had been busy pulling a jug of ale from the firkin in the corner of the kitchen. He poured a beaker for his father, and one for himself. "I can take you by boat," he offered. "The *Spry Lass* is a fine craft, and she can bear us along the Reach."

Gwillam's face betrayed his apprehension. "Are you sure you can find the way? I don't want another shipwreck!"

Gunnar said proudly, "You can trust the lad to guide you. He is a true son of the Mariner."

Katkin asked, "Where is my mirror, Jakob? I wanted to take it to St. Valery with me."

"I left it at your house, Grandmother."

She frowned. "Are you sure? I did not see it when I went to Ruthecombe this morning."

Shortly after she had returned to the island, Katkin walked over to the stone house she had shared with Huw. She asked no one to accompany her, thinking that she would best savor the memories, both bitter and sweet, alone. When she arrived, the front door stood wide open and rats had made themselves at home inside. They had eaten all the remaining food in the pantry, and chewed great holes in the woolen stuff piled by the fireplace.

The house reeked of sour milk. Katkin dumped the curds from the milk crock into a clean linen sheet and twisted out most the liquid, then left it hanging on the clothesline. In a few days, Poppy could salt it, making pounds of white cheese that she could then shape and coat in red wax, and leave to age in the cool stores. But Katkin did not plan to linger on Asaruthe long enough to sample the finished product. The damp and dreary cottage no longer felt like any kind of home, and she had her bleak mission to tend to in St. Valery.

Jakob interrupted her memories. "I was in a hurry, but I remember putting it on the bed. I took the toasting fork, nothing else."

"And you looked very fearsome when you came to rescue me with it," Poppy giggled. Jakob colored as Gwillam struck up a comic ditty about a mighty warrior who cut a wide swathe through his enemies with his trusty fireplace tool, Forkarnen.

Poppy reached under the table and squeezed his hand. "Never mind, Jakob," she whispered. "I shouldn't have made fun. You were wonderfully brave."

Jakob whispered in return, "Don't be sorry. Look at Dad's face. I haven't seen him smile like that in ages."

By the time Katkin and Gwillam were ready to depart for St. Valery, Poppy had already moved her things from Katkin and Huw's old cottage. She took over a bright and airy space that had once been Gwenn's spinning room. "It will be easier for me to take care of the livestock from here," she explained breezily to her mother. But Katkin had already noticed the amount of time that Poppy and Jakob were spending together.

When Poppy expressed an interest in herbs to prevent pregnancy, Katkin grew even more suspicious. "Do you need them?" she asked, a little too sharply.

"No... Not exactly. Not right now. But I might, sometime in the future. Perhaps you had better show me where you keep such things, just in case." While Katkin showed her the various preparations, Poppy busily looked in one of the medical texts.

"What about this one? Tansy, is it called?"

"That will cause miscarriage, and make you quite ill. It is a very dangerous herb."

"Oh," said Poppy, and carefully marked her place in the book.

"Take care," Katkin told her daughter quietly, as they stood waiting for Gwillam to finish packing his bag and join them outside Asavale. "Jakob isn't the ruffian he once was, but neither is he Lut. Don't get in over your head with him, or you might regret it later. There are other fish in the sea besides Gunnar Strong Arm's boys, you know."

Poppy gave her mother an odd glance. "I know he isn't Lut, but Jakob is a good man. He will take care of me, when the time comes."

Katkin gazed at her in confusion. "When the time comes for what, Poppy?"

Poppy dropped her eyes so that she might carefully smooth her muslin gown. Her hands trembled, just a bit. "Nothing. Look, here is Gwillam, at last. About time, you sluggard! Where is Jakob?"

"Talking to Ikor. He will be here soon." Just then, Gunnar limped to the front door, with Jakob behind him. Gwillam grinned at him. "Got your toasting fork all packed?"

Poppy gave her mother one last hug and went to stand behind Gunnar. Jakob came very close to her, and wrapped his arm around her waist. She rested against him for a moment. "Are you truly coming back?" she whispered. "What if Maia..."

"Don't worry. I won't leave you, I promise."

Twenty-One

Willow

Katkin dropped the hood that she had worn to stay warm in the frigid winter wind. It had not been necessary for her to hide her face for any other reason. No Guardsmen remained in the Abelard compound at Kaisset. When she knocked, Queen Roseberry herself answered the door.

Roseberry stared and then smiled in belated recognition. "Aunt! You have returned to us. Emile said you would come back, but mother did not believe him. Goodness, you look fair frozen. Come into the kitchen and warm yourself." Katkin stepped inside, somewhat cheered by Roseberry's breathless welcome. She continued, "Let me make you something hot to drink."

"Some coffee would be wonderful. I have been walking almost all day." As Roseberry bustled about the kitchen, Katkin reflected on her journey. Jakob had left them by the western shores of the Mistmere, close to St. Salle. She waited with Gwillam, just inside the fringe of trees, wondering how he would meet up with the other *kylathie* Huw had promised to send. But it was not long before a low whistle echoed through the early morning mist. Maia, now looking as hoydenish as she did when she first arrived on Asaruthe, stepped from the shadows, with four other lithe girls at her back. They carried packs and crossbows.

"Welcome to the hunting party," she said to Gwillam. "Patre didn't want me to come, but I insisted. Oh, and you can call me Rab again."

Gwillam smiled at this and shouldered his pack. "You will be all right, Katkin?"

"Of course. I will walk to Willow's before nightfall."

The woods had been quiet. Katkin had not seen a single soul

all day. Her mood, which had been somewhat buoyant when they reached Beaumarais, sank as surely as the sun making its way across the pale blue sky.

Roseberry interrupted her reverie. "Sorry, but there is no coffee to be had anywhere in the kingdom. We will have to drink roasted chicory and acorns."

"Anything warm to drink would be most welcome, but surely that is no job for a ruling Queen? Where are your servants?"

She roared with laughter at this. "Queen? There is no ruler in Beaumarais. Even Daddy hasn't been able to bring order to the country, not since Trissy passed on." She glanced guiltily over at Katkin, trying to judge her reaction. "You knew about that already, I hope?"

Katkin nodded as she dragged a settle over so that she could sit close to the fire. "I did. Poppy told me, a while ago. Perhaps if you went to St. Valery, the people would rally round..."

Roseberry's round face turned obstinate. "I don't want to be Queen! And anyway, my health wouldn't stand it."

Just then Yannick threw open the door and limped into the room. "Who are you talking to? Have those beggars returned again? I told them we had no..."

He caught sight of his sister-in-law's chestnut curls. "You! By the gods, this is most unexpected." He groped for his pistol, but Roseberry calmly stepped in between the General and his target.

"Put that away, at once, Daddy. Aunt Katkin is my guest."

He frowned, but his argument sounded half-hearted at best. "Roseberry, she is a traitor to the realm. I must arrest her."

"You *must* obey me, Daddy. I am your Queen." She glared at her father, who subsided at once, and holstered his pistol.

Katkin smiled inwardly at this, thinking that Roseberry was not averse to reigning when it suited her. Yannick limped to the table and dragged out a chair. He did not seem particularly upset, and Katkin got the impression that his threat to take her into custody had almost been done for the sake of appearances.

Roseberry had finished brewing the drink, and handed her father and aunt a steaming mug. Despite her protestations, Katkin thought Roseberry looked rather better than the last time she had seen her. Her eyes were sharp and bright, and she seemed to have slimmed down. Yannick, too, looked thinner, and care had etched many new lines on his face.

"Are you hungry?" Roseberry asked as Katkin took a sip of the bitter brew. "We don't have much, but you are welcome to some black bread and dripping."

Katkin shook her head, wondering on this poverty. The answers would no doubt be found in St. Valery and she meant to go there soon, but not without seeing her sister. "Where is Willow?"

A look passed between Yannick and Roseberry. "Mummy isn't well. She has taken to her bed and will receive no visitors. Only old Inge is allowed to tend to her now."

Yannick wrung his hands together. "Willow has the Bludseth." Tears sprang to his eyes. "She has fought very bravely but we don't expect her to last much longer."

Katkin jumped up, remembering Bastet's last word to her. *Willow*... "You must let me see her. Maybe I can help."

Yannick stood too, and his chair clattered backwards to the floor. "You would practice your filthy witchcraft under my roof again?" He took a step towards her with his fists clenched.

She did not back away. "Yes. Yes, I would. If I thought I could save my sister, I would not hesitate." Katkin stared at Yannick, her eyes blazing. His face softened, and he looked very old.

"Then by all means, please try. Prime God has not heeded my prayers, so why should I not embrace the old ways?" He passed the frayed sleeve of his uniform jacket across his eyes.

"Prime God is no more. And the old ways are dead too. We must let go of what is passed and find a new path."

Yannick pondered this gravely. "There will be no more Gods?"

Katkin shrugged. "There will always be Death. But I think He has greater things on His mind than our paltry troubles."

The darkened room reminded Katkin poignantly of the cave in which she had found Lalluna. Through the gloom, she saw that Willow lay on a high feather mattress, with several pillows behind her head. Her eyes were slack and she looked to be sleeping. Her breaths came and went, following one after another with effort.

Inge sat in a chair in the corner, also dozing. Roseberry shook the old cook's shoulder gently. "We will watch for awhile. There is fresh chicory in the kitchen. Have a cup and a bite to eat, Inge."

"Your mother has been mighty restless this afternoon, Miss Rose. She made me shut all the blinds. Said the light pained her eyes.

And she has been coughing something terrible."

Katkin sat on the edge of Willow's bed, looking at the livid red weals covering her sister's drawn face. The streaks extended onto her neck, and disappeared beneath the high-necked gown she wore. A crust of blood clung to the corners of her mouth.

"Willow? It is Katkin. How are you feeling?" She tried to make her voice sound untroubled.

Her sister's eyes fluttered open. "Katkin?" Willow clutched her hand. Her speech was low and raw, with frequent pauses for coughing. "I am so happy you have come back. When I heard you had gone with the Outlaw Glint, I thought..." She sighed and stirred in her bed. "Gods, I am sorry you have to see me like this."

"How on Yrth did you get the Bludseth? I thought you of all people would be safe from it."

Willow misunderstood her observation. "After Tristan died most of the Guard deserted. Turns out he had forgotten to pay them for quite some time. Without any kind of authority, law and order fled soon after. Bands of sick tramps roamed the countryside, breaking into houses, taking what food they could find. Roseberry and I were here alone when they attacked."

"I understand that, Willow. But you are of the kindreds, just as I am. You should be immune to the Bludseth."

"My mother was a serving girl," Willow said slowly, and then licked her cracked lips. "Father took her to his bed one night in a drunken rage, after he had fought with Mother. Later, when they reconciled, he sent her away, and Mother pretended that she had been pregnant with me."

Katkin stared at her sister's pale, sweaty countenance in shock. "I never heard that before. How did you find out?"

Willow gave a wan smile. "Nurse told me. She seemed rather pleased about the whole affair."

"So that is why she said she came for me instead of you! Did you know she was my grandmother?"

She shook her head. "No, but it does not surprise me. I often felt jealous, growing up, because I knew she favored you over me." Willow began to cough. She turned her face away from Katkin and curled over the side of the bed, obviously in grave pain. Yannick and Roseberry hurried to her side.

Yannick turned to Katkin, a desperate plea in his eyes.

Katkin's voice was gentle. "I will try, but I can make you no promises. Take Roseberry and wait outside."

He took her hand, gripping it hard. "For what it is worth, I am sorry I said all those things when the Unity took Berry. I know thirty years is a long time to wait for an apology."

"Come on, Daddy." Roseberry tugged at his arm. "Let Aunt do her work in peace. You can grovel later, when she has finished healing Mummy." Katkin could only nod hopefully as she watched them depart.

She helped Willow to sit up again and arranged her pillows. Her sister lay pale and unmoving, her lips a thin blue line of suffering.

"I am going to try something," Katkin said softly. "By your leave."

Willow's eyes opened halfway as she spoke with unaccustomed sourness. "I thought you said you had lost your gift?"

"I found it again, dear Willow. Under the trees." She closed her eyes and placed her hand on her sister's chest. "One thing you must remember though, before I begin. Sometimes I... go to sleep after I heal someone. It makes me very tired. So you must not be alarmed if that happens, all right?"

Willow whispered, "What will you do? Will it hurt?"

"No," said Katkin, resolutely. "It will not hurt you a bit."

She worried that she would not be able to reach the Deres and ask for their help. But the endless marches of St. Valery's Acre surrounded Kaisset and Katkin found the trees easily, by casting about with her mind. She felt them lend their strength, and it flowed from her fingertips into Willow. As the sickness left her sister, Katkin felt her own lungs begin to ache and then to burn. Soon, she experienced the terrible ravages of the Bludseth—felt the splitting pain in her head, the ache in every joint, and the crackling fire of the welts on her skin.

But slowly, exceedingly slowly, Willow's pain ceased.

Willow opened her eyes and stretched as Katkin pitched forward on to the bed. She did not wake when her sister shook her, nor when her overjoyed cries brought Yannick and Roseberry running. When Willow left her sickbed, they put Katkin into it, and waited. But still she did not stir.

People surrounded her, clawed at her—their faces scarred with ugly red wounds. "You must help us!" they cried, and Katkin backed away in terror, knowing she could do nothing without the trees. The pain in her chest made it hard to run, and her legs felt like lead. Still the needy ones chased her onwards.

She woke to Emile's voice, as he spoke softly to his mother. "Aunt has been muttering things in her sleep. I believe she is almost with us again."

"Emile? Katkin's tongue felt like a dusty stone lodged between her jaws.

A woman spoke first. "Thank the gods. Give her something to drink, Emi." A cool draught of water dribbled between her lips and loosened the stone somewhat. Katkin opened her eyes and rubbed away the blurriness. Then she found her sister's face and blinked in surprise.

"You are well?" she whispered.

Willow's eyes were bright and steady. "Indeed I am, but I have been very worried. When you told me you might go to sleep I did not know you meant for a whole week!"

Katkin, still groggy, tried to take this in and failed. "Did you say I have been sleeping for a week? That is not possible." Emile helped her sit up, and gave her some more water. A rumbling twinge in her chest made it difficult to swallow.

Emile spoke. "Mother is quite correct. But can you say why it is so? I remember when you saved my life you slept for an hour or two afterwards, at most."

Katkin looked around her, while trying to think of an explanation. The room was not a familiar one. Lanterns burned in niches scattered about the walls, but barely cut through the gloom. The rough curving stonework and high embrasures reminded her of the Citadel, but she knew it was not. She knew her former home as well as a good friend, but this place felt cold and strange.

"Where am I? Why did we leave Kaisset?"

"We had no choice," Willow said. "The trouble started after Inge went to the village for food. She told her family of my healing and they gossiped to others. Before long, the compound swarmed with those who had the sickness. They clamored to see you, wanting a cure." Katkin blanched at this, reminded of her dream. "When Yannick tried to send them away, the most desperate among them grew violent. They set fire to the barn, and attacked the main house.

We would have been lost if Emile and his Swallows had not come to the rescue. With their help we were able to creep away under cover of darkness."

"Oh, Willow, I am so sorry. But where on Yrth did you bring me?"

"This place is known to you, though I guess you have never been here," Emile said. "It is the Watchkeep on Split Island."

"*Maggrai's* Watchkeep?" Katkin struggled to sit up and the burning pain doubled. "Can it really be safe here?"

Yannick, who had been hanging back, limped over. "It is the *only* safe place in the kingdom at the moment. The Citadel has been overrun by ex-Guardsmen, and the City is in chaos. Thank the Gods for the Swallows."

Roseberry, somehow still lighthearted after all their troubles, chuckled. "I never thought to hear those words pass your lips, Daddy."

"Things change, Berry," he said mildly.

Katkin's eyes darted from face to face. "I still don't..."

Willow patted her hand with sisterly concern. "Don't fret, Katkin. Emile can explain it to you while I make you something to eat."

He sat by the bed. His similarity to her own people, the Anandi, struck Katkin once again. That used to make some kind of sense, but now given what she knew of her sister's true parentage, it made none at all.

"Willow?"

"Hmm?" her sister answered, as she fried eggs and black bread in a pan over a brazier.

"What was your mother's name?"

"Something quite unusual. Tanith, I think it was. I don't remember her at all."

Katkin settled back into her covers, ready now to listen to whatever tale Emile had to tell her. The Deres were still directing everything, and she had no complaints.

Emile stared at the empty space that had once held Maggrai's mirror and tugged at his ear. "Do you remember I once told you I was sent away?"

She nodded.

He frowned at the memory, but his voice held no bitterness. "I had been captured. They took me to the Citadel, but I won't dwell on what happened after. I endured many days of torment, and I remember little enough of it now. Eventually, I became Uncle Tristan's servant. He used me in his Chymericum, for by then I was deaf and dumb and no risk to his secret experiments."

Katkin sighed, knowing he had left a great deal of his terrible suffering unspoken. "But how did you escape? You said something to me about the Deres, though I did not know, then, what you meant."

"Tristan himself sent me to them."

"Tristan?" Katkin echoed in surprise. "He has not been known for such acts of kindness in the past."

"It was not he who first thought to do so," said Emile, pensively. "There was a woman with him—a very beautiful woman, dressed in a silvery gown. It seemed to me that she told him to place me in the Chronagine, so that it might be tested. When he turned away, she smiled at me, and moved her lips so that I might understand her words without hearing them."

"What did she say?"

"She told me not to fear. Her face was the last thing I saw before I was thrust screaming through a tunnel of light. Then I fell into darkness so complete I thought I had been blinded. I suppose I should have been afraid, but I knew nothing but peace. Perhaps it was the power of Azothe's words on me."

"How did you know her name?" said Katkin sharply. "I thought you said you were deaf."

"I learned her name after," he said, and blushed.

Willow brought the eggs, mashed and spread on top of the bread. Katkin nibbled a crust while Emile continued his tale. "The *Na*-Irais came. I could not see them, but their touch was gentle, and again I did not fear. When I could hear again and speak, they took me to a strange land, full of wonder. I heard the song of the trees, and learned that the Irais were their servants. The Deres and I spoke for a long while, but I have no memory of time passing."

"What a tale!" said Katkin, in an awestruck tone. "I have seen the Deres myself, and they are mighty. But what happened then?"

Emile gave her an oblique glance—half-curious and half-concerned. "An angel came to me as I wandered amongst the trees. He looked a lot like the Glint, but he had wings of grey, like a dove."

Katkin's mouth went dry again. "Did he say his name?"

"It was Ben'aryn. He said he had a favor to ask, and in return he would help me get back to Beaumarais." Emile smiled sheepishly. "Can you think what he asked me to do, Aunt?"

She spoke with certainty. "He is the friend you said wanted a lock of Dai's hair." But she wondered to herself what possible need Ben'aryn could have for such a thing. "Did he say anything else?"

Emile shook his head. "Nothing at all. Once I had agreed to his request, he touched my face and I fell into a deep sleep. I awoke in this room. And Azothe was here too, and she said she had been waiting for me. I felt afraid, for I knew the Master of this place, and I thought that she must be his servant. But then Azothe told me that he would soon be no more.

She was looking for an object, a globe of blue. I found it for her, locked away in a box under yon bench." He gestured at the wooden trestle table in the center of the room. "Azothe said she would soon have need of it, and told me to leave it on top, where she could find it when she returned. And then..." Emile fell silent and stared at the ground.

Katkin nodded, understanding a great deal more of her actions than he seemed to. "Then?"

"Eventually Azothe left me, using the *Mebbain*. She said she had business with the King. It took me a long time to find my own way out."

"How did you leave? Poppy and Jakob could find no exit."

"There is a set of steps leading down to the ground—it winds around the inside of the Tower walls. The trapdoor is cleverly hidden amongst the floorboards, and covered with a cabinet, over there." He pointed to the far wall. "I left the island by swimming the Ariane. The current took me far along the river before I could make my way to shore. Then I headed for the Acre. The Swallows were there, with Glint and Myrie, and they were glad to see me." He smiled. "The rest you know, Aunt."

No one said anything for a few moments. Willow prowled around the Watchkeep before turning to her husband. "What should we do now, Yannick? We cannot stay in this place forever."

Yannick gazed at Katkin, and then at his son. "There is work to be done, and it should begin—at once." He crossed the floor to Emile and threw an arm over his shoulders. "Will you and your

Swallows allow a stubborn old mule like me to join your ranks? 'Tis true we once fought on opposite sides of the battlefield, but now I think we share the same cause—bringing order back to Beaumarais."

Emile replied, without a trace of bitterness. "Well spoken, my father. We Swallows have ever been ready to fight for what is right. And Aunt Katkin will help as well, will she not?"

"Me? Surely Roseberry is the one you need. She is the Queen."

Roseberry snorted. "I have not set foot in the Citadel for years. My subjects have forgotten my face, if they knew it at all."

Katkin lay back on the bed. The brief interest she had felt when Emile told his tale withered and she felt nothing but calm indifference. "I am sorry, but I cannot be of any use to you. Why would the people listen to me, anyway? *My* son caused all the troubles they have now."

Willow took up the cause. "Because your reign is the last memory many of us have of peace and prosperity. Everyone knows that you abdicated under pressure from Philip Tremayne and the House of Deputies. I believe the City of Isle St. Valery would welcome you with rejoicing if you returned."

"Even if that were true, how could I get there? If the countryside is as lawless as you say, I would not be able to move without Bludseth sufferers dogging my every step. And there is nothing I can do for them either."

Willow looked at her in surprise. "Why not? You helped me."

She sighed and rubbed her breastbone, as the pain in her chest flared again. "I just don't think I have the strength."

Emile, grinning, agreed with her. "Aunt Katkin cannot be Queen if she is always sleeping. We will have to help the unfortunate ones some other way."

Willow brightened and looked over to Roseberry. "What about the Infirmarie?"

"You could not possibly make use of that. It is in a terrible state," Katkin objected listlessly. "And Lalluna is no more. How would you..."

"Leave that to me, Aunt," Roseberry interrupted, with a confident gleam in her eye. "Tris forced me to leave my Juvenead`, long ago. It has been my dearest wish to return to it, ever since.

---

* Apprenticeship in the Unity of Lalluna.

And Mummy knows everyone in the villages. She can help me find the other ex-Sisters of the Unity." Roseberry gazed at Katkin, and rubbed her chubby hands with glee. "As for our patron, we will have the Arkafina. The gentle Angel of Belladore will bring healing, I am sure of it."

The memory of her former home woke within Katkin a quiet kind of resolve, though the pain in her chest did not abate. She smiled tiredly. "All right, you have won me to the cause. I will help you, as much as I am able."

The sun rose over the island of Asaruthe. Poppy and Jakob had gotten up early, and trudged to Ruthecombe. Now they stood in the middle of Katkin's sickroom.

Poppy consulted the medicinal text she had bookmarked. "Help me find some things in the herb store—I need pennyroyal, blue cohosh and tansy."

Jakob frowned and shook his head, then began to sort through the boxes and packets of wrapped herbs that Katkin had left behind. One by one, he removed the three she had selected. "Are you sure?" he asked, for the hundredth time. "Why don't you wait a day or two, and think about it some more?"

She sighed patiently. "I have to take these herbs within a few weeks of conception or they won't work. The book says so. How much time elapsed while we were in the Vastness, I have no clue. So it is now or never, Jakob."

He did not care about the child, not exactly. Jakob knew it wasn't his. But he did care about Poppy, and he worried that she was making a terrible mistake. "It is dangerous for you to take these herbs, is it not?"

"Only a little," she lied. "I am quite sure I know what I am doing."

Glowering, Jakob slid into the chair on the other side of the table. Poppy kept her eyes on the open book that lay between them. Jakob flipped it shut. "I don't care who the baby's father is, and neither should you. We can raise it like it was ours. Dad won't tell anyone."

"I can't pretend it didn't happen! How can I bring that monster's child into the world?"

Jakob seized on a thin thread of hope. "Are you so sure it is his?

You told me you couldn't remember much of anything after you put the dress on. Maybe..."

Poppy blushed scarlet. "I am sure I would remember something like that!" But under Jakob's piercing blue-eyed stare, uncertainty began to gnaw at her. There had been two weeks, at least, between Madame's and the moment of Tristan's death in the Citadel Tower.

Jakob had been studying her face, watching for signs of hesitation. He took her hand and squeezed it. "Put those things away, Poppy. You don't need them. I will take care of you and the baby, I promise."

She sighed, but tried once more to convince him. "Jakob, you don't even like living on Asaruthe. You have said so, many times. If I have this baby, it will be one more thing that ties you to this island."

"I won't leave here anyway, not while Dad lives. I owe him that, after what happened with Ma and Pop. So why should we not raise the child together? Can you be happy with that, Poppy?"

"I guess so..." she said slowly. "But are you so sure that you can?"

Twenty-Two

Rimu

They decided to begin with the Infirmarie. For, as Roseberry remarked, "Once we have a place for the sick to rest and recuperate, then the rest of the citizenry will be able to live in peace."

"I hope so," murmured Katkin. "How many Swallows did you find to help us, Emile?"

Her nephew grinned. "Plenty, as long as the Infirmarie is not defended. Do you think that is likely, Sir?" he asked Yannick.

His father, who had removed the frayed uniform of the Black Guard and donned the faded black of the Swallows, shook his head. "It is doubtful. I think most of my former subordinates will be living high in the Citadel, not hanging about in Maggrai's old haunts. I never met the man who could bear to be in the same room as that demon. Except the King, of course."

Emile bent his dark head to a map of the Infirmarie grounds, hastily sketched by Katkin. His finger traced a smudge at the edge of the map. "There is a path over Mt. Hythea?"

Yannick looked over Emile's shoulder. "I know it well. Once on the summer solstice, I rode that way, with Roseberry in my arms—through a hidden pass close to the top of the mountain, and then down the other side. 'Tis steep and winding, but passable, with care." A look passed between him and Katkin, the memory unspoken but seemingly as close as yesterday. Yannick said matter-of-factly, "I can think of one sacrament that is best left unpracticed when the Infirmarie is reopened."

"Now that my Lady is no more, who can say what comfort the ill may find there, sacrament or no?" Katkin sighed.

Emile looked baffled and tried to get the strategizing back on track. "So it is possible to enter the Infirmarie precincts from above?"

"Yes," Katkin answered him. "The path winds past the entrance to the Temple, and through the cemetery, and ends by the back entrance to the Springhouse. It should be possible for men and horses to move along it, especially at night."

"Very well. I will send word to the Swallows. But how will we cross the Mistmere?"

"Leave that to me," Willow said. "I know many people in Kaisset with boats, and I am sure I can commandeer a few of them, for a good cause. Which reminds me—what shall we call our little group of revolutionaries?"

Katkin and Yannick shrugged.

Roseberry grinned. "How about the Salve?"

Emile took this up at once. "That is perfect! Beaumarais needs a potent cure to restore her to health. We will be that medicine."

"And if it is bitter to taste?" Katkin asked.

He did not seem daunted. "Many purgatives are, Aunt. But in the end, it is right to heal the body by whatever means are necessary, even if they are unpalatable. As a healer, you of all people should know this."

As Willow had promised, the requisitioned boats waited for them on the shores of the Mistmere. The members of the Salve, some ninety in all, embarked from Kaisset in sixteen overcrowded vessels.

The sea lay flat, like black glass, as they set off close to midnight. The moon, a dull quarter, hid her face behind a narrow band of clouds, leaving the dusty stars to light their way. Katkin wondered if Lalluna had somehow been able to bless their undertaking and the thought gave her forlorn hope.

"Let's move," Emile whispered. "Try to stay together as much as possible."

The timbers creaked and rocked as the former Swallows took to the oars. Yannick and Emile stood side by side in the lead boat, their enmity forgotten. Katkin took comfort in this, for if they could mend such a breach, then perhaps her country might find healing as well. But Emile and Roseberry would bring such a cure, if it existed. Not the former Queen Arkafina.

After an hour, the steep slopes of Hythea filled a quadrant of the nighttime sky with blackness. "There is the jetty," Yannick hissed. "We must bring the boats in one at a time, for there is not much shoreline."

The unloading took some time in the darkness, for the rickety jetty had many missing planks. Several of the Salve's members took unwelcome cold-water baths in the interim. At last, they all stood on the narrow shingled strip of land that skirted the base of the mountain.

Emile had gone ahead to find the start of the path. He returned, cursing quietly. "I cannot see a thing in this soup. Aunt, do you remember anything about the lay of the land here?"

Katkin walked to the edge of the scrubby woodland that clothed the side of Hythea. She could see nothing resembling a track. Stumbling slightly, she reached out to the nearest tree, and felt the electric shock of contact with the bark.

"Will you help me in this, also?" she whispered. "Deres, will you help?"

The clouds hiding the moon parted, and the dusky shadows fled. The track snaked up the side of the mountain, shining like a satin ribbon in the light.

"Here," Katkin called softly to the others. "The way is here."

The walk to the pass took two hard hours, and her chest ached abominably before they finished. The younger and fitter members of the Salve passed her, leaving Katkin dead last in the line. She wished then that she had stayed behind with Yannick, whose injury prevented him from making the climb. But Katkin struggled on regardless, and when the pass came into sight, she saw the others assembled at the top.

Emile hurried back to meet her. "Aunt, I am sorry we left you behind. Are you all right?" Her face looked haggard and grey in the moonlight. "Come and sit by me for a moment." He passed her a flask of brandy, after wiping the mouth carefully with a handkerchief. "Some liquid nerve?" He grinned—a charming flash of white in the darkness—and patted her arm.

Katkin took a long drink, feeling the warmth spread through her and drown the pain in her ribs. "What now?"

"The downhill part should go faster. Then we will spread out and reconnoiter. I will assign a couple of men to stay here with you."

"That won't be necessary. I am perfectly capable of walking *down* the track." Emile looked about to argue, and she added, "Anyway, I know the ways of the Infirmarie better than anyone here."

He passed her the flask again. "Very well, but this time stay close by me. I would not like to lose our Queen to the darkness."

Katkin shook her head, thinking he did not know how prescient that might be.

"I can see a light moving, just inside the window. There!" Emile whispered to Katkin as they stood behind the Springhouse with the rest of the Salve clustered at their back. She peered through the branches of an untidy elderberry bush at the side of the building to which he had directed her eyes. The cracks between the boarded up windows allowed hardly any view of the interior.

"Are you sure? I cannot see..." But as she squinted in the darkness she did catch sight of shadowy figures moving about. Katkin caught her breath. "Wait! There are three, maybe four people inside. What should we do? Retreat?"

Emile and the others snorted at this. "I think the odds are on our side, Aunt. There are ninety of us."

"There may be a hundred and ninety of *them*, all armed to the teeth. All we know is what we can see from this window."

Emile pointed left and right to his followers, and they crept through the dew-laden grass. "We will soon know more," he said as he watched them fade into the rosy dawn light. Meanwhile, after removing a whetstone from his pocket, he settled down to sharpen his battered sword.

Katkin watched him, amazed at his calm demeanor. He believed that they could take St. Valery with a force of less that one hundred ragged soldiers, many armed with nothing but short-bladed knives. She found this courage admirable, but Katkin still hoped to win the City back without more violence.

The second-in-command, Louis, squatted beside Emile. "Why the delay? The sun is rising. We should attack soon."

"Be patient, my friend. As soon as the scouts come back, we will know how many we are up against. Aunt is right. It shows no wisdom to dive into murky waters."

Ten minutes passed, while an early morning chorus of song from the resident birds filled the air. The sun would be shining on the jetty where Yannick waited with the boats, but under the shadow of Hythea, it was still quite dark. The scouts returned and whispered their reports to Emile. "Very well. Let us move. There are only five people visible in the windows. We should be able to capture them without much of a struggle."

Katkin let the others pass her, knowing she would be useless in any fighting. She watched as they broke open the door to the Springhouse. As the Salve made the first strike of the battle to free the Infirmarie, a volley of crossbow bolts scattered those crossing the threshold. Several found their marks.

As the surprised attackers staggered back, Katkin could hear shouts from inside. "Hurry! Get that door closed. Good work, Rab! Keep their leader covered." With a cry of alarm, she hurried forward.

"Don't shoot! We are friends." The door slammed in her face, and she knew those inside had not heard her words. The other Salve members retreated to the band of shrubs and Katkin went with them. She quickly thought of a new strategy. "Does anyone have a piece of paper?"

"They have Emile in there!" Louis hissed. "We need to do more than write them a polite note. Form up to attack," he ordered the others behind him.

"Wait! My son is in there, too. I heard him speak, just now. I need that paper." Someone handed Katkin a grubby bit of rolled parchment, and she pulled a charcoal from her pocket. A few seconds later she had written a terse message and tied it to a stone. She examined the back of the Springhouse. Boards covered the broken windows at ground level. The second tier, consisting of narrow panes of glass that opened outwards to release the steam from the bathing pools, looked miraculously intact. "Can you hit that high window from here?" she asked Louis.

He frowned. "I think so, but I still don't see..."

"Then throw this, and hurry. There has already been more fighting than necessary. We must try to prevent any more bloodshed."

Louis whipped the stone through the air, and it smote the window with the crash of breaking glass. Nothing happened for a minute or more, and as Katkin waited impatiently, the men behind her began to murmur.

"Form up," said Louis, more resolutely. Just when it seemed the Salve would attack, the door opened a crack, and a white cloth appeared. It fluttered for a moment in the shadows, like a timid dove, and then moved forward into the light.

"Gwillam!" shouted Katkin, and hurried to meet him.

"So you made this your headquarters?" Katkin asked Maia, as they sat together, sipping tea.

"It was the best place for us," she answered. "Many of the avisceti thought of the Infirmarie as home, so we were able to pick them off as they returned to their roosts. Poor creatures," she sighed. "Once Maggrai, their master, died, they had no will to keep hunting and killing. Most were almost dead from starvation when we found them."

"How many have you dispatched?"

"About fifty," Maia said with a shrug. "I don't think there are any left now."

Katkin saw a group of ragged Firaithi huddled in the corner of the bathing house. Several members of the Salve passed amongst them with bread and tea. "And where did you find those unfortunates?"

Gwillam joined them, and threw himself on the ground beside Maia. "The last of the corsfyre hunters? Maggrai had exhausted all the local stock of dead souls, so he sent them far afield, into the Vastness. When they returned, they seemed very surprised to find us here. Not that they could say so, of course," he added. "Their tongues have been cut out."

Katkin shuddered in horror. "You must take them to Mornguard soon, so that they may be reunited with their loved ones."

Her son grinned. "If you had timed your unprovoked attack a day later, we would already have been gone."

"I am sorry about that. But we had no way of knowing you had hidden yourselves in here."

"There is no need to feel bad. We are unhurt. And anyway, the man we captured... Emile? He already apologized, many times." Maia gazed over to where Emile stood, consulting with some of the injured Salve members.

Gwillam elbowed her in the ribs. "Stop eyeing him like that."

"Well he *is* very good-looking," she said, with a bright grin. "Too bad he is already taken."

Katkin could not help herself. "Really? How on Yrth do you know? I have not seen him show much of an interest in anyone."

"As soon as he laid eyes on Gwillam, he started asking questions," Maia added wickedly.

"What *sort* of questions?"

Gwillam guffawed. "Nothing like that, Katkin. He wanted to know if I had an older sister, named Azothe." He gave a self-conscious shrug. "Apparently I look like her, or something. So I told him about Poppy, and the haunted dress. He seemed very keen to see her again, and said he would go to Asaruthe as soon as he finished his business here in St. Valery."

"Really?" Katkin repeated in bafflement. "Poppy never mentioned it. But I suppose they did spend some time together, in the Watchkeep. She must have made quite an impression on him."

"I'd say she did," Maia agreed with a knowing smirk.

Gwillam and the others left the same day, escorting the bewildered Firaithi to Mornguard. Inside his shirt, he carried a leather pouch with forty-eight ruby red pieces of corsfyre to give to Myriadne. He knew these extra souls might further isolate her, but Gwillam was not as worried as he might have been. One of the hunters, a brave and lovely girl named Enfys, who was a crack shot with a crossbow, had taken a liking to him.

"Farewell, Katkin." Gwillam wiped a tear from his eye. "I hope I will see you again soon."

Katkin embraced him. "Of course. You may visit me whenever you like. And bring your friend with you." He had blushed at this. "She seems a fine partner for a future Tane, my son. I am sure your Patre will be very proud."

Maia had decreed that she would remain, "to help the Cause," as she put it. But Katkin believed she was more interested in Emile, for she overheard Maia questioning him about his plans to visit Asaruthe, and offering to show him the way by the worlds between.

Though Emile's relationship with Poppy made her curious, Katkin could not ask him about it. Emile spent his days in the City proper, overseeing the squads of Salvatores, who roamed the streets quelling trouble. And Katkin soon had other business to occupy her, for both invalids and former sisters had begun to arrive at the Infirmarie. Roseberry mobilized an army of willing hands to scrub and disinfect the main ward and treatment rooms.

"There is not as much damage to the main building as we feared," she informed Katkin. "Maggrai seems to have concentrated his evil work in one wing, and shut the rest of the rooms. We have found many supplies untouched."

Emile and Yannick, meanwhile, had entered into negotiations with the renegades at the Citadel. They begged Katkin to proclaim herself Queen once more, and order her Guard to reform. But Katkin, remembering her humiliation in front of the Chamber of Deputies, did not wish to force herself upon the citizens of Beaumarais.

"When the people call my name, as they did when I first became Queen Arkafina, then I will answer. Not before." She made no secret of the fact that she hoped that call would never come.

Willow, Yannick and Roseberry took over the Maitress' old quarters. Katkin slept in the Springhouse. It had always been her favorite place at the Infirmarie—the one place she felt at peace. Each time she looked at the statue of Lalluna, poised forlornly over the unfilled pools, the goddess' serene expression encouraged her to action.

"I will see that your healing waters once more spill freely, for all to make use of, My Lady. But it may well be my last gift to you and Beaumarais."

Those suffering from the Bludseth filled the main wards, keeping Roseberry and the other sisters busy with their treatment. Though they had some success ameliorating the worst symptoms, they found nothing amongst the stores of medicaments that stopped the inevitable advance of the disease.

One day in early autumn, Roseberry paid a visit to her aunt. Katkin, who had been on her hands and knees scrubbing the largest of the copper-bottomed bathing pools, stood wearily when she entered the Springhouse. "How are you, my dear?" she asked, noting that her niece seemed to be thriving on the demands of the Maitress' position.

"I am well, Aunt. Sister Salle has brought some tea for us." Roseberry tutted, "You look as though you are ready to drop. I thought I told you to go back to Acorn for a few days?"

Katkin shrugged as she accepted a cup of tea. "Louis has promised me that the water will be running again within a week and the pools must be ready to receive it. Then we can search for a cure to the Bludseth. It lies here, in the Springhouse, if it is anywhere."

Roseberry's eyes lit with hope. "Do you really believe that? For that is one of the reasons I came to see you, to tell you of a dream I had last night."

She sat beside Katkin on the edge of the main fountain, and looked to the high-beamed ceiling. "The dream brought me here, to the Springhouse. Some winged creature appeared, perhaps Lalluna, but, in truth, she looked more like you, Aunt. She went to the edge of the pool and opened her mouth, and some dark, sticky mixture began pouring out of her. I thought it looked like blood. It frightened me terribly, and I begged her to stop."

Roseberry paused and took a deep breath. Katkin waited, her heart pounding in her ears. "Her voice sounded like yours. She said, 'The cure will be found in the root of the tree.' Then she disappeared, and I awoke. Do you understand it?"

Katkin shook her head, though she knew she did.

"Perhaps it means there is some medicinal preparation we have overlooked in the treatment of the Bludseth. Something made from rootstocks. Is there any such thing?"

She shook her head again, and the hope in Roseberry's eyes faded. She spoke, in quiet desperation, of the overflowing beds in the main wing. "We need to find a new treatment soon, Aunt. Though we have done our best to contain the infection, new cases continue to break out. We will begin losing people soon—people we should be helping, because there is not enough medicine to slow the progress of the disease."

Katkin stared at the statue of Lalluna for a long while. "Ask your brother to send me another half-dozen men. If we can get the pipes reconnected, I may have an idea."

Roseberry brightened. "What is it? May I help in any way?"

"Yes, you can give me the key to the locked wing of the main building, where Maggrai kept his laboratory."

"Aunt! You can't think the answer is to be found in that filthy den. It is due to be demolished in a few days. I could persuade no one to enter and clean it out."

Gwillam wandered on Deres Tama. The stream of Sutun, now slowed to a trickle, ignored him as he wove a path through the trees, looking for Myrie. He had seen little of her since he returned to Mornguard with the other hunters. She had accepted the last of the stolen corsfyre from him, and swallowed it in his presence. Her form had increased, as he knew it would, and she seemed even more difficult to talk to.

But Enfys had become a comfort, in that. Gwillam decided he would find her in the village, and ask if she would wait with him.

Myrie called his name, just as he turned to leave the hill, and he saw her approaching from over Golden Ocean. She flew, on Lalluna's wings, until she alighted on the hill, close to the magnificent trees. Gwillam watched the blur of arms and legs curiously. She rarely left the shelter of Deres Tama, and had not been off the island since she arrived on the aermaran.

"Where have you been, Myrie?"

"To see our Mariner-Father" she said, in a few quiet voices. They sounded sad. "We had something important to tell him. And now, we are glad that you are here, dearest."

"W... Why?" asked Gwillam, a little discomfited by her somber tone.

She did not answer his question. Instead, she asked one of her own. "Does the one whose hand you hold when you walk beneath the trees make you happy?"

Gwillam looked baffled by this. "Enfys, you mean?"

"Yes. Enfys. Does she make you happy?"

He nodded shyly, but insisted, "Of course, she won't ever take your place, Myrie. You will always be my best friend."

The hundred mouths turned down a little. "We rather hoped she would. Take our place, that is. We have remained here for you, for we feared you would be unhappy if we did not. And yet we long to become the Guardian of the Vortice, as we are destined to do. To have so many thoughts and so many voices is... tiring."

"But... But I thought you had done that already?"

Much laughter at this. "No. But we would like to. Do you think we could?"

Gwillam understood. "If you do, then you will not be able to talk to me any more, is that it?"

A hundred blurred nods filled him with sorrow, but how could he refuse her? "But must you leave? Will I ever see you again?"

"We will be here, always," the voices answered, and they sounded just like the wind in the leaves of the trees.

Unshed tears tightened his throat, so that he could hardly speak. "Then do what you need to do, Myrie. I will never forget you."

He stepped within the cloud to receive her embrace. The arms brushed against him impersonally, without comfort. But after a single warm mouth touched his, Myrie walked away from him, towards the Deres. A gap, left by some long-forgotten calamity, stood between the third and fourth trees on the left. Myrie entered within it, and threw her hundred arms high. "Farewell, beloved. Bring your little ones to play beneath the trees, when the time comes. We will be here. Waiting..."

"Farewell, Myrie," he called, and added those names of the others that he knew. "Farewell, Nicholas. Farewell, Lalluna."

A single voice answered him. "Give my love to my Vessel. Tell her I have found peace, at last."

Leaves burst forth from her fingertips as Myrie began to change. Gwillam shaded his eyes as he watched her stretch towards the sun, her body disappearing into the trunk of a young and shapely euca-lypt. Her faces became shadows on the naked bark and her many legs plunged deep, anchoring her to the earth.

Within a minute, it had finished, and the wind sighed through the glistening leaves of the newest Guardian of the Vortice. Gwillam wiped the tears from his eyes and went to tell Enfys everything.

Poppy's pregnancy had begun to show, and she did not bother to disguise it. Jakob looked after her solicitously, but she could tell his heart lay elsewhere. Gunnar also seemed distracted, and spent a great deal of time by the graves of Gwenn and Arkady, deep in one-sided conversation. Poppy watched him with some concern, because he often forgot to eat or sleep unless she reminded him.

His bright blue eyes faded to grey, as though some dark shade consumed him from the inside out. He spoke little to his son, only reminding him now and again of what he needed to do before they abandoned the island of Asaruthe.

"The sheep will be all right. They have been here for a hundred years or more. But you must slaughter the cow before you leave. It would not be right to leave her alone. And take the dogs with you, of course."

"But Dad," said Jakob, now quite troubled. "We aren't going anywhere. Poppy and I plan to stay on Asaruthe for a long time. And you must stay with us. When the baby is born he will need a grandfather to teach him to sail."

Gunnar looked to the jetty where two boats lay moored, and spoke as though Jakob's words had not registered. "*Fair Drake* is a good enough boat for the journey across Golden Ocean, I reckon. You have sailed the *Spry Lass* many times on the Reach, so I will leave her for you and Poppy."

Jakob frowned. "What are you talking about? I just told you..."

He sighed patiently. "I have to go back to the Western Isles soon. Myrie came to see me the other day. She said your Ma and Inky are there, waiting."

"Ma is dead. So is Pop." Jakob glanced sideways at his father, wondering now about his sanity.

"Of course," was all Gunnar said in reply. Then he smiled, and his eyes regained some of their old sparkle. "Look, just don't worry about me, lad. I won't go anywhere far without telling you first. All right?"

He nodded, though he was not reassured.

"Now why don't you see what that girl of yours is up to? I saw her by the rocks, collecting eggs for supper. I am sure she could use a hand."

Poppy and Jakob took turns watching him for the next week, but Gunnar showed no signs of leaving Asaruthe. He spent time chocking the cracks in the stone walls of Ruthecombe, making the house airtight for winter. He chopped a huge pile of wood and peat for the cooking fires. He took long walks across the tops, and made sure the fences were secure. Gradually, they relaxed, thinking whatever madness had gripped him must surely have passed.

But Gunnar was only waiting for fine weather and an early offshore wind, so that he could take the *Fair Drake* out to sea without rowing. One morning, thirteen days after Myrie visited Asaruthe, the red sky of dawn saw him climb aboard the ship he had named for Gwenn Faircrow. He carried very little with him for this journey: a cloak, a knife, some lamp oil, flint and firesteel.

Tinder-dry chunks of willow filled the hold. He had seen to that last week when the young folk relaxed their vigil. Gunnar felt glad that they would have each other after he had gone. It was hard being alone on Asaruthe.

The wind and tide carried him straight out, as he had known they would. He watched the cliffs of the island receding, without regret. It had been a fine home, but now he must embark on his final voyage.

He let the *Fair Drake* drift with the current, until he could see no land in any direction. The Mariner had become a cipher in the vast domain of Golden Ocean, but he did not feel alone. Gunnar sat at the stern and smoked his pipe, listening to the waves as they whispered and sang—soft words of farewell, and Gods-speed

The wood he piled fore and aft, and then doused with lamp oil. He made a small fire, with steel and flint, placed so that the larger logs would ignite within a few minutes. Unhurriedly, Gunnar lay down close to the mastfish and placed his folded cloak neatly beneath his head. Then he removed a pouch from under his tunic, and drew from it a handful of spun gold curls.

Tenderly he stroked the hair against the line of his jaw and across his lips. He thought back to the first time he had seen her upon the beach in Celeste—standing before him like some pale Goddess, carven from the very essence of strength and beauty.

"Remember that day, love?" he whispered. "I swore to be true to you forever. Gwenn... Gwenn... Wait for me. I will soon be at your right hand and then we will part no more."

Gunnar made sure the logs were well ablaze before he withdrew the knife from his belt. The blade was quite sharp—he had seen to that, too. Carefully, he opened the veins in both wrists. It stung, a little, but the pain was nothing compared to the rheumatism that gripped his once-shattered bones like a vise every winter.

But that pain, like all pain, would soon be no more.

The fire grew searingly hot as it consumed the *Fair Drake's* salt-bleached bones, but Gunnar did not feel it. He was very, very tired. Slowly, he brought his bloodied hand to his lips, and kissed

Gwenn's fair hair once more. Then his eyelids sank gently down, as the waves of Golden Ocean rocked him to sleep.

A passing sea bird, alarmed by the smell of smoke, sped to the west, calling to its mate.

Twenty-Three

Oak

Katkin lit a candle and crept through the door of Maggrai's laboratory. A pestilential stench hung almost palpably in the air, and she paused long enough to place a handkerchief over her nose and mouth. The shadows fled as she moved forward, giving her glimpses of nightmarish racks and hanging ropes. Her courage almost failed her.

"Just find the notebooks, Katkin," she said out loud. "They must be here somewhere."

She pawed through a pile of damp papers on a table, looking for the formula for Broth. A cloud of bats exploded from the ceiling above her head, making Katkin shriek. She dropped the candle, but fortunately it did not extinguish itself. As she squatted to retrieve it, she saw that the table had a suspended shelf beneath the top. Several leather bound notebooks sat side by side. Katkin dragged them out, shuddering at the feel of the slimy damp that clung to her fingers.

Unwilling to face another moment in Maggrai's domain, she took the books back to the Springhouse. The building felt much more comfortable now that the workmen had finished reconnecting the pipes. Hot water spilled from the fountain and through a series of open gutters and waterfalls, before draining into the copper bathing pools. Katkin cleansed her hands in the water, feeling the steam permeate and calm her.

In the dim light of her candle, Katkin pored through Maggrai's notebooks. Much of the writing looked arcane and indecipherable—a twisted scrawl of symbols and letters. Halfway along the page, she saw a new hand had taken over the note-keeping. She recognized Tristan's neat and precise script. He had made a list of plants, beginning with Yellow Melilot, and including White Clover, Butcher's Broom and Horse Chestnut.

"Now we are getting somewhere." Katkin scanned several more pages.

Tristan had tried twelve different recipes for Broth, and tested each on twenty Bludseth sufferers. In the case of ten of the formulae, all of the test subjects had died. In the eleventh, over half had died, and the other eight improved.

Formula twelve turned out to be the cure that Tristan had been seeking. Katkin made a note of the ingredients and the method for mixing them. Of course, the main constituent had to be blood— lots of blood. She must combine it with extracts of several known anticoagulants and Mezereon,* and then place the mixture over heat until steam issued forth. Two drops placed under the tongue would halt the progress of the Bludseth; five would cure it outright, but cause an unpleasant tightening of the throat. Six or more would be fatal.

She finished her research as the bells chimed five o'clock. Katkin crossed the greensward, and the grass shone in the light of the full moon. She let herself into the closed wing of the main building again and lit her candle. The skittering of rats whispered around her as she crossed the stone floor, slippery with mold and damp.

"All right, Maggrai," she said cheerily, to keep her fears at bay. "Where did you keep the constituents for Broth, my friend?"

Cabinets and shelves filled the room, making candlelit search nigh on impossible, but Katkin did not want to wait until daylight revealed the full horrors of the laboratory, nor did she wish for any help. Roseberry would almost certainly try to stop her, if she knew what she had planned.

A shadow loomed in the corner, and Katkin thought for one terrible moment that Maggrai himself had come to assist her with her inquiries. But the dark object was nothing more frightening than a cupboard. She took her knife and jimmied the lock, then swung the doors back. Neatly labeled boxes and jars filled the shelves inside.

"This is more like it!" Katkin began to sort through the contents, finding the things she needed. But one box—the one labeled Mezereon—rattled uselessly.

---

* *Daphne Mezereum*. The berries are rich in Daphnetoxin and poisonous to humans

She swore and looked for another.

There was none. She took the rest of the ingredients and placed them in a basket along with a scalpel and a graduated container. She could undertake the painful task of bleeding herself in the comfort and cleanliness of the Springhouse. But first, she had to find Roseberry.

"Mezereon? Never heard of it. I don't think it grows around here anywhere. Why don't you ask Emi?"

"Do you think he could help?" Katkin asked, somewhat surprised that Roseberry's brother might be an expert on herb lore.

"He has traveled all over Yr, and he knows every kind of plant life you have ever heard of and many you have not," she answered proudly. "Emi will know where it may be found, if anyone does."

"Poppy!" Jakob cried, his voice sounding very distressed. "Come to the beach."

"Is it Ikor? Has he returned?" She dropped the distaff from her hand and let the spinning wheel come to a halt. Poppy ran outside, calling for Jakob.

He had not waited for her. She could see the top of his blond head disappearing below the level of the cliff tops. It took her far longer to make the climb, for her expanding waistline made her ungainly. She felt thoroughly puffed before she reached the sand.

Jakob squatted next to a single charred piece of wood, close to the high tide line. "What on Yrth is it?" Poppy asked.

"This," he answered, and rocked the curved timber under his hand. He sounded close to despair.

"That piece of driftwood? What is so important about it?"

He raised tear-filled eyes to meet hers. "It is part of the keel of the *Fair Drake*, Poppy. The tide must have washed it up, sometime in the night."

"The *Fair Drake*! My gods, are you sure?"

Jakob stroked the grain with his fingertips as he might a lover's face. "I shaped this myself, with fire and an adz. I know it like my own arm." He sat back and covered his face with his hands. "Don't you see what this means? Dad took the boat and then set fire to her. I should have seen it coming, what with all his crazy talk about Ma and Pop waiting for him. Why didn't I stop him?" He sobbed now, in earnest, and Poppy put her arms around him.

"Myrie said she would tell him when they came to Deres Tama," Poppy gently reminded him. "Ikor wanted to make the last journey with them, into the Shadow. Don't be angry at yourself, Jakob. He did what he wanted to do, right to the last."

He nodded forlornly, and wiped his eyes on his sleeve. Poppy watched as he easily lifted the blackened keel. A glint of gold shone bright underneath, cupped in a hollow of sand. She extricated the anchor, still attached to its chain, and solemnly placed it around Jakob's neck. "Lutyond wanted you to have this. You are the only son of the Mariner now."

They buried the remains of the *Fair Drake* next to the graves of Gwenn and Arkady. A third marker, sculpted of soft, rust-colored limestone, now stood in a line with the others. Jakob carefully carved an anchor on it, though he knew the wind would weather it to a cipher before a season passed.

"Farewell, Dad. I will try to be worthy of Lutyond's anchor—to be a true son of the Mariner. But it is hard, when I have so much to make up for." He shook his head sadly and turned away. As he climbed the cliff he thought of Poppy, and wondered how he would break the news that they were leaving Asaruthe for good.

Katkin, with her hair well covered and a scarf muffling her face and neck, left the Infirmarie for the first time since coming back to St. Valery. She hurried along Lampwright's Street, noting with pleasure the number of shops that were open for business, though their wares looked scant. Many had Salvatores standing guard outside to prevent trouble. The populace of St. Valery, although very worn-looking, moved about the City in relative peace. Katkin saw no Bludseth sufferers on the streets.

Emile had taken up residence in the Guard quarters on the mouth gate of the Yoke.* When Katkin arrived, he was just sitting down to a belated breakfast in the cobbled courtyard.

"Come in and welcome, Aunt! You look famished. Here, you may share in my breakfast. There is far too much for me." Katkin had developed a fierce appetite on the hour walk from the Infirmarie, and accepted guiltily, for his breakfast actually looked quite meager. She sniffed the air appreciatively. "Is that *real* coffee?"

He grinned as he cleared away the maps and plans littering the

---

* The land bridge that connects St. Valery to the mainland of Beaumarais.

breakfast table. "Indeed, Aunt. Some of the King's private stock, from Shadion, I believe. The Salve liberated it in a raid on the Citadel storehouse yesterday. We found many other foodstuffs there, and we plan a distribution on the Commons as soon as I can get enough men to supervise." Emile took the jug from the stovetop and poured a steaming cup for Katkin, then passed her a plate of toasted oatcakes spread with preserves.

Katkin sipped coffee as she told Emile of her errand. He studied the beautifully rendered botanical painting she had found in the Infirmarie library and then rubbed the back of his neck thoughtfully.

"I have seen this shrub. The flowers grace the highlands of Yr, and birds feast on the berries in the fall. But there is none here in Beaumarais, nor in her neighboring states."

Katkin's eyes filled with tears. "But I need some at once! It is very important."

"What do you need?" asked Maia, who had just come through the gate after an early morning patrol. She flopped down in the remaining chair and rested one booted foot on the table. Katkin frowned her disapproval at this unladylike behavior, as Emile explained her errand.

She glanced at the picture and then looked at Katkin with a raised eyebrow. "This grows on Asaruthe! On the highest part of the tops, close to the limestone quarry. Have you not seen it, Aunt?"

Katkin shook her head, a little chagrinned. "I rarely went to the quarry. The climb wore me out. Are you sure it is there?"

Maia nodded. "Would you like me to get some for you?" she asked, with an eagerness Katkin felt sure had nothing to do with Mezereon. After giving Emile a sly glance she said, "And you had better come with me, Emi. Otherwise I might get lost."

Emile gave an exasperated grin. "You know the way far better than I, Maia Adaryi. But I will come, nevertheless."

Maia hurriedly left to retrieve her leather satchel from the Salvatore camp on the shore of the Mistmere. Emile paced the narrow confines of the Guard's shed, obviously impatient to be on his way.

Katkin watched and wondered. Did the tasks he must leave behind worry him, or something else? She decided the time had come to find out. "What happened between you and Poppy at the Watchkeep?"

He whirled and stared at her. "I... What do you mean, Aunt?" The brilliant color on his cheeks spoke far more volubly.

"I *am* her mother, Emile. I think I have a right to know."

Emile blushed again, this time quite ferociously. "I don't... want you to think ill of me."

"Why would I?"

His voice, sounding dreamy and far away, drifted over her words. "She was so beautiful—and so afraid. When she asked me to make love to her, she made it sound as though I would be giving her the greatest boon she could wish for. I could not refuse, not when she had given my life back to me." He looked anxiously at his aunt through half-closed lids, waiting for her to speak sharp words.

Katkin spoke gently. "It is all right. I think no less of you for it. But I must warn you. Poppy has no memory of the things she did as Azothe. She may not recognize you or want to have anything to do with you. And she is on Asaruthe with a young man, one who risked his life for her."

Her words wounded him, but he tried hard not to show it.

Poppy's lip trembled as the first tears spilled onto her cheeks. "I don't want to leave Asaruthe. And you said you would take care of me, no matter what."

A cold rain fell, and the wind howled in the chimney, filling the front room of Asavale with the smell of peat. Jakob rubbed the smoke from his eyes, wishing they were already in Mornguard. "I *will* take care of you. But there is no reason for us to stay on this godsforsaken island now that Dad is gone. You would be much more comfortable at Mornguard, where your father and his wife could help with the baby. He would be glad if you came back—I heard him say so myself."

Poppy shivered and went to stand closer to the fire. How could she make Jakob understand? She could not go back to Mornguard, not when she was with child. The stain on her Patre's honor would be too great. The Anjali might very well strip him of his position as Tane. But Jakob, ignorant of the strict codes of the Firaithi, seemed determined to make her do just that.

She turned her back to the fire. "You can go, if you want. I am staying here. But anyway," she added cruelly. "Are you so sure Maia will have you back?"

He frowned. "That has nothing to do with it. Come on, Poppy. We have the *Spry Lass*, and a lot of silver coins that Dad left behind. Why should we stay here?"

"Because..."

Jakob waited, but she didn't finish her sentence. Poppy stared out the window at two bedraggled figures trudging through the yard in the driving rain.

He followed her eyes and then shouted in excitement. "My gods, that is Maia!" Jakob crossed the room and threw open the door, just as Maia and Emile reached the top of the stairs that led from the lower level. Maia flung herself immediately into Jakob's embrace.

"Your father said you fell!" she said breathlessly. "Then Gwillam told me you were all right. I have been waiting and waiting for you to come to St. Valery." She dragged Jakob's head down and kissed him. He responded with a passion that brought flames to Poppy's cheeks.

She looked beyond their display to the stranger who waited just inside the door. He seemed as mortified as she by Jakob and Maia's effusive reunion. Giving the lovers a wide berth, she made her way over to him.

"Welcome to Asaruthe. My name is Poppy Brunner." She held out her hand. As he took it, he raised his head and Poppy found herself gazing into the kindest and warmest brown eyes she had ever seen. When he squeezed her hand, she felt a curious thrill of recognition. "Very pleased to make your acquaintance, Miss Poppy Brunner. I am Emile Abelard, commander of the Salvatores of Beaumarais. Perhaps you would like to come back to the barn with me, for I think we need to talk, and those two might be best left to carry on their business without interruption from us."

Jakob and Maia did not notice when Poppy and Emile closed the door and trod the stairs downwards.

They sat on a bale of hay, and the animals clustered about them, sharing their warmth in the chilly barn. Emile had not yet released her hand, but Poppy did not mind at all. "Your mother told me you did not remember anything," he began. "Is this true?"

She gazed at his face again and nodded. "And yet I feel as though I know you, Emile. We must have met before now."

He grimaced. "In a way we have, though the meeting was less than felicitous, for neither of us were ourselves. When you first saw me, Tristan had made me his idiot assistant, and you were... Azothe."

Sounds and images fluttered about in her mind, like a flock of restless doves. She remembered the look of wretched fear he had given her through the glass of the Chronagine. "Your name was Mungo," Poppy said, with certainty. "I helped you escape from Tristan."

"You did," Emile agreed. "You saved my life, and for that I will be forever in your debt."

A torrent of memories broke free, and washed away the blankness. *The Watchkeep, a glowing globe of blue, a kiss...*

Many kisses, warm and tender.

Poppy's heart began to race. Emile sat beside her, holding her hand tightly in his. In the barn, the earthy smell of sheep filled the air, but the memory of patchouli hung between them like a ghost.

"Do you remember what we did after?"

The scent of pine trees and sun-dried linen. His breath, warm and sweet, on her cheek.

She had been very afraid.

Emile's strong arms held her close, as his soft whispers soothed her fears.

She hadn't wanted the miserable Tristan to be her first lover.

They had embarked on a gentle journey of discovery, as with patience and care he led her on the path to ecstasy. And after, though it had been her first time, he had been the one to cry.

"Yes I do," whispered Poppy. "Oh yes, I remember it well."

Emile brought her hand to his lips and kissed each fingertip. "Since then, not an hour has passed when I did not think of you. I gave you my heart that night in the Watchkeep."

Poppy looked at her swelling abdomen, fiercely glad now that Jakob had prevented her from taking the herbs. "You gave me something else as well," she giggled, perfectly aware of the absurdity of it all.

Emile threw his arms about her, and they fell backwards into a heap of loose hay. Many more warm and tender kisses followed before Emile spoke again. "Of that gift I am very, very glad. Will you be mine, Miss Poppy Brunner? I have a rebellion to manage in St. Valery, but when it is finished, I expect I shall be King."

A tiny pause followed, hardly noticeable, while Poppy thought once more of Lut Strong Arm and wondered what he would have said to it all. Then she kissed Emile again, and placed his hand on her belly so he could feel his child's first feisty kicks. "Yes," she said, with mock solemnity. "I believe Baby agrees that we should be yours forever and ever."

The sound of his joyous laughter filled the barn, and filtered up the stairs. Maia and Jakob broke from their long embrace. "Do you think Poppy will be all right?" Maia asked him. "She has been depending on you to look after her."

Jakob opened the loft door and peeked into the barn. "I think she will be fine," he said happily. "Just fine."

Emile found his aunt at the Springhouse and handed her a huge bundle of deep green leaves, red berries and roots. "We were not sure which part you wanted," he said sheepishly.

Katkin peered at him through the branches, thinking his eyes looked a little brighter than they had when he left. "Did you speak to Poppy?"

He grinned widely. "I did indeed. Will you mind me calling you Mother instead of Aunt before long? Poppy and I plan to marry as soon as she and Jakob arrive in St. Valery on the *Spry Lass*." He said nothing of the baby, thinking that Poppy would want to impart that happy news herself.

Katkin embraced him. "That is wonderful news, Emile! Have you told Willow yet?"

"I came straight here with the Mezereon, for you said you had need of it. But I go to see her now."

"Go on then," she said, smiling affectionately. "I have much work to do here."

Knowing that Poppy would soon arrive in St. Valery made Katkin even more determined to solve the riddle of the Bludseth. She pored over the notebook. Tristan's formula had called for a mutchkin of "darky" blood. Even with ruthless use of his subjects, ordinarily he would have needed two people to gather that much blood. But Katkin did not have any other Firaithi to act as donors—the last had left Beaumarais with Gwillam and the other hunters several weeks ago.

"I hope it will be enough, my Lady," Katkin said to Lalluna, whose statue loomed above the proceedings like a watchful angel.

She had the graduated container ready. Katkin passed the scalpel over the vein in her wrist. She watched dispassionately as the dark fluid began to drip into the bowl, a few drops at a time. Though she pumped her fingers into a fist repeatedly, she could see that the blood would begin to clot long before she had the required amount. Steeling herself, she cut much deeper with the scalpel. A stinging, throbbing ache chased up her arm and into her shoulder, but the blood flowed more freely.

Katkin began to feel lightheaded many minutes before she filled the container but she did not stanch the bleeding. Black spots danced before her eyes as she staggered to her makeshift laboratory. Her left hand had gone almost numb after she made the second cut, and Katkin could not hold on to the container. As a wave of nausea gripped her, she stumbled, and the precious fluid spilled to the floor. Within seconds, it had trickled its way into one of the drains.

She sank to the floor and cried. Above her head, the gaslights flickered. Lalluna's statue cast a wavering outline before her on the stone flags. Katkin looked up, noticing for the first time how much Lalluna's face resembled her own. "Are we the same poor creature after all? Both destined to live in some endless world of shadow?" The statue had no answer for her.

Sighing, Katkin hauled herself to the edge of the pool, picked up the container, and returned to the bench. Dragging over a chair, she sat, trying to ignore the throbbing pain in her wrist and the one in her temple. She had difficulty holding the scalpel in her left hand, but she managed to saw a jagged cut on her right wrist.

The pain in her head had become fearsome by the time she finished filling the bowl a second time. Neither hand worked, so she gripped the vessel between her forearms and carried it to the bench. Thankfully, Katkin had weighed all the other ingredients before beginning, and now she stirred them into the blood, using a stick clenched between her teeth.

But no matter how hard she tried, she could not light the gas burner in order to heat the mixture. Katkin singed her numbed fingers six or seven times before turning away in disgust. Realizing that she had little time left, she lurched towards the main pool. She thought fuzzily that she might be able to warm the Broth if she held it over the steaming water.

Blood loss caught her just as she reached it. Katkin fainted, striking the back of her head hard as she fell. The flask of Broth flew from her hands and tipped into the water. The darkness spread like a stain, until the whole pool had turned the color of her blood.

A dream, perhaps. He lifts her from the floor, and cradles her in the softness of his feathered arms. As he places her on the pallet, in the shadow of Lalluna, he says sadly, "Oh love, what you have suffered for my sake. But someday soon, I hope to make it up to you."

He bandages her wrists and prays she has enough blood left to remain in the living world.

"Remember, I am waiting to help you, when the time comes," he breathes, and kisses her lips. Then he is gone. A single feather of grey lies on her breast.

She woke to the splashing of many bathers, and heard their cries of joy.

Katkin opened her eyes. Willow sat by her side. "You did it! But oh, my sister, how close we came to losing you! Why did you not ask for help?"

Little of this made sense. "What... What did I do?" Memory returned. "I failed," she said desolately. "I could not light the burner, and then I fell. I fainted, Willow. The blood must have gone into the drain again."

Now Willow looked confused. "But we found you in your bed. You were pale, yes, but you did not seem injured, except for the bandages on your wrists. And the bathing pool..."

"Bandages?" Katkin held her hands before her face.

"Yes, bandages. When Roseberry saw the water, she said her dream had come true. We took the worst of the Bludseth sufferers, and brought them here. It was a miracle!"

"They were healed?" Katkin shook her head. It did not seem possible, when she had failed so utterly.

"We healed *everyone* in the Infirmarie while you slept. More are coming in from the villages all the time."

Katkin lay back on her bed, dead tired and somehow joyless, though she knew that Yr's long nightmare would soon be over. "What happens now?"

"Now I will take care of you, Katkin. You need rest and a lot of strengthening food and drink. And later, when you are better, the City is waiting with open arms. You will be Queen again, and everything will be as it should be."

"Tell Emile to recall the Chamber. I want to address them, as soon as they can be seated."

"But Katkin, you are hardly well enough to..."

"Tell him," Katkin broke in flatly. "I am well enough to say what I wish to say."

A single short battle cleared the Citadel. Yannick once more took command of the Guard, and set the men to work collecting rubbish and putting the City to rights. Isle St. Valery woke to a new day, and so did the villages, but the specter of starvation loomed large, with winter coming and so many men lost to the Bludseth.

Katkin gripped the podium with both hands, using it as a prop to keep her upright. The galleries overflowed with spectators, and more stood in the doorways, craning their heads to see the Arkafina, remarking on her pallor and her restored arm. The Deputies had been cheering for a full five minutes, and she waved her hand so that they would stop.

Emile, seeing how pale Katkin's face had become, cried, "Deputies, please come to order! Your former Queen wishes to speak." Finally, they settled down and waited for her words.

She cleared her throat to keep her voice from wavering. "I will not keep you long, Deputies. It is on a matter of prime importance that I address you today. There are some here who believe that the Queen Arkafina should return to the throne." More wild cheering at this. Katkin sighed and waved her hand again. "I say to you that Beaumarais needs a new leader—someone young, and strong, who will be with you for many years. I am not that person, Deputies." Silence dropped like a dark mantle over those present. "Your Queen, Roseberry, has told me that she wishes to remain at the Infirmarie, as Maitress, and indeed she has already done great works there. So we must find another to lead you henceforth."

Katkin looked over her shoulder, to where Emile and Poppy stood side by side. "Here is the man who would be your new King—Emile Abelard. As you doubtless know, Emile fought bravely to free his country from the cruel fist of the tyrant, Tristan Dinrhydan. The woman by his side is my daughter, Poppy Brunner. She bears the future heir to the throne. Together they will rule

Beaumarais wisely and well." Katkin swayed as her fatigue got the better of her. "Do you accept the counsel of your former Queen, the Arkafina?"

There were murmurs from the Deputies, and then one, a former Swallow, cried, "Emile! We are with you!" The others took up the pledge, as Katkin stepped from the podium. Emile and Poppy took her place, holding hands and waving to the crowded hall. Willow helped her sister into a wheeled invalid's chair and they left the Hall by the back entrance. Yannick pushed the chair along to the Citadel tower. Katkin curled up, to try and reduce the pain in her chest, and did not speak.

The monarch's private apartment still enjoyed the luxurious appointments of Tristan's reign. Yannick picked up Katkin and placed her in a comfortable velvet slipper chair. Willow gave her a cup of tea. "Thank goodness that is over," Katkin murmured.

Yannick stood before Katkin, still stunned by her announce-ment. "Are you sure this is what you want? The Deputies were ready to give you their full allegiance."

She nodded wearily. "The country must come first, and I have done what is best for Beaumarais—and myself. Emile and Poppy will be a fine King and Queen."

Yannick's eyes were bright with pride as he looked fondly over to Willow. "On that we have no quarrel, my dear. Emile has already been in negotiations with our neighbors to return their sovereignty. He is sure they will be eager to trade food for the use of the healing springs. There is much work to be done, but I believe the young folk are capable." He smiled wryly. "As for me, I plan to retire as well. Louis will become the leader of the Guard, and I will take charge of the rose gardens. But what will you do now?"

Katkin shrugged, thinking it did not matter.

Willow took her hand and squeezed it. "There is no need to think of the future, my Sister. You will come to the Infirmarie with Yannick and I. I will be able to look after you, and then once you have your strength back, you will find things to do with yourself. The Sisters would love to have another healer, especially one as gifted as you are, Kat."

But try as she may, Katkin could summon no enthusiasm for this plan or any other. She murmured, "I really just want to go back to Acorn."

"Acorn?" Willow's eyes brimmed with tears. "But I thought you would want to live in the City, with us! The baby will be coming soon, and we will be grandmothers together. Wouldn't you like that?"

"I won't be that far away, Willow. You can visit me whenever you like, and Poppy too. And of course I want to see the baby before..." She corrected herself. "After it is born, I mean."

Twenty-Four

Gingko

Poppy and Emile rode with Katkin to Acorn, and helped her settle in. The King had already sent many men to repair the doors and windows, and re-thatch the roof. An eager army of countrywomen, led by Willow, had cleaned the inside, banished the rats and spiders, and filled the pantry with preserves.

Katkin wandered around the main room, seeing the waxed shine on the wood floor and the new muslin curtains. The house was warm, and smelled sweetly of honey. She felt humbled and somewhat guilty about the amount of trouble her family had gone to for her. "It is beautiful. Just as I remember it."

That last part, though, was a lie. Acorn would never be the same. Not without Jacq.

They left her, with many promises of future visits, and many a backwards glance. "Come to the Citadel soon," Poppy called back, as she rode away on a beautiful white palfrey that had been a wedding gift from Emile. The clattering hooves of the King's personal guard faded into the afternoon haze, leaving Katkin alone.

She went inside and closed the door. Though she had been at the Infirmarie for many weeks, recuperating from the making of Broth, she still felt very weak. The pain in her chest, which had begun in Deres Tama, bothered her all the time now. Katkin rubbed her shoulder, and went to lay on her bed. She pulled aside the pretty flowered quilt, given to her by Willow, and stretched out on her back. The silence hummed in her ears, broken only by the occasional cluck of the hens outside.

After a time she fell asleep, and when she woke, darkness had fallen. Sighing, Katkin thought about dinner and decided it would be too much trouble to light the fire. She cast about for the quilt and pulled it over her. Then she slept again.

In sleep, there was no pain, and no loneliness.

The days dragged on. Winter came, with darkness and swirling snow. Jacq's brother Nathan, now a prosperous householder, dropped by each day and chopped wood for her. He had lost his wife to the Bludseth, and made no secret of the fact he would like another. Katkin rebuffed him, politely, and kept her distance.

Nathan, stung by her lack of interest, stopped coming. The pain in her chest remained.

Katkin stayed by the fire, wrapped in a blanket. She felt too cold to do much of anything else, and it hurt her to breathe when she moved around. She spent her time reading, or just gazing out the frosty glass of the windows. Willow and Yannick came to visit once or twice a week, and brought food and wine. Sometimes Katkin forgot to eat on other days.

"Poppy is well and sends her love," Willow said. "She is big as a house, now. The baby will not be long in coming."

Katkin felt the crushing weight in her chest lift just a little. She still found satisfaction in the joys of her children, for Gwillam had written to say that he and Enfys were also expecting a child.

Spring came, bright with promise. The Infirmarie treated the last cases of the Bludseth. The merchants of St. Valery reclaimed her position as a vital trading port on the Mistmere. Her neighbors gradually forgave the predations of Tristan's reign and settled the borders.

And Crown Prince Huw Yann Abelard arrived into the world.

As soon as the weather grew warm, his proud parents, the King and Queen of Beaumarais, brought him to see his grandmother. Poppy, whose difficult pregnancy had confined her to the Citadel, had not seen her mother in four months. Emile, busy with the affairs of the country, had not been to visit for five. The emaciated, white-haired woman who met them at the door, walking with the aid of a cane, stunned them both.

"Katkin?" Poppy whispered in a shocked voice. "Is that you?"

Her mother smiled, but her green eyes were bright with tears. "Of course it is me! No one else lives here, do they? Now, where is the little one? Bring him inside at once."

Emile carried the basket in and placed it on the kitchen table. Katkin stared at the tiny, dark-haired bundle for a long moment before she spoke. "He is beautiful," she said at last, with a satisfied sigh. "Looks just like his father." She and Poppy were soon deep in a discussion of colic and teething, as Emile wandered about the yard, with his contingent of guardsmen in tow. He stood for a long time peering in at the window, watching his wife and her mother talk, and fuss over his son.

Later, as he and Poppy rode home together in the carriage, with little Huw sleeping between them, he said, "I think we should ask Katkin to come back to St. Valery again."

Poppy tucked the blanket around little Huw, and kissed his forehead. "Oh? Why is that, my love? She has said many times she does not wish to leave her home."

"I know, but today I felt nothing but sorrow at Acorn. I do not believe it is the best place for her. She coughed a great deal, and several times I saw her grimace with pain. Your mother is not well, Poppy."

"I will send Aunt Willow to try and talk some sense into her tomorrow. We have plenty of room at the Citadel. And Huw would like to have his grandmother close by, wouldn't he?" She cooed at the baby, who yawned and slept on.

Emile smiled devotedly. "He already has the best and most beautiful mother in the world. He is very lucky and so am I."

Katkin went to bed early that night, after sipping a cup of hot milk laced with whiskey, honey and opium. The full moon lit the inside of Acorn, making it almost as bright as day. Her eyes rested on the things that Jacq had made for the house—the dresser, the china cupboard, the wrought iron pothook in the fireplace. His presence had a tangible quality, as though his spirit lingered somehow at Acorn. But she knew it did not.

"You left with Raven long ago, did you not, my husband?" she whispered. "Even your Sutun has gone away." Katkin sighed, feeling the opium wash through her, lessening the pain in her chest. She continued to chat with Jacq, as she did every night before sleep claimed her. "I saw our newest grandchild today. A very handsome little lad he is, too. And Poppy and Emile looked so happy together. You would have been very proud of the way Yannick's son has grown. He is a fine ruler, and his subjects adore him."

Katkin spent a few moments coughing, as her heart skipped about like a cat playing with a mouse. This arrhythmia had worsened in recent weeks, leaving her gasping for breath almost every night. More than anything, she wished she could find the forgetfulness of sleep. The long dark nights of winter and spring had been torture as pain kept her awake, night after night after night.

Once she could breathe again, she got out of bed and made herself another cup of milk. In it, she emptied the rest of the opium from her supply cupboard, much more than a standard dose. Katkin drank it and got back into bed. She knew it would not kill her, for nothing would, but perhaps the drug would bring her the blessed relief of an unbroken night's rest.

As she pulled the covers high, Katkin whispered, "Goodnight, my dearest Jacq. I wish I could lie in your arms, tonight of all nights."

Some time later, when two figures appeared at the bottom of her bed, Katkin had already drifted into a deep sleep. The first, a tall grey-winged creature who glowed with some internal light, spoke to his companion. "It is time." The second figure, an apple-faced man dressed in robes of purest black, nodded.

"I have given up my Sutun for her. So when I place them together, in the next turn of the Gyre, they will be just as any other of their kind would be. Life and death will be an endless dance between Radiance and Shadow."

Death nodded again. He never spoke.

Ben'aryn held something bulky in his arms, wrapped in a shroud of white silken stuff. Carefully, he laid it on the foot of the bed and pulled away the covering. He revealed a girl, of about sixteen years, with lank chestnut hair, and dull green eyes. Her freckles were dark against her pale, pale skin. She had no life in her, no anafireon, so she lay still, without breath or heartbeat.

Ben'aryn spoke to Death again. "I created this form from the cells I took from her cheek long ago. But transferring the anafireon from her old body to the new is beyond my skill. You must help me bring her to life."

The black robed figure gave him a measured look.

"I promised to take her somewhere far from here, and I will, in return for your help. The others are there already, and they will take care of her. I will not interfere in her life any further, I swear to you."

Death moved to the side of the white-haired woman that lay

upon the bed. Though sleep had softened the lines upon her face, she still looked a hundred years old, though she was but fifty-three. "She is very beautiful. May I say something to her, before you do what must be done?"

Death nodded.

Ben'aryn knelt, and placed his lips close to Katkin's ear. "Your sorrow in this life has been endless, my love, but now you will have peace. Peace and a chance to live again, with the ones you love best. I am sorry, more sorry than I can say, for causing you so much pain. I do not think that you will remember me, when you wake, but I will always remember you, in the silent spaces between the stars." After he had pressed his lips against hers for a long moment, he stood, and signaled Death to begin.

Katkin did not stir, but the corners of her mouth somehow lifted in an ethereal smile. Death took her hand, and the hand of the girl. The body on the bed twitched a few times, and then lay very still. Meanwhile, color appeared in the girl's cheeks, and her lips grew warm and her eyes vivid. She took a deep, sighing breath, as though she might wake at any moment.

Death stood back, as Ben'aryn picked up the living, breathing girl. He stared for a long moment at the hollow shell on the bed. Then he stepped away, and the light died.

When Willow came to visit her sister on the morrow, she mourned, thinking her dead. They would bury Katkin's remains in a grave under the oaks at Acorn, but her spirit had already taken wing in the arms of her angel.

Poppy wrote the inscription for the tablet:

Katrione Estelle du Chesne Benet, Queen Arkafina
Aged 53 Years
Beloved Healer of Beaumarais

Ben'aryn drifts now in quiet darkness, almost formless, almost pure energy. He gave his Sutun to his beloved, so he cannot die. But forgetfulness is a kind of death, and within the Shadow, he remembers very little. A flash of green, a tender smile, the soft touch of silk against his skin. In these dreams; in the knowledge that all is right in the world—that *he* has made things right, for her, Ben'aryn rests.

Epilogue

When the girl woke, she felt only confusion. She rubbed her eyes, and they felt gritty, as though she had been napping for a long time. A bird called, clear and melodious, as the sun beat through the dappled shade and light of the trees. She decided it had been the bird that woke her.

She stood and stretched, wondering about herself and where she had come from. A suitcase lay on the ground by her side. An engraved plate told the girl her first name, but provided no other information. Perhaps inside there might be some clue?

Some strange-looking clothes, carefully folded, and an ornate, silver-framed mirror rested in the bottom of the case. A generous lunch of sandwiches and some sort of drink in a sealed bottle lay alongside. As she dug under the clothes, her fingers brushed against something cold and hard. It frightened her even before she drew the object into the light—a long, thin-bladed dagger with a pearl handle. But entangled in the blade lay something beautiful—something that touched on the edge of memory. A feather, of green-flecked crystal, strung on a thong of leather. With trembling hands, she placed it round her neck and then buried the dagger back amongst the clothes.

Hunger trumped her other worries and she settled down to eat the sandwiches. The drink bottle proved to be more of a puzzle. Some incredible force seemed to hold tightly to the top, and she could not pry it off no matter how hard she tried.

"That soda looks mighty good," a voice said, and made her jump. A boy stood before her, very tall, but his gap-toothed smile looked friendly enough. "Want me to open it for you?"

She nodded warily.

He flipped the top off with his pocketknife and handed the bottle back to her. She gulped it quickly, for she had been thirsty. The drink tasted sweet and cold, with bubbles that tickled her nose.

The girl saw a second bottle of the bubbly drink amongst her things, and she offered it to the boy with a shy smile. "Thank you kindly, Miss. It sure is hot today." He sat beside her and pushed his cap back, then wiped the sweat from his forehead with a kerchief. His hair was dark, and quite curly. "My name is Jack," he said. "Jack

Bennett." He fixed her with a serious grey-eyed gaze. "And who might you be? I haven't seen you around here before."

"K... Katy," said the girl. "My name is Katy. I am sorry but I can't seem to remember anything else. I took a nap, and when I woke, I found myself here." She frowned a little and he patted her shoulder.

"Don't worry about it. Maybe you fell and hit your head. Sometimes that makes people forgetful. Do you think that is what happened?"

"I guess so." Her eyes filled with tears. "What should I do?"

"Would you like to come back to my house for awhile? My ma and pop would be glad to meet you."

"Is it far?"

Jack smiled and pointed to a nearby prominence, neatly divided into squares by trees and white fences. "See up there? That place on the hill?"

She saw it and her eyes went wide. "Such a big house!"

He shrugged modestly. "My father is the county judge. He has plenty of money, I guess. And he knows a lot of people. If you are lost, then I am sure he can help you find your way home." He grinned at her and held out his hand. "Shall we go?"

A horse chestnut came whizzing through the air and narrowly missed Jack's head. Hoots of laughter echoed through the leaves as a voice mocked, "Hey Jacky, who's your girlfriend?"

"Who is that mean boy?" Katy cried. "He almost hit you."

Jack raised his head skywards and shouted, "Take that, knucklehead!" He sent the chestnut whistling back into the tree with a wicked sidearm throw. It connected solidly, and the other boy gave a yelp of pain.

"That's Tom," Jack said to Katy. "He's all right, once you get to know him. We're on the same baseball team."

Katy looked mystified. "Bays-ball?"

Another boy, with blond hair cut flat on top and close to his scalp, dropped from the tree to land beside them. His faded blue trousers had stained and ripped knees. "Hi, baby! I'm Tom. And you are?" He gave her a dazzling smile and thrust out his hand. Katy's lip trembled a little.

"She's lost," said Jack, frowning. "So lay off. OK, Tom?"

Tom gazed at Katy and scratched his head. "I saw someone else

302

hanging around here a while ago. A crazy-looking guy, with long silver hair. Maybe she belongs with him."

"Truly?" Katy asked. "Did you see where he went?"

"Naw," Tom answered. He gave her a peculiarly knowing look, accompanied by a sly half-grin. "He might be your guardian angel. I am pretty sure I saw a set of wings."

"Didn't I tell you to lay off?" Jack snapped. "Come on, let's go. I'm getting pretty hungry. You coming with us, Katy?"

"All right. If you are sure your parents will not mind. I am hungry too."

"What, after all those sandwiches?" Tom teased. "I've never seen a girl put away so much food."

"Yes," she said, laughing. "I think I must have missed a few meals somehow."

"I'll get that." Jack made a grab for her case, but Tom beat him to it.

They argued good-naturedly all the way back to Jack's house. Her cares forgotten, Katy walked between them—with the comforting feeling she had heard it all before.

Appendix 1

The Nature of the Folium

The notes of Eira Adaryi, former Ydane of the Kindred of Chandra and present Stavekeeper of the Amaranthine.

Knowing that we might never again have the opportunity to communicate with the Irais, I asked the leader, Bastet, to explain to me the meaning and use of the Folium. Although Bastet had taken our language from the mind of the goddess Elleranne, it had grave difficulty communicating the subtle connotations of the leaves and their relationships to one another. Of our kind, only Elleranne, the *emma na Deres*, might have understood them, but she has departed.

I tried to distill the essence of its description into a single word that best captures the convoluted nature of each leaf; nevertheless, my understanding is still incomplete. In particular, the method of determining location within the Gyre by leaf color is incomprehensible to me.

Apple – birth

Ash – death

Aspen – discovery

Beech – loss

Birch – partnership

Cedar – reprieve

Chestnut – danger

Elm – separation

Eucalyptus – transcendency

Fir – sacrifice

Gingko – immortality

Hawthorn – understanding

Holly – deception

Larch – reunion

Locust – revenge

Nutmeg – passion

Oak – strength

Olive – victory

Plane – retribution

Poplar – reckoning

Redwood – courage

Rimu – loyalty

Rowan – beginning

Willow – healing

Yew – unhappiness

Appendix 2

Glossary

Acorn – Jacq and Katkin's stone cottage on the grounds of her late father's former estate, Tintaren. Burned down by the King's Guard after Jacq's arrest for spying, and rebuilt by Queen Arkafina during her reign.

Aermaran – The airship invented by Maggrai.

Ambits, Greater and lesser – The routes the Firaithi follow through Yr.

Anafiremad – Weapon for the destruction of anafireon.

Anafireon – The spirit of the living.

Ancarnen – The Mariner's sword.

Angellus – The enemy of the Amaranthine.

Asparitus – The Firaithi way of life; it means to take little and return much.

Astarene – The spirit body of the dead. *Pl. astaren.*

Autochthones – The Amaranthine name for the Firaithi.

Aviscet – A bird reanimated with corsfyre. *Pl. avisceti.*

Aza'thuwlas – An indeterminate time, neither future nor past. Also called Nowhen.

Azimity – The force which holds the whirling strands of time close to the Gyre.

Beaumarais – A small country in the continent of Yr. Bounded to the east by the Mistmere and Mardon to the west. The northern border is shared with Secuny and the southern with Spanja. The capital is Isle St. Valery, an important trading hub on the inland sea.

Black Guard – Tristan's secret army.

Bryn Mirain – The secret meeting grounds of the Firaithi.

Chamber of Deputies – The ruling body of Beaumarais, consisting of one hundred representatives elected biannually.

Chronagine – Tristan's invention for traveling beyond the outermost Pellicula.

Chymike – The mystical arts of severance and recombination. *Adj. chymerical.*

Citadel, The – The five-sided fortress that overlooks the City of Isle St. Valery. The abode of the ruling monarch and the Guard.

Corsfyre – The power source created by smelting anafireon.

Dai Irrakai – Amaranthine, seeker of the paths between the stars.

Daminem – Sisters of the Unity.

Deres – The trees.

Dinrhydan, The – Jacq Benet's code name. Translates as "true heart" in the old tongue. Also Tristan's middle name.

Eira – Huw Adaryi's sister.

Eydis – Stavebearer of the Amaranthine.

Fenacrist – The living. Radiant anafireon.

Feringhall – Eydis' house on the wild coast of Starruthe.

Firaithi – A wandering people, comprised of twenty Kindreds, who traverse Yr trading in horses and handcrafts.

Firemma – Discipline of Hana that keeps body and soul together after death. Lit. *spirit devotion.*

Fyn – A god of the Fynära, beloved of Lalluna.

Fynära – A marauding, seafaring race.

Geya – A Triple Goddess of the Amaranthine. Her sisters are Raven and Moonlight.

Gruagá – Firaithi name for the settled peoples of Yr. Means "white devil". *Pl. Gruagán*

Gyre – Everything that is or ever will be winds around the infinity of time in the Gyre.

Hana – The Eastern Star. Goddess of the Firaithi.

Ikor – Firai word for Uncle.

Ikora – Firai word for Aunt. *Pl. Ikoran.*

Irais – The servants of the Deres.

Juvenead – An apprenticeship in the Unity.

Juvenie – A Unity apprentice.

Keth Dirane – The name that the Amaranthine Raven was given by the Firaithi when she came to Yrth. *Lit. "Death's Shade".*

Keth'fell – Gwenn Faircrow's sword. Means "death crow" in the old tongue.

Kindreds, The – Divisions of the Firaithi people. Normally a group of around thirty to forty adults and children.

Kyan – Elders of the Firaithi.

Kylathie – Firai word for teenager.

Kymatre – Firai word for Grandmother.

Kypatre – Firai word for Grandfather.

Lathie – Firai word for child.

Lilies of the field – Firaithi expression for any forbidden drug.

Lutyond – The Divine Mariner, god of the Fynära.

Mardon – A neighboring but unfriendly country to the west of Beaumarais. Several wars have been fought between Mardon and Beaumarais over disputed territories. Citizens from Mardon are called the Mardonne.

Mebbain – Passageway to the worlds between.

Mistmere – The large inland sea that brings trade and exchange to Beaumarais. Isle St. Valery is on a peninsula that extends into the Mere.

Moera – The Goddess of Fate.

Moonlight – Amaranthine. Sister of Geya. Also called Lalluna.

Pellicle – Part of the Amaranthine system of addressing points on the Continua. *Pl. Pellicula.*

Periri – The lost Sutun.

Raven – Amaranthine. Sister of Geya. Also called Keth Dirane.

Secuny – The neighboring country to the northwest of Beaumarais.

Stavebearer – The leader of the Amaranthine.

Skyre – The heavenly reward of the Fynäran raiders, an eternity of feasting and fighting.

St. Valery's Acre – The vast forest that clothes the western shores of the Mistmere.

Sutun – The Irais name for the guardians of the anafireon.

Tane – Leader of a particular Firaithi Kindred. An inherited position passed from father to son.

Triske stones – The divination method used by the Firaithi. Consists of three octahedral bone carvings—each face incised with a different symbol.

Tsmar'enth – The moon gate. Firaithi expression for death.

Uri'el – Keepers of the astaren.

Wayfarers, The – The four planets beloved of the Firaithi. They are called Unda, Herd, Zephur and Ruber.

Yr – The continent on which Beaumarais is located.

Appendix 3

(Article from the Litchfield Gazette, April 21st, 19—)

LOST GIRL GRADUATES HIGH SCHOOL

A young woman with a mysterious past has succeeded in becoming the valedictorian of Litchfield High School.

When two local youths found the girl last year, she was unable to recollect anything other than her Christian name, Katy. After efforts by the police to discover her identity failed, Judge John Bennett and his wife Elizabeth, who had been sheltering the girl during the search for her family, applied to the 9th Circuit Court for guardianship. The judge further requested that the girl be known henceforth as Katherine Ellen Rain, a tribute to the location in which she was first found—the forest that is bordered by Ellendale Road and Rain's Road.

The pretty and popular Miss Rain lives with the Bennetts at their home, "White Oaks," on Schofield Hill. She was elected this year's Queen at the Knights of Litchfield Hunt Ball. Her escort, John David Bennett, Jr., the star pitcher of the Class A Litchfield Tigers, was King.

She and fellow Litchfield High classmate Thomas Deveney Finn, who was Salutatorian, have been granted full scholarships to Ohio State University. Both plan to study medicine.